SWEET RU...
Sweet D......

"It-would be better for you to stay with your father and me," Katherina's mother warned her, "than to marry a man you do not love."

Katherina snapped back: "Don't talk to me about love. Love is nonsense. There is affection between us. That is enough for a good marriage."

Her mother shook her head sadly. "Affection is one thing, Katya. But what about passion? There is passion in your blood. Russian passion. Someday it will demand that you let it out . . ."

Sweet
Rush
of
Passion
by Lynn Lowery

BANTAM BOOKS · TORONTO · NEW YORK · LONDON

SWEET RUSH OF PASSION
A Bantam Book | January 1978

ISBN 0–553–11486–7

Published simultaneously in the United States and Canada

Bantam Books are published by Bantam Books, Inc. Its trade-
mark, consisting of the words "Bantam Books" and the por-
trayal of a bantam, is registered in the United States Patent
Office and in other countries. Marca Registrada. Bantam
Books, Inc., 666 Fifth Avenue, New York, New York 10019.

For James—my fire, my love,
my passion, and my inspiration

Prologue

Katherina Andreievna huddled beneath the brightly embroidered comforter. Her heart pounded wildly, and a lump of apprehension grew in her throat.

The last guests had left the estate more than an hour before. At any moment, Count Pavel Pavlovich Ostrov would open the large oak door, crawl into bed beside her, and demand his full rights as a husband.

For the first time since the announcement of her engagement almost three months ago, Katherina felt a stab of uncertainty. The decision to marry Pavel Pavlovich had been hers alone. Indeed, her mother had tried desperately to talk her out of the match, but Katherina had been convinced that they would have a good marriage. The count was kind, intelligent, and jovial. Katherina had always felt at ease with him, and even though he was thirty years older than she, she was sure he had a great deal of affection for her. In her younger years, she had rejected the proposals of at least three rich and handsome young men, whom she judged empty-headed. Now, at twenty-five, she could no longer afford to be too choosy.

During the months of her engagement, life had been a flurry of uninterrupted activity. Her marriage to an influential member of Russia's Council of State was the most important social event of the season in Novgorod. Any doubts Katherina may have had were buried under the avalanche of details. Only now, as she lay shivering, waiting for the arrival of the stranger who was her husband, was she forced to consider all the implications of her decision, all the duties she had agreed to when she accepted Pavel Pavlovich's proposal.

Katherina shook herself, trying to release the tension she felt in her body. All brides felt nervous on their wedding nights—it was only natural. Surely she had nothing to fear. Pavel Pavlovich was such a gentle man that he was not likely to treat her harshly. Still, earlier in the evening, she had glimpsed a mysterious part of his nature.

As they had danced in the great ballroom of his Novgorod estate, the count had pulled Katherina close and whispered into her ear in an urgent voice, "Let us hope our well-wishers do not overstay their welcome. It is good to celebrate with friends and family, but I believe our own, more important, celebration is yet to come, eh?" He had chuckled then and regarded Katherina affectionately. "Ah—my dear young wife—you blush so prettily. It is hard to imagine that soon I will feel an even greater joy than that which envelops me now, as I hold you in my arms."

Hours later, after they closed the doors behind the last group of departing guests, Pavel Pavlovich had turned to her. "And now, my dear," he said, his gray eyes sparkling with anticipation, "the rest of the night is ours. Almost an hour ago I instructed the servants to begin filling the tub in your bedchamber with hot water and sweet-smelling oils, so you can bathe and relax a bit. But please," he murmured, gently squeezing her hands, "do not keep me waiting too much longer. The wait has already been more than unbearable."

Now, bathed and perfumed and dressed in the special nightgown her mother had lovingly sewn for her, Katherina found the wait equally unbearable.

Her gown was made of the sheerest white silk. Katherina was accustomed to the high-necked, long-sleeved gowns of flannel or wool that kept her warm through northern Russia's cold nights, but this gown, designed to stir a new husband's passions, had only tiny puffed sleeves, and it scooped low in front to expose the tops of her breasts, where it was tied with a white satin ribbon. A second satin ribbon was woven through the fabric and tied in a bow just beneath her breasts. Katherina Andreievna wondered if her husband would notice the care with which the nightgown had been made. If only he would come and at last put her mind at rest! At least his presence could answer some of the questions that suddenly assailed her.

Just what did he expect of her? What could she offer that would give him the unbounded joy of which he spoke? He must know that she was totally inexperienced in any type of physical love. Or did he suppose that because of her age she must have had some passing affair?

And what of Pavel Pavlovich's own experience? He was fifty-five, and it was hard to imagine that he had never bedded a woman. He was still an impressive figure of a man, although he had grown a bit plump with age. His head was still covered with chestnut hair, only lightly speckled with gray, and his muscles were still firm and well-developed. In his youth he must have been quite handsome—and his looks, along with his title and his influence with the Czar, undoubtedly made him highly sought after and irresistible to many women.

Most likely, Katherina thought, he had had a string of willing young women in his day. Perhaps he had even taken some of them in this room, in the very bed that was soon to become their marriage bed. Perhaps even now he kept a mistress somewhere in the environs of Novgorod, or in St. Petersburg where he owned another house and spent most of his time. Katherina wondered if he would compare her performance tonight with that of other women. What if she did not satisfy his expectations? Was there a chance that he might even consider divorce? Although the Orthodox church officially frowned on divorce for the lower classes, it was easy enough for the rich and influential to arrange one. She had heard rumors that even Czar Aleksandr's own son had been divorced.

As the moments passed and she strained to hear the sound of the count's footsteps, Katherina became more and more apprehensive. She wondered if she would suffer much pain. She had heard gossip among the servants that some women absolutely drenched the bed linen with blood during their wedding nights. Surely so much blood must indicate indefinable pain. She recalled hearing talk of women submitting to their husbands only because it was their duty and searching for any excuse that would keep their husbands from their beds.

Yet she knew all women could not feel such distaste, for she thought of how infinitely happy her mother always appeared and of the loving looks that passed between her father and mother, even after forty years of marriage. On reflection, Katherina felt that at least some of their joy must have originated in the bedroom. Even now, after bearing eleven children, Katherina's mother still emerged from her room very often with a radiance caused by something more than a sound night's sleep.

Thinking about her parents helped Katherina to relax. Perhaps, she hoped fervently, her own marriage could turn out to be just as rewarding. As she concentrated on the happiness that had surrounded her as she grew up, her nervousness began to change to longing. A warm ache of desire began to spread through her body. She tried to guess how she would feel at the moment of total union with her husband, how it might feel to have the muscular body of a man pressing against her own nakedness, moving inside her, and what kind of tingling she might experience with the rush of new sensations. Suddenly, sweat seemed to be streaming from her every pore. She felt like a child waiting excitedly to open a birthday package, unsure of what might be inside, but convinced that whatever it was it would make her happy.

At last there was a light rap at the door. "Are you ready for me, Katherina Andreievna?" Pavel Pavlovich's gentle voice came through the door.

Katherina sat up in bed and carefully folded the comforter to her waist. "Yes, I am ready, dear Pavel Pavlovich," she called truthfully, only a slight quiver in her voice.

Before she finished speaking, her husband had entered the room. The count wore a maroon satin dressing gown that shimmered in the light of the candle he carried in one hand. The fingers of his other hand curled around the neck of a champagne bottle and the stems of two sparkling crystal goblets. Without taking his eyes from his young wife, the count closed the door behind him and walked eagerly toward the bed.

"My dear little Katya," he whispered, "you look even more beautiful than I have dreamed you would in the months since you agreed to become my wife."

Katherina's golden hair, piled atop her head like a crown during the wedding ceremony, now tumbled over her shoulders, shining against her skin, her nightgown, and the polished wood of the headboard.

She smiled demurely at her husband's compliment and watched shyly as he put down his candle and set the two goblets on the table beside the bed.

He stood for a moment, watching her breasts rise and fall as she breathed. He could faintly see the pink blush of her nipples through the thin silk of her gown. He longed for the day when he would watch his own babies—their babies—suckle on those inviting young breasts. Until that day, perhaps he could know the joy of caressing her pink and ivory flesh with his own eager tongue. But not tonight, he quickly told himself, as he felt hot desire building in his groin. No doubt the girl was still too nervous and innocent for such a show of passion. He must go slowly with her, no matter how tempting her body appeared, so she could discover for herself all the pleasures of love.

He filled the two goblets and handed one to Katherina. "Now, let us toast the joys of marriage, my dear. The private joys that only a husband and wife can share." Katherina obediently held her glass aloft as he clinked his own against it. She had to use both of her shaking hands to keep from spilling the champagne as she brought it to her lips.

Watching her leaning back against the high headboard, her husband felt almost uncontrollably anxious to consummate their marriage. How fitting, he thought, that the headboard was carved with the crest of the Ostrov family. In a few moments his precious Katherina Andreievna—his sweet, often-dreamed-of Katya—would become an Ostrov in more than name alone.

The count drained his glass and removed his dressing gown. Katherina watched him over the rim of her glass. When he moved, she could see his muscles, still firm and strong, flexing under his white linen nightshirt. She wondered how he would look if he removed the nightshirt, too, and the thought made her blush.

Pavel Pavlovich sat down on the edge of the bed and smiled at his wife. Taking her hand, he asked, "Are you nervous, my dear Katya?"

Katherina Andreievna shook her head, afraid that if she spoke her voice would betray her.

"Good." The count brushed a lock of golden hair away from her face. "You know, you need not be afraid of me, Katya. I will be very gentle with you, and I promise not to hurt you. But I must warn you, in case your mother has not already done so, that you may feel a bit of pain at first. I can assure you it will pass quickly, and afterward you will know only the sweet delights of love."

Katherina smiled and took another swallow of champagne, trying to dissolve the lump in her throat. Touched by her husband's concern for her feelings, she blinked to cover the tears that clouded her eyes, and she directed all her attention to draining her glass.

Pavel Pavlovich took the empty glass from her and set it aside with his own. Then he leaned toward her and with a slow, smooth motion he drew the cover down until all of Katherina's shivering form was revealed to him. Her nightgown, drenched with perspiration, clung to her body. The count exhaled in slow rapture as he traced his fingertips over her firm breasts, down to her small waist and the curve of her hips. His hand slid inward from her hips, briefly patting the quivering flesh between her thighs. Impulsively he bent and kissed the spot. He was overwhelmingly aware that only a thin piece of silk separated him from her most private, most precious possession, which he would soon claim as his own. Katherina remained motionless, holding her breath as she watched him.

"My dear, you have been perspiring," the count said with real concern. "Are you feeling quite all right?"

Katherina considered telling him she was ill. Then he would go away, and the inevitable would at least be postponed. But she thought again of her mother's radiance in the mornings, and she was suddenly overwhelmed with the desire to discover for herself the cause of that radiance. She quickly found her voice. "Pavel Pavlovich—I assure you I am not ill. In fact, I have never felt more perfect than at this moment."

He beamed his approval. "Good. Then shall I extinguish the candles and join you in our bed?"

"Please do," Katherina whispered.

For an instant his face was illuminated by the last glimmer of the candles. Then the only light in the room came from the dull glow of the fire dying in the fireplace.

Pavel Pavlovich slid into the bed beside Katherina and drew the comforter up. She felt his warmth as he took her in his arms. His fingers found the white satin ribbons of her nightgown and quickly untied them. The next moment his hands were moving over the flesh of her breasts, stroking, caressing, kneading, gently massaging. Katherina felt her breasts tighten until her nipples stood hard and erect under his fingertips. She stiffened, surprised at the unexpected effect a man's hands could have on a woman's body.

"You must relax, my dearest Katya," the count whispered in her ear. "Relax and accept what happens." Secretly he was pleased at his new wife's shyness, since he took it as proof that no other man had so much as touched her.

He buried his face between her breasts, letting her sweetness wash over him, intoxicating him with desire. Feeling the nervous thumping of her heart, he again cautioned himself to go slowly. With an effort, he lifted his head and gently kissed each of her breasts.

He pressed his lips against hers, and Katherina could taste and smell the stale saltiness of the caviar he had consumed during their wedding party. No matter how often she was told it was a delicacy, Katherina could barely stomach caviar. Mixed with the vodka and champagne on her husband's breath, she found it unbearable. She turned her face away from his and gasped for air.

"Is something wrong, my dear?" the count asked as he moved his mouth to her throbbing throat.

"No—," she stammered, "your kiss simply took my breath away."

He smiled to himself, thrilled that, even at his age, he could so stir a young woman.

He inched her nightgown off, all the while murmuring words of encouragement. He dropped his own nightshirt to the floor beside the bed and poised his naked body above hers. Katherina lay rigid, waiting, as he lowered himself onto her. She could feel the matted hairs of his chest brushing against her breasts. His groin felt heavy on hers.

For a moment he lay motionless, then he slowly moved a hand down her body and massaged her belly. Katherina began to relax, and as his hand slid lower, her loins began to throb and ache for fulfillment. She stifled a gasp of pleasure as he gently nudged her thighs apart.

For the next several minutes, the count fumbled between her legs. Katherina, unable to imagine what was happening, felt her desire drain away, to be replaced with more and more tension as each second passed. Their bodies had become so coated with sweat that she was afraid they would slide out of the bed before they ever completed their union. After what seemed an eternity of uncertainty, his probing found an entrance.

Katherina felt an excruciating flash of pain, and what had begun in her throat as a gasp now filled the room as a scream. Instantly ashamed of her reaction, she dug her fingernails into her husband's back and sobbed quietly into his shoulder until the ordeal was over.

Afterward, Pavel Pavlovich assured her that the marriage act would never again be so painful. She sobbed acceptance of his words and begged him to forgive her for screaming. Long after he had fallen into a contented sleep, Katherina lay awake pondering the night's experience. Had her mother ever felt as she felt that night? Had her mother's wedding night been so full of hope that had exploded into so much pain? Perhaps, as Pavel Pavlovich insisted, the next time would be so much better.

As she drifted toward sleep, she recalled the discussion she had with her mother the day she announced that she would marry the count.

"Katya—I know he is a good man," her mother had said, "but to marry someone thirty years older than you is not good."

"He cares for me, mama," Katherina had replied. "And it is high time I made a life of my own. I cannot live with you and papa forever."

"It would be better for you to stay with us," her mother had sighed, "than to marry a man you do not love."

Then Katherina had snapped back, "Don't talk to

me about love. Love is nonsense. There is affection between us—that is enough for a good marriage."

Her mother shook her head sadly. "Affection is one thing, Katya. But what about passion? There is passion in your blood. Russian passion. Someday it will demand that you let it out. You cannot change that."

"And how do you know there is no passion between Pavel Pavlovich and me?"

Again her mother shook her head. "Passion is something that sparks even at the first meeting. If you felt it for the count, you would not need to ask about it."

Katherina had shaken her own head then and stomped away. At the time, she had no illusions about passion. She wanted only a kind and gentle husband who would give her a good home and show her some of the empire. Count Pavel Pavlovich Ostrov offered her that, and she was sure it was all any woman could possibly hope for.

Now, as she lay beside her sleeping husband, she realized that she wanted something more. She wanted that indefinable quality—that passion—that her mother had found with her father. Perhaps tomorrow, free from the tension and fatigue of their wedding, she would find it. Katherina Andreievna fell asleep praying that she would.

The next morning, Pavel Pavlovich made no mention of their problems of the night before. Throughout the day, he seemed relaxed and jovial, and Katherina made every effort to match his mood. Since her husband gave no indication that he was disappointed in her performance, Katherina began to hope that she had reacted exactly as he had expected her to. Perhaps all women screamed on their wedding nights.

After the evening meal, Katherina gratefully accepted a second glass of wine, hoping to still the quivering anticipation that was again creeping through her body. While Pavel Pavlovich sipped his cognac, she retired to soak in a hot, soapy tub, designed to relax her even more. When Pavel Pavlovich knocked at the bedroom door later in the evening, Katherina was sitting up in bed reading a book of Vasili Andreievich Zhukovsky's poetry. As her husband entered the room, she paused at the line, "When I was loved, I sang, by you inspired."

"You look lovely, as always, Katya," Pavel Pavlovich whispered as he climbed into the bed and extinguished the candles.

In the dark, Katherina involuntarily tensed again as her husband took her in his arms.

"Katya," he murmured comfortingly, "there is no need for us to consummate our love every night. At my age a man's needs become a bit less urgent than those of a youth. If you would prefer—"

"Please, Pavel Pavlovich," Katherina interrupted him, "I want to be a good wife and—," she stammered, "to prove—to you and to myself—that there will be no repetition of my behavior of last night."

"As you wish, my dear." He kissed her lightly and lowered his body over hers.

Again he fumbled for several minutes while Katherina lay tensed beneath him. As the clock in the downstairs salon boomed the hour, she began to squirm nervously, partly to dissolve her own tensions and partly from a blind hope of somehow aiding her husband in his nervous probings. He raised himself on his elbows and rocked his body over hers, tickling the points of her breasts with his chest, drawing his groin over her smooth stomach. Then, with a quiet grunt, he lowered himself again and resumed his probing. Only when the salon clock boomed the half hour did he finally roll away from her and groan as he swung his feet to the floor.

"Pavel Pavlovich," Katherina asked in a frightened voice, "is something the matter?"

He reached out and stroked her cheek before responding hoarsely, "I suspect nothing serious. I've always heard that a man of my age, because of fatigue, excitement, or whatever, might occasionally experience these difficulties. But it is something that never before happened to me—" His voice trailed off as he got out of bed. "Try to go to sleep, Katherina Andreievna. I think I will go and get a glass of cognac."

But Katherina could not sleep. She felt sure that she had caused her husband's problems. If only she had not screamed last night like some fragile ninny! Now she would be forced to live still another night and day without any taste of the incomparable happiness for which she longed—if indeed she was ever destined to sample it. Perhaps she had so displeased her husband that he would never wish to bed her again. When Pavel Pavlovich slid back into bed, Katherina Andreievna pretended to be asleep, but tears of disappointment were stinging her cheeks.

When Katherina awoke the next morning, her husband was no longer beside her. She got out of bed, slipped into a dressing gown, and went to find him. The sweet smell of his pipe tobacco led her to the room that had been his private bedchamber before their marriage. Although the door was ajar, she thought it only proper to knock before intruding. But as she raised her hand to knock, she froze in horror at the sight that greeted her. The count was folding a ruffled shirt into a half-filled portmanteau.

"Pavel Pavlovich," Katherina said, trying to control the quaking in her voice, "are you planning a trip somewhere?"

The count looked up and waved her cheerily into the room. "Why yes, my dear. Since it looks to be such a splendid day, I thought we might start for St. Petersburg this afternoon. The Council of State has already convened, and I should be there to fulfill my duties to the empire." He lay the shirt in his bag and went to kiss Katherina on the forehead.

"Did you say *we* might start—," she asked weakly.

"But surely you cannot object, my dear! I know we had talked about waiting until next week to make the trip, but there is so little social life in Novgorod, and I must confess I am anxious to show off my charming new bride. In a few weeks, Czar Aleksandr will be returning to the Winter Palace, and the social season will be in full swing."

"I don't object at all, dear Pavel Pavlovich," Katherina said, almost laughing with relief. "It's just that I—" she stopped herself, embarrassed to admit that she had imagined he was leaving her, that she thought he was disgusted with her failures in their marriage bed.

"What is it, my dear?" Pavel Pavlovich's gentle eyes caught the troubled look on her face.

"It's just that I have a great deal to prepare," she said quickly. "I'd better attend to my own packing." She kissed him on the cheek and bustled back toward her bedchamber, calling to her servants as she went.

St. Petersburg! St. Petersburg would give their marriage a new start, perhaps even a spark of that elusive ingredient—that Russian passion she so desperately wished to discover.

Chapter 1

Katherina Andreievna stood staring at her wardrobe. There was nothing in it—nothing she would want to wear to the evening's ball. At home in Novgorod she had always prided herself on being one of the most fashionably dressed young women, but here in St. Petersburg, the capital of the Russian Empire, where everyone dressed in the latest Paris designs, her gowns looked pitifully provincial. Pavel Pavlovich had told her to engage a dressmaker, but it would take weeks, at the very least, for her first gowns to be finished.

Turning away in disgust, Katherina went to her balcony window, unlatched the door, and stepped outside. An icy finger of November wind, fresh with the salt scent of the Gulf of Finland, scratched her face. She breathed in, looking out over the city with a sense of exhilaration. Compared to Novgorod, St. Petersburg seemed like a different world. Novgorod, with its ancient walled kremlin, had been Russia's capital when savage tribes still roamed much of what was now the civilized empire. But when Peter the Great planned St. Petersburg little more than a century ago, he had conceived it as a totally new European-style city.

Unlike the old cities, St. Petersburg did not even have a kremlin. Petropavlovsky Fortress, where the city began, was not a kremlin in the traditional sense. Kremlins, thought Katherina Andreievna, had musty onion-domed cathedrals, like Saint Sophia's in Novgorod. Petropavlovsky Cathedral had a glimmering golden spire that stretched joyfully toward the heavens. Staring at the spire in the distance, Katherina felt her spirits surge with it. It seemed like a beacon welcoming her to a new life in a new city.

Looking down from her balcony, she contemplated the ice already forming on one of the city's many canals. She looked forward to the spring and summer, when St. Petersburg would become the Venice of the North.

Katherina Andreievna tried to remember who had described the city to her in that way. One of the women at the ball last night. Or was it the night before? She had been in St. Petersburg only a week, and already the faces were becoming an indistinguishable blur. But the image of one face returned to her memory again and again, each time etched in sharp detail.

It was the face of a young officer in the Imperial Army, surely no more than twenty-five years old. Katherina Andreievna had seen him at a ball three nights ago, and, although he was always on the other side of the ballroom, she remembered him better than any of the hundreds of others to whom Pavel Pavlovich had proudly introduced her. She had felt sure he was looking at her during the evening. Now she recalled his dark curly hair and his piercing black eyes that seemed to say, *I do what I want, and I get what I want.*

Katherina Andreievna laughed softly to herself. Perhaps that was what she found so interesting about him—the very willfulness of his expression. People said that she was willful, too, and it was true that she usually got what she wanted. She had married Count Pavel Pavlovich Ostrov despite the pleading and protests of her mother, and now she had a lavish house in St. Petersburg, the shining capital of the Russian Empire.

Except for occasional ventures to other parts of the sprawling empire, Katherina could now expect to spend most of her life in the city she had dreamed about since she was a child. Like most Russian noblemen, the count seldom traveled to his country estate. He appeared in Novgorod from time to time to collect taxes and for brief vacations, but he preferred city life, and his work on the Council of State took much of his time.

Katherina sighed contentedly, then pursed her lips as she considered the one part of her life that seemed incomplete. She wondered if she would ever know the ecstasy that some women felt when they made love with their husbands. When she and the count had arrived in St. Petersburg, he had quietly installed himself in a separate bedroom, and he had made no further mention of the physical part of their marriage.

Once or twice Katherina had considered speaking to him about the subject, but he seemed so completely happy that she saw no reason to upset the balance of their life. Perhaps she would be happier not discovering any more about physical love. When she considered her two encounters with Pavel Pavlovich in bed, she had no desire to repeat any part of either episode.

"Madame—you'll catch your death standing out there," Masha called, shooing her mistress back into the bedroom. The servant, Katherina's maid, closed the balcony doors and announced, "There is someone in the sitting room to see you."

"Is it the dressmaker?"

"No, madame."

Katherina Andreievna sighed. Probably a middle-aged matron she had met at least three times in the last week but would not recognize. It was so embarrassing. They all spoke impeccable French, and her own French was atrocious. She had only learned a few basics from a cousin who once spent a summer in St. Petersburg. In Novgorod, everyone spoke Russian. Bracing herself for the worst, she demanded, "Well, who is it?"

"A young man," Masha replied. "He says his name is Aleksandr Sergeievich Belikov."

Katherina turned away. "I don't know him. Tell him to go away. Obviously he has the wrong house."

Masha shrugged and scurried downstairs with the message. Katherina, realizing that she had become chilled on the balcony, looked for a shawl. After allowing enough time for the intruder to receive her message and leave, she decided to go downstairs to see if the samovar was hot. A cup or two of hot tea would warm her up.

Halfway down the stairs, she met Masha, who was almost in tears. "He insists he knows you, madame," the servant said. "I tried to persuade him to leave, but he won't. He says he must see you."

"Why didn't you threaten to have Dmitri throw him out?" Katherina said.

"I did, and he threatened to send the Czar's whole army after me."

"All right, Masha," Katherina said. "I will handle this." The Czar's whole army, indeed, she thought. Who does this person think he is, intimidating a poor servant who is simply following her mistress's orders. Katherina continued down the stairs, followed by Masha, who anxiously waited to see her mistress lash into the intruder. At the foot of the stairs, Katherina turned and threw open the double doors to the sitting room. Before her, a smug look of triumph on his face, sat the young officer whose face she had moments ago envisioned.

Katherina Andreievna stood there, uncertain of what to do or say, and he stood and walked toward her. Although she did not offer her hand, he took it from her side, kissing it softly. Katherina Andreievna felt a tingle run up her arm and down her back. Telling herself she was still shivering from the cold, she snatched her hand away and turned to her maid. "That will be all, Masha."

The servant backed off, looking dejected. Katherina tried to compose herself. Turning back to her visitor, she said, "I'm sorry, the count is not at home."

Aleksandr Sergeievich's eyes danced. "That's just as well. I did not come to see your father. I came to call on you."

"The count is my husband. I am the Countess Ostrova. Surely you knew that," Katherina said.

"Forgive me, madame," he bowed in mock penitence. "I simply assumed that such a great difference in age meant—"

"Obviously you assumed too much," she said. "Tell me, is it the fashion in St. Petersburg for officers of the Imperial Army to pay social visits to married women?"

"It is—when the women are as beautiful as you." He smiled. "I had thought scores of others would have been here before me."

Katherina felt a flush creeping up her neck. She knew he was only flattering her, but she was not used to compliments. No one but Pavel Pavlovich had ever called her beautiful. She was also aware of his perfect French and of her clumsy attempts at the language.

"Then perhaps you learned your French while consorting with the wife of the French ambassador," she snapped.

"Did you learn yours from the French ambassador himself?"

While Katherina Andreievna wondered how to respond to his impudence, Aleksandr Sergeievich settled into a chair. "Actually," he said, "I learned my French at Tsarskoe Selo. Along with Latin, Greek, and assorted other subjects."

"But I thought Tsarskoe Selo was the Czar's school," Katherina said.

"It is. At least it is in one of his palaces and is under his direction. But many young noblemen are schooled there. I received my commission as an honor when I graduated." Sensing that Katherina was relaxing, Aleksandr asked, "How do you like Peter's city?"

"What I have seen is lovely," she replied. She wondered how she could sit and have a civil conversation with this impudent intruder, but she continued. "Actually, though, I have seen very little. The count is occupied at the Senate each day with whatever business the Council of State attends to. And he does not think I should explore a strange city alone. At night we rush from one ball to the next, and I barely have a chance to glimpse one or two buildings through the shadows."

"Perhaps I could help." Aleksandr Sergeievich smiled. "I have lived in St. Petersburg all my life, and I would be happy to show you around."

Katherina stiffened. "I hardly think the count would approve."

At that moment, Count Ostrov strode into the room, jovial as always. "What would I not approve of, my dear?" He bent to kiss her forehead, and Katherina silently thanked him for his show of affection.

Before she could answer, Aleksandr stood to introduce himself. "Count Ostrov, I am Aleksandr Sergeievich Belikov."

"Of course, my boy," the count clapped him on the shoulder. "I know your uncle, Pyotr Dmitrievich, well. He often speaks proudly of you, and I can see why." He surveyed the young officer approvingly.

Aleksandr warmed to the praise, and, all charm, he continued. "I was just telling the countess I would be happy to help her become acquainted with our city —but she seems to think you would disapprove."

"Disapprove? Nonsense," said Pavel Pavlovich. "I think that is a splendid idea. Katherina Andreievna and I both thank you for your generosity." He glanced at Katherina and she smiled weakly. "The fresh air will put some color in your cheeks, my dear. A young woman should not be closed up in a house all day. It's most unfortunate that my work for the Council of State keeps me from showing you the city myself, but this young man offers a perfect solution to the problem."

"Good," Aleksandr smiled broadly. "I shall bring a carriage tomorrow at two o'clock."

Pavel Pavlovich led him to the door. "Thank you again, young man. The countess needs some diversion. Give my greetings to Pyotr Dmitrievich."

As her husband came back into the sitting room, Katherina Andreievna looked at him in wonderment. "Pavel Pavlovich, do you really think it is wise for me to be seen with that young man? I've heard that gossip flies in St. Petersburg."

Pavel Pavlovich chuckled. "My dear, I have complete trust in you. I would be a fool to have married someone as young as you if I was plagued with petty jealousies."

He offered her his arm, and they went to supper, the subject closed.

When Aleksandr Sergeievich arrived the next afternoon, Katherina Andreievna was still in bed. Lying
in bed that morning, thinking of how he had kissed
her hand and of the tingle that his touch had sent
through her body, she knew that she had not shivered
from the cold. In fact, she reluctantly admitted to
herself, she had felt more than a strange tingling.
She had felt a throbbing in her loins similar to what
she had felt on her wedding night—before her desire
had dissolved into screams of pain. But with the young
officer, the throbbing had been much more insistent.
She knew she could not allow herself to see this
strangely attractive brash young man again. If she
refused him today, perhaps he would desert her for an
easier conquest.

All morning she lay in bed complaining to Masha
and the other servants that she felt faint and had a
headache. If they believed she was ill, Katherina reasoned, they would be more convincing when they
turned Belikov away. Now she sat up in bed, her door
slightly ajar so she could hear the exchange between
the servants and the officer. He arrived just as the
clock in the foyer struck two, and Masha began her
well-rehearsed speech.

"The Countess Ostrova sends her deepest regrets,
but she finds she is not well enough to venture out in
the cold today."

"Is that true?" Aleksandr's voice sounded apprehensive. "She seemed in the most perfect health yesterday."

"During the evening she was struck with an attack
of faintness, and she has not yet fully recovered,"
Masha continued, just as Katherina Andreievna had
instructed her.

The officer's voice became more agitated. "Perhaps

your mistress is simply avoiding me again today. Does she forget that Count Ostrov himself made the arrangements for this outing?"

"I can assure you, she does not." Masha's voice began to waver.

"Then perhaps I can be afforded the luxury of speaking with her personally."

"Forgive me, sir," Masha's voice quivered more noticeably, "but that would be quite impossible. She is truly indisposed. In fact, she is still in bed."

Without stopping to answer her, Aleksandr galloped up the stairs.

Masha hurried behind him, wailing, "Please, sir, I beg you. Do not bother the countess. Have pity on a poor servant."

In her bed, Katherina Andreievna silently cursed the young officer for his arrogance, but she felt her heart quickening.

Striding to her half-closed door, Aleksandr Sergeievich kicked it open and stood glowering at Katherina. Masha cowered behind him, sobbing, "Forgive me, mistress. I could not stop him."

Avoiding Aleksandr's eyes, Katherina Andreievna looked pityingly at Masha. "Masha," she said gently, "please go and get me some fresh tea." As Masha fled, thankful to be spared Katherina's wrath, Aleksandr stroke to Katherina's bedside and sat on the edge of the bed. Even through the heavy comforters, she felt as if his body was searing her thigh. Katherina forced herself to move her leg away, but he only settled himself more comfortably.

"I was sorry to hear of your illness, Countess Ostrova," Aleksandr Sergeievich said sarcastically.

"Yes, I had so looked forward to today's outing." She returned his sarcasm.

"Perhaps I should find a doctor for you."

"No," Katherina said firmly, trying to sound convincing. "I'm sure I am simply exhausted from the constant round of social events. I'm not accustomed to the pace of St. Petersburg society. I expect I will recover with a little rest."

"Let us hope so. It would be a pity to rob St. Petersburg of a gem such as yourself." Aleksandr smiled wryly, and Katherina wished she could slap away his sarcastic look.

Suddenly his expression changed, as though a mask had fallen from his face. Leaning over her, one hand on either side of her shoulders, he said, "Why do you avoid me so carefully?" His dark eyes seemed to bore into her very brain. He leaned closer, his nose nearly touching hers. Katherina Andreievna squirmed under the comforter and hoped that he did not notice the increasingly rapid rise and fall of her breasts, but when she looked into his eyes, she knew that he could see everything.

A voice inside her told her to push him away, but her arms seemed paralyzed at her sides. His eyes were flashing like the medals on his chest, and she felt both terror and exhilaration knowing he was about to kiss her. And after the kiss, what more might he demand from her, here in her bedchamber? As she felt her body throbbing again, she wondered if she had the strength to deny him anything. His nose brushed hers, and she parted her lips.

He sat up abruptly, hearing the clatter of dishes. Masha, bringing tea and tea cakes, had dropped her tray in the doorway. Totally embarrassed by her own clumsiness and the scene she had just interrupted, she burst into tears and collapsed on the floor. To Katherina Andreievna's astonishment, Aleksandr Sergeievich jumped up from the bed to comfort the servant. Piling the pieces of china back onto the tray, he mopped up the spilled tea with his own handkerchief. Masha sobbed her thanks and scurried away with her tray of broken dishes.

Standing in the doorway, Aleksandr Sergeievich refolded the wet handkerchief and put it in his pocket. "Perhaps tomorrow at two o'clock you will be more disposed to join me," he said.

"Perhaps," Katherina Andreievna answered.

Then he was gone.

When Pavel Pavlovich arrived home, Katherina was still in bed. He asked about her day and sympathized about her illness. He seemed particularly sorry that she had been unable to join the young officer for a tour of St. Petersburg.

"It was a splendid, crisp day, my dear, and I had so looked forward to seeing some color in your cheeks from the jaunt in the fresh air. And, of course, I was anxious to hear your impressions of young Belikov—to see if he is everything Pyotr Dmitrievich is constantly crowing about."

I'm sure he is all that his uncle says, Katherina thought—and much, much more.

They shared dinner in her bedroom, the count insisting that she get the full measure of a day's rest.

"And did young Belikov leave word that he would call for you again tomorrow?" Pavel Pavlovich asked between bites.

"Yes, I believe he did."

"Then if you feel up to it, by all means you must go," the count said.

"Of course; if you insist, dearest."

She convinced him that he should attend that

evening's ball without her. She intended to go to sleep early, she said, with the hopes of a full recovery by the next day.

"Then I shall sit with you until you feel drowsy," Pavel Pavlovich said.

"Please don't trouble yourself, dearest. I insist that you not be late. You must consider the feelings of your hostess. Her soiree would be quite a flop if she did not have the benefit of the handsomest, wittiest count in the empire being there for the entire evening."

The count's chest swelled, and Katherina Andreievna reminded herself to compliment him more often. Dear, kind, gentle Pavel Pavlovich—he deserved at least that.

"To please you, I will go," he said, kissing her lightly on the cheek. "Sleep well, my dear. Let us hope tomorrow brings you good health."

After Pavel Pavlovich left, Katherina Andreievna called Masha to close the curtains and close the door to her room. But she was awake long after she heard Pavel Pavlovich come home and go to bed.

Finally, no more than an hour before dawn, Katherina Andreievna made her decision. When Aleksandr Sergeievich arrived the next day, she would be ready to go with him. She would not—could not—risk another scene like the one Masha had interrupted that afternoon. She felt sure she could trust Masha's discretion although she wondered how Masha had explained the broken dishes to the suspicious cook. But the other house servants worried Katherina. They had lost no time in indicating their disapproval of Pavel Pavlovich's choice of a wife.

The situation would be much better controlled in a carriage, Katherina Andreievna told herself. Besides, Belikov would be so busy describing his beloved city that he would not even have time to look at her.

There had been a fresh snow during the night, and, to Katherina Andreievna's relief, Aleksandr Sergeievich called for her in a troika instead of a carriage. Climbing happily into the sleigh, Katherina felt sure that Belikov would not behave indiscreetly in an open troika, with all of St. Petersburg looking on.

The icy wind stung their faces, and Katherina Andreievna snuggled beneath the troika's heavy fur lap robes, enjoying the day and the view of the city. She exchanged pleasantries with Aleksandr Sergeievich, and gradually all of the tensions of the day before drained away.

The driver sped them to the heart of St. Petersburg, past the pastel-painted Winter Palace and across the Palace Bridge toward Petropavlovsky Fortress. Below them, the partly frozen Neva moved sluggishly. As they crossed the bridge, Katherina caught a glimpse of the golden spire of the Admiralty, the center of the Imperial fleet. So much of St. Petersburg seemed to be painted in gold, and Katherina felt that it was an omen of the shining, rich life the city offered her.

At the center of the fortress, Aleksandr ordered the driver to stop. Springing from the troika, he turned to lift Katherina down. Even through her layers of capes and clothing, his touch felt oddly gentle, and Katherina felt the now-familiar tingle run through her flesh.

Leaving the troika behind, they walked to the Petropavlovsky Cathedral. He put his hand on her arm to steady her on the icy streets, and she felt a rush of warmth.

At the foot of the cathedral steps, they stopped to gaze at the golden spire; though she could barely see its face, Katherina was sure the angel atop the spire smiled at her. Then they climbed the steps and Aleksandr opened the cathedral door. In the stillness, all of the icons glittered at them. Katherina stood in awe as Aleksandr whispered to her that the funeral of every Czar since Peter the Great had taken place there.

The cathedral was only the beginning of her tour. There was more within the fortress walls than Katherina had ever imagined. Aleksandr led her to the house of Peter the Great, built by his soldiers in only three days in 1703. Katherina marveled that Peter, the greatest of all czars, had ruled from this simple one-story cabin. By comparison, even the most barren farmer's shack in Novgorod seemed luxurious.

They examined each gate of the fortress, and they visited Boat House, which housed Peter the Great's own boat—the Grandfather of the Russian Fleet. There was one group of buildings that Aleksandr Sergeievich seemed to avoid. Katherina wondered why, but she did not ask.

As they climbed into the troika once more, Katherina wished that the afternoon could continue, even though her face and her feet felt frozen in the harsh November weather. On the way back, Aleksandr Sergeievich seemed somehow elated, and he continued to point out various landmarks as they flew past. Anyone viewing him from the street would have thought him a perfect gentleman, but beneath the lap robe his leg pressed insistently against Katherina Andreievna's. She hoped he couldn't feel her own leg—quivering in answer—through her heavy petticoats and his high military boots.

In front of the Ostrov house, the count was descending from his carriage. He turned at the sound of troika bells to see Katherina and Aleksandr approach. Hurrying to the side of the troika, he surveyed his wife with approval.

"My dear, you look much better indeed today."

"Thank you, Pavel Pavlovich," she murmured, wishing that Aleksandr Sergeievich would withdraw his leg.

"I must thank you again, Belikov, for your kindness to my wife."

"It is I who must thank you, sir, for allowing me the honor of her company."

The count looked pleased with the officer's humility. He reached up to swing his wife from the troika and gave her his customary kiss on the forehead.

"Well, my dear, did you see all there is to see of St. Petersburg?" the count asked.

"We saw quite a lot," she replied.

"Actually, Count Ostrov," Aleksandr cut in, "we spent most of the afternoon at Petropavlovsky Fortress. The countess seemed quite fascinated with all of the historical sites. Perhaps, with your permission, I could show her more of the city on another day."

"An excellent idea," said the count. "You know, Katherina Andreievna, St. Petersburg will be your home for more than half of every year, so it would be wise for you to know the city well. You have my permission, Belikov, to call for my wife whenever she wishes."

"Countess Ostrova," Aleksandr said, "may I suggest tomorrow at two o'clock?"

"I would be delighted." Katherina Andreievna smiled.

Chapter 2

What was to be only tomorrow stretched on into the next week. Katherina Andreievna learned every street, every bridge, every cathedral, every palace, and every monument in St. Petersburg. And whenever she thought, with disappointment, that they must have covered the entire city, Aleksandr Sergeievich thought of more things to show her. At night, riding with Pavel Pavlovich on the way to their seemingly endless social engagements, Katherina would point out various sights and recite what she had learned. Pavel Pavlovich seemed delighted with her newfound knowledge, with the fact that her afternoons were so fully occupied, and with her overwhelmingly cheery spirits.

Toward the end of the second week, Aleksandr Sergeievich called for Katherina Andreievna in midmorning. He wanted to show her Tsarskoe Selo, where he had studied for so many years. It was a long trip, and Katherina thought it would probably be their last day together. If they had to reach so far south of St. Petersburg, they must have come to the end of their legitimate meetings. And, much as she had come to treasure her time with Aleksandr Sergeievich, she was convinced that she could not go on seeing him when there was no longer any ostensible reason to do so. Even Pavel Pavlovich, with all his understanding, could not approve of that.

They traveled by carriage, sharing a picnic lunch on the way, but Katherina Andreievna was too preoccupied to take much notice of the palaces and the

16

school at Tsarskoe Selo. For Aleksandr's sake, she tried to act gay, and she spiced much of her conversation with light laughter; however, her facade broke down during the journey back to St. Petersburg.

For most of the way back, Katherina was silent, trying to drive the gloom from her mind. Aleksandr Sergeievich also seemed unusually quiet. Then the carriage rolled into the outskirts of St. Petersburg, and the reality became too much for Katherina Andreievna. Tears began to roll down her cheeks, hesitating on her chin and then dropping to her cape. Aleksandr watched her from the corner of his eye, and then, without a word, he turned to her and began catching her tears with his kisses.

He kissed her eyes, her cheeks, her chin, the tip of her nose. And then his lips were on hers. Night after night, Katherina had lain awake thinking of that day in her bedroom when they had come so close, assuring herself that if such a thing ever happened again she would push him away. Now she knew that she had only been waiting for that kiss to be fulfilled. Her arms moved around him and her lips answered his. Ripples of excitement flowed from her lips to her belly, and her body felt liquified. She moaned ever so softly as they inhaled each other's presence, reluctant to interrupt the soft contact of their lips.

Neither Aleksandr nor Katherina noticed when the carriage stopped. They were both suspended within a moment of joy. Then the driver knocked on the carriage door. "Monsieur Belikov, we have arrived at the home of the countess," he said.

Katherina tore herself from Aleksandr's arms. Without waiting to be helped from the carriage, she bolted past the startled driver and ran into her house.

As a servant took her cape, Katherina heard Pavel Pavlovich's voice upstairs. Not wishing to face him before composing herself, she went to the sitting room and asked Masha to bring her some tea. The cup shook in her hand, and she narrowly missed spilling the tea on her bodice, but she forced herself to drink it slowly, breathing deeply and avoiding Masha's astonished stares. By the time Pavel Pavlovich entered the room, she felt steady.

"I was getting worried about you, Katherina Andreievna." The count bent to kiss her.

"I'm sorry. I'm afraid we tried to see too much today. But I think we have covered all of the city now, and I do not expect to be going out with Monsieur Belikov again." If she told that to Pavel Pavlovich, perhaps she could keep herself from seeing Aleksandr Sergeievich again.

"What a pity. We will have to find some other afternoon diversion for you."

"Yes," Katherina agreed. "Perhaps French lessons."

"What?" The count seemed shocked.

"My French is so awkward. I feel I must embarrass you when we go out in society."

"Katherina Andreievna," the count said, "you could never embarrass me. But," he said, and he shrugged, "if you would like a tutor, perhaps we could look into the matter. Your happiness is most important, my dear."

After dinner as she dressed for the evening, Katherina Andreievna resolved to forget the afternoon. Aleksandr Sergeievich had not said anything about the next day, and that was good. If he sent her any future invitations, she would firmly refuse. She must not do anything more to betray the trust Pavel Pavlovich had placed in her.

As the evening began, Katherina took special pains to laugh at her husband's witty remarks. She watched him glow as he introduced her to various people, and she smiled at him continuously as they danced. He was, she thought, the perfect husband, and she must strive to be a more perfect wife.

The first time Katherina Andreievna saw Aleksandr Sergeievich across the room, she quickly looked away, but it was only a moment before Pavel Pavlovich saw him.

"Aha," said the count, "I see young Belikov is here tonight." Before Katherina could respond, they were waltzing toward him.

Belikov and Ostrov exchanged their usual pleasantries. The count thanked the officer effusively for his generosity, and Belikov responded just as effusively. Just when Katherina was thinking they must have run out of ways to compliment one another, Pavel Pavlovich recognized someone.

"Ah, my dear friend Dmitri Ivanovich has just arrived. I have not seen him since last winter. I must go and greet him." He turned to Aleksandr. "Could I impose upon you to amuse the countess for a few moments?"

"I would be honored, Count Ostrov."

"Katherina Andreievna, you will excuse me for a moment, won't you?" the count asked. Katherina smiled weakly and nodded to her husband.

As the count hurried away, Aleksandr offered Katherina his arm. "Would you care to dance, Countess Ostrova?"

"Of course."

Katherina felt her body tremble in his arms. With an effort, she held her head high, although she desperately wanted to rest it on Aleksandr's shoulder, to brush her cheek against his. She forced herself to stare at the flower arrangements on a table across the room, afraid to let her eyes meet his.

"Why didn't you tell me you would be here?" Katherina whispered.

"Why didn't you tell me?" Aleksandr said. "Never mind. I had hoped to see you tonight. You left in such a hurry this afternoon you didn't give me time to tell you. I'll call for you tomorrow at two o'clock."

"That is impossible." She kept staring at the flowers.

"Oh." He sounded disappointed. "Do you have another appointment?"

"Yes."

He held her more firmly and whispered, "Katherina Andreievna—look at me, please."

She sucked in her breath. In all their meetings he had never called her by her first name and patronymic. The endearment caught her by surprise, and she flashed a glance at him. His eyes caught hers, and his look was full of such gentle pleading that she could not take her eyes away.

"Will you be ready tomorrow at two?" he asked.

"I can't. I told Pavel Pavlovich there was nothing left for us to see—that I would not be going out with you again."

"The count need never know about this meeting. Please, I must see you at least one more time."

Katherina Andreievna looked into his dark eyes and she knew she could not refuse him. And even if she tried, she could no longer refuse herself.

To Katherina's delight, the dressmaker arrived the next morning with three of the gowns she had ordered. She had been up at dawn, trying on every dress in her wardrobe, wondering what to wear that afternoon. If this was to be her last afternoon with Aleksandr Sergeievich, she wanted to look perfect. When Masha came in to announce the dressmaker's arrival, she was amazed by the pile of discarded dresses on Katherina's bed.

Katherina was thrilled with the dressmaker's excellent workmanship and even more pleased with her timing. Now there were three more dresses from which to choose. She promised the dressmaker a bonus payment for her fast work and hurried back upstairs to try on the creations.

Katherina lay the dresses across her bed: a burgundy velvet gown with traces of white ermine and tiny pearls at the neckline; a deep green satin gown with rosebuds embroidered at the hem; and a royal blue brocade. Katherina knew at once that she would wear the brocade. Its color closely matched her eyes and provided a perfect contrast to her golden hair and fair skin.

She dressed herself, not bothering to call Masha, and stood before the mirror admiring her reflection. The neckline was cut low and square; the bodice fitted tightly, emphasizing her nearly perfect figure. She strained to look over her shoulder at the back where the dress was cut low and fastened with tiny ivory buttons. Below her waist, the material was draped to fall in the slightest hint of a train.

When Katherina called Masha to arrange her hair, her choice of gowns was confirmed. "Madame," the servant gasped, "I have never seen you look more beautiful. Surely that fabric was woven for you alone."

"Thank you, Masha." Katherina looked at herself again with approval. "Now perhaps you can do something equally stunning with my hair."

Masha looked shocked. "But you don't mean to wear such an exquisite gown for the rest of the day! I will be happy to help you change to another dress."

"That won't be necessary, Masha."

"Begging your pardon, madame, I only thought you would wish to save that gown for a special evening—perhaps one of the Christmas balls next month."

"Masha," Katherina said sharply, "it is not your place to question what I wear." Then, seeing how upset her servant had become, Katherina softened. "It feels so wonderful to have a new dress of fine fabric. I would like to keep it on for a while. Perhaps it will drive away the dreariness of the day."

Masha said no more but began vigorously brushing Katherina's hair and piling it in a cascade of curls. Katherina had never looked better. She readily forgave Masha her insolence as she stared at the reflection in the mirror.

Aleksandr Sergeievich arrived precisely at two o'clock. From the sitting room window, Katherina watched him slow his troika in front of the house. She wondered why he was alone and had not even brought a driver. Before any of the servants could answer the door, she slipped on her cloak and ran out to meet him.

"It's good to see you, Katherina Andreievna," he said, lifting her into the sleigh. "I was afraid you might have changed your mind about meeting me."

"I never break an appointment," Katherina said softly.

"Except, of course, when you are ill," he teased.

"Of course." She smiled back sweetly as he clucked to the horses. "Where are we going today, Aleksandr Sergeievich?" She had practiced calling him that when she was alone, and now the name seemed perfectly natural to her.

He smiled more broadly, in appreciation, and replied, "That is to be a surprise."

They rode silently through the city, their legs intertwined beneath the lap robe. Five blocks from the

Ostrov house, they turned down a street, stopping in front of a house only a little less elaborate than the Ostrov's. A waiting groom took the horses as Aleksandr led Katherina to the door. He opened the door without knocking, and they stepped inside.

Katherina stared at the crystal chandelier that was suspended over the stairway.

"Well, what do you think of my house?" he asked.

"Your house?"

He nodded. "It was a gift from mother and father for my twenty-first birthday."

She spun around, absorbing small details, then looking again at the chandelier. "It's lovely," Katherina breathed.

Aleksandr placed his hands on her shoulders. "Let me take your cloak, and then I will show you around."

As he slipped off her cloak, she turned to face him. Seeing her in her new gown, his mouth fell open. "You look more beautiful than any vision in any of my dreams," he said.

She reached up and put her arms around his neck. Her half-bared breasts swelled under the brocade, and he stared in enchantment. Dropping her cloak to the floor, he swept his arms around her and drew her closer. Slowly, as if afraid the vision would disappear, he bent to kiss each of the ivory half moons. She felt her breasts tense and stand upright at his touch. For a moment she was afraid her bodice would burst from the beating of her heart.

Drawing away at last, he led her to the parlor. "I was afraid," he admitted, "that you would not come with me if I told you I was bringing you here."

"Aleksandr Sergeievich," she murmured, "I am afraid I could not have stayed away."

They sat together on a velvet love seat, quiet for a moment. Katherina Andreievna welcomed the soft light in his dark eyes that said, *I want you, but I will not take you without your permission.* She knew he could see her answer in her own eyes. *I am yours. Take me now, before the waiting drives me insane.*

Again their arms entwined and their mouths pressed together, exploring, each drinking deeply of the other's passion. He moved his mouth to her throat, her shoulder, her chest, her breasts, planting kisses that rocked her whole body with tremors of desire. As his lips wandered tenderly, she felt him carefully unbuttoning her dress.

"What about your servants?" she whispered.

Still kissing her, he said, "I sent them all away for the day."

She rubbed her face in his hair as he peeled away her gown and cast it aside. Within minutes, their bodies were locked in love, and Katherina was lost in a feeling of happiness she had thought impossible. This time there was no pain, just mounting desire that reached its pinnacle in their final moment of fulfillment.

"Katya—my sweet, beautiful Katya," he whispered.

"Sasha," she breathed in joy. She knew she would never again call him anything else.

They lay together on the love seat, breathing deeply, not noticing how cramped they were. They had stayed that way for at least half an hour, dozing, caressing each other, when Katherina heard noises at the door.

"Sasha," she whispered, "someone is knocking at the door."

The knocking got louder, and Aleksandr pulled her closer to him.

"Perhaps you should answer," she whispered. "Perhaps it is something important."

"Nothing is more important than you, my love," he

replied. "If I do not answer, whoever it is will go away."

The knocking continued for five minutes, but eventually the caller went away and the house grew silent again.

Aleksandr raised himself on an elbow to study Katherina. "I think it is time for you to see more of my house." He smiled. Lifting her from the love seat, he kissed her again. Katherina felt a new fire growing within her as she returned the kiss—and the soft, sweet, almost electrifying kiss continued as he carried her from the parlor, up the marble staircase, and into his bedroom.

Aleksandr's bed was completely curtained in velvet. Finding the opening in the curtains, he gently laid Katherina on the bed.

Overwhelmed by her flood of feeling, Katherina felt as if she were a balalaika and Aleksandr the musical artist, coaxing beautiful music from her, making her sing as no one else ever would. Now she responded to him even more passionately than before, and his moans of pleasure fueled her own desires. She felt as if he understood her every sensation, as if he knew before she did what would bring her excitement to an almost unbearable height and how to give her unnameable pleasure. They continued to lie together, embracing their happiness, until the clock in the hall struck five.

"Sasha," she whispered, "I must—"

"I know," he said dismally. "I'll get your clothes."

While he went downstairs, Katherina lay in the curtained bed, dreading the moment when she would have to return home. At last she understood what her mother had meant when she had said, "Katya, there is passion in your blood. You cannot change that." She knew she would never want to change it.

Aleksandr returned. "Shall I help you to dress, madame," he said, trying to mimic Masha.

Katherina dissolved in laughter, then stopped herself to reprove him. "Sasha, you should not make fun of Masha. She is a good and loyal servant. I am sure she never told a soul about the scene in my bedroom last week."

"My love," he said gravely, "you no longer need other servants. In return for your love, I will be your servant until the end of time."

"It is impossible for you to be my servant," she said, smiling, "for you have already enslaved me."

When she arrived home, Katherina Andreievna crept through the door and up to her room. She was surprised and relieved not to hear Pavel Pavlovich's voice, though she wondered what business kept him so late. Perhaps he was napping in his room. She slipped out of the blue brocade into an everyday dress and went to the count's bedroom. The door was wide open, but he was nowhere in sight. She returned to her own room and looked in the mirror. Her hair was in total disarray. After several minutes of trying to fix it, she called Masha.

Masha clucked at the tangle of curls but said nothing. Katherina explained that she had taken a nap and had later gone out on her balcony. "The wind today is positively ferocious," she said. Masha nodded.

"By the way, Masha," Katherina quickly changed the subject, "have there been any messages from the count this afternoon?"

"None that I know of, madame."

"How strange that he is so late today."

"Yes, madame." Masha finished with Katherina's hair, and Katherina dismissed her.

Katherina waited in the sitting room until 7:30. The

servants brought her dinner, but she waved it away. Could something have happened to Pavel Pavlovich? Could something have happened at the very moment she was being unfaithful?

At 8:30 she called a servant to take a message to the Senate building to see if Pavel Pavlovich was still there. Just as she was about to send the messenger out the door, Pavel Pavlovich came in.

He looked as if he had aged five years, and Katherina feared that, somehow, he had found out about her day. Perhaps someone had seen her in the troika with Aleksandr Sergeievich and thought they looked too gay. How could she have let her own joy and desire hurt Pavel Pavlovich?

Summoning all her courage, she said, "Pavel Pavlovich, what is the matter?"

He looked at her, his eyes hollow. "The Czar is dead."

Katherina gasped. She knew Pavel Pavlovich considered himself a personal friend of Czar Aleksandr. He had often told her how he looked forward to presenting her at court.

"Was he at the Winter Palace or at Tavrychesky Palace?" Katherina asked, remembering how Aleksandr Sergeievich had driven her around both estates.

"He was at Taganrog."

"Taganrog?" Katherina could not remember any palace by that name.

"A city on the Sea of Azov," Pavel Pavlovich said wearily. "He died a few days ago—suddenly. The message reached us today."

Katherina remembered that Czar Aleksandr had no children. "But who will be the new Czar?"

"Grand Duke Mikhail has gone to Poland to summon Grand Duke Constantine, Czar Aleksandr's oldest brother. He is our new Czar." Pavel Pavlovich sighed. "It has been a long day, my dear. And the days ahead promise to be no better. If you will excuse me, I think I would like to go to bed." He kissed her softly on the forehead and trudged upstairs.

Chapter 3

The death of Czar Aleksandr threw all of St. Petersburg into an uproar. Parties all over the city were canceled as the empire went into mourning. Every dressmaker in St. Petersburg was besieged with requests for black dresses. Katherina thought of how, only a week before, Aleksandr Sergeievich had shown her Petropavlovsky Cathedral and told her about the funerals of the czars. Everyone wondered about the new Czar, who had almost been forgotten since he moved to Poland several years before. But the Senate, the Council of State, and the military prepared to take their oaths of loyalty to him.

Pavel Pavlovich's days at the Council of State grew longer, and he looked more and more weary each night when he returned home. To everyone's surprise, Constantine was not at all anxious to ascend the throne. He remained in Warsaw, sending his youngest brother, Grand Duke Mikhail, scurrying back to St. Petersburg with his news.

Over dinner, Pavel Pavlovich grumbled to Katherina that the empire would be better off without Constantine. He had had the poor taste to divorce his first wife and marry a Polish Catholic countess, and now he could never offer the empire an Orthodox heir. But there seemed no alternative, and the count resigned himself to the upcoming oath of loyalty. Already citizens all over the empire were displaying portraits of the Most High Czar Constantine.

Katherina Andreievna listened to her husband with

forced interest, for her mind and heart were far from affairs of state. It mattered little to her if the next Czar's name was Constantine, or if he ruled from Warsaw or St. Petersburg. What mattered was that she had not heard from Aleksandr Sergeievich in four days.

The afternoons stretched before her as she sat waiting and worrying, and the evenings offered no break as she waited for her husband and then sat listening to his problems and those of the empire. Was it possible, she wondered, that she had misread the feelings that showed in Aleksandr Sergeievich's eyes? Was she only another conquest—a passing fancy—for a willful, spoiled young officer?

On the fifth day, Katherina Andreievna resolved to go to Aleksandr Sergeievich's house. She could not sit and wait any longer. But she could not ask a servant to drive her there. She would go alone, on foot, and she would not even let Masha see her leave.

Rushing through St. Petersburg, Katherina pulled her cloak close, hoping that no one would recognize her. She stopped once and almost turned back, but the thought of waiting again, alone in her house, pushed her on. At Aleksandr's door, she did not hesitate. She knocked sharply, nervously wondering what she would say if one of his servants answered. What message could she leave if she were told he was not at home?

Her worries turned out to be useless. No one answered the door. Remembering how, five days before, she and Aleksandr had lain listening to someone knocking, she pounded on the door with both fists. Enraged, she pounded, kicked, and finally tried to open the door, but it was no use.

Hot tears of disappointment flooded her face as she stumbled home. Crossing a street, she narrowly missed colliding with a troika. She slipped on a patch of ice, falling in the street and tearing her dress, and she picked herself up and stumbled on.

Why, why—why had no one answered the door? Had he sent the servants away for the day while he made love to someone more beautiful than she? Could he now be avoiding her as she had once avoided him? Perhaps she expected too much. She had been overwhelmed by her first taste of passion and had lost her ability to think and act rationally. Filled with embarrassment, Katherina wondered if she could ever stand to even look at Aleksandr again.

Then another idea began to take shape in Katherina's mind. Perhaps Aleksandr had gone away out of concern for her. Perhaps he realized that she could not leave Pavel Pavlovich—and he was trying to spare her the agony of seeing him again. He may even have felt concern for Pavel Pavlovich, knowing how the scandal could ruin the good count's life. Surely the Belikov family owned at least one country estate. Aleksandr Sergeievich was probably there right now, pondering what to do—for her, for himself, and for the count.

Her new theory made Katherina Andreievna feel better. It made Aleksandr Sergeievich seem warm and noble—just the way she wanted to think of him. She easily convinced herself she was right, and she hurried home.

Masha, visibly agitated, met Katherina at the door.

"Madame, where have you been? I have been searching everywhere for you."

"I went for a walk, Masha," Katherina said.

"But you have been gone two hours. There is a messenger here, and he refuses to leave without seeing you. He says he was instructed to deliver his message to you alone."

Katherina's heart pounded. "Where is he?"

"In the sitting room, madame. I could not keep him standing in the hall all this time—"

Katherina rushed into the sitting room, closing the doors behind her.

The messenger rose uncertainly, skeptically surveying Katherina's torn dress. "Are you the Countess Ostrova?"

"Yes. I'm told you have a message for me." Katherina held out her hand, and the young man gave her a letter. It was sealed with red wax that bore the imprint of a military button.

Turning her back to the messenger, Katherina broke the seal. Silently, she thanked Aleksandr for writing in Russian and sparing her the problems of stumbling over French.

My beloved Katya,

Please forgive me for not writing to you sooner. I can only say that it has been impossible and I have been tortured with the fear that you may have thought I deserted you. But you must know, dearest Katya, that, having tasted your sweet love, I am forever under your power.

I cannot explain to you what has kept me from your side. The explanation would be too difficult for me and the knowledge too dangerous for you. Suffice it to say that my work concerns the future welfare of the entire empire. Nothing less significant could keep me away.

With your permission, I shall fly to you at the first opportunity. I send you my love, beloved Katya, and pray that you will keep it warm within your heart.

Your own Sasha

Tears of joy clouded Katherina's eyes. She slipped the letter into the bosom of her dress. Without looking at the messenger, she asked, "Can you carry a message in reply?"

"Yes, Countess Ostrova. I was instructed to wait for your reply."

Nodding, Katherina went to the desk. Through blurred eyes she located pen, ink, and paper. The words poured out without her having to think about them.

My dearest Sasha,
    I am yours. The days without you have seemed endless, but your words have renewed my strength. I pray that you will come to me soon, my dear one, or send me word and I will gladly come to you. I dream of you both day and night, and send you love that continues to grow stronger.

Your own, always, Katya

When the messenger was gone, Katherina went upstairs. In the privacy of her bedroom, she read the letter again, whispering the words and memorizing each one. That night she slept with the letter clutched beneath her pillow, and the next day she carried it again in her dress, against her breast.

Mulling over Aleksandr's words, Katherina wondered about his important work. Perhaps he had been sent to Warsaw to guard Czar Constantine on his journey to St. Petersburg. But surely Pavel Pavlovich would have heard if that were the case, and he would have mentioned it to Katherina. She worried about the dangers Aleksandr faced, and she resolved to find out more about his work.

Each day Katherina waited for Aleksandr Sergeievich to come to her or send for her or send a message. After a week passed, an unfamiliar carriage stopped before the Ostrov house. Katherina met the driver at the door and he handed her a note that was sealed

with the familiar red wax. Scarcely stopping to scan
the lines, she grabbed her cape and hurried out the
door after the driver. Snug in the carriage, rolling
through St. Petersburg's streets, Katherina read the
note again.

> My dear one,
>   I can no longer wait for the joy of your caresses.
> I write this in haste so I may see you all the
> sooner. You will not recognize this driver, but he
> is a trusted friend. Come with him, my dear
> Katya, and he will speed you to me. Please hurry,
> my love, the waiting is unbearable.
>
> *Your Sasha*

The carriage rolled to the outskirts of the city and
stopped before a house Katherina did not recognize.
As the driver helped her down, Katherina wondered
why they had not gone to Aleksandr Sergeievich's
house. She hesitated a moment in the street. Then
the door flew open and Sasha rushed down the steps
toward her.

"My dear, dear Katya," he cried, swinging her into
his arms. Before she could respond, he was carrying
her into the house.

As Aleksandr set her on her feet, she examined the
house in amazement. "Sasha," she breathed, "don't tell
me this is your house, too? Perhaps a twenty-second
birthday present?"

He laughed, his dark eyes flashing. "No, I have only
one house of my own. This belongs to a friend."

Katherina took in the surroundings. "It must be a
very rich friend—and very generous."

"Katya," Aleksandr said softly, "I had hoped we
would not spend the whole afternoon discussing my
friends."

She moved close to him and brushed his cheek with her lips. "I'm sorry, Sasha. I can't help myself. There is so much I don't know about you. So much I want to learn."

He kissed her. "You will know everything, I promise you, but for today we have so little time." He led her to an upstairs bedroom, and she could feel the passion pulsing through her body again, the heat of it melting her, her desire taking over.

They shared love in soft slowness, each learning the other's body, each giving exquisite physical expression to the love that engulfed their very souls. Their moments of joy stretched into hours, and their happiness swelled with every movement.

As they slowly dressed, savoring each moment they had together, Katherina spoke eagerly of seeing him again the next day.

Taking her face in his hands, Aleksandr Sergeievich looked at her, his eyes full of sadness. "Katya—we cannot meet tomorrow."

"Then the following day?" She read the answer in his eyes before he opened his mouth. "Then when, Sasha? Surely we won't have to wait another two weeks?"

He shrugged and turned away.

"Sasha," Katherina said firmly, "I will not leave you until I know I will see you again."

"You *will* see me again, but—," he faltered, "I cannot say when."

"Then I am not leaving."

"You must leave," he pleaded. "In a short time I must leave, too."

"Then I will go with you."

"No," he responded sharply. Then he sat down on the bed and pulled her onto his lap. "Katya," he said, rubbing her neck with his fingertips, "I would love to have you with me—always—but I love you too much to put you in danger. You must go home and have faith that we will be together again soon."

"And what about you? How can I show my love if I leave you when you say you are in danger?"

He smiled and kissed her nose. "I have responsibilities, and so do you. If my work is successful, Mother Russia will be a better place to live. If not—" He looked away.

"Sasha," Katherina said urgently, "at least tell me what kind of work you are involved in."

He shook his head. "If we fail, it would be better for you not to know. That is why you must not be seen with me now—why we could not take the chance of meeting at my house." Seeing the worry in her eyes, he changed his tone. "But we will not fail. Do not worry about me, sweet Katya. Just knowing you are waiting will make the work go smoothly. In a short time, a few weeks at most, it will all be behind us. Then I will gladly answer any questions you ask. Then we can plan our future."

Riding home, Katherina thought about a future with Aleksandr Sergeievich. She was tantalized by the image of a lifetime with him, sharing a home, perhaps even children. Children—that thought brought her abruptly back to reality. What about Pavel Pavlovich? It would be easier if she hated him—if he were cruel, miserly, and inconsiderate. But he was not. He was warm, kind, affectionate. He had taken her away from the dull life of Novgorod and showered her with everything she had asked for from the moment of their marriage. She could not think of hurting him in any way, even for her own happiness. But neither could she think of leaving Aleksandr Sergeievich. She could not hurt him—or herself—in that way.

Perhaps she and Aleksandr Sergeievich could continue to have their separate life of love while she remained married to Pavel Pavlovich. Katherina Andreievna was certain they could be discreet. Surely Aleksandr Sergeievich would agree. He would not want to wound Pavel Pavlovich in any way either. Katherina shuddered as she thought of what Pavel Pavlovich would do if he learned of the liaison. Society would force him to challenge Aleksandr Sergeievich to a duel. And one of them would die. But, she resolved, there would be no duel because Pavel Pavlovich would never know.

At home, as she waited for her husband to return from the Council of State, Katherina Andreievna became surer with every passing moment that she could keep her secret from Pavel Pavlovich. Even if some hint of gossip reached his ears, he would be unlikely to believe it. He had told her himself that he was too old to engage in petty jealousies. And he thought too highly of both her and Aleksandr Sergeievich to believe any vicious rumors. Unless—a new problem loomed in Katherina's mind, and its enormity overwhelmed her. Unless he had absolute proof. What if she should bear a child? What if, even now, she was carrying Aleksandr Sergeievich's child? Katherina knew what she had to do. She had no choice in the matter. And she would have to do it tonight.

That night at dinner, Pavel Pavlovich seemed especially agitated. Constantine had sent word that he would not accept the throne, and he refused to travel to St. Petersburg to make an official announcement. At the same time, the Senate had discovered docu-

ments—signed by the late Czar and Constantine—
that renounced Constantine's right to the throne and
named his next brother, Grand Duke Nikolai, as the
successor. All this had happened after the army, the
Senate, and the Council of State had already declared
allegiance to Constantine.

"It is all Constantine's fault," Pavel Pavlovich grumbled. "If he had not left the church to marry that
Polish whore, the empire would not be in this quan-
dary. The whole fiasco makes a mockery of the divine
authority of the Czar. Can you imagine what will
happen when the troublemakers among the serfs find
out about this? Who is your *Batiushka*? they will say.
He is not appointed by God, he is appointed by a
piece of paper."

Katherina tried to act as though she was concerned.
"Perhaps they will not find out," she said, trying to
soothe him. "News travels slowly to the provinces.
Perhaps Grand Duke Nikolai will ascend the throne,
and no one will be the wiser."

"I hope so." Pavel Pavlovich sighed. "But it seems
entirely unlikely, my dear. There are rumblings in the
army. Nikolai is unpopular with the officers, and now
even he seems hesitant to become Czar."

Katherina forced a smile. "The empire will survive,
Pavel Pavlovich. It has survived hard times before.
Even the burning of Moscow. Our struggles make us
strong."

Pavel Pavlovich smiled back. "I certainly hope you
are right, my dear. But it is wrong for me to burden
your pretty head with the problems of the empire.
I'm afraid I've been very tiresome."

"Not at all, Pavel Pavlovich. I find your conversation
fascinating."

They ate in silence for a few moments, and Katherina thought uneasily about how to bring up the next subject. Finally, she forced another smile and said softly, "Pavel Pavlovich, I've been thinking. We have been married more than a month now, and you have been a perfect husband in every way."

"No more perfect than you, Katherina Andreievna."

She blushed slightly. "You are too kind to me, Pavel Pavlovich, and I know I have been less than perfect to you."

"I'm sure I don't know what you mean, my dear." He gazed at her affectionately.

"I know I have not fulfilled all of my marital obligations, and you have been too good to pressure me."

The count continued to look at her questioningly and she blushed more fully. "Please understand. It is difficult for me to talk about this. The subject is so delicate." Beneath the table, she nudged his foot with her own.

At last he smiled. "Katherina Andreievna," he whispered fondly, "if you find it distasteful, there is no need to pursue the subject. But I appreciate your efforts to take my mind off my worries."

"No, I—" She faltered. "I want only to be a good wife, Pavel Pavlovich."

"I do not want to force anything on you, Katherina Andreievna. I want you to be sure you are ready."

"I am ready," she said, patting his hand. Pavel Pavlovich looked at her, his eyes sparkling with affection.

After dinner they sat for a while in the sitting room, reading and drinking tea. From time to time, Katherina could feel Pavel Pavlovich gazing at her with intense anticipation. Finally, she could stand the waiting no longer. Yawning, she closed her book of poetry.

"I think I will prepare for bed, Pavel Pavlovich."

He followed her to the sitting room doors. "By all

means, my dear. You look tired." Then he added hopefully, "I hope you are not too tired?" She shook her
head. "Good." He kissed her nose, then her forehead.
"I will be coming up shortly."

Katherina prepared for bed quickly, extinguishing
her lamps and crawling beneath the comforter long
before she heard Pavel Pavlovich coming up the
stairs. She waited uncertainly while he undressed in
his own room. Then she heard him at the door.

"May I come in, Katherina Andreievna?" His tone
was gentle and solicitous.

"Of course, Pavel Pavlovich."

There was none of the pain of their earlier union,
but there was none of the joy she felt with Aleksandr
Sergeievich. Katherina lay wondering if her husband
could sense her indifference. Apparently he could not.

"My lovely Katya, my lovely wife," Pavel Pavlovich
murmured.

Katherina tried to respond by calling him Pasha,
but the name stuck in her throat. It sounded too much
like Sasha. Instead she whispered, "My dear, dear
husband."

Afterward he lay beside her, gently patting her
breast. "Katherina Andreievna," he whispered, "you
have rekindled the joys of my youth. You are in truth
an angel of a wife." He kissed her lightly and sat up in
bed. "But I think that I shall leave you now, my dear.
I don't wish to disturb your rest when I leave in the
morning for the Council of State."

"Thank you, Pavel Pavlovich. You are, I am sure, the
most considerate of husbands." Katherina meant those
words with all her heart.

He kissed her again before he got up. "I shall look
forward to my next visit to your bed with great joy."

As he left the room, Katherina sighed, grateful that

he would not be spending the entire night with her. Knowing he was her husband, she felt ashamed of her thoughts. But hard as she tried she could not shake the wish that Aleksandr Sergeievich, not Pavel Pavlovich, had just shared her bed.

Chapter 4

Ten days passed, and Pavel Pavlovich visited Katherina Andreievna's bed three more times. Each time she welcomed him with resignation, aided by her visions of Aleksandr Sergeievich. And each time Pavel Pavlovich went away convinced that his wife had reacted with all the passion a good, moral woman could be expected to show.

By day, Katherina Andreievna waited and worried about Aleksandr Sergeievich, wondering when his work would be completed—when the danger, whatever it might be, would be past. She listened to all of Pavel Pavlovich's grumblings and expoundings with renewed interest, hoping to detect some clue, but nothing he said seemed remotely related to Aleksandr Sergeievich. And she dared not ask, fearing that her voice, her face, her manner might reveal her feelings for the young officer.

On December 13, Pavel Pavlovich came to dinner more relaxed than he had been since the Czar's death. "It is settled," he announced. "Nikolai will be Czar. Tomorrow the troops assemble at Senate Square to take the oath of loyalty to him. The metropolitan of Moscow has found documents in Uspensky Cathedral declaring Nikolai the successor to Aleksandr. And Constantine's final renunciation of the throne has arrived from Warsaw. At last we will have a Czar, and one who has a good Orthodox wife and a son baptized in Orthodoxy."

"That is good news, Pavel Pavlovich," Katherina

said. "Now perhaps your long days at the Council of State will be getting shorter. I'm afraid you have been working much too hard."

"I must agree that I have been getting weary, but," he said, smiling tenderly at his wife, "it is a blessing to know I can share my evenings with you, Katherina Andreievna."

Katherina returned his smile absently, her thoughts in another part of St. Petersburg. Perhaps now, she thought, with the empire under the firm control of a new Czar, Aleksandr Sergeievich's perilous work would be ended and she could look forward to a joyous reunion.

Katherina Andreievna arose early on December 14. The anticipation of seeing Aleksandr Sergeievich again had kept her awake for most of the night. She felt sure she would see him very soon. The oath-taking ceremony for the new Czar was scheduled for the morning. Perhaps Aleksandr would even call for her that afternoon.

She strolled to her balcony, opening the doors to the frigid December air. The canal below was now solidly frozen; a light snow had fallen during the night, leaving a thin frosting on the ice. Katherina could hear troika bells in the street, and they seemed to echo the merriment she felt in her heart.

As Masha arranged her hair, Katherina smiled, imagining Aleksandr Sergeievich, his buttons and medals flashing in the sunlight on Senate Square. For a few moments she considered sneaking off to the square to watch him take his oath. Then she discarded the idea. She would spend the morning making herself beautiful in case Aleksandr came for her that afternoon.

Katherina hummed to herself and imagined the

hours and days to come. After the midday meal, she stationed herself near a window in the sitting room so she could watch for her loved one. As the hallway clock ticked, Katherina fidgeted with the curtains.

Masha, entering the room uncertainly, said, "Is something wrong, madame?"

"No, nothing at all," Katherina replied, and she tried to look engrossed in the book lying open in her lap. As soon as Masha left the room she found herself staring out the window again.

As the clock struck two, Katherina decided to go upstairs to her balcony. If she stood on tiptoe, she knew she could just see a patch of Senate Square. At least she might be able to see whether the troops were still assembled there.

The moment she unlatched the balcony door, she began to hear the noise of a crowd. Straining to see past the half-finished dome of Saint Isaac's Cathedral, she caught sight of some green uniforms, and she wondered why the soldiers were still there, for state ceremonies were usually precisely on time. The brisk December wind muffled the sounds of the crowd, and she could only hear an occasional crescendo in the noise. None of the shouts were distinct.

Katherina stayed on the balcony, shivering in the crisp air. The noise from the crowd grew louder, and then Katherina heard the crack of a rifle shot—no doubt a military salute to the new Czar. Perhaps the ceremony was over at last. She waited for the noise to subside and the garrison to leave the square. Instead, the shouts swelled louder. Impulsively, Katherina rushed from the balcony and ran downstairs.

Grabbing her cape, she hurried outside. Like many of the nobility, the Ostrov house was only a few blocks from Senate Square. She could easily walk there in a few minutes. Katherina stumbled as she hurried through the rutted snow. She tried to explain to herself why she was going, but she could not. She simply knew that she had to see for herself what was happening on the square. She had to find Aleksandr Sergeievich and know that he was safe.

The streets around the square were jammed with people. Katherina struggled to push herself through the crowd, pressing toward the towering bronze equestrian statue of Peter the Great. As she pushed, she caught fragments of conversation.

"Is he dead?"

"Where is the animal who fired the shot?"

"He was a fool to be here."

"Is he dead?"

In confusion, Katherina turned to an old woman next to her. "Who is everyone talking about, babushka?"

The woman shook her head uneasily. "Governor General Miloradovich. He tried to talk to the soldiers, and they shot him. Shot him right in front of the bronze horseman."

Katherina sucked in her breath and stood on tiptoe to see the statue of Peter the Great; a group of men was clustered at its base. She thought of how she had met General Miloradovich only weeks ago at a soiree. He was an old and distinguished gentleman, who, she was convinced, could not have said or done anything to deserve murder. She watched in horror as the troops fell aside and a few soldiers carried away the body of the old general. Then the ranks closed again and the jeers of the mob continued.

Katherina fought her way along the edge of the mob, searching for Aleksandr Sergeievich. She recognized the uniforms of some of his regiment milling around the bronze horseman, but she could not pick him out of the crowd. The sun reflecting off the snow, the rifles, and the gilded buildings distorted her vision as she strained to see.

Suddenly a hush fell over the crowd as people pointed to the Senate entrance. Standing in the archway, his arm raised in the sign of blessing, was Metropolitan Serafim, head of the Orthodox church in St. Petersburg. As the crowd quieted, the metropolitan began to speak. But before his words could reach Katherina's ears, they were drowned out by the jeers of the soldiers around her.

"Go back to your cathedral, father, and pray for our souls," someone yelled. All around the monument others took up the cry. "Go and pray for us!" The words reverberated through the square, more a demand than an entreaty. Katherina was shocked and afraid. She had never heard anyone address even a priest, much less a metropolitan, with such disrespect. Serafim stood a while longer, waiting for the crowd to quiet again. When the noise continued, he shrugged and walked back into the Senate building.

Almost at once, another figure appeared under the archway. Katherina did not recognize the young man, and she turned questioning eyes to the man beside her.

"It is the Grand Duke Mikhail," the man said simply.

Mikhail stood only a moment in the doorway, then strode directly toward the bronze horseman. The soldiers treated him without deference, as if he were no more important than they.

From the dome of Saint Isaac's, one of the workmen shouted, "Shoot him, too. Let's see what kind of revolutionaries you are."

Revolutionaries. The word sent a chill through Katherina Andreievna's body. She remembered her grandfather telling her once about a revolution led by a peasant named Pugachev, but that had been ages ago, when even Pavel Pavlovich was just a young child. Was this gathering on the square a new revolution? Could Aleksandr Sergeievich possibly be involved in such a thing? No. She was sure he could not. She pushed farther into the center of the square until she was standing among the soldiers themselves. Some of them turned to her and told her to get out of the square, to go home. But she ignored them, still searching for Aleksandr Sergeievich. As she got closer to the monument, she saw Grand Duke Mikhail walk toward the Senate archway. She held her breath until he disappeared safely inside the building.

For more than half an hour, Katherina wandered among the troops looking for Aleksandr Sergeievich. A few times she asked some young officers if they had seen him, but they simply shook their heads and turned away from her.

Katherina wondered whether Pavel Pavlovich were on the square. What would he say if he saw her? But there were thousands of people there; it was unlikely that he would see her. Unless, of course, he was watching from a window of the Senate building. Katherina Andreievna pulled her cape closer and decided it was useless to worry. The crowd was quieter now, waiting to see what would happen next. Perhaps even the Czar Nikolai himself would appear.

The Czar did not appear. He sent his artillery to speak for him. No one on the square noticed the cannon being removed from the Admiralty and wheeled into place. When the first shot was fired, the crowd panicked. Even the soldiers tried to scatter, but there was nowhere for them to go. The surrounding streets were completely blocked by the retreating mob. Some of the soldiers headed for the frozen Neva, but the second cannon blast cracked the ice, and the water

began to seep through. Loyal troops were closing in
on the revolutionaries.

Katherina Andreievna stood frozen in the square,
still searching for Aleksandr Sergeievich, not knowing
where to go. She stared toward the Senate building.
There was a familiar figure. Could that be Aleksandr?
She ran toward him, bumping into fleeing soldiers, calling his name. All around her, people were
screaming to their friends and comrades. Aleksandr
turned away, and Katherina had the sick realization
that he could not hear her. As she tripped and fell
over a discarded rifle, she saw him break into a
run.

"Sasha," she shouted. Unknown hands helped her
to her feet. She looked around frantically, but he had
disappeared. Katherina wandered about aimlessly until she was forced to admit to herself that it was useless to stay. Perhaps Aleksandr Sergeievich would
send word to her at home.

It was late evening before Pavel Pavlovich arrived
home. Katherina had waited nervously, pacing her
room, trying to understand how Aleksandr Sergeievich could be a revolutionary. In the end, she knew it
made no difference to her. A label could not change
her feelings. He was still her Sasha, the only person
who could awaken her passions.

Over dinner, Katherina inquired casually about
the day's events. "Pavel Pavlovich, was there a disturbance today on Senate Square?"

"I did not want to trouble you with it," he said.
"How did you know about it?"

"I had gone to the balcony to get some air, and I
could hear shouting and gunshots."

Pavel Pavlovich sighed. "Yes, there was some trouble. Part of the garrison refused to take the oath of loyalty."

"But why?"

"I'm sure I don't know. Some of them said it was impossible because they had already taken an oath to Constantine, but I am sure there was more to it than that. There have been dissidents in the Imperial Army for some time now."

"Were there many of these dissidents?" Katherina asked.

"I watched from the Senate building, and my guess is that there were about three thousand of them. The loyal troops outnumbered them three to one. They could have crushed the rebels easily, but Czar Nikolai did not want to begin his reign with bloodshed. Unfortunately, there was bloodshed after all. The rebels murdered General Miloradovich."

"Oh, no!" It was not difficult for Katherina to sound shocked, for she was still genuinely horrified by the murder.

"He went to them in good faith, to try to talk them out of their foolishness—and someone shot him. Later, Metropolitan Serafim and Grand Duke Mikhail went, too. Only God kept those barbarians from shooting them as well." Pavel Pavlovich shook his head. "It is a sad way for Nikolai to begin his reign."

"What will happen to the rebels now?" Katherina tried to sound offhanded and unconcerned.

Pavel Pavlovich shrugged. "Some of them were captured immediately, some escaped, but they will all be punished." His eyes flashed contempt. "No doubt some of them are languishing in Petropavlovsky right now."

Katherina was confused. "Where? In the cathedral?"

Pavel Pavlovich smiled indulgently. "Of course not, my dear. I see your tour last month of Petropavlovsky omitted the less aesthetic aspects of the fortress. Perhaps you did not see the prison. In the last hundred years, the worst enemies of the czars have died there."

Katherina paled, suddenly remembering the buildings Aleksandr Sergeievich had so carefully avoided. Seeing her reaction, Pavel Pavlovich patted her hand. "You must not worry about it, Katherina Andreievna. The Czar will see that all the criminals are justly punished."

She tried to smile. He could not know that was precisely what she was worried about.

Chapter 5

Katherina Andreievna told Pavel Pavlovich that she was exhausted, and she retired immediately after dinner. Thinking she was merely upset by the problems of the empire, the count accompanied her to her bedroom door, kissed her lightly, and told her again not to worry.

"Remember," he smiled, "you told me yourself that our struggles make us strong."

Katherina nodded as she stepped into her room and closed the door. She listened as the count continued down the hallway to his own room. Without bothering to undress, she crawled into bed.

All night she lay awake, worrying about Aleksandr Sergeievich. Had he escaped? Was he at that moment sleeping safely in his own house, or in a friend's house? Perhaps he was fleeing St. Petersburg, on his way to some provincial hiding place. Or perhaps he was lying in Petropavlovsky Prison. The possibility that he was in prison horrified Katherina Andreievna. She had never seen the inside of a prison, but she imagined it to be a million times more terrible than the home of Baba Yaga, the fairy-tale witch her nurse had told her about as a child.

She tried to convince herself that Aleksandr Sergeievich was not a revolutionary at all. Hadn't Pavel Pavlovich said there were three times as many loyal soldiers as rebels on the square? But the memories of Aleskandr's secrecy during the last weeks—and the nightmare vision of him fleeing the Czar's cannons—

dissolved any doubts. Katherina knew that Aleksandr was part of the unexplainable revolution, and she fervently prayed that he would escape with his life. She wondered if God would accept a prayer for a man who slept with another man's wife and dared to question the power of a Czar appointed by God Himself.

As dawn sent slivers of sunshine into her room, Katherina, still wide awake, threw off the covers and went to her mirror. She quickly rearranged her hair, smoothing the wisps that had come loose during the night. Her dress was badly wrinkled, but she did not bother to change. Anyway, it would be covered by her cloak. She listened behind the closed door of her room as servants brought Pavel Pavlovich his breakfast. It seemed forever before she heard them carry away the tray, then heard the click of Pavel Pavlovich's boots on the stairs. He spoke to his servants in muffled tones, probably trying not to wake her. Finally, the door to the street closed behind him.

Katherina hesitated a few more moments, giving the servants time to retire to their own quarters, then she carefully swung open her door and crept into the hall. She closed the door to her room, hoping Masha and the other servants would think she was asleep and not to be disturbed, tiptoed down the stairs, and slipped into her cloak. The sound of the clock striking nine covered the sounds of the front door opening and closing.

Katherina had never been on the streets of St. Petersburg so early in the morning. She found them crowded. Carriages were driving noblemen to the Senate, and servants were rushing to be first at the market. Keeping her eyes lowered, she wove her way through the pushing peasants as she hurried through the streets to Aleksandr Sergeievich's house.

She knocked and only a moment passed before a sleepy-eyed servant opened the door.

"I would like to speak to your master," Katherina said firmly.

"The master is not at home." The servant yawned.

"If he is asleep, I will be glad to wait until he arises."

"The master is not at home," the servant repeated more firmly.

Fear enveloped Katherina, but she forced herself to continue the conversation. "Perhaps you can tell me where to reach him?"

The servant shrugged. "He has been at the family estate at Sestroretsk for the last fortnight."

At last Katherina understood. The servant had been instructed to tell any callers that Aleksandr was away, to protect himself and his revolutionary comrades. If only she could break through the servant's protectiveness. "You needn't worry that I mean your master any harm," Katherina said gently. "I am—" She stopped. What could she say? I am his lover? His sister? Surely the servant would know she was not a member of the family. If he caught her in a lie, he would trust her even less.

"It does not matter who you are," the servant said. "If I recognized you as Monsieur Belikov's own mother I would tell you the same thing. He has gone to Sestroretsk."

"Did he at least leave word when he would return?" Katherina was becoming desperate.

"I've told you all I know." The servant turned and closed the door as Katherina stumbled back to the street.

Perhaps he *had* told her all. he knew. If Aleksandr Sergeievich had not told her about the revolution, it seemed unlikely that he would confide in a servant. Katherina cursed her stupidity for ever going to his house. But where else could she go for information? She knew she could not sit at home, waiting for news that might be days or even weeks in coming. If Aleksandr Sergeievich had escaped somewhere, it might be too dangerous for him to attempt to send her news at all. Perhaps she could try the house where they had had their last meeting, but that was on the outskirts of the city, and Katherina was not sure she could find it. And, not knowing to whom it belonged, it would be impossible to ask anyone for directions. There was only one way to be sure Aleksandr Sergeievich was not in prison. She would have to go to the prison herself.

Threading her way through the city toward Petropavlovsky Fortress, Katherina Andreievna shuddered with fear. As she passed her own house, she considered stopping to get Masha. She could confess everything, swear Masha to secrecy, and take her along for moral support. But Katherina discarded the idea almost immediately. She knew she had to go alone, even though she felt like a poor orphan being sent by her stepmother into the clutches of Baba Yaga.

As Katherina crossed the Palace Bridge, the fortress's forty-foot walls looked grim and threatening. She crept uneasily through the gate, staring at the battlements—sixty-five feet thick—that now seemed to her a symbol of the Czar's steadfast power. Even the golden spire of the cathedral brought her no joy. It pointed to the threatening December sky as if to emphasize the terrible wrath of God. Katherina wanted to flee, to run all the way back to Novgorod, where life had been so much simpler, but she forced herself to approach the prison with an air of dignified composure.

Katherina had hoped to slip into the prison unnoticed, but a guard challenged her at the door, barring her way with a saber-tipped rifle. "Where do you think you are going, madame?" His tone was brusque, not even tinged with the respect to which Katherina was accustomed.

"I would—like—to visit a prisoner," she stammered.

"Oh you would? And what is that prisoner's name?"

Katherina hesitated, wondering if she should give Aleksandr Sergeievich's name. If he was not in prison, could her inquiry incriminate him? Would the guard's superiors reward him if he supplied the name of another rebel?

"You can't very well visit someone if you don't know his name," the guard snapped. "Can you?"

"Well," Katherina said, blushing, "the fact is, I know his face, but I don't know his name."

"That seems highly unlikely for a noblewoman such as yourself."

"Please," she pleaded, "are there soldiers imprisoned here from the disturbance yesterday on Senate Square?"

"Perhaps."

"The person I wish to see may be among them. Couldn't you direct me to them?"

"Perhaps I could." The guard seemed disinterested.

In desperation, Katherina slipped several rubles into his hand.

"Yes," he nodded, still not changing his expression, "perhaps I could direct you to them." He called another guard; the two men whispered for a few moments and exchanged some of Katherina's money; and then the second guard nodded to her to follow.

Their footsteps echoed in the stone corridors. The

prison smelled damp and musty. Katherina was glad it was dark so she could not see all the insects and rodents that were surely hiding in the shadows. Near the end of the long corridor, the guard stopped before a heavy iron door, holding his lantern up to its small iron-barred window and indicating with his chin that Katherina should look inside.

Standing on tiptoe, she surveyed the men sitting and lying listlessly on the cold stone floor. They had all been stripped of their military medals and gear, and one night in the prison had robbed them all of the proud rebellious bearing she had seen on Senate Square the day before. Katherina carefully focused on each of them, but Aleksandr Sergeievich was not among them. Shaking her head, she shrank back from the door.

The scene was repeated at each of the next five cells, each time with the same result. Katherina began to have renewed hope that Aleksandr Sergeievich had escaped. Then, as she stretched to see into the window of the sixth cell, she saw him. He was sitting on the floor, his back rigid against the stone wall. His clothes and body were soiled, and his dark hair was badly tousled. Katherina wanted to run her fingers lovingly through his hair, smoothing it, bringing his head to rest on her breast. Even in this horrible situation he looked the most handsome and the strongest of all the soldiers.

Pressing her face against the window bars, she called in a sharp whisper, "Sasha!" Every face in the cell turned to look at her. Aleksandr Sergeievich sprang up and rushed to the door.

"Katya, what are you doing here?" he asked in a pleased whisper.

"Looking for you, of course." She heard the guard

move away as she pressed closer to the heavy iron door. Straining to hold herself at the window, her mouth met Aleksandr's as she kissed him, hungry for him, aching for him.

Pulling away at last, he gazed at her, his eyes overflowing with love. "But how did you know to come here?"

"I saw you on Senate Square yesterday, and Pavel Pavlovich said that anyone who was caught would probably be imprisoned here."

"Pavel Pavlovich—does he know I'm—"

"No," Katherina cut him off, "he doesn't even know I was there. He thinks I just heard the noise from my balcony."

Aleksandr Sergeievich relaxed. "Good. The count is a good man, but I'm afraid he could not bring himself to understand my position. I don't want him to think ill of me—or of you."

Then his eyes clouded again. "But Katya, you should not have come. What if someone saw you? What about the guards? It could be dangerous for you—you could be implicated in the revolution. You must think of your own safety, and of the count's."

Katherina smiled bravely. "I would not worry about the guards. And I'm quite sure no one else saw me. Besides, even if my very life were in danger I would have come—to see for myself that you are alive." He smiled, and they stared longingly at one another while Katherina tried to phrase the question that was haunting her. "Why—Sasha? Why did you get involved in a revolution?"

"For the good of Russia." He said it simply, as if the answer were obvious.

"But you have a good life, a good home."

"No," he whispered, "no one in Russia, from the

lowest serf to the highest noble, no one but the Czar and his family has a good enough life. The Czar steals our land, our power, our very God-given freedoms."

"But the Czar is appointed by God."

"Come, Katya," Aleksandr said, "you know better than to believe that. Surely Pavel Pavlovich has told you. The Czar is appointed by the Czar. And the Czar makes his own rules. Russia needs a constitution that will protect the people's rights."

Katherina sighed. "But what has all this talk of freedom and a constitution gained you, Sasha? What will happen to you now, locked up in this terrible place?"

"Perhaps nothing will happen to me. I joined the secret societies only recently. It would be difficult for them to prove my involvement. And, of course, Uncle Pyotr is a good friend of both the Council of State and the Romanov family. I am sure he will say a few words for my character."

"Can he save you?"

"I think so, though he will probably never forgive me for this involvement."

"And then what will become of your revolution?"

Aleksandr shrugged. "This was not the time for it. Those of us who escape the Czar's wrath will see that it does not die—but we will be more careful. The next time we strike, we will not fail," he whispered fiercely. Then, seeing the renewed fright in Katherina's eyes, he softened his tone. "You must not worry, Katya. You and I will still have our future together. I wish we could plan the when and where at this moment, but for now I can only promise you a someday."

"I can't allow you to stand here forever, Madame." The gruff voice of the guard interrupted them.

"Of course," Katherina replied. "You've been very kind, and we both thank you for it." She stretched to brush Aleksandr's lips with her own, and she forced a smile as she saw a veil of sadness fall over his eyes. "Until someday," she murmured.

Outside the prison, the midday sun stung Katherina's eyes, forcing the tears that she had held back as she talked with Aleksandr. Blinded by the light and by her tears, she stumbled into the cathedral to compose herself. A caretaker, polishing the icons on the walls, stopped to stare at her. As she quietly sat down, he continued his work. Katherina mopped away her tears, breathing deeply. She closed her eyes, but she found herself confronted by terrible images of Aleksandr Sergeievich lying in the cold, damp prison while rats scurried over his arms and legs and nibbled through his clothing. Her eyes flew open and she stifled a scream. The caretaker looked at her fearfully, and she forced her eyes to focus on a flickering candle on the central altar. Concentrating on the flame, she gradually managed to calm herself. After twenty minutes, she rose slowly, crossed herself, and left the cathedral.

At home, Katherina Andreievna tried to rest before Pavel Pavlovich arrived, but whenever she closed her eyes, she saw horrible images of Aleksandr in prison. She wondered how long it would take Aleksandr Sergeievich's uncle to gain his release. Even one more night in the cell was too frightening to imagine. She wondered if the guards who accepted her money today could be persuaded to open Aleksandr's cell and let him escape. Perhaps they would accept some of her jewelry, some pieces Pavel Pavlovich had never seen and so would never miss. The thought of returning to the prison made her shudder, but the thought of her beloved Sasha locked up with the vermin was even worse.

At dinner, Pavel Pavlovich politely inquired about how Katherina had spent the day.

"Oh, nothing very exciting," she replied. "I slept late, read a bit, played the piano, and I took a nap this afternoon."

The count smiled at his wife. "Count Anitchkov thought he saw you crossing the Palace Bridge this afternoon, but I assured him he must have been mistaken."

"I'm sure I don't know how one could recognize anyone under a heavy winter cloak."

They finished the meal with light conversation, and Masha and another servant, Anna, came to clear away their plates.

Masha stopped on her way out the door. "Oh, madame, I almost forgot to tell you. The dressmaker called while you were out. She said she will return tomorrow at three."

"Thank you, Masha." Katherina stared at her hands, conscious that Pavel Pavlovich was studying her.

After the servants left, he spoke softly. "I was under the impression that you did not go out today, my dear."

Katherina did not respond.

"I am sure you would not purposely deceive me," he pressed. "Is there something you forgot to mention to me?"

"I did go out, today," Katherina said slowly. "To Petropavlovsky Cathedral—to pray."

"So Count Anitchkov was not mistaken." Pavel Pavlovich paused as Katherina nodded. "That is quite a long walk for a cold December day. I should think you would have preferred to go to Our Lady of Kazan. It is so much closer."

"But Petropavlovsky seems so much more splendid to me. And," she groped for the words, "as the birthplace of St. Petersburg, it seemed the most fitting place to pray for the future of Mother Russia."

"I see." The count was silent for a moment; then he asked gently, "Katherina Andreievna, why didn't you tell me before that you had gone there?"

She shrugged. "I was afraid you would not approve."

"I don't approve," he said. "I don't believe it is safe for you to be out on the streets alone. I do not want to frighten you, my dear, but these are strange times in St. Petersburg. One of the rebels still lurking in the streets from yesterday's exhibition could easily have kidnapped you. A young, beautiful countess would be quite a prize. Of course I would pay any price for your return, but I cringe to think of what those barbarians might do to you in the meantime." He was silent a moment, like a chastening father waiting for his words to sink in. "You must promise that if you wish to go out in the future, you will ask Aleksei to drive you."

He waited for her response, and she choked out a whisper, "Yes, Pavel Pavlovich, I promise."

"Good. Now then," the count continued in a lighter tone, "I have been saving a piece of good news for you. Czar Nikolai has appointed me a member of his special commission of inquiry to examine the rebellion and the attempted revolution. We shall see that the rebels are brought to justice and made an example of for the God-fearing people of the empire."

Katherina Andreievna turned white. Visions of Aleksandr Sergeievich being "made an example of" raced through her mind. Her husband watched her in shock.

"What is the matter, Katherina Andreievna?" he

asked. "You do not seem very pleased. Need I explain what a great honor it is to be chosen to serve on such an important commission? The Czar has placed extraordinary trust in me."

"Of course he has, and I am very proud of you, Pavel Pavlovich. It is just that I—," she stumbled over her thoughts, "I hate to anticipate the long hours of work and strain this will mean for you."

"Nonsense. There is no strain in dispensing justice. It is simply a question of right and wrong. For the sake of the empire, the guilty must be punished, and I must accept the role I am called upon to play."

Before the count could continue his lofty speech, his servant Ivan broke in. "Count Ostrov, Pyotr Dmitrievich Belikov is here to see you."

"Ah, what a pleasant surprise, it is good to see you back in St. Petersburg." The count, followed by Katherina Andreievna, went to the sitting room to greet his friend. After the two men embraced, the count presented his wife. "Pyotr Dmitrievich, I have been wanting you to meet Katherina Andreievna for some time now. I had hoped you would call on us sooner."

"I am most honored to make your acquaintance, Countess Ostrova." Pyotr Dmitrievich kissed Katherina's hand.

"Your nephew, Aleksandr Sergeievich, was most gracious in helping Katherina become acquainted with St. Petersburg," said the count.

"Yes, he mentioned that fact to me." Pyotr Dmitrievich eyed Katherina uneasily, shifting his weight from one foot to the other.

"Pyotr Dmitrievich, you do not seem your usual self," the count said. "Is something troubling you?"

"Yes—there is something," he admitted. "I'm sorry

to disrupt your evening, Pavel Pavlovich, but I'm afraid this is not merely a social call. Would it be too much of an imposition for us to talk privately?"

"Not at all." Pavel Pavlovich turned to Katherina. "Would you mind, my dear?"

"Of course not." Nodding to their visitor, Katherina Andreievna stepped out of the sitting room, and Pavel Pavlovich closed its heavy double doors. For a moment Katherina hesitated outside, listening.

"Now, what is the problem, my friend?" Pavel Pavlovich asked. "You know I will do whatever is possible to help."

"I'm not sure you will think it so easy," said Pyotr Dmitrievich. "The problem concerns Aleksandr Sergeievich." He lowered his voice, and Katherina leaned closer to the door. At the same moment, Pavel Pavlovich's servant, Ivan, appeared in the dining room doorway. He flashed a disapproving glance at Katherina, and she quickly turned and flounced up the stairs to her room.

Pyotr Dmitrievich stayed more than an hour. Katherina, fidgeting in her room, heard him leave, then listened to Pavel Pavlovich pacing in the sitting room. Finally, the count trudged up the stairs. Katherina greeted him at her door. "Your friend's visit seems to have tired you, Pavel Pavlovich."

"Yes," he said, "my new position appears to be more complicated than I had anticipated."

"Would it help to talk about it?"

"Perhaps you are right, Katherina Andreievna." He called Ivan to bring him some cognac, then settled into a chair in her room. "It seems that young Aleksandr Sergeievich Belikov is mixed up among the revolutionaries." He sighed.

"Mixed up with the revolutionaries? In what way?" Katherina hoped she sounded incredulous.

Pavel Pavlovich shrugged. "Who can say? A young, impressionable mind. A product of the too-liberal education at Tsarskoe Selo. The romantic spirit of youth that believes in the principle of freedom at all costs. At any rate, he is among those imprisoned at Petropavlovsky Fortress."

Katherina cringed, remembering her visit. "How horrible."

The count nodded. "Yes, I'm afraid the prison can be horrible." He was silent for a moment, studying the swirling cognac in his glass. "Pyotr Dmitrievich is convinced the lad had nothing to do with the revolution, that he merely joined with the rabble on the square. He wants me to secure his nephew's release."

"And will you?" Katherina felt her heart quicken.

He shrugged halfheartedly. "I would like to. Pyotr Dmitrievich is an old and dear friend. And, in the short time we have known him, young Belikov has shown true friendship to both of us. But Czar Nikolai will not be impressed with personal friendships. He only wants subjects who are friends to the empire, friends to the Czar. I must be careful not to let personal feelings interfere with the course of justice."

"But if young Belikov is really not guilty—"

"I will see that he is interviewed fairly," said the count. "That is all I promised Pyotr Dmitrievich, all I can promise anyone. But," he said wearily, "for all of our sakes, I pray to God that he is innocent."

Chapter 6

More than a week passed, and during that time Pavel
Pavlovich and his commission interviewed the men
who were participants in the insurrection. Katherina
did not go to the prison again for fear of being seen
by her husband or one of his associates. She wondered how Pavel Pavlovich would weigh Aleksandr
Sergeievich's case if he knew of their liaison. Each
evening she waited tensely, hoping her husband
would mention the young officer, and each night she
went to bed with her hopes frustrated.

Gradually, Katherina gathered bits of information.
The revolutionaries were members of secret societies
located in both the northern and southern cities of the
empire. They were mostly upper-class intellectuals
and members of the military, people who—Pavel
Pavlovich said—should know better. All of them
wanted to free the serfs, an act that would undoubtedly throw the empire into chaos. The northern groups
wanted a constitution, a two-house legislature, and a
complete reorganization of regional government. In
fact, many of their plans were modeled after the government of that fledgling nation—the United States
of America. Pavel Pavlovich said it was absolutely
absurd to even consider replacing a governmental
system that had been developing for hundreds of
years with one that was less than fifty years old.

During the entire week, Katherina slept for only a
few hours. She was afraid to close her eyes and thus

see the progressively worsening visions of Aleksandr Sergeievich in prison. By the fifth day, she imagined that the rats had eaten one whole foot, leaving a ghastly bleeding stump, and that the mice had carried away huge tufts of Aleksandr's hair to build a nest. When exhaustion drowned her in sleep, Katherina had vivid nightmares of her beloved fleeing from Senate Square and being torn in two by the Czar's cannons. She began sleeping with a pillow over her face so that Pavel Pavlovich could not hear her when she awoke screaming.

On the afternoon of Christmas Eve, Katherina Andreievna sat in the sitting room, depressed and disheartened. She had agreed with Pavel Pavlovich's suggestion to forgo a festive celebration as they continued to mourn the deaths of Czar Aleksandr and General Miloradovich. The idea had suited Katherina, since she knew it would be futile for her to attempt a gay holiday attitude while she worried so about Aleksandr Sergeievich. But now, the house depressed her even more. She thought of her parents' house in Novgorod. It would be gaily decorated with lacquered wooden ornaments and delicate straw figures. She could almost smell the holiday cookies and tea cakes fresh from her mother's oven, and she imagined her family toasting the holiday with *braga*, the traditional nectar of Novgorod that always made her head spin with dizzy, happy images.

For the first time since her marriage, Katherina felt homesick. How often when she was growing up she had wished for an escape, for fewer family members to bother her. Now she wished for just one person from her family to comfort her, to wipe away the tears that she hid each day from Pavel Pavlovich.

Katherina Andreievna was so caught up in her sadness that she did not hear the knock at the front door or the servants going to answer it. When Masha entered to announce a visitor, she was startled and embarrassed. There was no place for her to escape and hide her tears, so she turned away from the sitting room door, blotted her face as well as she could, and directed Masha to show the visitor in. She heard someone enter the room and then heard the click of the closing doors. Courtesy demanded that she turn and greet her visitor, but she continued to stare at the wall, waiting for the intruder to speak.

"Merry Christmas, Katya."

Only one person could utter her name so tenderly, and, filled with astonishment and relief, she whirled about and ran into his arms. "Merry Christmas, Sasha," she said, although she could scarcely find her voice as their lips met. The intensity of their twin desire was electrifying, and when she finally stepped back to look at him, all the terrible imagery of the past week finally dissolved. He was thinner from his ten days in prison, and his face looked pale, but his eyes still shone with the same dark fire, and his arms were still firm and strong around her.

"Did you—escape?" she asked in confusion.

He smiled and kissed her nose. "No—I was released. Owing to the influence of your husband."

"Oh." She sighed happily and nestled her head on his shoulder.

He took her chin in his hands, tilted her face toward his, and searched her eyes. "Katherina Andreievna—did you ask him to do it? Does he know about us?"

"No. I have told him nothing. Your uncle was here to plead your case, and perhaps I added a bit of subtle influence, but the decision was Pavel Pavlovich's own. I know it was difficult for him. He takes his duties to the empire very seriously."

"Your husband is a fine man—a credit to Russia," Aleksandr Sergeievich said sincerely.

They gazed at each other, letting the joy of reunion seep through their bodies. But Katherina sensed his sadness, and she tried to allay it. "You look wonderfully well, Sasha—much better than I would have dreamed possible."

"Yes." He sat down on the love seat, indicating that she should join him. "I was fortunate in that they did not treat me too badly."

"When were you released?" She sat beside him, her head on his chest.

"About two hours ago. I would have come directly here, but I wanted to go home and wash and change clothes first." He hesitated, uncertain whether to continue. "I wanted you to remember me looking well."

"Remember you?" Katherina sat up straight and stared at him. "What do you mean—remember you?"

He sighed. "The commission has recommended that I leave St. Petersburg immediately."

"But whatever for? If you are innocent, they have nothing more to say to you—"

"Katya, no one connected with our movement will ever be judged fully innocent. It is true they cannot saddle me with guilt, but, believe me, it is better for me to accept a brief exile and move beyond the Czar's wrath."

"But where will you go, Sasha?"

He shrugged. "I have not decided yet. Perhaps to one of the outlying provinces. Perhaps to the Caucasus. Life there is freer, I'm told, farther from the long arm of the Czar."

"I will come with you," Katherina said.

Aleksandr smiled. "That would be a fine way to

thank Count Ostrov for releasing me—by running off with his wife. No, Katya," he said, "you must stay here. I will not take you with me when I have no idea what kind of life I can offer you. This separation will only be temporary, I promise you. In time, the memories of December 14 will fade, and I will be able to return to St. Petersburg."

"And I will have grown wrinkled and ugly from the waiting and the worrying."

"No, Katya," he insisted. "If we both live to be three hundred years old you will still be beautiful and desirable to me. You must never stop believing in our someday. If we both want it and believe in it, we will surely have it—someday."

He took her in his arms and kissed her, and tremors of delight rippled through her body. Her own lips and mouth answered in overwhelming urgency, and she felt his body trembling. Their passion was like a volcano waiting to erupt—hot, impatient, fueled by the knowledge that this moment was the beginning of a long separation. "Sasha," she whispered fiercely, "I want you so badly—now—please."

"Oh, my sweet Katya," he murmured, "I wish that it were possible."

"It is," she said between kisses.

"But what about your servants?"

The dizzying heat of her desire obliterated Katherina's reasoning powers. "They will not intrude when the doors are closed," she insisted.

"But perhaps they can hear us," he whispered, kissing her.

"Sasha—please. Don't deny us these few moments when months of emptiness lie before us." She did not have to plead further, for their passion had reached a height that neither could control.

Their flesh came together greedily, sensation piled

on top of sensation, his hardness insistent, her burning fluidity demanding, sustaining their ecstasy almost beyond endurance.

Lying in cramped contentment on the love seat, Katherina pressed closer to Aleksandr's quivering flesh, not wanting to give in to the impending moment of separation. At last Aleksandr sat up, gently lifting her body with his own. With sad tenderness, he kissed her forehead, her nose, her lips.

Katherina turned to him with glistening eyes. "Must you really leave today?"

"I wish the answer were no. But—" He finished the thought by pulling on his boots.

"Surely you could stay another day. For Christmas. No one would persecute you on Christmas."

"There is no Christmas in St. Petersburg this year. Ask my comrades in Petropavlovsky Fortress about Christmas. They will tell you it does not exist."

Katherina took his hand. "At least we had our moment of Christmas, Sasha. Thank you for the only gift I have prayed for."

He smiled lovingly and kissed her once more. "Wait for me, Katya. When I can I will send you news. When it is safe, I will bring the news myself."

Katherina impulsively tore a button from the sleeve of her dress and pressed it into his hand. Half smiling, he kissed the gift and dropped it into his pocket. Then he snapped a button from his uniform, handed it to her, walked to the door, and let himself out.

Katherina was still rubbing the golden button, with its insignia of the Imperial Army, when she heard troika bells outside. Through the window she saw Pavel Pavlovich dismounting from his sleigh. She scurried up the stairs to hide her memento.

As Katherina walked back down the stairs, Pavel Pavlovich looked up from the foyer where Ivan was taking his cloak. "Ah, Katherina Andreievna," he said, "you are looking lovely today."

"Thank you, Pavel Pavlovich," she said as they walked into the sitting room.

"Tell me, my dear, was that young Aleksandr Belikov I saw walking away from our house?"

"Yes, it was. He came to wish us a Merry Christmas and to thank you for getting him released from the prison," Katherina said smoothly.

"He should not thank me," the count replied. "It was the decision of the entire commission."

"He seemed to think you were instrumental in convincing the others of his innocence."

"Perhaps I was," the count admitted. "At any rate, it would be a great blow to Russia to sacrifice so fine a young man because of one moment of ill-informed indiscretion. Some of the others are merely rabble —overeducated pompous trash. But young Belikov has breeding. He comes from a good family, and I have no doubt that one day he will do great things for Russia." He paused and smiled affectionately at Katherina Andreievna. "That young man needs the stabilizing influence of a good woman like you, Katherina Andreievna."

"Perhaps—someday—he will have that, Pavel Pavlovich."

A few days after Christmas, news reached St. Petersburg that one of the rebel leaders had been discovered near Kiev, and each day brought more news of him and the force he commanded that was eight hundred strong. Katherina couldn't help wondering whether Aleksandr Sergeievich had joined that force and if he would be captured again. She knew that even Pavel Pavlovich could not arrange to have him released a second time. She prayed that he had gone directly to the Caucasus and that he had not traveled there by way of Kiev.

Early in January, the Czar's forces met the rebel army. Those revolutionaries who were not killed in the battle were rounded up and returned to the capital to face imprisonment and inquisition by the Czar's commission. Katherina listened carefully as Pavel Pavlovich expounded on the deeds and identities of the newest prisoners. The names Muravyov-Apostol and Bestuzhev-Ryumin were repeated again and again, but Aleksandr Sergeievich Belikov was never mentioned, and Pyotr Dmitrievich Belikov did not call on the count, so Katherina assumed with relief that her beloved was safe somewhere within the sprawling Russian Empire.

Winter dragged on, and Katherina Andreievna became more and more bored with life in St. Petersburg. The cold weather seemed relentless, even the gilding on the spires of the Admiralty and Petropavlovsky Cathedral looked gaudy and unattractive, the troika bells no longer sounded merry, and fresh hot tea from the samovar tasted stale and bitter. The one thing that motivated her to get out of bed each morning was the hope of receiving word from Aleksandr Sergeievich. She rarely left the house, fearful of missing a message, but no news came, and her prized button from Aleksandr's uniform began to tarnish from constant handling.

Much as she longed for Aleksandr Sergeievich, Katherina Andreievna admitted to herself that it was safer for him to be away from St. Petersburg. In the months after the insurrection, the city was overrun with secret police—under the direction of Czar Nikolai's trusted friend, General Benckendorff. Pavel Pavlovich was sometimes gone all night, involved as he was in his work on the commission of inquiry.

Though he never spoke to her about the actual inter-rogations, Katherina pieced together some information from the strange hours he was keeping and from rumors whispered among the house servants. She knew that prisoners were sometimes yanked from their cells in the middle of the night to face brightly lighted rooms where the commission—or even Czar Nikolai himself—questioned them. She heard that those who did not cooperate were thrown into chains and isolated in dungeons. She even heard that some had died from the strains of interrogation.

When Pavel Pavlovich did come home, he seemed weary and withdrawn. He seldom spoke, even at meals, and he abandoned his visits to Katherina's bed. Katherina sympathized with him, for he hated the harsh role imposed on him by Czar Nikolai, but at the same time he felt a firm commitment to his country and his sovereign. She could not, would not, envision her gentle, considerate husband in the role of inquisitor. Instead, she idealized him as liberator of her beloved Sasha.

As the ice melted on the Neva and its canals, Pavel Pavlovich's work with the commission continued. Still no word came from Aleksandr Sergeievich, and the long-awaited springtime now seemed to Katherina as bleak as the winter just passed. Without her beloved, the Venice of the North offered neither charm nor romance.

By summer, the Czar's special commission had examined more than 600 people who had been connected in some way with the revolution. A special high court sentenced 121 of the conspirators. Hearing their fates, Katherina was again thankful that Aleksandr Sergeievich was safely far away. Five of the rebel leaders were sentenced to be drawn and quartered. Most of the others were exiled to Siberia, some for a life of hard labor, others for shorter terms, but everyone knew that even a short term in Siberia could quickly turn into a life sentence. As the proverb said, The road to Siberia is wide; the lane back is narrow.

In July, having observed a proper period of mourning for Czar Aleksandr, Czar Nikolai celebrated his coronation in Petropavlovsky Cathedral with an awesome display of splendor and power. It was customary for czars to be crowned in Uspensky Cathedral in the ancient capital of Moscow, but Czar Nikolai had important business to attend to in St. Petersburg. The same day he was crowned, the five rebel leaders, whose sentences had been commuted, were hanged— in an equally awesome display of power and absolute authority.

Katherina Andreievna and Pavel Pavlovich joined countless foreign and Russian dignitaries in witnessing the coronation. On their way to the coronation ball, they passed the five corpses that hung at the fortress walls as lifeless symbols for future rebels. Shuddering, Katherina hoped that the coronation and the executions also symbolized the end of a nightmare and the beginning of a new Russian era.

Not to mention the safe return of Aleksandr Sergeievich.

Chapter 7

With the matter of the revolutionaries finally resolved, Czar Nikolai felt free to move his court to Moscow for a few months. His eastern subjects had still not seen their new ruler, and he was anxious to establish his authority in all parts of the empire.

Pavel Pavlovich, relieved of the trying and distasteful task of serving on the commission of inquiry, began to pay more attention to Katherina Andreievna. Although she tried to make a show of cheerfulness, she found herself slipping deeper into a depression as each day passed without news from Aleksandr Sergeievich. Her husband watched her and worried about how to bring more happiness into his young wife's life. Thinking she was overcome by the oppressive nature of the last few months in St. Petersburg, he decided she needed a change of scene. At dinner one night, a few weeks after Czar Nikolai had departed for Moscow, he made his announcement.

"Katherina Andreievna, I have decided that both you and I need a vacation. Some time away from St. Petersburg would be good for both of us. These last months have been too filled with sadness."

"Do you propose to go to our estate in Novgorod?" Katherina tried to sound unconcerned.

"No. Novgorod is too near—and too familiar. I have decided we shall go to Moscow."

"Moscow?" Katherina was alarmed. A visit to Novgorod would take a few weeks at most. She knew Pavel Pavlovich quickly tired of country life and never stayed long at the estate, but Moscow was worlds away. The visit could extend into months, and what if Aleksandr Sergeievich returned to St. Petersburg while she was gone? Would he think she had deserted him? That she had tired of waiting for him?

"I thought you would be more pleased, my dear."

"Pavel Pavlovich," Katherina said, "I am touched by your proposal. You know I have often dreamed of visiting Moscow, but perhaps it would be better to postpone such a trip. I know you are exhausted from your service on the Czar's commission, and the long journey to Moscow might be too tiring."

"Nonsense, my dear. I am not such an old and feeble man that I am too weak to travel. The fresh air of the journey will be good for me. And with Czar Nikolai in residence, the Moscow social life is bound to be exciting. Perhaps," he said, patting her hand affectionately, "we could even consider it the honeymoon I never gave you."

Katherina smiled, then quickly looked away.

"There is no need for you to worry about details," the count continued. "I have already instructed the servants to begin packing. Your Masha and my Ivan will accompany us, and we will leave the day after tomorrow."

The swiftness of the decision was too much for Katherina. Announcing that she had a headache, she bolted from the table and rushed to her room, leaving her husband to ponder her unpredictable behavior. She quickly undressed and got into bed, knowing that Pavel Pavlovich would soon be knocking on her door to inquire about her health. She must find a way to change his plans. But how?

Within an hour, Pavel Pavlovich came upstairs and rapped softly at Katherina's door. "Katherina Andreievna," he whispered, "is there anything I can do for you? Shall I ask Anna to bring you some tea and brandy?" Katherina did not answer. She was afraid her husband would want to talk more about their trip to Moscow, and she could not talk about it until she had time to think. Pavel Pavlovich came to her bedside as she lay still, breathing evenly, as if asleep. He stood over her a moment, listening to her breathing, then he gently kissed her forehead and quietly left the room.

By the time the night was half over, Katherina realized that there was no way she could convince Pavel Pavlovich to cancel the trip to Moscow. She could delay their departure by pretending to be ill, but after a day or two Pavel Pavlovich would summon a doctor, and her deception would probably be uncovered. Resigning herself, she began to concentrate on how to leave a message for Aleksandr Sergeievich. Masha was the only servant she trusted, and Masha would be with her in Moscow. She thought of the others—Anna, Dmitri Aleksei, Petrushka. All of them were Pavel Pavlovich's servants—loyal to him, but politely disapproving of her. If Aleksandr Sergeievich came calling for her, they would probably tell him the Ostrovs were in Moscow—nothing more. If she asked them to say more, or gave them a written message to deliver, most likely they would gladly deliver her message—straight to Pavel Pavlovich.

Katherina Andreievna got out of bed and went to her balcony. Perhaps the breeze from the Gulf of Finland would stir the hot July air and help her to think more clearly. St. Petersburg was asleep; the bright full moon watched over the city. Katherina stared at the moon's reflection in the rippling canal and wondered if Aleksandr Sergeievich's servants could be trusted. Perhaps at least some of them could. She thought of her visit to his house the day

after the revolution, when the servant insisted that his
master was in Sestroretsk. If he was loyal enough to
protect Aleksandr Sergeievich then, surely he could
be trusted to keep and deliver a message now. At
any rate, there was no one else to whom she could
turn. She went to her bureau for pen, ink, and paper.
Returning to the balcony, she balanced the paper on
the railing, and wrote her note to him.

My dearest Sasha—
Should you return and find that I am gone please
do not think that I have tired of waiting and have
deserted you. All these months, I have waited
faithfully, and, though I am far from St. Petersburg now I still wait for you with a loving heart.
   Pavel Pavlovich insists that we follow the Czar
to Moscow for a vacation, and all of my excuses
are too feeble to dissuade him. I cannot say how
long we shall be gone, but can only guess that we
shall return before the Neva freezes.
   Please wait for me, beloved Sasha as I have
waited for you these many months. I pray continuously for your safe return to my arms. I am
writing this by the full moon's light hoping that
it will make the fates smile on our love in the
future. I cannot send you my love, for it is already
completely in your possession.
                                   Your own, always,
                                       Katya

Carefully folding the letter, Katherina returned to
bed. She tucked the message under her pillow, hoping to infuse it with even more of her love.

In the morning, Pavel Pavlovich, free from responsibilities now that the Council of State had re-
cessed, knocked on Katherina's door. He was carrying
her breakfast tray.

"Good morning, Katherina Andreievna," he said cheerily as he set the tray across her lap and bent to kiss her forehead. "I hope you slept well and are feeling better today."

"Yes, thank you, Pavel Pavlovich. The night's rest has made me look forward to our coming journey."

"Good." He sat down on the edge of the bed and moved to prop up her pillow behind her. Katherina quickly slid her letter beneath her, almost upsetting the tray. Catching the tray, Pavel Pavlovich looked at her quizzically.

She smiled sweetly. "I guess I am just excited about going to Moscow." She resettled the tray on her lap and began to eat the bowl of warm kasha.

The count was obviously pleased. "Katherina Andreievna," he said, "I thought I would call on my friend Pyotr Dmitrievich this morning. Perhaps you would like to accompany me. I would so like the two of you to become better acquainted."

"Pavel Pavlovich, I would truly enjoy a visit with your friend, but I think it would be better for me to stay home and oversee the arrangements for our trip."

"As I told you last night, my dear, there is nothing for you to worry about. The servants are quite capable."

"I know they are, but I would feel better if I took some part in the preparations. Besides," she said, "I'm afraid I would not be very good company. I'm much too excited about our trip to offer interesting conversation. Perhaps you could carry my greetings to Pyotr Dmitrievich and suggest that we might entertain him at dinner one night soon after we return from Moscow."

"Very well, my dear," Pavel Pavlovich said. "I shall go alone and extend your greetings and your invitation." He rose and kissed her on the forehead again. "I won't be gone more than an hour or two. See that you don't exhaust yourself in my absence."

"Enjoy your visit, Pavel Pavlovich," she said, and then she wondered if she had made a mistake. Perhaps Pyotr Dmitrievich had some word of Aleksandr Sergeievich. No, she assured herself, Aleksandr would send word to her before anyone else. It was more important that she use the time to deliver her message to Aleksandr's house. She looked toward her balcony, and her gaze fell on the pen and ink still on the railing where she had left them the night before. Sliding the breakfast tray from her lap, she rushed to the balcony to put them away. In her haste, she knocked the ink from the railing, and it fell to the canal below, dissipating in a murky cloud. Katherina turned away quickly, telling herself it was silly to accept the accident as any kind of omen. She dressed herself and called Masha to take away the half-finished breakfast tray.

As soon as Katherina heard Pavel Pavlovich leave the house, she tucked the letter into the bosom of her dress, crept downstairs, and let herself out. Months had passed since her last visit to Aleksandr Sergeievich's house, but her feet knew the way. As she approached his door, her heart pounded eagerly, and her mind was flooded with memories of her first visit there. The door knocker was badly tarnished, she thought disapprovingly, the servants had become lax in their master's absence.

She knocked and waited breathlessly for an answer. For ten minutes Katherina stood at the door knocking and waiting, knocking and waiting. A servant woman, carrying the day's marketing to a neighboring house, stopped and stared at Katherina.

"You won't get any answer there, madame," the

servant called. "No one has lived in that house for months."

"I'm sure you're mistaken," Katherina answered. "I've heard the master here has a large staff of servan's."

"He did have a large staff," the servant called, "but before he left last Christmas he gave all of them their freedom."

Katherina was shocked. "Are you quite sure?"

"Yes, madame," the woman nodded. "It seemed to me like a rather unusual thing for a rich young man to do, but I always thought there was something strange about that young Belikov."

Suddenly embarrassed at being seen, and remembering how viciously gossip circulated among St. Petersburg house servants, Katherina stepped back from the door. "Belikov?" she cried. "Did you say the master's name was Belikov?"

"Yes, madame. Aleksandr Sergeievich Belikov."

"Oh my goodness!" Katherina rushed back into the street. "How embarrassing! I have the wrong house entirely. I told my driver to leave me at the house of Madame Benshikov. How could he make such a mistake?" She hurried away, leaving the servant staring after her.

Wandering in the streets, Katherina wondered how she could deliver her message. Perhaps she could slip it beneath the door and hope that Aleksandr Sergeievich would eventually return to his deserted house and find it. But what if mice had overrun the house? Would they eat the paper or shred it and use it to build nests? What if one of Aleksandr's relatives came to check on his house? Would they find the note and read it? Suppose it was Pyotr Dmitrievich? Could he guess who Katya was? And if he did, would he keep the secret from his dear friend, Pavel Pavlovich? Hundreds of possibilities haunted Katherina's imagination, but the fact remained that she knew of no other way to leave a message for Aleksandr's Sergeievich. She walked back to his house, watching for neighboring house servants, and, when she was sure that no curious eyes were peeking from behind the neighbors' curtains, she stepped to the door and slid her letter beneath it. Still fearful of being watched, she jumped back from the door, and hurried toward home. One bright corner of the paper protruded from beneath the door.

As she approached her own house, Pavel Pavlovich's carriage was just arriving. Katherina slipped between two neighboring houses and waited for him to enter their door. Then she slowly walked to the door, hoping that she could slip in unnoticed. She met Masha in the foyer, and, at the same moment, Pavel Pavlovich appeared at the top of the stairway.

"Ah, I was looking for you, my dear," the count said as he walked down the stairs. "I expected to find you packing."

"Oh, Pavel Pavlovich—the dressmaker had not delivered some of my summer dresses, so I went to see if she had finished them," Katherina said. "I had hoped to take them with me to Moscow, but I shall have to make do with what I have."

"Katherina Andreievna," her husband said with a hint of sternness, "I've told you not to go out alone. If you had waited for me to return, I could have taken you in the carriage."

"But it's much too lovely a day not to walk," Katherina said gaily. "Besides, I did not go alone. Masha accompanied me."

Pavel Pavlovich, not noticing Masha's expression, softened, and he chuckled. "Well, I suppose it is useless to try to change the willful young woman I married. And I suppose that St. Petersburg is a safer place now that the echoes of revolution have been dispelled." He took Katherina's arm. "Let Masha do your packing. Come and sit with me a bit." The confused servant scurried upstairs as Katherina and the count went into the sitting room.

"Did you enjoy your visit with Pyotr Dmitrievich?" Katherina asked.

"Oh yes," her husband said. "He is off to his country estate next week. He sent his greetings and his regrets that you did not accompany me. He is anxious to visit with you, since his nephew delivered such glowing reports of your intelligence and wit."

"His nephew?"

"Surely you have not forgotten young Aleksandr Belikov, my dear. Pyotr Dmitrievich seemed a bit concerned that he has not heard from the young man since his departure from St. Petersburg, but I told him not to worry. Russia is a vast empire with thousands of tempting young women to amuse a free young man. Young Belikov is probably much too busy to bother writing to his old uncle in St. Petersburg." The count chuckled.

"I'm quite sure you are right, Pavel Pavlovich." Katherina smiled.

They arrived in Moscow in mid-August, after traveling slowly by carriage, stopping at several small towns along the way. They spent only one night at the count's Novgorod estate and only a few hours visiting with Katherina Andreievna's parents. As they drove through the endless silver birch forests, Katherina wondered what the landscape was like in the Caucasus and if Aleksandr Sergeievich was indeed there. They spent nights in Okulovka, Bologoye, Torzhok, and a number of other small towns, each of which

offered only the most rustic of inns. In each case,
Katherina was forced to share a room with her husband, who, as he had promised, did everything possible to make the trip seem like a honeymoon. Katherina resigned herself to his attentions, acting the
dutiful, if not joyful, wife. Most nights she lay awake,
uncomfortably listening to Pavel Pavlovich breathing beside her, as she continued to wonder where
Aleksandr Sergeievich was and what he was doing.

Much as she had opposed the trip, Katherina could
not help feeling exhilarated by her first sight of Moscow. The imposing Spasskaya Tower—gateway to the
Kremlin—seemed to symbolize the feelings of power
and pride that existed in this ancient city that had
risen again, like a phoenix, after the disastrous fires
of Napoleon's occupation. The silver and gold domes
of Uspensky Cathedral and Blagoveshchensky Cathedral glittered invitingly, and the red, green, yellow,
and blue striped domes of Saint Basil's Cathedral
looked to Katherina like a vision from an ancient fairy
tale.

They stayed at the mansion of Prince Dolgochev,
an old military comrade of Pavel Pavlovich, who
was a distant relative of the Czar. The prince, a
widower who lived there without any other family,
allotted them twenty-five of his mansion's one hundred rooms, but, to Katherina's despair, Pavel Pavlovich still chose to share a bedroom with her. Since
she was his wife, she knew she could not complain,
but she hoped that the honeymoon would end by
the time they returned to St. Petersburg.

Their first week in Moscow was spent attending
exquisite balls. Even with Czar Nikolai in residence,
the atmosphere here seemed gayer and freer than
in St. Petersburg. The residents were all acutely
aware of the revolution and its aftermath, but they

seemed less intimidated than people in St. Petersburg. General Benckendorff's gendarmes were less noticeable, and the newspaper, *Moskovsky Telegraf*, offered a full discussion of political ideas—even daring to criticize the autocracy from time to time. The Czar and his court were ringed by the sturdy walls of the Kremlin, and the Muscovites, secure in the knowledge that he would soon return to St. Petersburg, continued to live as they wished.

A week after their arrival, Pavel Pavlovich announced that he was going to the Kremlin to pay his respects to the Czar. Katherina smiled, thinking how her husband's lifetime in state service had conditioned him to follow his sovereign even during a supposed vacation. While Pavel Pavlovich was gone, the prince supplied Katherina with a carriage and driver, and she took Masha with her to explore the city.

As they drove around the red brick walls of the triangular-shaped Kremlin, Katherina realized that Moscow was much like Novgorod, but on a much grander scale. The two cities were nearly the same age and had similarly Slavic styles of architecture. There was none of the Western European influence that made St. Petersburg look like the capital of a foreign country. From the Kremlin, Moscow ranged out in rings of boulevards. They drove across the winding Moscow River, and the driver pointed out the two buildings of Moscow University, built at the end of the last century, then rebuilt after the fires of 1812. As they drove around the Novodevichy Monastery, itself a miniature kremlin, the driver explained that Czarina Sophia, wife of Ivan the Great, was buried in the monastery's Smolensky Cathedral.

As the carriage crossed the river again to return to the center of Moscow, Katherina ordered the driver to stop, for approaching the carriage on horseback was a familiar figure. Katherina blinked, unable to believe what she was seeing. She stood up in the carriage to gain a better view. At that moment the rider caught sight of her golden hair, and he spurred his horse to the side of the carriage. Aware that Masha and the driver were watching her, Katherina sat down and phrased her words carefully.

"Good day to you, Aleksandr Sergeievich."

He looked at the two servants and replied, "How pleasant to see you, Countess Ostrova."

She controlled the quiver in her voice. "Where are you going on this beautiful day?"

"To Novodevichy Monastery for a time of prayer."

"I did not know it was possible to enter the monastery walls," Katherina said.

"It is if you know the abbot," he said. "Perhaps you would like to accompany me. The cathedral is quite beautiful."

Katherina turned to the driver. "Do you think there is time for us to return there for a few moments, Yuri?"

"Certainly, countess, if you wish." He clucked to the horses and turned the carriage around. Katherina smiled happily as Aleksandr rode beside the carriage.

Leaving the servants to mind the carriage and horses, Katherina Andreievna and Aleksandr Sergeievich entered the monastery gate. No one questioned them as they walked, arm in arm, to the Smolensky Cathedral. Its soaring gilded domes and glittering icons made no impression on Katherina. Her eyes never wavered from the flashing eyes of Aleksandr Sergeievich. The cathedral was empty, and Katherina, weak with excitement, sank to her knees on the stone floor.

"Sasha, where have you been all these months? Have you tried to reach me in St. Petersburg? Have you been there? Why are you in Moscow? When did you get here? Why haven't I seen you at any of the balls?" The questions tumbled out rapidly.

He laughed, his eyes dancing. "Katya, do you expect me to answer everything at once?"

"I'm sorry," she said. "I have worried and waited for so many endless months, longing just to hear from you, to know that you are safe. And now I find you where I never expected you." She smiled. "To think I tried to convince Pavel Pavlovich we should not come to Moscow. If I had known I would find you here, I would have suggested the trip myself!"

He took her hand and kissed it. "Katya, I have worried and longed for you all these months as well, but I was afraid to send you a message. Even in the Caucasus there is talk of Benckendorff's gendarmes—and of the long arm of the Czar's wrath. I was afraid that communication from an exile might somehow endanger you. But I could stand it no longer. The Caucasus is beautiful, lush, green, but without you it seemed barren and desolate. That is why I have come to Moscow."

Katherina shook her head. "Sasha, I'm afraid I do not understand."

"Life without you—my love—is no life at all, so I have come to beg a full pardon of the Czar and request permission to resume residence in St. Petersburg. I want to return with his blessing, so I need not fear for myself or for you."

Katherina sucked in her breath. "Do you really think Czar Nikolai will grant you a pardon, Sasha?"

"I am almost sure of it," he said. "Czar Nikolai has succeeded in making the example he wished. Now he will want to gain his subjects' love with a show of mercy. Just last week, he personally summoned the poet Pushkin and granted him pardon and release from exile."

"But was this Pushkin a member of the revolution?" Katherina asked.

"No—Czar Aleksandr had already exiled him from St. Petersburg before the uprising took place. But had he been in the city, he would surely have joined us on Senate Square. Some of his writings are quite revolutionary."

"And you are certain that Czar Nikolai pardoned him?"

"Yes," Aleksandr assured her, "I understand they had quite a friendly audience." Seeing the doubt in her eyes, he took her hand again. "You must not worry, Katya. Meeting you today is a sign that fortune will smile on my plea. My audience with the Czar is tomorrow at two o'clock. If you meet me in Saint Basil's Cathedral at three o'clock, I will have good news."

"I will meet you, Sasha. And until then I shall pray for you—for both of us." Katherina squeezed his hand and then returned to her waiting carriage.

The next morning Katherina Andreievna and Pavel Pavlovich were enjoying a leisurely breakfast of blinis and fresh fruit when the count's servant, Ivan, burst into the room.

"There is a messenger here from Czar Nikolai," Ivan announced. "He says the Czar requests your presence at an audience one hour from now."

"Tell the messenger I shall be there," said Pavel Pavlovich.

"You don't understand," Ivan said. "He wants to see both you and the countess."

The count raised his eyebrows, but he answered,

"Very well. When the Czar summons, his subjects must obey." As Ivan left the room, Pavel Pavlovich turned to Katherina Andreievna. "It's strange that Czar Nikolai did not mention this audience to me yesterday," he said. Then he got up from the table and kissed Katherina affectionately on the forehead. "Perhaps word of your beauty has finally reached the Czar."

Katherina had attended many social functions at which the Czar was present, but she had never met him face-to-face. She dressed carefully for the audience, as if her appearance would somehow determine the fate of Aleksandr Sergeievich.

As they hurried to their carriage, Pavel Pavlovich looked at her. "Katherina Andreievna," he breathed, "surely all the women in the court will envy your beauty, and all the men will envy me for having so lovely a wife."

They entered the Kremlin through the Spasskaya Tower Gate. Looking at the huge icon of the Savior that hung above the gate, Katherina hoped it symbolized the redemption of Aleksandr Sergeievich— and of herself. Their carriage rolled past the towering belfry of Ivan the Great, between the centuries-old Uspensky Cathedral and Arkhangelsky Cathedral, and they stopped in front of the magnificent Granovitaya Palace. As Pavel Pavlovich helped her from the carriage, Katherina Andreievna stared in awe at the thousands of faceted stones set in the wall of the palace. It was like some splendid crown.

Czar Nikolai received them in a hall that was constructed of polished marble and granite. As they bowed and walked toward their sovereign, he smiled and addressed Katherina. "It is a great joy to meet you at last, Countess Ostrova. I hope you will forgive me for keeping your husband from you so often in these last months. He is indeed a dedicated patriot to leave a beautiful woman such as you each day to serve his Czar and the empire."

Katherina blushed and curtsied humbly, and Pavel Pavlovich's chest swelled with pride.

The Czar motioned to them to sit down, and he continued. "My dear Count Ostrov, I have asked you here today, first to meet this lovely lady, but also to talk to you about an important matter of state. As you no doubt have heard, the Persians have threatened our territories in the Caucasus almost since the beginning of my reign."

"Yes." Pavel Pavlovich nodded. "I have heard."

"General Yermolov has been commanding our troops in the area, but I have begun to doubt his effectiveness. Only this morning I learned that he has lost Yelizavetpol and that he came quite close to losing the city of Tiflis. I think there is need for immediate action, and that is why I summoned you on such short notice. There is another general—Paskevich—in the region, who may be better equipped to assume command. I would like you to journey to the Caucasus and evaluate for me the effectiveness of both men."

"This is a great honor," Pavel Pavlovich murmured, "but why do you find me worthy of the mission?"

The Czar smiled. "There is no reason to be so humble, my dear count. I am well acquainted with your records from the Polish campaigns and during the time we drove Napoleon Bonaparte from our soil. I think you are a shrewd judge of military effectiveness and can serve me as an excellent adviser." The Czar paused and glanced at Katherina. "However, I can understand that you may feel reluctant to leave your lovely wife. Therefore, I propose that you take her with you. If you establish headquarters in Kislovodsk or Pyatigorsk, she should be quite far enough from the fighting to remain safe."

Katherina listened in horror. How could she go to the Caucasus now, when Aleksandr Sergeievich was sure to be returning to St. Petersburg? Why hadn't the Czar sent them months before, when she had longed to see her beloved? The color drained from her face, and the Czar looked at her in surprise.

"There is no need to worry, Countess Ostrova," he said. "Kislovodsk and Pyatigorsk are quite Russian. You will not meet any of the barbarians found in the Persian regions of the Caucasus."

Pavel Pavlovich looked at his wife in dismay. "Katherina Andreievna is just surprised at our good fortune," he said quickly.

The Czar nodded. "I would like you to leave without delay, before Yermolov surrenders more of our lands. I will provide some of my own carriages to afford the countess the greatest comfort on the journey, and a small company of militia will accompany you to ensure a safe journey. Can you be prepared to leave at noon?"

"We will be ready, Your Gracious Majesty," Pavel Pavlovich replied. "The countess and I both thank you for conferring this honor upon me—and for your generosity in seeing to our comfort." The Czar dismissed them, and Pavel Pavlovich led the stunned Katherina outside.

"The Czar has placed a great trust in me," Pavel Pavlovich said. "I was surprised you were not more gracious in accepting his generosity."

"Pavel Pavlovich—," Katherina blurted, "I don't wish to go to the Caucasus."

"Nonsense, my dear. It will be a great adventure. And think, you will not be spending another cold winter in St. Petersburg."

"But I can't be ready to leave at noon."

"Katherina Andreievna," her husband said, "I'm afraid you do not understand. One does not question the plans made by Czar Nikolai. As I told the Czar—both you and I will be ready."

Chapter 8

All the way back to Prince Dolgochev's mansion, Katherina was silent, trying to devise an escape from the Czar's wretched plan. She wondered if, somehow, the Czar's secret police had discovered her relationship with Aleksandr Sergeievich. Perhaps Czar Nikolai, in friendship to the count, intended to separate her from her lover by sending her to the Caucasus while he allowed Aleksandr Sergeievich to return to St. Petersburg, or perhaps God Himself was punishing her for ever loving Aleksandr Sergeievich and for violating her sacred marriage vows.

Pavel Pavlovich tried to chat with his wife. "Pyatigorsk or Kislovodsk will be lovely places to stay, Katherina. They are both such famed resorts that I cannot decide which to choose. Perhaps we shall station ourselves for some months at Pyatigorsk and then move to Kislovodsk. That way we can sample the mineral waters of both spas. Does that plan suit you?"

Katherina did not respond.

"Come, come, my dear," the count cajoled. "I know you are sorry to leave Moscow so soon, but I can assure you we shall return in the future. And the social life in Pyatigorsk may be just as exciting as in Moscow or St. Petersburg. Many prominent families travel there to enjoy the healing and invigorating effects of the mineral springs."

Katherina remained silent. She was not interested in any social life without Aleksandr Sergeievich.

She knew she must somehow slip away from Prince Dolgochev's and meet Aleksandr Sergeievich as they had planned. He could take her with him back to St. Petersburg, and perhaps they could find a country villa, where no one knew them, to begin a new life together.

"Katherina Andreievna, you told me when you became my wife that you dreamed of exploring the empire. On this trip we can discover unseen parts of Russia together."

Pavel Pavlovich's gentle, consoling tone intruded on Katherina's thoughts. How could she think of deserting him when he had always been so kind, so understanding? The thought of repaying his goodness with her own selfish cruelty made Katherina feel ashamed, but the fear of losing her beloved Sasha quickly drowned her guilt and shame. After all the months she had hungered for him, Katherina was sure she would rather be condemned to an eternity in hell than be separated from him again. Pavel Pavlovich would recover, she told herself. He loved her, but without the all-consuming passion she felt from Aleksandr Sergeievich. Surely the count could overcome any feelings of loss by even more dedicated service to his Czar and country.

But with all her rationalizations, Katherina admitted to herself that she could never tell Pavel Pavlovich, face-to-face, that she was leaving him or that she loved Aleksandr Sergeievich. She was sure she could not bear the hurt look in his eyes, the questions about how he had failed her, or the pleas to reconsider and remain with him. She knew that, in his loving, forgiving way, he would blame himself or Aleksandr Sergeievich, but he would never blame her. No, she could not tell him or even hint anything to him. She would have to slip away without him seeing her. Perhaps while he said a private good-bye to Prince Dolgochev.

Even when he found her gone, she felt sure he would not keep the Czar's militia waiting. He would leave for the Caucasus without her because his Czar requested it and because nothing could alter his sense of duty. And he would have plenty of time on the long journey south to recover from her treachery. Perhaps he would even find a more deserving woman—who would fully devote her own life to his.

As if sensing Katherina's plans, Pavel Pavlovich stayed by her side. From the moment they reached Prince Dolgochev's mansion, he followed her from room to room, helping her gather up their belongings. He sat watching her fold her dresses as he gave Ivan instructions for the journey. No matter what she did, she was always in view of his searching eyes.

As noon grew nearer, Katherina began to despair of having the opportunity to escape. Dropping one of her half-folded dresses, she said distractedly, "Oh —the book of poems I brought from St. Petersburg— I believe I left it in the garden yesterday." As she began to rush from the room, Pavel Pavlovich gently laid a restraining hand on her arm.

"There is no need to upset yourself, my dear. I'll call Masha and ask her to retrieve the book." From the doorway, he called the servant and told her to go to the garden.

After Masha left, Katherina feigned another sudden recollection, stamping her foot in mock annoyance with herself. "How stupid of me," she said. "Now I remember, I didn't leave it in the garden at all. I was reading it yesterday evening in the green sitting room." Again she started for the door.

"Then there is no need to concern yourself," Pavel Pavlovich said. "Masha will go through the sitting room on her way to the garden. No doubt she will see the book herself. Really, Katherina, you must try to be more relaxed. With the servants' help, we shall be ready long before the Czar's escort arrives. And I'm sure the prince would be happy to send us anything we might leave behind."

"Of course you are right," she said, forcing a smile. "You are always so sensible, Pavel Pavlovich. I'm sure that Masha, Ivan, and I can manage without further problems. Perhaps you would like to seek out the prince, to thank him for his hospitality."

"Don't you wish to thank him as well, Katherina Andreievna? I am sure he would be offended if he were denied the chance to view your beauty one more time." The count smiled fondly at his wife.

"Of course. I'll join you in a few minutes. As soon as I am sure that everything is in order for the journey."

Pavel Pavlovich did not move. "I am in no hurry, my dear. There is more than enough time for us to see the prince together."

"I only thought that as old friends you might wish a few moments in private," Katherina coaxed.

"You are very thoughtful, my dear. But, as my wife, you are part of me. Having you with me is in no way an invasion of privacy. Whatever pleasantries the prince and I exchange can only be enhanced by your presence."

Katherina smiled weakly and returned to her packing. Together they said their good-byes to Prince Dolgochev, who invited them to return at any time.

And when Czar Nikolai's carriages and militia arrived a few minutes before noon, Katherina Andreievna and Pavel Pavlovich greeted them together.

As their small caravan rolled past Saint Basil's Cathedral, Katherina stared until her eyes clouded with tears.

The count placed a comforting arm around her and brushed her cheek with his lips. "Don't fret, Katherina. I promise you we shall return someday for a longer stay."

The word *someday* evoked Katherina's treasured vision of Aleksandr Sergeievich, and she thought of how, in a few hours, he would be waiting for her in Saint Basil's—waiting for someone who would never come. Turning away from her confused husband, Katherina tried unsuccessfully to stifle her sobs. As they crossed the Moscow River, she caught a glimpse of Novodevichy Monastery's Smolensky Cathedral, the golden domes swimming in her blurred vision as she recalled being there just the day before.

Katherina wondered what Aleksandr Sergeievich would do when she did not appear. How long would he wait? What would he think? Would he try to locate her through some of his friends in Moscow? Her mind raced over their conversation, and she cursed herself for not mentioning to him where she was staying. If only he knew to go to Prince Dolgochev's, he could at least learn where she had gone—and why. If only she had known where he was staying, at least she might have found a way to send him a message.

During the first days of the journey, as they rode through the towns south of Moscow, Katherina entertained thoughts of running away and finding her way back, but she feared that, as a woman traveling alone, she would attract too much attention, making her instant bait for murderers and thieves. A dead lover would be of no use to Aleksandr Sergeievich, and, even if she escaped the criminals, the Czar's militia would certainly find her.

As their carriages left the birch forests of the north and entered the unfamiliar steppes, she discarded all thoughts of escaping. The flat plains, rich with black earth, soon became monotonous, and Katherina knew she would lose her way. She had heard that wild tribesmen and unruly cossacks still roamed the area, and she had no wish to confront any of them. Besides, she was no longer sure that Aleksandr Sergeievich was still in Moscow. Perhaps by this time he had left to search for her.

Katherina prayed that he had gone back to St. Petersburg. At least he would find the message she had left before departing for Moscow, and he would know that she would never willingly agree to desert him. She consoled herself by thinking she would send a letter to his St. Petersburg house as soon as they reached Pyatigorsk. During the long, boring days of jostling over the dirt paths that served as roads, she occupied her mind by composing the letter.

South of Kharkov the group abandoned the rough roads for the swift waters of the Don, and later the Kuban, rivers. The rocky motion of the riverboats made Katherina feel sick, but she welcomed any change from the seemingly endless flat farmlands, and she was willing to endure anything that would speed them toward their destination.

Throughout the journey, Pavel Pavlovich was even more solicitous than usual. Still blaming himself for Katherina's tearfulness as they left Moscow, he watched her moods closely and seldom left her side. Katherina tried to respond cheerfully to his attentions, although she often wished he would be less thoughtful, so she would not feel as guilty about her desire for escape.

From the Kuban River, it was less than two days' journey to Pyatigorsk, on the Podkumok River. The landscape became less monotonous as they neared the majestic Caucasus Mountains. Pyatigorsk was a sparkling town that had grown only in the last few years, after the Russian gentry had discovered the mineral springs. Cherry trees dotted the streets and yards, and the mountains provided a breathtaking backdrop. Even at the end of summer the highest peaks were frosted with snow, providing a stunning contrast to the warm springs that flowed at their base.

Not wishing to leave Katherina in a hotel for several months, Pavel Pavlovich rented a fairly large stone house and hired a cook and a housekeeper, both natives of the region.

From her window, Katherina could look down on the main boulevard of the town, or she could look up at the soaring peak of Mount Elbrus, the highest mountain in Europe. A pleasant tangle of grapevines, flowers, and fruit trees made up a garden beside the house, and a low stone wall bordered a cobbled courtyard in front of the house. Gazing at the peaceful surroundings, it was hard for Katherina to envision the events to the south, on the other side of the main Caucasus chain, where young men such as her own Aleksandr Sergeievich were dying as Russia and Persia battled for control of the Transcaucasian lands.

On their first day in Pyatigorsk, Pavel Pavlovich walked with Katherina Andreievna along the main boulevard and up a hill to the mineral water spa. Katherina's ears strained at the variety of unfamiliar languages and dialects being spoken around her. The town was filled with wealthy Russians and Ukrainians, there to enjoy the resort, and with Russian soldiers who were sent to the spa to recover from their war injuries. But Katherina saw and heard just as many Caucasian and Turkic tribesmen—Chechen, Circassians, Kabardins, Karachai, and Balkars—with their exotic slanted eyes and their strange style of dress. Wide-eyed, she surveyed the men's *beshmets*, silk smocks that were partially covered by loose, open tunics—called *cherkeskas*. Many of the women wore flowing embroidered robes. Their long dark braided hair was partially covered by veils and headbands, and some of the men wore heavy fur hats.

Use of the spa itself was limited to the Russian nobles and soldiers, who were provided with wicker-encased glasses to dip in the healing waters of its well. Katherina went with Pavel Pavlovich to sample the water. It had a strong sulfur taste that made her wrinkle her nose.

Pavel Pavlovich laughed. "You don't like the medicinal waters, my dear?" He laughed again as Katherina shook her head and poured the remaining contents of her glass into the nearest bush. "Well, then, let us go and walk on the terrace. Perhaps we shall see someone I know."

He offered her his arm, and they strolled along the stone terrace. Katherina looked with pity at the young soldiers. Some struggled to walk on crutches, some had their arms in slings, and some simply lay drinking the waters, unable to move because they had lost a limb to the war. Young fair-haired girls, daughters of the vacationing nobility, flirted with a few of the most handsome soldiers, but most of the men simply talked among themselves, unhappily eyeing the parade of rich, spoiled young women. Katherina was glad that Aleksandr Sergeievich was far from this scene, that he had returned from the Caucasus unharmed.

They walked to the end of the terrace without meeting anyone whom Pavel Pavlovich knew, but as they turned back toward the well, a voice stopped them.

"Ah, Count Ostrov! What brings you to Pyatigorsk?"

Pavel Pavlovich turned questioning eyes to the speaker, a gray-haired man of about his own age.

"Ah, forgive me," the man said. "I should not be so familiar. It is obvious you do not recognize me."

"I must admit I do not," said the count.

"Nor should I have expected you to. We met at the house of my cousin, Aleksei Strelkov, some years ago in St. Petersburg. I am Grigorii Mikhailovich Strelkov."

"Ah yes," said the count. "Now I remember. Aleksei Aleksandrovich's cousin from Moscow!"

"Yes." Strelkov nodded. "I did not mean to intrude, but it was such a joy to see a familiar face. Most of my friends returned to Moscow weeks ago."

"Think nothing of it," the count replied. "We have just arrived ourselves, and it is a pleasure to see you. Allow me to present my wife, Katherina Andreievna."

"I am most charmed," Strelkov said, pressing his lips to her hand.

"Have you been in Pyatigorsk long?" the count asked.

"Two months. It has been most pleasant," Strelkov sighed, "but I have begun to miss the northern cities."

"Then you are planning to return to Moscow soon?"

"No, to St. Petersburg, to spend some time with Aleksei Aleksandrovich. I leave in three days. And may I inquire as to your plans?"

"We will no doubt stay the winter," Pavel Pavlovich replied. "I have been sent by Czar Nikolai on official business. Katherina will stay in Pyatigorsk while I travel over the mountains."

"I am sure you will both find your stay most pleasant," Strelkov said. "Pyatigorsk is a delightful town. I wish I could stay to chat longer, but, unfortunately, I have an appointment within the hour. Perhaps I will see you here again tomorrow." Strelkov nodded to Katherina and the count and went on his way.

As they strolled back to the main boulevard, an idea began to form in Katherina's head. Perhaps she could ask this Grigorii Strelkov to personally carry her message to Aleksandr Sergeievich. It would, no doubt, arrive more quickly than through the notoriously slow Russian postal system. But, of course, there was the danger that he would mention the errand to his cousin, who in turn might inform Pavel Pavlovich.

"You seem very pensive, my dear," Pavel Pavlovich said, breaking in on Katherina's thoughts.

"I was just trying to place this Aleksei Aleksandrovich Strelkov in my mind. I cannot recall meeting him at any of the St. Petersburg social events."

"I doubt that you ever did. I understand he spends a good deal of the year at his country estate now. I knew him several years ago, when he was a Senate member, but I can't recall seeing him at all in the last year or two."

"Perhaps you were just too busy." Katherina smiled as she realized there was less risk than she had originally imagined in sending a message through Strelkov. "And what of his cousin—the man we just met —Grigorii Strelkov? What do you know of him?"

"As I recall, he is a professor of foreign languages at the Moscow University. A very likable, intelligent fellow. It's a pity he is leaving so soon, or I would ask him to look in on you while I am away. Perhaps he could even give you those French lessons you have been wanting." The count smiled fondly at Katherina.

"But it is not necessary for anyone to look in on me," Katherina said quickly. "Masha and I can get on quite well by ourselves."

"Still, I feel uncomfortable leaving you alone in a strange place without a man to look after you. I had planned to have Ivan accompany me, but perhaps I should leave him behind. I would feel more relaxed knowing someone I could trust would be seeing to your welfare."

"Nonsense, Pavel Pavlovich. I am sure you have no cause for worry."

Pavel Pavlovich shook his head. "I may be away for months. When winter sets in, it may be impossible to get through the mountain passes. I should have had the foresight to ask the Czar if a few of the militia that accompanied us here could stay to look after you. Unfortunately, they are already on their way across the mountains to join General Paskevich's troops." The count paused. "Perhaps I could commission another member of the Imperial Army to watch over you. There is a fort a few miles outside of town. I plan to ride there tomorrow to arrange an escort for my journey to review General Yermolov's forces. I will check into the matter then."

Katherina sighed, hoping this proposed military

bodyguard would not make her a prisoner in her own home. On the other hand, without Aleksandr Sergeievich, she would have very little desire to go anywhere anyway.

Pavel Pavlovich sighed as well. "I hate to leave this lovely town so soon—but I was not sent here simply for a vacation."

"Surely the Czar could not object to your enjoying a few more days rest after our journey," Katherina said.

Her husband shook his head. "No, if the garrison commander agrees to provide the necessary escort, I will leave the day after tomorrow."

They walked the rest of the way to their house in silence, and Katherina planned her activities for the next day.

That night, listening to Pavel Pavlovich breathing heavily beside her, Katherina reviewed the plans she had formulated during the afternoon and evening. While Pavel Pavlovich visited the fort, she would return to the spa, staying all day if necessary, until she talked with Grigorii Strelkov. But she would not ask Strelkov to carry a message to St. Petersburg, as she had originally planned. Instead, she would ask him to take her with him to the capital. At first she had hesitated to consider this alternative, fearful of traveling with a strange man, but Pavel Pavlovich had, unknowingly, put her at ease. If her husband would consider asking Strelkov to watch over her in Pyatigorsk, the man must be completely moral and trustworthy. And, she assured herself, this would be the kindest way to leave Pavel Pavlovich. He would already have left Pyatigorsk when she departed, and by the time he returned, he would be accustomed to life without her. Katherina fell asleep, happily dreaming of her coming reunion with Aleksandr Sergeievich.

Pavel Pavlovich, accompanied by Ivan, left for the army fort early the next morning. Kissing Katherina softly on the cheek, he said, "I shall try to return early, my dear, but I may not be back before suppertime. Perhaps you and Masha would enjoy a walk to the spa while I am gone. You needn't drink the water." He chuckled.

"Yes—perhaps we will go."

From the garden, Katherina watched Pavel Pavlovich and Ivan ride away. Then she rushed inside and called Masha to help her dress and then accompany her to the mineral springs.

At midmorning, the spa was quite uncrowded. Katherina, with Masha beside her, strolled up and down the terrace looking for Grigorii Strelkov. As they passed a group of soldiers for the fifth time, the young men began to smile as if they thought Katherina and Masha were flirting with them.

Masha blushed and murmured, "Please, madame, could we stop at the end of the terrace and view the scenery for a few moments? These soldiers make me feel so nervous."

"Nonsense," Katherina snapped. "You can see the scenery just as well if we continue walking. The soldiers will not bother us." She turned at the end of the terrace and began to walk back. With an unhappy sigh, Masha followed her mistress.

This time, as they passed the soldiers, one of them stood up, leaning on his crutch, and extended his hand to Katherina. "Ah, madame, you are more beautiful than the acacia or the cherry trees in bloom," he said. "And your companion is more lovely than the snowcapped peaks at sunset."

Masha blushed again, and Katherina pushed the

soldier's hand away. The two women hurried to the end of the terrace, where Katherina finally agreed to sit down.

Masha glanced back at the soldiers and begged her mistress, "Madame, couldn't we return to the house now? I feel so uncomfortable sitting here as if I am on display. Surely we have seen all there is to see at the spa."

"Really, Masha," Katherina said, "you must learn to compose yourself better in the presence of men. You are an attractive young woman, and it is only natural for them to notice you."

"But I am so unaccustomed to attention." Masha glanced nervously at the soldiers.

"Very well, then," Katherina relented. "We will take a stroll to the well. But I am not prepared to leave the spa for the day."

As they returned from the well, Katherina caught sight of Grigorii Strelkov walking toward the far end of the terrace. She motioned to a bench and told Masha, "Wait here. There is someone I must see."

"Couldn't I come with you, madame?" Masha pleaded.

"Stop acting like a child," Katherina replied. "No one is going to harm you here. I will only be a moment." Before her servant could plead more, Katherina turned and hurried toward Strelkov.

As Katherina approached him, Strelkov smiled. "How pleasant to see you again, Countess Ostrova."

"I am pleased to see you as well, Monsieur Strelkov."

"Where is the count today? I trust he is not ill?"

"No. He had business to attend to. But he did direct me to look for you here today," Katherina said. "We have a rather important request to make of you."

"Oh?" Strelkov raised his eyebrows.

Katherina continued smoothly, "You did say you were leaving for St. Petersburg the day after tomorrow, did you not?"

"Yes." He nodded.

"We would be much indebted to you if you would agree to take me with you." Strelkov's mouth fell open, and Katherina quickly explained, "We received word only yesterday that my mother is quite ill. I wish to return to her in St. Petersburg immediately, and unfortunately Pavel Pavlovich has business for the Czar that may detain him for months. Since you are traveling to St. Petersburg, Pavel Pavlovich felt that perhaps it would not be too much trouble for you to take me with you—and he was sure I would be safe with you."

Grigorii Strelkov shook his head. "I would, of course, be honored and pleased to have your company, countess, but you may wish to reconsider. I had planned to travel alone, and without the greatest of comforts. I'm afraid you might find the trip much too difficult."

"Please," Katherina begged. "You are the only person in Pyatigorsk who is leaving soon for St. Petersburg. And I must see my mother before it is too late."

"Can you ride a horse?" Strelkov asked.

"Of course." Katherina tried to sound convincing. In fact, she had ridden in the fields of Novgorod as a child, but she had not been on a horse since a frisky stallion threw her at the age of ten.

"Well, perhaps I should speak with the count. If— after I explain the hazards of the trip—he feels it will not be too hard for you and he is willing to entrust you to my care, I will certainly agree."

"But I'm afraid he won't be home before evening," Katherina said quickly, "and we would so like to spend the evening alone together. He leaves on his mission tomorrow, and with me in St. Petersburg and him in Transcaucasia we will probably be separated for months."

"I understand," Strelkov said. "But I hardly know what else to suggest."

"I will tell Pavel Pavlovich about your misgivings myself," Katherina promised. "If he thinks I should not make the trip I will meet you at the well at two o'clock tomorrow to tell you. Otherwise, I will be prepared to leave the morning after next. You can call for me at the stone house up on the hill at the far end of the boulevard."

"Very well," Strelkov agreed, although he seemed hesitant. "If I do not see you tomorrow, I will call for you the following morning. Is six o'clock all right? It is always best to get an early start on a long journey."

"I will be ready." Katherina smiled sweetly. "Thank you for your kindness, Grigorii Mikhailovich. I am quite sure that Pavel Pavlovich will agree to the plans, and we shall soon be traveling together to St. Petersburg. Good day to you now." She turned and walked back to Masha, who, to Katherina's surprise, was talking amiably with a fair-haired young officer.

Embarrassed by Katherina's sudden appearance, Masha sprang to her feet. "Do you wish to depart now, madame?" she asked meekly.

Katherina smiled in amusement. "I am in no hurry, Masha. When you have finished your conversation, you may find me at the well." She smiled again and walked away, leaving the girl totally confused by her mistress's sudden change of mood.

Chapter 9

Katherina hummed all the way back to the house. It had been easier than she had imagined it would be to convince Grigorii Strelkov of her need to go to St. Petersburg, and now her body tingled at the prospect of finding Aleksandr Sergeievich at the end of her journey. She hated the prospect of riding horseback all the way to St. Petersburg, but she was certain she could endure much worse in return for the lifetime of happiness that lay ahead. Katherina was so enveloped in her own thoughts that she did not even notice Masha's soaring spirits and flushed face.

The strong smell of shashlik greeted Katherina and Masha as they entered the house, and Katherina thought of another reason to be glad that she would be leaving Pyatigorsk. She was not at all certain that she could ever become accustomed to the heavily spiced foods or the thick soured goat's milk—called yogurt—served by the cook. Like most Russians, she was used to dishes topped with sour cream, but this yogurt had a strange, unappetizing odor and taste.

Despite her distaste for the food, Katherina smiled at Tamara, the cook, an olive-skinned beauty who had long braided black hair, before she went to the garden to pick some flowers. Today Katherina could smile at anyone. She would even make special efforts to please Pavel Pavlovich and enjoy his attentions tonight. At least she would leave him with happy memories of their last night together.

As she arranged the flowers for their supper table,

Katherina heard noises in the courtyard. Looking out the window, she saw Pavel Pavlovich and Ivan dismounting. A third person had already dismounted, but his horse blocked him from view. Katherina wondered if Pavel Pavlovich had brought a member of his escort to spend the night and discuss their traveling plans. At least, she thought gratefully, there would be an extra mouth to share the shashlik. She went to the kitchen to tell Tamara there would be a guest at dinner.

When she returned to the parlor, the three men had already entered. Katherina froze in the doorway as her eyes focused on the visitor. Rushing to support her, Pavel Pavlovich gazed at his wife in concern.

"Are you all right, Katherina Andreievna?" he asked as he helped her to a chair.

"Yes. Forgive me," she smiled wanly. "I'm afraid I spent too long in the sun today, and my head is throbbing."

"Ah." He kissed her forehead. "Then I'm sure you will feel better after you have rested and had a bit to eat and drink." He turned to their guest, who was still standing in the shadows. "Come in, Aleksandr Sergeievich, and sit down."

Aleksandr strolled to a chair opposite Katherina's.

Composing herself, Katherina spoke. "What a strange coincidence that we should meet you again in Pyatigorsk, Monsieur Belikov."

"I was just remarking the same thing to your husband," Aleksandr said. "It is a pleasure indeed to see you once again, Countess Ostrova."

"Will you be traveling with the count to Transcaucasia?" she asked, trying to keep a casual tone.

"No," he replied, and Katherina felt a faint flush begin to move up her neck.

Pavel Pavlovich broke in. "I count it as an extraordinary piece of good fortune that I found young Belikov at the fort. As I told you yesterday, my dear, I had hoped to find someone to look after you in my absence. I was about to mention that fact to the garrison commander when Aleksandr Sergeievich came in. Naturally, I was most pleased to find someone I know and trust, and someone you know as well. I explained my need to the commander, and he immediately offered to assign young Belikov to our house. Since I will be on a mission for Czar Nikolai, he agreed that the assignment would be quite proper. Aleksandr Sergeievich will stay here while I am gone."

"Here?" Katherina asked in a tremulous voice, not trusting her own ears.

"Yes. There is an extra bedroom in the house, and he can sleep there. I am most concerned that you not be left alone at night, my dear."

Katherina turned to Aleksandr Sergeievich. "Pavel Pavlovich is such a worrier. I've tried to convince him I will be quite safe here with Masha and the other servants. Czar Nikolai himself assured us that Pyatigorsk is quite civilized."

"Your husband has good reason for concern," Aleksandr Sergeievich said evenly. "I am afraid our good Czar exaggerated the safety of the area. Many of the Circassian tribesmen are less than pleased to be ruled by Russia, and one never knows what they might attempt. Besides," he said, smiling broadly, "I must thank the count. I could not have imagined a more pleasant assignment."

Pavel Pavlovich beamed. "I am sure the arrangement suits us all."

As they prepared for bed that night, Pavel Pavlovich looked at Katherina affectionately. "I know you did not want me to arrange for a protector or escort for you, my dear, but I was only concerned for your safety."

"I quite understand," she said, kissing his cheek, "and I do appreciate your concern."

"With young Belikov to protect you, you can move about Pyatigorsk freely and in complete safety."

"Perhaps it will be better than having only Masha to accompany me," Katherina agreed. "Some of the soldiers at the spa this afternoon were rather insolent. I'm afraid poor Masha was quite embarrassed."

"I'm glad you can finally see my viewpoint," the count said. "Perhaps you will even wish to attend some evening parties with young Belikov."

"Pavel Pavlovich, do you really think that would be proper?"

"With my permission, how could it be improper? As I've told you before, Katherina Andreievna, I have infinite trust in you. And I don't care a bit what anyone else might think."

They extinguished the lamp and got into bed. In the darkness, Katherina could almost imagine that the body moving against hers belonged to Aleksandr Sergeievich. As she concentrated on the image of his curly hair and flashing black eyes, she responded to her husband more tenderly than ever before, and, once, she had to bury her face in his shoulder to muffle the cry of "Sasha" that involuntarily escaped from her throat. Pavel Pavlovich held her closer, murmuring, "Oh, my Katya, I shall miss you so."

Afterward, she lay with her heart pounding, wondering how she could sleep the night next to Pavel Pavlovich when her dearest Sasha was in the next room. When she closed her eyes, she saw him again, sitting across the supper table, a thin veil of merriment covering the smoky look of passion in his eyes. How could she be so blessed, to have him here with her to share months of uninterrupted love? Just thinking of him now, so near, inflamed her body. She felt sure Pavel Pavlovich would awake at any moment, concerned that she was suffering from a fever.

Katherina tried to sleep, telling herself that sleep would speed the morning, Pavel Pavlovich's departure, and her time alone with Aleksandr Sergeievich, but every time she thought of Aleksandr, her heart thumped more insistently, driving away all possibility of sleep.

For a few moments she lay listening to the regular breathing of Pavel Pavlovich. Then she slipped from their bed.

In the hallway, she could see a sliver of light shining from beneath Aleksandr Sergeievich's door. Without knocking, she slowly inched open the door and went into the room. He was sitting at the desk, fully clothed, writing a letter.

At the sound of her footsteps, he looked up. "Katya!"

She stepped closer, her thin summer nightgown clinging to her legs and body. Aleksandr stared in enchantment. "Katya—what are you doing here?" he whispered.

"I couldn't sleep." Her breasts rose and fell beneath her gown. Aleksandr thought she looked like an angel of the night with her golden hair falling past her shoulders and shimmering in the lamplight. He jumped from his chair and gathered her into his arms, feeling her firm, almost naked body nestle against him. His hands melted into the silky softness of her hair, and his lips caught hers.

"Sasha," she moaned. "Take me. Take me."

A cough in the next room interrupted their embrace. Aleksandr stepped back. She opened her mouth to protest, but he covered it gently with his hand.

"Katya," he whispered, "you must go. What if the count awakes and finds you gone?"

"But I can't sleep for thinking of you."

He indicated his unused bed and the half-written letter. "Neither can I—but we must wait. After all these months, we can survive one more night."

She shook her head. "I don't think I can."

"You must," he murmured, taking her by the shoulders and steering her toward the door. He kissed her nose and murmured, "Until tomorrow—Katya."

Unable to control her throbbing heart, Katherina paced in the parlor for almost an hour. When she returned to her room, she saw the light still escaping from beneath Aleksandr's door. She hesitated, battling with her passions, then sighed and forced herself to enter her own room. The door creaked as she closed it, and Pavel Pavlovich turned in the bed.

"Is something wrong, Katherina Andreievna?" he whispered.

"No. I just can't seem to fall asleep. I keep thinking of you leaving tomorrow. It will be your first time away from me since our marriage." Katherina tried to control her voice, hoping her husband would misinterpret the reason for her restlessness.

"I know." Pavel Pavlovich sighed. "I wish this mission were not necessary. I had looked forward to celebrating our first anniversary together, but it seems unlikely that I shall be able to return in time." He paused and sighed again. "Shall I wake Tamara and ask her to brew you some tea to calm you and help you sleep?"

"No—please don't disturb her. I'm sorry I awakened you, Pavel Pavlovich, but if I had stayed in bed I'm afraid my tossing and turning would have disturbed you more."

"Don't concern yourself, my dear. Come back to bed now, and try to sleep."

As Katherina returned to bed, her husband fondly patted her cheek and murmured, "I thank God each day that I have been blessed with such an angel for a wife."

Pavel Pavlovich's military escort arrived at seven the next morning. Before he left, the count walked with Katherina in the dew-soaked garden, telling her again to enjoy her time in Pyatigorsk as best she could. He promised to write her whenever possible, but he cautioned her not to be too anxious for his letters. "The Daryal Pass through the Caucasus may soon be blocked by snow, so you must understand, my dear, if the messengers cannot get through."

Katherina nodded, willing his departure to be over soon.

As Pavel Pavlovich bent to kiss her, his gray eyes clouded over. "I shall miss you, Katherina Andreievna, and shall dream about you each night. We will have our anniversary celebration when I return, all right?"

She nodded and brushed his cheek with her lips. Hearing the sounds of his escort mounting, Pavel Pavlovich turned away and walked to his horse. He mounted and looked down at Aleksandr Sergeievich, who was standing in the doorway of the house.

"I am trusting in you, Aleksandr Sergeievich, to keep my wife safe until my return," said the count.

"You needn't worry," Aleksandr replied. "I will guard her as if she were my own wife."

Pleased with the young officer's dedicated response, the count nodded at Katherina and Aleksandr and then signaled to the escort commander that he was prepared to leave.

Katherina Andreievna and Aleksandr Sergeievich watched as the group rode through the gate, down the hill, down the main boulevard of Pyatigorsk, and out of sight. Then Aleksandr scooped Katherina off her feet and carried her, laughing, into the house.

He strode directly to his bedroom, where he dropped her gently on his bed. "It seems," he laughed, "that we have some unfinished business to attend to."

As he went to close the door, Katherina sat up and teased, "You mean you did not finish your letter?"

"No, as a matter of fact I did not. It was impossible to concentrate on Uncle Pyotr when my mind kept wandering to you—lying beside the count." He sat on the edge of the bed, removed his boots, and dropped them to the floor. Then he turned and pulled her down on the bed.

Her blood raced at the sight of his smoldering eyes. Their lips met again, in a fiery continuation of the night before, and his tongue explored every crevice of her mouth, coaxing little whimpers of delight from her throat. She responded without hesitation, gliding her tongue over his teeth until a low growl of desire rose from his chest and crept down her throat, making her tremble.

As they kissed, he quickly unfastened her dress, his fingers stroking the willing flesh beneath it. Katherina had especially chosen the dress, knowing it was easy to unfasten and remove. She slid her hands beneath his loose peasant-style shirt and felt the heat of his back. His lips traveled slowly down her body, following her dress as he inched it toward her hips. He stopped to kiss her breasts, caressing each of

them with his tongue as the nipples tightened into
hard buttons of desire and she moaned in rapturous
appreciation.

By the time her dress had reached her waist,
Katherina felt she would go mad. Her passion took
over, and it was as though she had no choice but to
follow the dictates of her body. She wanted everything and she wanted it right away. Kicking and
squirming, she sent her dress and petticoats flying.
She had purposely not bothered to put on other un-
derclothes that morning, so now she lay naked, shuddering with the desire that had been building in her
for so many months.

Aleksandr gazed at her, tantalized by the promise
of her smooth ivory skin. Then he wrenched his shirt
over his head, ripping one sleeve in the fury of his
movement, and, trembling, he kissed her half-open
mouth.

Still kissing, they struggled together to free him
from his trousers. As they rocked on the bed, he
loosened the pins that held her hair in its curls and
buried his face in her golden hair.

And then their bodies became one, and their
spirits soared higher than the loftiest peaks of the
Caucasus. In all her months of dreaming, Katherina
had imagined only a small fraction of the joy that
now consumed her. She nibbled greedily at Aleksandr's lips and tongue, moaning and whimpering
uncontrollably as she felt him inside of her, until she
could no longer distinguish her own body from his as
their twin tremors of passion continued to build. Her
head was spinning, and she was sure their bed was
spiraling toward the ceiling, about to propel them
through the roof and out above the main boulevard
of Pyatigorsk. She wanted to scream with fulfillment,
but instead she plunged her mouth deeper into

Aleksandr's, drowning her own sounds in his moans of rapture.

They lay exhausted, the bed drenched with the effects of their passions, falling in and out of sleep, murmuring endearments. Waking for the fourth time, Katherina felt her body aching again with desire, every muscle shivering. She pressed closer to Aleksandr and found the same yearning growing in him even as he slept. Unable and unwilling to stop herself, she molded her feverish body against his. His arms encircled her and his muscles tensed in readiness. "Mmmm," he murmured in pleased surprise, and once again their desire found release, only now with less urgency. With exquisite tenderness, Aleksandr slowly, slowly brought her every nerve to a pitch still new to her, and this time she did not stifle her cries of ecstasy but cried out to him so he could know the infinite pleasure his love was exacting from her body.

Succumbing at last to exhaustion, Aleksandr and Katherina fell into a sound sleep in each other's arms. At noon, Masha rapped on Aleksandr's bedroom door.

"Sir—," she called. "Monsieur Belikov?"

Aleksandr pulled Katherina closer. "What is it?" he asked.

"The midday meal is ready, sir."

"All right," Aleksandr sighed. "I will be out in a few minutes."

They listened for the sound of Masha's receding footsteps, but she remained at the door. "Sir?" she ventured again.

"What is it?"

"Would you know where the countess is? I can't find her in her bedroom or anywhere else in the house."

"Did you look in the garden?"

"Only from the window, sir."

"Then perhaps you had better go out and look there more carefully."

"Yes, sir," Masha replied meekly.

As they heard her walking away, Aleksandr whispered to Katherina, "Perhaps you better go back to your room." Nodding, she slid from the bed, picked up her clothing, and slipped out the bedroom door.

She dressed quickly, and, by the time Masha returned from the garden, Katherina was sitting in the parlor.

"Madame, I have been looking everywhere for you!"

"I was walking in the garden."

"But I've just returned from the garden."

Katherina shrugged. "Well, apparently you missed me." At that moment Aleksandr Sergeievich appeared in the parlor doorway and Katherina changed the subject. "Is Tamara ready to serve our meal?"

"Yes, madame."

As they walked to the dining room, Masha stared at Katherina's hair, hastily plaited in two long braids, in the style of the peasants and tribeswomen.

"Is something wrong, Masha?" Katherina snapped.

"No, madame. But I would have been happy to arrange your hair if you had called me this morning."

"There was no reason to bother you," Katherina replied. "I think braids are quite suitable when I am spending the day at home. After all, we are not in Moscow or St. Petersburg, and there seems little chance that anyone will be calling on me."

"Yes, madame." Masha retreated to the kitchen.

After the meal—a spicy lamb stew that smelled to Katherina exactly like a herdsman's lamb's-wool cap —Katherina and Aleksandr walked in the garden. They sat beneath an apple tree, and Katherina picked an apple to purge her mouth of the strong aftertaste of the dinner. Taking a bite of the apple, she studied Aleksandr, who was relaxing on the grass beside her.

"I am sure Pavel Pavlovich told you how we came to be in Pyatigorsk," she said, "but you have not yet even hinted at how you came to be here, Sasha."

Aleksandr's eyes danced mischievously. "It seems that we have not yet had much time for idle conversation." He laughed.

Katherina laughed with him, unashamed of her passions. "But perhaps now, while we have a moment's rest, you will be so kind as to fill me in on your adventures."

"The afternoon after we met in Moscow, I had my audience with Czar Nikolai. He was friendly and sympathetic, but he was also unwilling to grant what I requested. However, he offered me a bargain—a compromise, so to speak."

"A bargain with the Czar?" Katherina seemed surprised.

Aleksandr grinned. "Of course—according to the Czar's own rules. He pointed out that he was in need of good soldiers to quell the Persian invasions. If I would serve for two years, and if I received a good report from my commander, he would agree to grant me my full pardon. Otherwise," Aleksandr shrugged, "I could look forward to a life in exile."

"Two years," Katherina repeated hollowly. "But what about the pardon you said he granted the poet, Pushkin?"

"I ventured to ask him the same thing, and he replied that Pushkin is a dreaming poet, a literary genius it's true, but of little use on the battlefield. Since I, on the other hand, had the misfortune to be trained as a soldier, I could serve the empire well on the Persian front—a small price to pay for Czar Nikolai's favor. I was assigned to a Moscow regiment and told we would depart the next morning."

"Did you go to Saint Basil's afterward to meet me?"

"Yes, but my audience with the Czar took so long that I did not arrive there until four o'clock. When I did not find you waiting, I assumed you had left for another pressing engagement."

"Were you angry with me, Sasha?"

"Of course not. In a way I was relieved. I didn't think I could stand to say good-bye to you again."

"If only you knew how I wept when we left Moscow!" Tears formed again in Katherina's eyes as she remembered that journey, and Aleksandr kissed each eye tenderly.

"At first," he continued, "I thought I would not go with the regiment. I planned to slip out of Moscow and somehow make my way back to St. Petersburg. But I knew I would be hunted as a deserter, and, with Benckendorff's police at work in St. Petersburg, I might never have gotten near you without endangering both of our lives. And so I spent the evening composing a letter to you. It is probably waiting for you in St. Petersburg right now."

Katherina smiled and squeezed Aleksandr's hand. "And when did you arrive in Pyatigorsk?"

"We got to the fort three days ago. We were to take three days rest and then continue through the Daryal Pass to the Kura River valley. You can imagine my surprise when I saw Count Ostrov at the fort. Even then I never imagined that you would be in Pyatigorsk with him."

"And when he offered you the position of being my protector?"

"At first, I almost asked my commander for a different assignment."

"But why?" Katherina looked confused. She was sure he loved her as strongly as ever.

"There seemed something dishonest about professing to watch over you for the count when all the time I wanted you only for myself. But then I thought of the job going to someone else—of someone else enjoying your nearness, your laughter, your smiles—"

"But Sasha," Katherina interrupted, "surely you must know I would never share myself with other men."

"Of course I know that, but I could not bear to think of another man even sharing your house. The count is your husband, and I begrudge even him the small kisses and looks of affection he exchanges with you." He paused and stared at the apple tree ruffling in the breeze above them. "But he is a very fine man. Never once did he mention the unpleasantness of our last dealings in St. Petersburg. He made it clear that he thinks very highly of me." He paused again, groping for the right words. "Katya, we must be very careful not to hurt him."

"I know, Sasha—I know." She looked away as her eyes clouded again. "But we must also take care not to hurt ourselves," she whispered.

Katherina Andreievna and Aleksandr Sergeievich sat in the parlor that night long after Masha, Tamara, and Lizaveta, the housekeeper, had retired. The sun had set, and the room was dark, but they did not bother to light a lamp. They sat without speaking, enjoying each other's presence and cherishing the opening moments of their first night together. Katherina felt like a nervous bride, longing to realize their love in bed, but unwilling to disturb the quiet moments beforehand. After their morning of lovemaking and their past interludes, it seemed strange that she should feel so shy, but she could not help feeling that this night, like a wedding night, was the beginning of a new life. The beginning of their someday.

She yawned and dropped her head on Aleksandr Sergeievich's shoulder. He stroked her cheek. Then he stood, pulling her up beside him, and led her to her bedroom. At the door, he hesitated until Katherina entered and pulled him in after her. She closed the door and they began to undress in silence.

Aleksandr watched breathlessly as Katherina moved about in the thin sliver of moonlight that shone through her window. She dropped her dress and petticoats over a chair, not bothering to put on a nightgown; then she slowly unbraided her hair, letting it fall like a thin golden veil over her perfectly formed ivory breasts. Her hair and skin shimmered in the pale light, making her seem to Aleksandr like a spirit of love. He dropped his own clothes as Katherina held out her arms, and he rushed to her as if afraid she would vanish. They stood for a long moment in the shaft of mystical light.

They made love in sweet softness, each discovering untapped wells of tenderness and passion in the other. The slow rhythm of their movements soothed away Katherina's worries about Pavel Pavlovich, making her feel secure and sheltered. "Sasha," she breathed, "my love for you stretches farther than all of Mother Russia."

"And I love you as much, my Katya."

She lay for a long time with her head on his chest, lulled by the regular thumping of his heart. Then he slowly slid from beneath her and sat up in bed.

Katherina caught him by the waist. "Where are you going?"

"To my own bedroom." He swung his feet to the floor.

"But this is your bedroom, Sasha. My bed is your bed."

He shook his head. "Your Masha would not think so —nor would the other servants."

"But there is no way for them to know. You can leave early in the morning—before they arise. Stay with me tonight, Sasha," she pleaded. "I need your body beside me."

When she sat up and kissed his mouth, she did not have to plead anymore.

Chapter 10

At six o'clock in the morning, a loud and insistent knocking at the front door woke Masha. Katherina Andreievna and Aleksandr Sergeievich, wrapped in their own sublime curtain of happiness, were oblivious to the noise. Masha lay listening, hoping the intruder would go away. The knocking only became louder and more insistent. Masha wondered why Monsieur Belikov, who had been engaged to protect them, did not go to the door, but it seemed obvious that he was not getting up, so Masha dragged herself from her bed and crept to the door.

When she opened the door a crack, she could see that the visitor was a well-dressed gentleman—not the Circassian ruffian she had imagined would greet her.

"Is this the house of Countess Ostrova?" the gentleman asked.

"Yes," Masha responded, opening the door wider. "But why do you ask?"

"I was to meet her here this morning. Is she prepared to leave?"

Masha shook her head in confusion. "I'm afraid there's been some terrible mistake, sir. The countess is still asleep, and she mentioned nothing to me about a trip."

The man became impatient. "Perhaps you'd better wake your mistress, so I might talk to her myself—but hurry—I don't wish to delay the start of my journey any longer than necessary."

"Yes, sir." Masha showed the gentleman into the parlor and hurried to Katherina's bedroom.

In her nervousness, she forgot to knock. She opened the door, babbling as she stepped inside. "Madame, there is a man—" Her eyes fell on the bed and she stopped in midsentence. Warm from their lovemaking, Katherina and Aleksandr had pushed the blankets from their shoulders and they lay with her bare breasts and his bare chest exposed.

Startled from her dreams by Masha's intrusion, Katherina pulled the covers to her chin and guiltily tried to reprove the servant. "Masha, how could you come in without so much as knocking?"

Katherina's voice shook Masha from her trance. Her hand flew to her mouth to stifle a sob as she turned and ran from the room. Thinking Masha's behavior very odd, and worried about what the girl might do next, Katherina slipped into a dressing gown and rushed after her.

"Masha," Katherina called as she ran toward the parlor, "whatever is the matter with you this morning?" She saw her sobbing servant run through the front door, and she was about to hurry after her when a movement in the parlor caught her eye. Turning, she met the disapproving glare of Grigorii Strelkov as he paced in the parlor.

"In case your servant did not tell you, madame, it is now half-past six," he announced in a biting whisper, "and I was of the understanding that you would be prepared for departure at six o'clock."

Katherina, dumbfounded by Strelkov's presence, stood with her mouth half-open, staring at the man. In all her excitement over Aleksandr Sergeievich's arrival and their first day and night together, her mind had erased her agreement with Strelkov. Even now, as she tried to recall their conversation, it seemed remote and unreal. There was no reason for her to go to St. Petersburg now. Didn't everyone know that?

"Well," he snapped, "am I to be kept waiting all day? Go and get yourself dressed before any more of the morning slips away."

"I'm afraid I will not be traveling with you, Monsieur Strelkov," Katherina said slowly and deliberately. "If you wish to leave, you may do so immediately."

"No," he responded. "You have already upset my travel plans, and now I must demand an explanation. Am I to assume the good count decided you should not undertake so strenuous a journey?"

"Yes," Katherina said, hoping he would be satisfied with the answer and would leave her alone.

"Then why," he demanded, "didn't you meet me yesterday as you said you would? Why do you waste my time so thoughtlessly? And what about your dear sick mother, whom you were so anxious to see?"

Katherina shrugged helplessly. Then from behind her she heard the cool voice of Aleksandr Sergeievich. "You needn't treat the countess so harshly," he said. Katherina turned to see that he had dressed in trousers and a peasant shirt, and he stood in the doorway, calmly staring at Grigorii Strelkov.

"But I'm afraid she has treated me most unfairly," Streklov explained. "She came to me, begging to be allowed to accompany me to St. Petersburg so she might visit her sick mother. We made an agreement, and now she tries to shrug it off, as if my own time and worry were of no consequence."

"All right." Aleksandr strode toward Strelkov, his

eyes snapping with fury, and the older man shrank back a step. "Since you so callously demand an explanation, you shall have it. There is no longer any need for the countess to journey to St. Petersburg. Her mother died last week, and by now she is in the grave. I have been riding day and night to bring her the message, and I arrived only late last night."

"Oh!" Strelkov's mouth fell open in horror. "Oh. Lord have mercy. I had no idea." He turned to Katherina. "My dear Countess Ostrova, I am deeply sorry. If only you had told me, I would never—"

"Can't you understand that the countess finds it difficult to talk about her loss?" Aleksandr interrupted.

"Why, yes—of course." Strelkov became flustered under Aleksandr's piercing gaze.

"If you had been any kind of gentleman, you would have accepted her first explanation and been on your way. But it is obvious that you find it necessary to bully a woman."

Strelkov's eyes darted between Aleksandr and the door.

"Yes—get out," Aleksandr said. "Don't delay your journey any longer. Leave the countess alone with her grief."

Nodding to Katherina, Strelkov hurried out of the house. Aleksandr stalked after him and slammed the door.

"Oh, Sasha," Katherina rushed to embrace him. "I'm so glad you came in when you did. I would never have expected Grigorii Strelkov to have such a temper!"

Aleksandr cradled her in his arms, tenderly kissing her nose, her velvety earlobe. His fingertips softly massaged the nape of her neck as he lifted her chin and gazed into her clear eyes. "So, you were going to St. Petersburg, were you, Katya?"

She nodded. "I had to, Sasha. I had to see you. But then, when Pavel Pavlovich brought you here, I forgot all about my plans. I was supposed to meet Grigorii Strelkov at the spa yesterday if I decided not to make the journey. But the day with you was so perfect—how could I remember such a thing?"

She buried her head in his chest and Aleksandr felt her tears through his thin cotton shirt. "It's all right, Katya," he soothed, stroking her back. "Strelkov is gone now. And I love you for what you tried to do. It would have been a hard journey to St. Petersburg, my brave devoted little Katya."

"But if I found you there, it would have been worth it." Katherina smiled. She pressed closer to his comforting body, rubbing her cheek against his chest. Suddenly she lifted her face to search his eyes. "Oh, Sasha—do you think Strelkov will make trouble for us? What if he tells his cousin in St. Petersburg about our encounter? What if he tells Pavel Pavlovich?"

Aleksandr grinned. "I don't think we have to worry. What would he say? That he tried to bully a grieving woman and was put in his place by a young man he did not even know? No, I think Grigorii Strelkov will want to forget this morning. And the long trip to St. Petersburg will help dull his memory."

Katherina rested her head on his chest again. "I hope you are right. At any rate, I guess it is silly to worry. Besides, Pavel Pavlovich hardly knows Grigorii Strelkov, and he seldom sees his cousin in St. Petersburg." She paused and sighed. "But Sasha—did you have to say my mother was dead?"

He smiled, kissing her face. "It was the first and most convincing explanation I could think of. You started the story, my love, by telling Strelkov your mother was ill; I simply finished it. Don't worry, your mother will never find out. And even if. she does, I am sure she will forgive us."

"At least I will not be traveling with that frightful man," Katherina said. "If I had known his temper, I don't think I would have had the courage to ask him."

Aleksandr smiled wryly. "You know, if the count had not found me at the fort, we might have passed each other—you on your way to St. Petersburg, me on my way through the Caucasus—without ever knowing. And what would you have done alone in St. Petersburg?"

"I would have found your message and traveled back to the Caucasus." Katherina laughed. "But let's not think of that, Sasha. We are here, together. Surely the fates are smiling on us."

She stretched up to kiss him, flicking her tongue teasingly into his mouth. His hands found the sash of her dressing gown, and the gown fell open so that her naked body was brushing against him. Through his thin shirt he could feel her breasts grow taut against his chest, and she could feel the desire rising hard in his body. Devouring each other's kisses, they inched toward the bedroom. Aleksandr's shirt was now damp with the perspiration of their mingled desires. He buried his hands in her silky hair, and Katherina felt her body tingle with feverish anticipation. Then, in the doorway, Katherina felt his hands fall away. Now he held her gently, but without the crush of passion she had felt only a moment before. He slowly moved his mouth away from hers, and she could feel him tremble, as if battling his sudden restraint.

"Sasha," she moaned, "don't stop now. Please—don't stop now."

She pressed closer to him, trying to catch his lips again. But he moved his mouth away, softly kissing her ear, gently coaxing her back from the brink of passion.

"Sasha, I want you! Don't you want me, too?"

He stroked her back and carefully pulled her dressing gown closed again. "Katya, Katya," he whispered, "I always want you. But I think we have forgotten about your Masha. Where is she now?"

"Oh!" Katherina gasped. "Strelkov's visit has made me lose my senses. Poor Masha! I must find her and talk to her." Tying her sash, she hurried out the front door.

Katherina found Masha cowering in the garden. Hearing Katherina's footsteps on the pebbled path, the servant turned her tearstained face toward her mistress. "Are you still angry with me, madame?" Masha sobbed.

"No, Masha. I should not have been angry at all."

"That man in the parlor—he was so impatient. He made me so uncomfortable and had me so confused—"

"Forget about that man, Masha," Katherina said. "I understand he treated you badly, but he is gone now."

"But he said you were going to go away somewhere with him."

"No, Masha—I am not going anywhere with anyone."

"Would you go, madame, and leave me in a strange town full of strange people?"

"Of course not, Masha." Katherina put her arm around the quivering servant girl. "You have always served me well, and it would be wrong for me to leave you anywhere." As she brushed away Masha's tears, she felt a twinge of guilt over her original plans.

"Wouldn't you leave me, even to punish me for—," Masha faltered and began sobbing again.

"For what, Masha?"

"For what I saw in your bedroom," Masha blurted, and fresh tears streamed down her face.

"Masha," Katherina said steadily, "you and I must have a serious talk. Not as a mistress to a servant, but as one woman to another."

Flattered by this new treatment, Masha stifled her sobs. She fixed her glazed eyes on Katherina and waited for her to speak.

"Masha," Katherina said, "Aleksandr Sergeievich, I mean Monsieur Belikov, and I are—in love."

Masha exhaled slowly, her eyes wide. "But you are married to Count Ostrov!"

"Yes. And he is a very good man and a good husband. I married the count because I saw in him so many good qualities and because I enjoyed his company. But when I married him I hadn't the faintest conception of what love meant. I never dreamed any woman could find the joy I've found with Aleksandr Sergeievich! Masha, until you experience it yourself, you cannot possibly imagine how it feels to be in love and to be loved. If I tried to describe it to you, you would not believe me." Katherina felt her face flush and her skin tingle.

"Does Count Ostrov know you love Monsieur Belikov?"

"No, of course not," Katherina said. "And you must never do or say anything to let him know. When the time is right, I will tell him. But neither Monsieur Belikov nor I wishes him any harm."

Masha looked hurt. "Madame, you know without asking that you can trust me."

"Yes, of course I do." Katherina patted Masha's shoulder.

They sat in silence for a few moments, then Masha spoke. "Madame, perhaps I understand about love better than you think."

"Why is that, Masha?" Katherina asked absently.

"Because I think—perhaps—I am in love, too."

"You? In love? Why, that is wonderful news, Masha!" Katherina said, embracing the girl. "But who? Where? How did you meet?"

Masha's face glowed. "Do you remember two days ago at the spa when you left me alone?"

"Of course I remember. You were afraid to wait by yourself."

"But did I seem afraid when you returned?"

Katherina tried to remember. Then she recalled how her own elation about going to St. Petersburg had blotted out her awareness of Masha. "No—," she said. "You were talking to someone—a young blond soldier, I believe."

"Yes—yes," Masha nodded enthusiastically. "He is the most wonderful person I have ever met. Not at all like those other animals who made me feel so nervous. Vladimir Nikolaievich makes me feel so relaxed, so happy, so important."

Katherina had never seen Masha's face glow with so much joy. "I'm sure he is a fine young man, Masha. Have you seen him again since your first meeting?"

"Yes—," Masha admitted. "I slipped away yesterday morning. I would have asked your permission, but I could not find you anywhere."

Katherina smiled, remembering how she had spent

the morning. "You needn't apologize, Masha. You did the right thing. Some people live a whole lifetime and never experience love. Those of us fortunate enough to find it must enjoy whatever happiness we are given."

Again they were silent, each thinking of the man she loved. Then Katherina noticed that more tears were rolling down Masha's cheeks. "Now what is the matter, Masha?" she asked gently.

"I—I am glad you have found such happiness, but—"

"But what?"

"But the priests say it is a sin for a woman to lie with a man who is not her husband."

Katherina sighed. "Masha, what Aleksandr Sergeievich and I feel cannot be a sin."

"They say that you will burn in hell for such a sin," Masha continued tearfully. "And I don't want you to burn in hell."

"Masha, the priests just want to scare people," Katherina said boldly. "Everyone knows that even they do not follow all the teachings they proclaim. Perhaps it is a sin to give your body thoughtlessly to someone you do not care for—or someone who does not care for you. But I am sure that love can never be a sin."

Masha stared at Katherina, and Katherina continued, as much to convince herself as her servant. "Don't the priests say that God commands us to love one another?"

"Yes." Masha nodded.

"Then isn't it foolish to suppose God would punish a person for loving another person?"

"I—I guess so. I don't know. I'm so confused."

"Masha, there is no need to be confused," Katherina

said. "It is simple to understand, just as I explained it. Love makes everything simple."

But Katherina Andreievna knew in her heart that love did not make things simple at all.

Chapter 11

Now that Masha was aware of their relationship, Aleksandr Sergeievich and Katherina Andreievna became more relaxed. They no longer felt forced to call each other Monsieur Belikov or Countess Ostrova in her presence, and they no longer worried about her seeing them entering or leaving Katherina's bedroom. Katherina noted happily that Masha seemed to slip away more and more often in the afternoon and evening for a rendezvous with Vladimir Nikolaievich. And, since they saw Tamara or Lizaveta only at mealtimes, Katherina and Aleksandr felt as if they had the house and grounds entirely to themselves.

Lying in bed one morning when Aleksandr was still asleep, Katherina reflected on how the month they had spent together was like a delicious, endless honeymoon. The house and garden were their private palace of love, already overflowing with memories. Content with each other, they had never ventured to the main boulevard of Pyatigorsk, to the spa, or anywhere else, and each day was lovelier and more fulfilling than the day before.

Aleksandr Sergeievich rolled toward her, lazily opening his sleepy eyes, gazing at her shimmering halo of golden hair. His arms enfolded her as she kissed him good-morning.

"And what have you been thinking of, my darling Katya?" he murmured, propping his head on one elbow.

"Not thinking, Sasha—dreaming. Our life has become a beautiful dream, hasn't it?"

"Yes—a beautiful dream." He closed his eyes and rolled away. "A beautiful dream—the perfect description—and how unfortunate for both of us."

She sat up and pulled him back toward her. "Unfortunate? What do you mean, Sasha?"

He opened his eyes again and Katherina could see that they were brimming with tears. "Dreams end, Katya. Dreams always end. We must wake up whether we want to or not." Aleksandr swung himself out of the bed.

"Sasha—don't!" Katherina reached for him, but he shook her hands away. He slid into his trousers and left the room.

Katherina sat dumbfounded, staring after him. Then she fumbled for her dressing gown. As she hurried to put it on, the silky sash fell away, sliding off the bed. Katherina pulled the robe closed and, holding it with one hand, hurried after Aleksandr.

She expected to find him in the garden, beneath their favorite apple tree, but there was no sign of him. Katherina wandered in the garden, past the black locust and acacia trees and around the tangle of grapevines that were heavy with their purple fruit. The pebbles of the garden path hurt her bare feet, but she kept searching as tears began to stream down her face.

She found Aleksandr standing by the garden's small sundial, rubbing his fingers over its inscription: *A clock to mark life's sunny hours.* His shirt lay on the path beside him. Katherina placed her hand over his, holding it tightly as the tears continued to streak her cheeks.

"Please don't ever walk out on me again, Sasha," she whispered. "Promise me that."

He turned and took her in his arms. "Oh, Katya, I'm sorry if I hurt you, but these last days have made me so happy that it gives me great pain knowing they cannot continue."

"Sasha—don't say that!"

He brought his finger to her lips to silence her. "I must say it, Katya. We must admit it. The count will return, I will be sent back to the fort and across the mountains—and then we will be separated again. Only God can say for how long—"

"No, Sasha," she cut him off. "Perhaps Pavel Pavlovich will not return. Perhaps you will not be sent away. And we will not be separated. We can't know what tomorrow will bring. We can only hold the happiness we are blessed with today."

"Katya," he choked. "My sweet Katya—I want to believe that!"

"Then do believe it, Sasha! Believe it for me!"

She reached up and put her arms around his neck, and her dressing gown fell open so that her breasts were brushing his chest. Pulling his mouth down to her own, she nibbled greedily at his lips, then slowly ran her tongue along them, forcing them to separate. Within a few seconds, she felt all resistance drain out of his body. His hands slid into her open gown and caressed her softly curving buttocks. Then one hand slipped lower to the velvety pocket of her inner thigh. With a low groan, Katherina parted her legs and arched her body against his.

His fingers traced teasing, tantalizing patterns as they wandered slowly toward their target. She was burning—waiting, but not wanting him too fast—and her mouth found his, and then his wandering fingers found the heat of her, throbbing, pulsing. She moaned in breathless delight as hot flashes of desire swept through her belly, building in a wild chain reaction until her whole body shuddered uncontrollably under his touch.

Katherina felt her feet leave the ground as her legs wound around him and she opened herself to him, her body meeting his own pulsating loins. As his touch drove her almost beyond the brink of passion, all logic deserted her. "Stop!" she cried, when the joy became too great for her to believe. Then in the same breath, "Don't stop now. Never stop. Please. *Never!*"

"Oh—my God," she sobbed. "Love me, Sasha. Please love me. Take me. Take me now. Now." Her body arched in a frenzy of desire. "Please, Sasha, please. Please—now—"

His kisses quieted her pleas as he carried her to a secluded area of the garden. For a moment, Katherina removed her arms from his neck as she tore off her drenched dressing gown. Kneeling, he laid her down on the cool grass that was still damp with dew. His fingers continued to work their magic as he caressed her, prolonging the sweetness. He inched off his trousers and cast them aside. All the while, his eyes traveled lovingly over her waiting, trembling body, her golden hair spread like a beam of sunlight over the grass. He could sense her every muscle straining toward him, pleading for him to give release to her pent-up passions, begging for fulfillment.

"My beautiful, beautiful Katya," Aleksandr murmured. Then he began to kiss her, starting at her toes, which curled in tense anticipation. His kisses moved slowly up the inside of her legs until she wondered as she strained toward his mouth whether she would not die of joy in sensation. He kept on kissing her, licking her, caressing her, the fire inside of her giving way to small explosions until his mouth reached hers, he hungrily took her, and they fell together toward the abyss of ecstasy.

Their morning of love lulled Katherina Andreievna and Aleksandr Sergeievich into blessed forgetfulness, but the magic was dispelled soon after they returned to the house.

The moment she entered the parlor Katherina saw the letter propped against a vase on the table. Her name showed clearly on the outside. Hoping Aleksandr would not notice, she brushed past it and hurried toward her room. She would not allow anything to spoil their day. But her plans to ignore the letter were quickly crushed.

"Katya," Aleksandr asked, "didn't you see? There is a letter here for you."

"I think I should go and get dressed," she said.

Aleksandr Sergeievich picked up the letter and followed her. "I think you should read it," he said, waving the letter in front of her nose.

"Of course I will read it. But not just now. It is almost noon. I should get dressed for dinner." Katherina dodged the waving letter and went to her wardrobe.

"It will only take a few moments to read, Katya. It might be important." Again he held the letter before her. "We can't simply close our eyes to reality."

"No," she said. "But sometimes we can hold it off for a while."

"Only for a while, Katya," he said as he put his hands on her shoulders. "Only for a while. Come," he drew her toward the bed and pulled her into his lap. "Shall I open it for you?"

She sighed. "No, I will. Give it to me."

Aleksandr handed her the letter and, with shaking hands, she tore away the seal. Katherina could almost hear Pavel Pavlovich speaking to her.

My dear Katherina Andreievna,

I hope you will forgive me, my dear little wife, for being so long in writing, but the responsibilities of my assignment have kept me entirely without any free moments. How I miss my evenings with you, and your excellent talent for taking my mind from my worries! I fear that Czar Nikolai's assessment of General Yermolov is correct. He seems much too hesitant in making military decisions, although he is still quite popular with his troops. Perhaps his judgment has been hampered by his age, although I understand that he is still a few years younger than I.

I have heard that General Paskevich has met with a good deal of success in his campaigns along the Kura River, and I leave tomorrow to observe his leadership. Forgive me, Katherina Andreievna, for it now appears certain that I shall not be able to return to Pyatigorsk in time for our anniversary. But now is the time to visit Paskevich, and I must put my responsibilities to the empire before personal considerations.

I hope I have not bored you with all this description of military effectiveness. I trust that you have been putting your time in Pyatigorsk to good use, enjoying the pleasures of the spa and the beauties of the community. When you can, please write to me of your activities, for I long to hear from you, my dear wife.

Give my regards to young Aleksandr Belikov. I hope he is caring for you as well as I would myself.

Your affectionate husband,
Pavel Pavlovich

Katherina dropped the letter and walked to her wardrobe. "Well," she sighed, "at least we know he will be away a while longer."

"Katya," Aleksandr said, "you know you must answer his letter. He is your husband, and you owe him at least that much."

"I know—but I don't know what I can write to him."

"Write as you would talk to him. Describe how the garden has changed since he left, or what Tamara has cooked for us—but do it today. If you put it off, it will only become more difficult."

"But it is pointless to write," Katherina said. "How will my letter ever get to him?"

"I will carry the letter to the fort myself. No doubt someone there will soon be leaving to join Paskevich's forces."

"Oh." She began to dress, unable to think of anything more to say.

"Today, Katya?" Aleksandr pressed.

"All right," she agreed. "I will write to him after dinner, and you can take the letter to the fort tomorrow."

Katherina brooded about what to write to Pavel Pavlovich. In the year they had been married, she had never found it difficult to talk to him, but that was before she had lived with Aleksandr Sergeievich, sharing with him more intimacy in their first days together than she could imagine in a lifetime with Pavel Pavlovich. In the past month, she had come to think of Aleksandr Sergeievich as her husband; and Pavel Pavlovich hovered in the back of her mind as a distant, benevolent uncle. She had closed her mind to reality, and now she found it impossible to think of Pavel Pavlovich as her husband.

Several times she sat down to compose a letter, but each time she was disappointed with her efforts. Stalling for time, she carefully burned the crumbled pages over a candle. Once she even started to write about her feelings for Aleksandr Sergeievich, explaining that she had never intended to fall in love with him and begging Pavel Pavlovich's forgiveness. But when she stopped to think of Pavel Pavlovich receiving such a letter when he was lonely and far from home, she could not finish it, and she crumpled the paper in disgust.

Once again, she began, "Dear Pavel Pavlovich," but her hand seemed paralyzed. For a long time she stared at the salutation, trying to concentrate on chatty, gay things to write. She did not hear Aleksandr Sergeievich come in behind her, and she was not aware of him as he looked over her shoulder at the empty page.

"I was happy to receive your letter today," Aleksandr began.

His voice startled Katherina and she turned so suddenly that she almost upset the inkwell. Putting his hands on her shoulders to calm her, he smiled. "Just write," he whispered, "before it is time for supper."

Katherina turned back to her desk, and Aleksandr began again: "I was happy to receive your letter today, and to know that you are well. I hope that you are finding at least a few moments to relax and enjoy the beautiful scenery that must surround you, for I shall expect a full description when you return." He paused to allow Katherina time to catch up. "There is a very little news here. Pyatigorsk seems to be quite a quiet town, and there has been no sign at all of the Circassian discontent you spoke of before you left. Tamara is slowly making me accustomed to Caucasian cookery, though I must admit I crave some real sour cream instead of this yogurt she insists on serving!" At that Aleksandr squeezed her shoulders playfully, and Katherina laughed. "All is well here, so you must not worry about us, Pavel

Pavlovich. I shall look forward to your next letter. Your affectionate wife, Katherina Andreievna."

As Katherina finished writing the last line, Aleksandr Sergeievich walked to the window and stared out at the setting sun. "There—that wasn't so difficult, was it?"

"Oh, Sasha!" Katherina cried. "What must you think of me! I suppose you wonder why I married Pavel Pavlovich when now I cannot even write him a simple letter. But you must understand that things were different when I married him. I hadn't met you. I didn't know a thing about love. I thought love was some silly peasant-girl notion that had no place in my life. I thought the affection I felt for Pavel Pavlovich was enough. Nothing in me believed there could be more. I did not know—"

He turned away from the window and took her in his arms. "Katya, Katya, I do understand. You must never think I do not. Before I found you, I had tasted the lust and empty physical fulfillment that all young noblemen and soldiers seek. I had laughed at the very thought of romance, calling it a poet's creation. When my friends spoke to me of their romantic interests, I laughed in their faces and stalked off to find a new bed partner for the night —but you awakened something unknown to me. At first I refused to admit that it could be love—until the very thought of you began to consume my whole life."

"At least you were not married. You are not being unfaithful to someone after you pledged that person your life before God." Katherina sobbed out her guilt.

"And yet," Aleksandr said, "I am even more guilty than you. Perhaps I should not have pursued you. Knowing you were married, I should have kept away from the beginning, when you resisted me so strongly. It is my fault for forcing myself on you and causing you this torment."

"No, Sasha," she insisted. "It is not your fault."

He stepped away and held her chin in his hand, so that he could read the slightest nuance in her eyes. "Katya—tell me truthfully—with your heart and with your mind. If you tell me to leave this house, I will go away now and make sure that I never see you again. I will see that another soldier comes to protect you until the count returns, but I will not tempt you or myself. I will do as you say, Katya. Will you tell me to leave?"

Her eyes never wavered as she answered in a clear, steady voice, "I would rather burn in hell!"

That night, for the first time since Aleksandr Sergeievich had begun sharing her bed, Katherina could not sleep. She cuddled against him, trying to lose herself in his warm flesh, but her mind refused to stop working. Ever since Pavel Pavlovich left, she had pushed away all thoughts of his return. Even that morning, when Aleksandr Sergeievich had voiced his fears, she had refused to accept them. But the letter from Pavel Pavlovich was a terrible tangible reminder that he would return—and he would expect to be greeted by an affectionate wife, willing to perform all her marital duties.

The thought of Pavel Pavlovich sleeping beside her while Aleksandr Sergeievich fought for the Czar somewhere across the mountains made Katherina's head throb. She felt she could never again accept the count as her husband.

Aleksandr Sergeievich stirred in his sleep, hugging her closer to him, and Katherina resolved that she would never give up his tenderness or his passion for a calm, comfortable, but totally unstimulating, life with Pavel Pavlovich. Why hadn't she listened to her mother's lectures about passion and her pleas that she not marry Pavel Pavlovich? Of course, if she had remained unmarried, hidden in Novgorod, she would still be scoffing at the idea of love and passion, and she would never have tasted the sweetness that came with unbridled love. It was too late now for regrets. All she could do was try to plan a better future.

Until that day, Katherina had convinced herself that she and Aleksandr Sergeievich had built an almost perfect existence in Pyatigorsk. She had thought that only Pavel Pavlovich was the loser, and, since he was so far away and could not know he was being hurt, Katherina seldom worried about him. Now she found herself forced to admit that all three of them—she, Aleksandr Sergeievich, and Pavel Pavlovich—suffered as a result of the situation. After the past month, she knew she could never again pretend to be a good wife to Pavel Pavlovich. Even if he did not sense it, he would be cheated of some part of her, and her own guilt, which had surfaced that afternoon, would continue to gnaw at her.

And what about Aleksandr Sergeievich? Katherina saw the hurt in his eyes when he had accused himself of causing her grief. She thought of him offering to leave her so she could live without guilt, and she knew that she could not allow such feelings to continue tearing at his heart. She feared that guilt and remorse, if allowed to grow, would ruin their relationship as they attempted to hide their feelings —not only from Pavel Pavlovich but from each other.

I will not allow that to happen, Katherina Andreievna swore to herself. She resolved that no one and nothing would rob her and Aleksandr Sergeievich of their happiness. When Pavel Pavlovich returned to Pyatigorsk, he would find that they had gone. She would convince Aleksandr Sergeievich that it was the only way to solve their problems—and that it was the fairest solution for all three of them.

Chapter 12

In the morning, Katherina watched silently as Aleksandr Sergeievich prepared to ride to the fort with her letter. As he mounted his black stallion, she held his right leg and looked up at him.

"I want to go with you, Sasha."

"But you have always said you don't want to leave the house and grounds."

"I don't as long as I have you near. But it will be too empty, too lonely, with you gone all day."

"You shouldn't be lonely. You have Masha, Tamara, Lizaveta."

"Masha has already left to meet her Vladimir Nikolaievich. Sometimes I think she is almost as much in love as we are. And Tamara and Lizaveta are no company. I can hardly understand their dialect. I need to be with you, Sasha. Please take me with you."

"Katya," Aleksandr sighed, "I will be home before evening. Besides—you know we have only one horse. The count and his Ivan took the others."

"Am I so heavy that this strong animal cannot carry me as well as you?"

"It's a long ride to the fort. You would be uncomfortable sharing my saddle."

"How could I be uncomfortable when I have you to lean against?"

Aleksandr Sergeievich was silent, trying to compose a logical answer. Sensing that he was about to capitulate, Katherina continued. "Please, Sasha. I long for some fresh air and open spaces."

He sighed again. "All right, Katya. How could I ride off and leave you when you beg so convincingly? I would have to be made of stone." He leaned over and scooped her into the saddle in front of him.

Katherina smiled sweetly, leaning back and rubbing against his chest. "Won't you be glad for my company on the long ride?"

"Of course," he admitted as he kissed her ear.

For more than an hour they rode southwest of Pyatigorsk, between the Caucasus foothills and the rippling Podkumok River. They rode through high grasses in gentle ravines, past groves of linden trees. Katherina caught glimpses of shepherds tending their flocks along the lower mountain slopes. As they neared the fort, Katherina felt Aleksandr Sergeievich tighten the reins, slowing the horse to a walk.

"Is something wrong, Sasha?"

"No. It's just that I feel certain now that I should not have brought you. A military garrison is no place for a beautiful young woman. Every man there will be coming out to gawk at you."

"So, let them stare." She tossed her head. "I'm not afraid of their eyes when I have you beside me. Or perhaps you are ashamed to be seen with me," she teased. "Perhaps you would rather that I wait out here where the other soldiers cannot see me."

"Don't be absurd, Katya. Those peaceful shepherds we just saw would go wild at the sight of an unescorted woman."

"Well then, I suggest we ride on to the fort and attend to our business."

Aleksandr chuckled. "You seem to leave me very little choice, my love." He gave the horse its head and they galloped toward the fort.

As Aleksandr had predicted, almost the whole garrison turned out to view Katherina Andreievna. The streets, nearly empty when they entered the gates, quickly filled with curious onlookers. Katherina flushed as she overheard their loud, lusty assessments of her.

"Ah, that one is a beauty. Spirited too, no doubt. See how she braids her hair like the wild women of the tribes?"

"She probably does that to keep it from tangling when she rolls and squirms in bed," another soldier smirked. "What I wouldn't give for a tumble with her! I didn't know that her kind, with the fair skin and golden hair, could be had in these parts. All I've seen are dark-haired slant-eyed creatures that smell like dirty sheep."

The soldiers roared with laughter, and the whispered question swept through the crowd. "What would it take to lure a woman like that away from her man?"

Katherina felt the flush spreading, painting her face and neck a deep red. Aleksandr's arms tightened around her and his knuckles went white as he gripped the reins in barely contained fury. She jostled herself in the saddle to press closer to him.

"I warned you that these soldiers are animals," he whispered in her ear.

"But don't they even know who you are? Have they no respect for a fellow officer and his woman?"

"Katya, the men I arrived with are long gone over the Caucasus to fight the Persians. Since then, hun-

dreds of others have come and gone, and I've had
little chance to become acquainted with those stationed here more permanently. As for respect, I suspect that these men have been deprived of female
companionship for long enough that any flicker of
respect they once had has been drowned by their
animal lusts."

"Oh!" Katherina drew in her breath sharply and
said no more. After all, she had prevailed upon
Aleksandr Sergeievich to bring her with him.

Aleksandr stopped the horse in front of an impressive stone building. Dismounting, he threw the reins
over the hitching post and turned to lift Katherina from the saddle. Katherina was glad to feel her
feet on the ground again. Though she had not wished
to complain, she had been quite uncomfortable wear-
ing a dress and riding astride the horse in the small
space allowed her in the saddle.

Aleksandr took her arm and led her to the building. "This is the commander's headquarters.
No one will dare to bother us here. And the commander will know who can be trusted to carry your
letter."

A guard at the door stopped them, but he let them
pass after Aleksandr explained the nature of their
business. Inside, a clerk led them to the office of
the commander—General Bugov.

Seeing Katherina, Bugov, a portly gray-haired man,
stood up with an exclamation of delight. "Ah, Belikov,
I see you have brought a lady with you. What a very
pleasant surprise." He hurried to offer Katherina a
chair.

"General Bugov," Aleksandr said stiffly, "may I
present the Countess Ostrova?"

"Ah—the countess." Bugov smiled at Katherina.

"Your husband is an impressive man, Countess Ostrova, and quite concerned with your welfare. He insisted that I release Belikov here to look after you in his absence. I trust that you have no complaints regarding his performance?"

"None whatsoever," Katherina said, returning his smile.

Bugov turned to Aleksandr. "So, Belikov, what business brings you to the fort, away from the considerable pleasures of Pyatigorsk?"

"Actually, it is Countess Ostrova's business. She has written a letter to her husband, and she wishes someone to deliver it." Aleksandr took the letter from his pocket. "I had intended to bring it here myself, but the countess wished to ride along to see some of the country."

"I see," Bugov nodded. "As a matter of fact, one of my men carried a letter from the count to Pyatigorsk only yesterday." He studied Katherina for a moment. "You are indeed a devoted wife to answer him so quickly. I hope the count realizes his good fortune in being married to so fine a woman."

Katherina flushed and lowered her eyes.

"I hope," Bugov continued, "that all is well with the count, and that his mission is progressing smoothly."

"Yes, quite smoothly," Katherina said. "He goes now to join General Paskevich's troops. I had hoped that a detachment from your fort might be traveling there soon and that someone among them might carry my letter."

"Yes, of course. As a matter of fact, I have troops leaving here tomorrow. I hope that is soon enough to suit you."

"Yes, thank you, general." Katherina nodded, and Aleksandr handed the letter to Bugov.

The general ran his fingers along the edges of the letter, then propped it up on his desk. "I will personally see that your letter is entrusted to responsible hands, Countess Ostrova," he said. "In the meantime, perhaps you will both be so kind as to join me for tea. I am sure you could use some refreshment and rest after your trip from Pyatigorsk."

"You are too kind, general," Katherina replied meekly.

"Not at all. If you will excuse me, I will call someone to bring us refreshment." He turned at the door. "Feel free to look around, countess. I imagine you have seldom visited a fort, but Belikov here should be able to answer any questions you have."

When General Bugov returned, he found Katherina and Aleksandr studying a large map that was hanging on the wall behind his desk.

"Interested in geography, are you?" the general asked.

"I was just showing the countess where her husband has been and where he is traveling now," Aleksandr said.

"You know, when he writes to me of the Kura River or of some of the towns in the region, I have no idea where he is," Katherina added. "It is so helpful to see all of these places on paper—to know where we are, and how far away he is."

"I understand. It is most unfortunate that the Persian hostilities prevent you from traveling with your husband." A Circassian maid carried in tea and tea cakes, and the general nodded to Katherina and Aleksandr to be seated.

"Since I married the count," Katherina sighed, "we have done so much traveling—first to St. Petersburg, then Moscow, and then the long journey to Pyatigorsk. It has been so exciting, but also confusing. If only I had a map to help me sort out where I am and where I've been, it would be a great help to me in keeping my journal." She sighed again and sipped her tea thoughtfully.

"But surely a man in your husband's position has maps he can show you," the general said.

Katherina shook her head. "If he has, he has never seen fit to mention the fact to me. But of course, this assignment from Czar Nikolai came so suddenly that we had little time to discuss the matter. I did not want to bother the count with my personal questions, and now that he is gone I would not think of disturbing any of his papers for so trivial a matter." Katherina paused, aware that Aleksandr was studying her curiously. She took a bite from a tea cake and sipped some more tea.

"Still," she said, fluttering her eyelashes, "with the count gone my days seem so long, and it would be such a pleasant diversion to trace our travels on a map."

"My dear countess," Bugov said, "I am sure I can arrange for you to have a map. I know this is rather irregular, since our maps are intended for military purposes, but I can see no harm in providing one to the wife of a highly respected Russian citizen who is, even now, performing a service for his Czar."

"Oh, but I couldn't trouble you," Katherina said in mock despair. "You have already been more than kind to me."

"I assure you, it is no trouble at all, Countess Ostrova." Bugov rose and went to his office door. "I'll simply ask my aide to find a map for you."

As the general stepped out of the room, Aleksandr

whispered to Katherina, "Why all this sudden interest in maps, Katya? And—I don't recall your keeping a journal."

"Never mind," she hissed, her eye on the door. "I'll explain it to you later."

General Bugov reentered and handed Katherina a bulky folded map. "I'm afraid this is all we could spare," he said. "It includes not only our own empire, but a good deal of Europe as well. However, I think you will find it of some help."

"I am sure it will be perfect," Katherina smiled. "Perhaps," she turned to Aleksandr, "you could hang it on the wall above my desk for me."

"Certainly, countess," he replied stiffly. Then he rose and addressed the general. "I think I should escort the countess back to Pyatigorsk now. No doubt the count would wish her home well before twilight."

"That is wise planning," Bugov replied. "One never knows what to expect of the Circassians in these parts." He gallantly offered Katherina his arm. Outside, he watched in confusion as Aleksandr unhitched his horse. "But where is the countess's horse?" he asked.

"I'm afraid she does not have one," Aleksandr said. "The count and his manservant took their mounts to Transcaucasia, and only my own remained."

"I was so insistent about riding here today that Monsieur Belikov was kind enough to share his horse with me," Katherina quickly explained.

"But my dear countess, that is unthinkable! You must have been extremely uncomfortable on such a long ride." Without waiting for a response, Bugov turned to his aide. "Dmitriev, go to the stable and bring around my chestnut mare."

"Oh, but I can't take your horse. I assure you my ride was quite comfortable."

"I really must insist, Countess Ostrova. I have several horses of my own, and I rarely have reason to ride anyway."

"But I have no idea when I could return it—"

Bugov cut her off. "It is not necessary to talk of returning it, my dear countess. Please accept the horse as a small thanks for the pleasure of your company this afternoon. Perhaps Belikov will bring you to visit again."

Dmitriev was leading the saddled mare toward them, and Katherina relented as graciously as possible. "Well, perhaps I shall accept your horse as a loan until my husband returns. At that time we can make arrangements to return her to you. In the meantime, General Bugov, I must thank you again for your hospitality and generosity."

"I assure you, Countess Ostrova, the pleasure is all mine." The general helped her mount the mare and watched as she and Aleksandr Sergeievich cantered toward the gate.

As they rode out of the fort, Aleksandr Sergeievich chuckled softly. "General Bugov is quite taken with you, Katya."

"Nonsense, Sasha. He was just being courteous—out of respect to my husband."

"Oh—really? I think if you had even hinted at it he would gladly have climbed to the top of Mount Elbrus to please you."

"You are exaggerating, Sasha. Or are you jealous?"

"Do I have reason to be?" His dark eyes sparkled with laughter.

"What do you think?" Her own eyes danced in response.

"Are you going to tell me now why you are suddenly so interested in maps?"

"I told you—I'll explain later." She laughed. For the rest of the ride, Katherina chattered aimlessly about the scenery, leading the conversation away from any talk of maps.

Only after supper, when Tamara and Lizaveta had retired to their rooms, did Katherina bring out the map. She spread it ceremoniously on the parlor floor, and she brought two lamps so they could see it clearly.

"Well," Aleksandr teased, "is it later yet?"

"Yes," she replied, kissing him on the ear. "You have been very patient, so now I will explain. I wanted the map because we need it."

"Katya, that explains nothing. Why do we need a map?"

"We need it because I have decided we are going to leave Pyatigorsk."

"You have decided!" he bellowed with a sudden rage that caught Katherina off guard. "You have decided! What about me?"

Alarmed by his unexpected anger, Katherina whispered, "Sasha—hush. You will rouse the servants."

He glared at her, but he lowered his voice. "All right. I'll be quieter. But please explain to me why you thought to make such a decision without so much as consulting me?"

There was still an undertone of anger in his voice, and Katherina chose her words carefully. "Sasha—listen to me. I have been thinking about this ever since I received the letter from Pavel Pavlovich yesterday afternoon. I am convinced it is the only sensible course of action. And I know that when you think about it calmly you will be forced to agree with me."

"Are you forgetting, Katya, that I am a member of the Imperial Army, assigned by Czar Nikolai himself to remain in the Caucasus for two years?"

"Are *you* forgetting, Sasha, that in the month you have been here, no one from the fort has thought to check on you? By the time anyone discovered your disappearance, we would be far away."

He shook his head as he paced the small parlor. "No. Nowhere in Russia is far enough. With his network of gendarmes, the Czar can see to the farthest reaches of his empire. It would be only a matter of time, Katya, before we would be hunted down. And you would be in just as much danger as I."

"Then it is obvious that we must leave the empire. We must seek refuge in a foreign country."

Aleksandr stopped pacing to stare at her. "Katherina Andreievna, have you gone mad? Do you really know what you are saying? You cannot be serious about leaving Russia. It is our homeland. Our lives are rooted here. For all the abuses of the Czar, I have never thought, even for an instant, of leaving the homeland!"

"Would you rather think of leaving me?" Katherina asked in a biting whisper.

"Katya, I beg of you, do not confuse the question—"

"No." She cut him off abruptly. "Think about it, Sasha. Think about the things you said yesterday morning. I know now that you were right to worry, and I won't stay here and wait for Pavel Pavlovich to return and claim me for his wife. I won't wave you off to war knowing full well you might never return to me. I love Russia as much as you do, Sasha—but, if I am forced to choose between the homeland and you, there is no question that I must choose you. Perhaps I was wrong to think your choice would be the same as mine!"

She turned away, not wanting him to see the tears of frustration in her eyes. When he came up behind her and placed his hands on her shoulders, she shook him away roughly.

For a few strained moments they both remained silent. Then Aleksandr spoke. "My choice is the same as yours, Katya. But what about your husband? We must think of how he will feel when he returns to find we have betrayed him. He has, after all, tried to give you a good life. And he has always treated me well."

She turned slowly to face him. "I know. I have thought of Pavel Pavlovich. But don't you see? This will be best for him as well as for us. I can't go on deceiving him, pretending to be his wife while I deny him the greatest part of me. When he returns, I know he will be hurt, but he is a strong man and he will recover. It will be better for him than the slow, burning hurt of living with someone who is longing for another."

Aleksandr sighed, taking her face in his hands. "Perhaps you are right, Katya. I'm not sure anymore what is the right thing to do, but I know that my worst fear in life is losing you."

"Then trust me, Sasha." She kissed his hands. "Trust me now, as I have always trusted you."

She knelt to study the map, and he sat by her side.

"I don't know, Katya," Aleksandr shook his head. "We are in a most difficult position here. None of the foreign borders are easily accessible, and whatever route we choose will present all kinds of dangers."

His finger traced a line across the Caucasus. "Here is our closest neighbor—Persia—but I think we must rule out this line of flight. Even if we were to traverse the mountains and safely slip through the battlefront, we would hardly be welcome in the Persian Empire. In fact, we would probably be shot immediately as Russian spies. Unless of course they tortured us first, in the hopes of gaining valuable information."

Katherina shuddered. Then she pushed his finger slightly west. "Here—what about the Ottoman Empire?"

"Hardly a better choice than Persia. Russian relations with the Turks have been uneasy for years. I suspect that hostilities may erupt at any moment."

Katherina stared at the map. The Black Sea penned them in on the west, and the Caspian Sea on the east. "What are we to do, Sasha?" she moaned.

Now that he had agreed to their flight, Aleksandr appeared coolly competent. His finger traced a line westward, along the northern border of the Caucasus Mountains. "Perhaps we can travel this way, to the straits of the Sea of Azov. No doubt we could pay some fisherman to transport us the short distance to the Crimea. Then, if we travel across the peninsula, perhaps we can find a boat to carry us across this arm of the Black Sea and into the Danube River. I think we might be able to find refuge in the Austrian

Empire." He hesitated. "If we get there safely. We would still have to travel some distance up the Danube and Prut rivers before we would be free of both Russia and Turkey."

"Of course we will get there safely," Katherina said, a bit of bravado showing in her voice.

Aleksandr shrugged. "I am not so sure. It is a difficult route—over mountains and hilly country. We could be murdered by Circassians before we even left the Caucasus, or we could be apprehended by gendarmes before we reach the Danube. There is a long distance to travel in the Russian Empire before we reach safety. It is a better plan than traveling to Persia, but it is not safe by any estimation. I am not at all sure I could let myself expose you to such dangers."

Katherina brought her finger to his' lips and stared into his eyes. "Are *you* willing to take the risk, Sasha?"

Without blinking, he answered, "Yes, darling Katya—for the chance of living a lifetime with you."

"Then do not worry about me," she said, flinging her arms around his neck. "With you, I can face whatever comes." She buried her face in his neck, hungrily sucking at his flesh. His arms welcomed her and his lips quickly found hers.

Neither of them noticed as the lamps burned down, slowly shrouding the parlor in darkness. The map, their key to their future, seemed as softly inviting as a down mattress.

Dawn was already beginning to streak the sky when Aleksandr Sergeievich gently lifted Katherina Andreievna and carried her to their bed. Her golden hair tumbled over his shoulders, and she sighed sleepily as she clung to him. Aleksandr felt himself aroused, and the feeling quickly overcame his drowsiness. Katherina's body pressed against his, signaling soft acceptance once again.

Chapter 13

They slept until almost noon, exhausted by their journey to the fort and the night of lovemaking that had followed. When they finally awoke, both were filled with renewed resolve that they would never again be separated from one another. As he watched Katherina braid her hair, Aleksandr announced that he planned to go to the village to get some provisions for their trip.

"Since we have made our decision," he said, "I think we should plan to leave tomorrow—as early in the morning as possible."

Katherina nodded, glad that he was taking charge, but she could not keep the tears from filling her eyes when she thought of leaving the place they had shared as their first home.

Aleksandr looked away, concentrating unnecessarily on drawing on his boots. He knew exactly what Katherina was thinking, but he could not allow her to see the tears welling in his own eyes. If they capitulated to their feelings for the past, their future would be lost.

He cleared his throat and tried to steady his strained voice. "I think you should stay here while I am gone. Choose a few pieces of clothing to pack; make whatever other preparations you think necessary. Try to sleep a bit if you can." He touched her cheek. "It will be a tiring trip." He turned to leave the room, but he stopped at the door. "Oh—Katya, I think it would be best if you did not let the servants know our plans. It will be safer for us—and for them."

Katherina nodded slowly. "Tamara and Lizaveta need not know anything—but I must tell Masha. She has been so understanding, and she would be devastated if we left without a word." Katherina's thoughts flew to the day she had spoken to Masha in the garden, when the girl had worried that her mistress would desert her. She hesitated, then added, "I think I must ask her if she wishes to come with us."

Aleksandr's eyebrows lifted. "Katya, do you really think it wise to endanger her life, too?"

Katherina shrugged. "It will be her choice. But Masha has been with me almost all of my life. She has been good and loyal, and I could never live with myself if I simply deserted her."

"All right. Talk to her. But make sure she understands that it will not be an easy journey. And be sure she realizes she need not come with us."

"I will." She kissed him, and he left for the town.

Katherina found Masha in her bedroom in the servants' wing, trying to choose from among four dresses that were carefully laid out on her bed. Her mistress's sudden entrance startled her and the girl's face flushed with embarrassment.

"Madame," she stammered, "forgive me, but I did not hear you call. Is there something I have neglected to do?"

Katherina smiled. "Relax, Masha. I did not call you, and you have taken care of your chores as well as you always do." She pushed aside one of the dresses and sat on the edge of the bed. "I simply wanted to speak to you privately."

The servant stared at her, and Katherina patted a place on the bed beside her. As Masha sat down,

Katherina said quietly, "Aleksandr Sergeievich and I are leaving Pyatigorsk."

Masha's mouth dropped open and her eyes widened. "Leaving Pyatigorsk?" she repeated hollowly.

Katherina nodded. "Yes. In fact, if all goes well, we will be leaving Russia."

"Oh, no, madame! You cannot be serious about leaving Russia. What are you saying?"

"Masha, I am quite serious. We leave tomorrow. It is the only way we can continue our life together—without interference from Count Ostrov or the Czar and his armies. Our time together has been so precious that we cannot bear to have it end."

Masha clapped her hands over her ears and shook her head. "Please, do not tell me more about your love and the problems it brings. It is not my place to question your decisions—or even to know about them. I am just a servant girl."

Startled by her reaction, Katherina rose and walked to the door. "I'm sorry, Masha," she said. "I can see that it is wrong for me to burden you with Aleksandr's and my personal problems. I simply remembered our talk in the garden last month, when I promised you I would not desert you in a strange city."

She opened the door to leave, but Masha's soft whisper stopped her. "At what time do you plan to leave?"

Katherina closed the door again and turned to face her servant. "Why do you ask?" she said, already knowing the answer.

"I shall, of course, come with you," Masha replied steadily. "That is, if you will have me."

"Oh, Masha," Katherina rushed to embrace her. "I had so wanted you with us." She hugged the girl as tears of joy filled her eyes. Then she remembered Aleksandr's warnings, and she pulled back. "But you have to understand that you must not come with us unless you are absolutely sure you want to. It will be a very difficult and dangerous journey. For Sasha and me it is worth the struggle, but perhaps you should think again, Masha. Perhaps you will find in your heart that you would rather stay behind."

Masha shook her head.

"You needn't worry, you know, that we will leave you homeless and penniless. I have money and jewelry you can have. You can go free, with my blessings and best wishes. Or, if you choose to remain at this house, I am sure the count will see that you are well cared for. Pavel Pavlovich is a fair man. He will not blame you for my leaving."

"I said I will go with you," Masha said quietly. "I will not change my mind."

"But what about your Vladimir Nikolaievich? Surely you do not intend to leave him behind?"

Masha shrugged. "I have no choice. His injuries are healed now, and he must go to rejoin his regiment. We are to have our last meeting today."

"Oh, Masha—I'm so sorry." Katherina embraced her again in genuine concern. "But then perhaps you should remain in the Caucasus. He will be allowed a leave from time to time and you could at least look forward to some days together."

"No. It's impossible. He is being sent to Poland. How can I follow him there when I know neither the land nor the people? I think it is better to say good-bye to him today. If the Almighty Father wishes us to be reunited, He will find the way, and the time, and the place. In the meantime, if I travel with you, at least I will not have the time to pine for Vladimir Nikolaievich."

Katherina squeezed Masha's hand. "I wish I could share your faith, Masha. Are you sure of your decision?"

"Nothing you say—and no dangers you describe— can change my mind."

"Sasha and I will both be glad to have you with us." Katherina smiled. "Now, let us go find you a gown that will forever imprint your beauty in Vladimir Nikolaievich's mind. You must choose one of mine."

With Masha safely on her way to meet her beloved, Katherina forced herself to face a more difficult problem—one that had been nagging at her ever since she decided to leave Pyatigorsk. She knew she would have to leave a message for Pavel Pavlovich. It would be too cruel to desert him without an explanation, to leave him sadly groping for a reason, imagining all the worst possibilities. Above all, she wanted him to know that their separation was not his fault, and she hoped that somehow she could keep him from feeling bitter toward her.

At first she tried to write an objective, reasonable letter, but the words seemed too cold and unfeeling to be of any help to her deserted husband. Crumpling the paper, she began again, this time letting her emotions pour out and hoping that Pavel Pavlovich could accept the sincerity of what she wrote.

My dear Pavel Pavlovich,
  By this time, you have no doubt searched the house and have been told that I am gone. I cannot blame you if you think of me now with bitterness and hatred, but I hope that you will be able to read my words and find at least a small amount of understanding in your heart.
  The truth is, I have always cared for you, and the affection I felt as you took me for your wife has only deepened through the months of our marriage. I know this may be hard to accept, but I have gone away at least partly out of concern

for you. My presence in your life would only be a type of robbery, and I am afraid you might learn to hate me if you discovered all that my heart has kept from you.

Despite my affection for you, I find that from the beginning I have been most unfair to you, and I must confess my total guilt. My dear mother warned me about the passion that flows in my veins, but I was too proud to accept her advice—until I met Aleksandr Sergeievich and it was too late. Please try to understand, my dear Pavel Pavlovich, that both Sasha and I struggled with our feelings at first. Neither of us wished you any harm, and we have kept our relationship secret for so long because we did not wish to hurt you in any way. Our decision to leave caused us both a great deal of anguish, but we believe that it is the best solution for all of us.

I am not going to tell you where we are going, and I hope that you will not attempt to follow us or send others after us. On reflection, I think you will agree that would only cause more heartbreak for everyone involved. Please do not question Tamara or Lizaveta. We have told them nothing, nor have we confided in anyone else, either in Pyatigorsk or at the fort.

I know very little about these matters, but I should think that since I deserted you, both the church and the state would consider you worthy of an honorable divorce. If that is what you wish, please do not hesitate to have our marriage dissolved.

Pavel Pavlovich, I hope with all my heart and soul that the future will bring you a woman more worthy of your love and protection than I. I pray that you may one day share a love and passion as consuming and fulfilling as Sasha and I share.

Both Sasha and I regard you with only the greatest affection and respect. I know that you have enriched my life immeasurably, and I only hope that I have brought you some small measure of joy. I shall always live with the hope that you can find it in your heart to understand and forgive me. And I shall always think of you, dear Pavel Pavlovich, treasuring the times you shared with me. For the future, I wish you nothing less than the ecstasy of love given and love returned.

Affectionately,
Katherina Andreievna

As she folded the letter, Katherina saw her tears fall on the page, blurring the ink. She considered tearing it up and writing a clean copy, but she changed her mind, hoping the tearstains would help convince Pavel Pavlovich of her struggle and her sincerity. Although she knew she would never see him again, it was strangely important for her to feel that he would forgive her and accept her explanation as genuine.

With shaking hands, she sealed the letter, dripping too much wax on the page so it ran in a messy streak. She wrote his name on the outside in bold black letters. She took the letter to the parlor and propped it against a vase, where Pavel Pavlovich would be sure to notice it. She returned to the bedroom, threw herself across the bed, and slept until Aleksandr Sergeievich returned to kiss her awake.

They spent their last evening in the garden, wandering aimlessly until the sun had set, then lying together on the grassy spot they had consecrated with their lovemaking only a few days before. Neither Katherina nor Aleksandr noticed the dew spreading through their clothing; they lay in each other's arms, gazing at the starry expanse of sky. Only a year before, Katherina mused, she was beginning a new life in St. Petersburg, thrilled with the excitement of her first days in the capital. Now she waited on the threshold of another new life that promised to be far more fulfilling than anything she had ever imagined in St. Petersburg.

Aleksandr Sergeievich rolled toward her, playfully kissing her nose. "What are you thinking about, Katya? You are much too quiet tonight."

"Oh—nothing." She rubbed her nose against his.

"You are sorry to be leaving tomorrow, aren't you?"

"No," she lied, rolling away from him and propping her head in her hands.

He reached over to stroke her hair. "It's nothing to be ashamed of, Katya. I feel sad to leave here, too." His voice cracked. "I will always remember this place as our first home. Every room, every tree, every garden path is etched in my mind and heart. We had a peace and security here that we may never again find anywhere."

"And now, because of my plans, we are leaving," Katherina said.

"Not because of your plans, Katya. Because our dream could not continue unchanged. The end was inevitable here, so we must go in search of another beginning." He gently pulled her into his arms, cradling her head against his chest.

"Oh Sasha," she sobbed, "if only we had met earlier. Perhaps we would not feel forced to leave our homeland."

"Hush," he soothed. "We cannot change our yesterdays. We can only plan for our tomorrows. If you want to stay, it's not too late to change our plans."

"No. I think we have made the right choice."

"I'm sure we have."

"But Sasha—why do I feel so—frightened?" She stumbled over the last word as if it pained her to utter it.

He laughed softly. "Do you think I do not feel

afraid? Only a fool would face a journey like ours and say he was not afraid. It's natural to feel fear when you face something unknown. Even a happy bride feels some apprehension as she nears her wedding night. But you and I and Masha are strong enough and sensible enough to meet whatever obstacles come our way."

She pressed closer to him, feeling the rise and fall of his chest. At least, she thought, I will always have my Sasha with me. That alone is enough reassurance for the future. But poor Masha—how will she fare without her Vladimir Nikolaievich?

As the moon slipped behind a cloud, Katherina could feel the desire rising in Aleksandr's body and her own body responding with the now-familiar throbbing.

"Shall we add one more happy memory of this garden?" he whispered.

"At least one more, Sasha. The night is still young!"

Chapter 14

At five o'clock in the morning, the sun was just beginning to scatter a few rays across the ridges of the Caucasus. Aleksandr Sergeievich was already in the stable, saddling his black stallion and General Bugov's chestnut mare.

Having dressed and braided her hair, Katherina went to Masha's room. Not until she entered the room, closing the door softly behind her, did she realize Masha was not there. The four dresses still lay across the bed, exactly as they had been the day before. The bed was unwrinkled except for the spots where Katherina and Masha had sat during their talk.

Katherina tiptoed through the house, checking the parlor, the dining room, the kitchen, Aleksandr Sergeievich's room. When she found no sign of Masha, her puzzlement turned to panic. Masha was much too dependable to disappear without leaving any message. Katherina went back to the servants' wing, quietly opening the doors to Tamara's and Lizaveta's rooms, careful not to wake them. She looked in Ivan's empty room. Finally, she ran to find Aleksandr Sergeievich.

He met her at the front door, almost colliding with her. "Are you in such a hurry to leave?" he teased, catching her in his arms. Then he looked at her face, and the merriment drained from his voice. "Katya—what is the matter?"

"I can't find Masha," she blurted. "I don't think she

came home last night. Oh Sasha—I'm afraid something has happened to her!"

"Katya, Katya, calm down," he shook her gently by the shoulders. "Now slow down and explain what you are talking about."

Katherina took a deep breath. "I went to wake her but she was not in her room. I looked everywhere in the house—and there is simply no sign of her."

"She is probably just saying good-bye to the garden. Come, we'll go and find her now." Aleksandr steered Katherina toward the pebbled path.

"No." Katherina held back. "I don't think we will find her there. Sasha—her bed was not even slept in."

"At least come with me and look." He led her past the locust trees and up and down the garden paths, but, as Katherina had predicted, they did not find Masha.

"Perhaps she decided to run off with her young soldier," Aleksandr said.

"No. No. She made it clear to me yesterday that he was being sent to Poland today—and she was coming with us. Besides, Masha is far too responsible and considerate to run off without a word. Something is wrong. Sasha—I know it."

"Now Katya, you must not jump to any conclusions." Aleksandr put his arm around her. "Love often makes people act irresponsibly. Perhaps she just lost track of the time."

"Sasha, I won't leave without her."

"Of course not, Katya. I wouldn't ask you to. Now why don't we go and sit in the parlor and wait for her? She might have stayed out all night with her young man. You know how difficult it is to say good-bye. She'll probably be arriving any moment now."

They waited until eight o'clock. Katherina paced the parlor. Aleksandr tried to cajole her into sitting quietly and drinking a cup of tea, but she refused to be comforted.

"Something is wrong, Sasha. I know something is wrong."

Shortly after eight o'clock, Tamara and Lizaveta arose. Tamara timidly asked if they would care to have breakfast. Before Katherina could reply, Aleksandr agreed that they would be ready to eat in the dining room in fifteen minutes.

As Tamara hurried away to prepare the meal, Katherina whispered, "Sasha, how could you? I cannot possibly eat."

"You can eat, and you will," he replied. "You need to keep up your strength. You have already exhausted yourself with worry."

"What does it matter? I'm not going anywhere. We can't leave until we find out what has become of Masha."

"No, we can't," he said. "At any rate, we won't be leaving today. It's already too late to begin the journey. I'm going out to unload the horses. When I return we will have breakfast. If Masha has not returned by the time we are finished, I will go and look for her." He strode from the room before Katherina could protest further.

They ate their meal in silence. Katherina was too upset to speak, and Aleksandr had wearied of offering her empty words of comfort. In fact, as the minutes passed, he too became more and more worried. Where had Masha disappeared to? They both wondered how long their trip would be delayed, but their concern far outweighed their irritation as they sat listening for someone to come through the door. Katherina thought she would gag when Tamara placed a bowl of warm kasha before her, but a glance at Aleksandr convinced her that she should eat the buckwheat groats without complaining. It was a struggle to swallow each bite, but she forced herself to finish the kasha, a slice of gray bread with butter, and a cup of tea.

As Tamara cleared the dishes, she remarked off-handedly, "It's odd I have not seen Masha today. Is she feeling ill?"

"I don't know," Katherina choked. "I haven't seen her either." Her eyes filled with tears, and Tamara gave her a strange look before leaving the room.

"Katya," Aleksandr said, "you must try to control yourself." He rose from the table and kissed her tenderly. "Now, where was Masha going to meet her beloved yesterday?"

"At the spa, I think. She always met him there."

"All right, I will go there now and inquire about them. Do you know his name?"

"Only that Masha called him Vladimir Nikolaie-vich. She never told me his family name."

"Well, perhaps that will be enough." Aleksandr kissed her again and started for the door.

Katherina rushed after him. "I'll come with you, Sasha."

"No," he replied. "I think it would be better for you to stay here. Perhaps Masha will return while I am gone. She may need you, and we wouldn't want her to think we left without her." He put his arms around her. "Try to relax a little while I am gone, Katya. I am sure that in time everything will be all right."

She watched from the window as he hurried down the hill toward the main boulevard. Oh God, she thought feverishly, please let Sasha find her. Please let her be all right.

As the day went on and the clock chimed noon, Katherina began to lose hope. Why hasn't he returned yet? Why hadn't she insisted on going with him? Anything would be better than pacing from one window to the next, praying for some glimpse of Masha, of Aleksandr, of the two of them returning together.

At one o'clock, Tamara entered quietly and asked if Katherina was prepared for dinner.

"No," Katherina replied sharply, "I don't wish to be served until Monsieur Belikov returns." In the next instant, she realized how harsh she must have sounded, but when she turned to apologize, the shocked servant had already fled. She began pacing even more furiously, wondering how many times she had snapped at Masha, and whether Masha harbored those harsh words in her heart. As she turned to the window again, she saw Aleksandr Sergeievich trudging up the hill—alone.

Katherina ran out of the house and rushed into his arms as he entered the courtyard. "Sasha, did you—" His grim expression answered her question before she finished asking it.

He shook his head hopelessly. "I talked to everyone I could find—at the spa, on the streets, in the stores, at the bazaar. A few of the soldiers at the spa remembered seeing them early yesterday afternoon, but no one could tell me when they left or where they might have been bound." He held her close as they walked back to the house. "I don't know where to go now, Katya—unless—"

"*Unless* what?" she pounced anxiously on the word.

He sighed. "Unless someone at the fort might know something about this Vladimir Nikolaievich and where he and Masha might have gone."

"Then we must go to the fort immediately and

find out." Katherina hungrily seized the new bit of hope.

"Perhaps tomorrow. If I leave now I won't arrive there until late afternoon. And I could not return until well after dark."

"It must be today, Sasha. I can't wait until tomorrow," she insisted. "I would not be able to sleep for worrying. I am not asking you to go alone. I will go with you."

"No. You will stay here. Remember your reception the last time we went to the fort?"

"I don't care about that. They can look and leer all they want, but I *will* find out about Masha." Her eyes flashed. "Please, Sasha—can't you see? I'll go mad if I have to sit here alone imagining all the things that could have happened to her. If you won't take me, I'll go myself."

Her determination was too much for Aleksandr Sergeievich. He touched her cheek. "All right. We will go to the fort this afternoon. I'll saddle the horses now."

Katherina smiled. "I knew you would understand. I'll ask Tamara to bring us some food, and then we can be on our way."

When they arrived at the fort, Katherina was too lost in her own thoughts to hear the soldiers' rude remarks. How she hoped that someone there would know something that could help them find Masha, or at least assure them that she was safe. Even when one of the more rowdy men grabbed at the bridle of her mount, she simply turned the horse's head and continued riding toward General Bugov's office.

The general received them with obvious pleasure. "Ah, my dear Countess Ostrova, I had not expected the honor of seeing you again so soon."

Katherina forced a polite smile. "Nor had I expected to be calling on you so soon, General Bugov."

Noting the strain in her voice, General Bugov arched his eyebrows in concern. "But I hope there is nothing wrong," he said as he ushered Katherina and Aleksandr into his office.

"As a matter of fact, general," Aleksandr said, "the countess is very upset today. We hope that someone here at the fort may be able to solve her problem."

"Indeed? I hope it is nothing too serious?"

"Her maidservant has disappeared."

"Really, Belikov, why do you bring such a problem to me?" the general snapped. "It was my understanding that you were commissioned to watch over Count Ostrov's household. If you find the task too difficult, perhaps I had best replace you with another—more capable—officer."

"I was commissioned to see to the safety of the countess," Aleksandr replied coldly.

"But surely that protection should also extend to her servants—particularly one who is obviously so dear to the countess."

Seeing Aleksandr about to retort more angrily, Katherina interceded. "Please, general, you must not blame Monsieur Belikov. I can assure you his performance has been above reproach. The fact is, my servant, Masha, had fallen in love with a young officer whom she met at the spa in Pyatigorsk. He was there recuperating from injuries. Yesterday afternoon she went, with my blessings, to meet him. But—," Katherina's voice broke, and she whispered the last words, "she never returned."

"Did you look for her yesterday, Belikov?" General Bugov asked.

Before Aleksandr could respond, Katherina said, "He offered to go out, but I asked him to stay with me at the house. I'm afraid I've become a dreadful coward since I've heard how ferocious the Circassians can be. I simply couldn't bear the thought of staying alone after dark. At any rate, I thought Masha would return. You see—it was her last night with the young man, and I knew they would find it hard to say good-bye. But then this morning I became concerned when I found she wasn't at home."

"I see." The general stroked his chin. "Have you considered the possibility that your servant may have eloped with the soldier in question?"

"That is highly improbable, General Bugov. Masha has been with me almost all my life, and I can assure you she is far too responsible to run off without so much as leaving a message."

General Bugov shrugged. "Of course. But love can do strange things to these silly little servant girls."

"I hardly think the countess considers her Masha a silly little servant girl," Aleksandr cut in.

Bugov stared at him in cold silence, then turned back to Katherina. "If you'll forgive my saying so, my dear countess, I fail to see how I can be of any help to you. If the girl is gone, she is gone. Surely you can find another equally satisfying servant."

"I don't want another servant," Katherina insisted. "Masha is not just a servant. She is an important person, a part of my life—"

This time Aleksandr Sergeievich interrupted. "We were hoping, general," he said with exaggerated politeness, "that you might be able to give us some information about the soldier whom Masha went to meet."

Bugov shrugged. "Perhaps. What is the young man's name?"

"Vladimir Nikolaievich."

"And his surname?"

"I'm afraid we don't know," Katherina whispered.

"Then how do you expect me to help you? There are probably hundreds of Vladimir Nikolaieviches connected with this fort."

"This one was scheduled to depart for Poland today," Aleksandr said. "Perhaps that will help you."

Bugov sighed. "Very well. I will check with the expediting officer to see whether we sent a Vladimir Nikolaievich to Poland today." He rose stiffly and lumbered out of the room.

"What a pompous nincompoop he has turned out to be," Aleksandr muttered. "Of course, I've no doubt he would have been more solicitous if you had come yourself."

"Sasha, please," Katherina whispered. "Try to conceal your temper, or the general may become even more difficult. We can't let ourselves forget that he is still your commanding officer. And what will happen to all our plans if he takes you away from our house?"

"I suppose you are right," Aleksandr grumbled. "I'll try to keep myself in check—but the man is so exasperating."

General Bugov was gone for more than half an hour. When he returned, he wore the self-congratulatory expression of a man who has just had his suspicions confirmed. Ignoring Aleksandr Sergeievich, he walked to Katherina Andreievna and looked down at her like an indulgent father.

"Well, my dear countess, it appears that a Vladimir Nikolaievich Gorolski was scheduled to leave for Poland today, but he did not report for duty this morning and his regiment was forced to depart without him." Bugov paused, pressing his fingertips together as a slow smile spread across his face. "It seems that we can only assume that Gorolski and your servant have run off together. Of course, in time, he will be apprehended. These cowardly deserters never get far. And at that time we can also return your servant to you—if you still want her."

Katherina sprang from her chair, her eyes snapping with rage. "I thought, my dear general, that I had already made it clear to you—Masha and her young man did not elope. I know her better than to believe that."

Surprised by her sudden anger, Bugov adopted a more conciliatory tone. "I know this is difficult for you to accept, my dear young woman, but you must realize that your servant's actions are by no means a reflection on you. Sometimes we find, to our surprise, that we do not know a person as well as we had imagined. Especially when that person is a mere serf."

"I have already told you that I do not consider Masha a mere serf," Katherina cried. "And I'll thank you not to address me as though I were some stupid child. Perhaps you have forgotten who I am? Or who my husband is?"

At that, the general turned away from her and addressed himself to Aleksandr Sergeievich. "It is obvious that the countess is hysterical. I see no point in continuing this interview. Perhaps you will be so kind as to escort her from my office."

Aleksandr rose, controlling his anger with difficulty. "If you'll forgive me, general, you seem to have been less than helpful—"

"I can hardly be responsible for every indiscreet little servant girl in the Caucasus," Bugov snorted. "You're an officer, Belikov. I would have expected you to know that."

"No one has so much as suggested that you should be—"

Aleksandr's words were cut short by a violent knocking at the office door. "General Bugov—General Bugov, sir," an insistent voice shouted.

Bugov glared at Aleksandr, then strode to the door and flung it open. "Well, what is it?" he barked at the breathless soldier.

"The Circassians, sir. They've—"

"They've what?"

"They've begun to attack again! A riding party on its way from Kislovodsk to Pyatigorsk was waylaid today. One of the men from the group just rode in to tell about it. And there is talk of skirmishes going on last night across the river at Essentuki. And then there was that man from Pyatigorsk who stopped here last night."

"What man? No one reported anything to me about a man from Pyatigorsk."

The soldier shifted uneasily. "No, sir. You were asleep at the time, and no one thought it urgent enough to wake you. It was obvious that the man had been drinking heavily, so he well may have imagined everything. You know the effects of this Circassian wine." He laughed nervously.

"Get to the point, young man. What did he say?"

"Only that he had been riding along the edge of the mountains and he thought he heard a disturbance."

"What sort of disturbance?"

The soldier shrugged. "Horses—shouting in a strange language—a woman's screams."

Katherina, listening from her seat in the office, gasped and collapsed in her chair. During his discussion with the soldier, Bugov had forgotten his visitors. Now he turned to see Katherina's pale face. He cleared his throat uncertainly and turned back to the soldier. "Perhaps I had better talk to this man from Kislovodsk. Is he here?"

"Yes, sir, general. I'll bring him right in."

"No," Bugov said quickly. "I'll speak to him outside." He started through the door, then stopped to address Aleksandr, his tone almost apologetic. "Please wait here until I return. I'll send a maid in with some tea for the countess."

When the general returned, he was visibly shaken. Glancing at Katherina Andreievna, he asked Aleksandr to have a word with him outside. Both men were shocked when Katherina shook off her dazed expression and addressed them in a firm tone.

"I think I should take part in whatever discussion you have."

General Bugov coughed uneasily, looking to Aleksandr Sergeievich for support. "I had only thought to spare the countess any unnecessary emotional trauma."

"No—the countess is right," Aleksandr said. "She has every right to hear whatever news you would tell me."

"Well, it is really very little. Nothing that can be called conclusive evidence, by any means."

"Please, general," Katherina demanded, "be so kind as to spare me any further suspense."

He cleared his throat and shrugged. "Very well. The man from Kislovodsk reports that he was riding with a group of five men and their lady friends when they were accosted by a band of about twenty Circassians. He said the tribesmen at first appeared ferocious, but they were subdued when he and his friends gave them money and jewelry."

"What about the man who came last night from Pyatigorsk?" Katherina asked anxiously.

"I talked with the soldiers who interviewed him

and they say he claimed to hear screams in the bluffs about twenty minutes' ride east of here. It was dark and he was concerned about his own welfare, so he did not stop to investigate. Instead, he rode to the fort with his story—"

"Surely someone investigated the area this morning," Aleksandr interrupted impatiently.

General Bugov looked embarrassed. "Alas, no. The soldiers who interviewed the man did not credit his story. They say he was barely sober enough to talk coherently, and they assumed that a man in his state could easily exaggerate any sounds he heard in the mountains. So they sent him on his way and gave the matter no further thought—until today's reports started to come in."

Aleksandr paced the office, trying to control his rage. "Tell me, general," he said bitterly, "do your officers always act so irresponsibly, without so much as consulting their superior?"

Before the general could reply, Katherina threw out her own question. "Have you at least dispatched someone to the area now?"

Bugov sighed and shook his head. "I'm afraid that is impossible, Countess Ostrova. It is already twilight, and it would be dark before a search party could arrive there—if there is indeed anything to find."

"Well, can't they carry lanterns?" she cried. "If a drunken man from Pyatigorsk can ride in the mountains at night, surely a regiment of brave soldiers from the Imperial Army can do the same."

Aleksandr put a comforting hand on her arm. "I'm afraid the general is right, madame. It would be foolish to go searching in the mountains at night when we have reports of Circassian hostilities. The tribesmen know the mountains much more intimately than any Russian ever could. It would be better to wait until morning."

"No," she shrieked, "I won't wait! Maybe Masha can't wait. If you are all too cowardly, I will go myself." She stomped out of the office and rushed over to General Bugov's chestnut mare.

As she tried to mount, Aleksandr caught her by the waist, pulling her foot from the stirrup and carrying her struggling body away from the horse. "Try to be sensible, for God's sake!" he said through clenched teeth. "If the Circassians took or harmed Masha, they wouldn't hesitate to do the same to you. I won't let you go out there tonight. I'll keep you here if I have to sit on you all night." He carried her back into the office, past the astonished General Bugov, and deposited her in a chair.

Giving in at last, Katherina began to weep. "I just want to find Masha."

"I can assure you, Countess Ostrova," the general said soothingly, "that I shall dispatch a search party by the first light of dawn. But please try to calm yourself. After all, we have no way of knowing at this point if the woman who screamed was actually your servant—and we must still consider the possibility that the man might have imagined the sound."

"I'm sure it was Masha," Katherina sobbed.

"Well," Bugov said, "we shall know soon enough. In the meantime, I must insist that you spend the night at the fort. It would be unthinkable for you to ride back to Pyatigorsk under the current conditions. I will give you the use of my quarters." Surprised by the angry glint of jealousy in Aleksandr Sergeievich's eyes, he hastily added, "I shall, of course, sleep in the barracks, along with the rest of the soldiers and Belikov here. If you wish, you are most welcome to remain at the fort tomorrow until the search party returns."

"No. I won't wait here. I will accompany the party."

Afraid that she might burst into hysterics again, the general nodded grimly. "Well, we shall see tomorrow, Countess Ostrova."

Chapter 15

Katherina Andreievna found it impossible to sleep. It was her first night in more than a month without Aleksandr Sergeievich beside her, and tonight, of all nights, she needed his comforting warmth.

The general, obviously embarrassed by his earlier outbursts and by the news of Circassian attacks, had been exceedingly kind at dinner. He had shared his finest wine with Katherina and Aleksandr and had attempted to entertain them with light anecdotes. Neither found him very amusing, though they managed to smile and control their tempers. Katherina desperately wanted a moment alone with Aleksandr, but there was no way to arrange it without arousing General Bugov's suspicions. When she announced that she was exhausted and wished to retire, the general himself escorted her to his quarters, leaving Aleksandr to stare after them helplessly. At the door, he discreetly kissed her hand and wished her a pleasant night.

As she tossed and turned on the general's uncomfortable straw-stuffed mattress, Katherina worried about Masha. Had the drunken rider from Pyatigorsk really heard Masha scream? Where was she now? Was she even alive? And what might the Circassian ruffians have done to her? The last question had been haunting her all evening. She had wanted to ask Aleksandr Sergeievich and General Bugov, but she had been too afraid of the answers they might give her. All night she struggled to push the possibilities from her mind. Toward morning, when she began to feel drowsy, she got up and paced in the small bedchamber, afraid that if she fell asleep the search party might leave without her.

Katherina was the first person outside as the sun began to come up. Seeing her unwavering determination, General Bugov did not even attempt to dissuade her from riding with the party. To everyone's astonishment, he announced that he would personally lead the detail. As the party of twenty-five rode out of the fort, Aleksandr Sergeievich maneuvered his stallion beside Katherina's mare. He held his horse back a bit until the others were out of earshot, then he spoke quietly.

"I missed you last night, Katya."

"And I missed you, Sasha. Let us hope we are never forced to spend another night apart."

She slumped forward on her mount, too tired to hold herself erect, and Aleksandr watched her in concern.

"Are you sure you feel strong enough to ride with this party? The search could take all day—or longer. Perhaps it would be better for me to take you home. General Bugov can send a messenger to Pyatigorsk to tell us what they find."

"I didn't sleep at all last night," she admitted, "but I am strong enough. I'll be all right."

Aleksandr regarded her doubtfully, but he did not argue. The party reached the bottom of the bluffs and began winding up the slopes. For an hour, the detail, divided into groups of five, combed the region, moving carefully among the low trees and bushes. Katherina was leaning forward, resting her head on her mare's neck and staring at the ground, when she saw something.

"My necklace!" she screamed. Both Aleksandr Sergeievich and General Bugov spurred their horses to her side as she pointed to a delicate gold chain caught on the curling tendril of a wild grapevine. Aleksandr jumped from his horse to retrieve the chain.

"I fastened it around Masha's neck myself," Katherina explained, "just before she left to meet Vladimir Nikolaievich. She must be somewhere near us."

"Yes. Unless of course the Circassians—" General Bugov swallowed the end of his thought.

"Unless what?" Katherina turned fearful eyes to the general as Aleksandr shot him a piercing glare.

"Uh, nothing—nothing at all, my dear countess. I must stop thinking aloud," he mumbled. Then, with a falsely hearty air, he continued, "Well—we must keep searching!"

Not more than ten yards away, Aleksandr Sergeievich suddenly reined in his horse. Coming up behind him, Katherina let her eyes study the ground until her gaze froze on a bit of pale green brocade—the fabric of the dress she had lent Masha—protruding from under a low bush. With a gasp, she slid from the mare and lifted the branches. Aleksandr Sergeievich stood behind her, his hands on her shoulders, as they stared at the two bodies.

The young blond soldier's face was horribly contorted. His chest had been tightly bound with strips of green brocade, torn from Masha's dress, but the dark splotches showed that blood had soaked through the makeshift bandage. Masha lay unmoving, her head on his chest, her arms tightly clutching his body. Her face was completely drained of color.

When Katherina could stand the sight no longer, she dropped the branches, turning away as sobs racked her body. Oblivious to the soldiers gathering around them, Aleksandr took her in his arms as she stood there crying. For a few moments the other soldiers stood still in silent respect. Then General Bugov gestured to two of them to pick up the bodies.

As they disengaged Masha's body from Vladimir Nikolaievich's, one of the soldiers jumped back in shock.

"My God, general," he exclaimed, "the girl is still breathing!"

The words penetrated the fog of grief that had enveloped Katherina Andreievna, and she jerked her head from Aleksandr's chest. Shaking off his embrace, she fell to her knees beside her servant. Laying her head on Masha's chest, she could feel a slight rise and fall. Fresh tears of relief rushed from her eyes as she gently shook the girl and murmured, "Masha, Masha—speak to me."

Except for her slow, weak breathing, Masha remained immobile, her eyes closed and her pale face devoid of expression. Katherina was vaguely aware of the soldiers lifting away the body of Vladimir Nikolaievich and mumbling about his terrible death. She wondered if Masha knew that her beloved was dead, and how she would feel when she awoke and learned that he was forever gone from her life. But would she awake? Was her body capable of shaking off all the pain, the exhaustion, and the terrible memories that possessed her? Or had they found her alive only to suffer the slow pain of losing her again. Katherina stared at the expressionless face and thought of how it had beamed only a few days before as Masha talked about her Vladimir Nikolaievich.

She felt Aleksandr Sergeievich's hands on her shoulders, gently pulling her to her feet. "Katya," he whispered in her ear, "you know Masha cannot hear you now. She is unconscious, and we must get her home so we can care for her properly."

Katherina nodded, falling back against the steadying strength of his body.

General Bugov watched them, begrudging Aleksandr his smooth familiarity with the young countess and wishing he could be the one to comfort her. The mere thought of holding her soft body in his arms and burying his hands in the shimmering golden silk of her hair electrified him. He cursed himself for being such a gentleman when he had surrendered his quarters to her the night before. Perhaps if he had been bolder he could have shared the room—and the bed —with her. Perhaps she would even have welcomed his attentions. It seemed obvious that her relationship with Belikov was less than formal and proper. Ah, these flighty St. Petersburg women! He wondered if Count Ostrov knew the sort of woman he had married, and he resolved that someday he would savor at least a few moments of this woman's charms.

The soldiers lifted Masha's body to a horse. General Bugov designated four soldiers to accompany him, Katherina, Aleksandr, and Masha to Pyatigorsk. The others were directed to continue combing the area for further clues and then to take Vladimir Nikolaievich's body back to the fort for burial.

At the house in Pyatigorsk, Katherina watched anxiously as Aleksandr carried Masha to her bed. General Bugov hovered nearby, still observing the unmistakable rapport that existed between Katherina and Aleksandr. While Katherina carefully undressed and bathed Masha, Aleksandr rushed down the hill in search of a doctor. The general discreetly retreated to the parlor, where he sat contemplating Belikov's extreme good fortune.

Katherina peeled away the tattered dress, horrified at the scratches and bruises that covered Masha's body. Her nausea almost made her turn away when she located a ragged gash in her servant's shoulder, but she forced herself to carefully cleanse the wound of dirt, dried blood, and bits of ragged brocade. She felt sure Masha would scream in pain when she touched the gruesome spot, but the girl did not respond.

Before Katherina had finished, the doctor arrived. After a thorough examination, he announced that there was little he could do for the girl. She was suffering from severe emotional and physical exhaustion, and she appeared to have lost a good deal of blood from her wound, which the doctor supposed was inflicted by a knife. He added that two nights of exposure on the mountain slopes had probably drained her body of whatever strength she had left after her struggle. Taking Katherina's arm, he led her out of Masha's bedroom to the hallway, where Aleksandr Sergeievich waited.

"If you keep her warm and allow her to rest," the doctor said, "I suspect there is a good chance for recovery."

"You suspect?" Katherina echoed uneasily.

"Well, madame, you must understand what the poor girl has been through. The human body, particularly the frail body of a woman, can only endure so much. But if she has managed to survive so far, it seems likely that she will pull through. In the meantime, you might instruct your cook to prepare some soup so it will be ready if she regains consciousness."

Katherina nodded. "Thank you for your trouble, doctor."

As they neared the front door, the doctor turned to Aleksandr, addressing him in a voice so low that Katherina could not make out his words.

"Doctor," she said, "if your remarks concern Masha, I would like to hear as well."

The doctor flushed with embarrassment. "It is rather a delicate matter to discuss, madame. I thought perhaps I could spare you, and the young man could pass on the information when it seemed appropriate."

"I think I have seen enough today to be beyond shock," Katherina replied. "Please share your information with me."

The doctor hesitated, looking doubtfully at Aleksandr, who nodded. "I was simply saying that the young lady appears to have been—" He hesitated again, then whispered, "Molested by the ruffians."

"Oh!" Katherina gasped and reached out to Aleksandr for support.

"I'm sorry," the doctor said quickly, "but I thought someone should know, in case she becomes delirious and alludes to the attacks in her ravings. Or in case—," he stopped and shrugged, "but that is too remote and distasteful a possibility to consider right now." He eyed the door. "If you'll excuse me, I really must get back."

Katherina, murmuring "Poor, poor Masha," leaned on Aleksandr as they turned away from the door. General Bugov's voice startled them as they walked into the parlor.

"I hope you will accept my heartfelt condolences, Countess Ostrova."

Katherina froze and stammered, "General—forgive me—in all my concern about Masha I did not realize you were still here."

"I quite understand." Bugov's eyes moved to Aleksandr's arm, which tightened defiantly around Katherina's waist. "I was hoping to have a few words with your servant. Perhaps she could describe the attack."

"I'm afraid that is quite impossible." Katherina stiffened. "She is still unconscious, and even the doctor cannot say when she will regain her senses. If you will excuse me, I think I should go sit with her. I wouldn't want her to awake and find herself all alone."

"By all means, go to her." The general bowed graciously. "Perhaps I can wait a bit longer, in case she regains consciousness."

"It might be better for you to go," Aleksandr said coolly, "while there is still daylight."

The general glared at Aleksandr and said, "Of course, I could spend the night in Pyatigorsk—if there were a place for my men and me to sleep."

He stared at Katherina meaningfully, but, before she could offer her house, Aleksandr said, "Surely you are not afraid to ride back in twilight with an armed guard to escort you, general?" He drained the sarcasm from his voice when Katherina nudged him. "As you can see for yourself, the countess's house could hardly sleep five soldiers comfortably. And, I think you will agree, the poor woman needs some privacy after her grueling experiences today."

Approached with such logic, the general had no choice. If he pressed himself on the countess now, he would seem impolite and unfeeling, and that would only make their future relationship more difficult. He would prefer to court her than to force himself on her. "Of course she does," he said gallantly. "But you *will* send me word, Countess Ostrova, when the girl begins to recover?"

Katherina nodded, and the general smiled. "Good." He bowed deeply and kissed Katherina's hand. "I wish your servant a speedy recovery. And to you, my dear countess, I wish a restful night and a pleasant tomorrow."

Katherina's night was not restful. Despite Aleksandr's coaxing, she refused to go to bed. She stayed by Masha's bedside, dozing occasionally, then waking to stare in disbelief at the unconscious girl. Midway through the night, unable to sleep without her, Aleksandr joined her at the bedside. Until morning, he held her hand, waiting and watching in silence.

For three days they sat with the unmoving servant, leaving the room for only a few moments, taking their meals beside the bed. After the first day, Aleksandr gave up trying to coax Katherina from the room. Although he was concerned by the dark circles that began to shadow her eyes, he loved her more than ever for her dedication to the girl. He shared the vigil in silence, hoping that his presence helped to fire her dwindling supply of strength.

On the fourth day, Masha began to stir. She thrashed deliriously in the bed, moaning, "Vladimir, Vladimir! Vladimir—help me!" Katherina mopped the girl's feverish brow, grateful that she had shown some signs of life.

That night, as Katherina sat slumped over in exhaustion, her head resting on the bed, Masha sat up suddenly, waking her mistress as she struggled to get out of bed.

"Where is Vladimir Nikolaievich?" she demanded. "I must find Vladimir Nikolaievich!"

"Masha, Masha," Katherina said, gently pushing her back onto the bed, "you must rest. It is nighttime."

"But I must see Vladimir Nikolaievich!"

"Not now, Masha. It is time to sleep now."

"Is my Vladimir Nikolaievich sleeping?"

"Yes, Masha, he is sleeping," Katherina assured her, though the words tore at her heart. Perhaps Masha did not know that her beloved was dead. Or had her fevered mind simply refused to accept the fact? At any rate, Masha was recovering. For the first time since Masha's disappearance, Katherina fell into a relaxed sleep by Masha's bedside.

When Katherina awoke the next morning, Masha was already sitting propped up in bed, and Aleksandr Sergeievich was feeding her from a bowl of hot kasha. He stopped to kiss Katherina.

"See how much improved our patient is today?" he said.

"Masha, are you really all right?" Katherina studied the servant's face. Masha's eyes looked clear, and her cheeks, though still pale, had the faintest blush.

"Yes—," Masha said, "I think I am all right—but I ache all over—and I am so hungry!"

"Then you must eat!" Katherina said. "Sasha, go and get her some soup. And perhaps some yogurt." She skipped to the window and opened the curtains, chattering happily about the beautiful sunny day.

"Madame." Masha's strained voice interrupted Katherina's chatter.

"What is it, Masha?"

"Is Vladimir Nikolaievich here, too?"

"Vladimir Nikolaievich?" Katherina stared out the window as she tried to find words. "No—Masha, he is at the fort."

Katherina heard Masha try to smother her sobs, but she could not bear to turn and look at her.

"He's dead, isn't he?" Masha asked in a small voice.

Still staring out the window, Katherina could not answer.

"You needn't be afraid to admit it, madame. For me, it is probably just as well."

Katherina whirled and stared at Masha in amazement.

Trying to hold her voice steady, Masha continued.

"He could never want me after what they did to me. No man could ever want me now—at least not as a wife." She buried her face in the pillow, her body shaking with sobs.

Trembling with helpless rage at the unknown attackers, Katherina rushed to the bed and gathered Masha into her arms. "Masha—you must never think that. What happened was not your fault. No one could possibly blame you for it."

"Oh my God!" she moaned as her tears wet Katherina's bosom. "Why did they have to kill him? Why did they do it? We tried to give them what they wanted. Forgive me, madame—I gave them your jewelry. I thought it could save us."

"It's all right, Masha." Katherina's tears mixed with those of her servant.

"But it was not all right. I thought it would save us, but they killed him anyway. And then, what they did to me—I wish they would have killed me, too." Her body convulsed with sobs as she remembered.

When Aleksandr Sergeievich returned, he found his brave Katya, who had been so strong these last days, collapsing under the strain. Her sobs now blended with Masha's, making it hard to discern which woman was comforting the other. Setting aside the food, he took both women into his arms, gradually calming them.

Over the next days, as Masha recovered, her woeful story emerged. Wanting to enjoy their last evening in perfect solitude, the young couple had ridden to the mountain slopes outside of town. The air was fresh and clear, and, cuddling together on Vladimir Nikolaievich's horse, they had lost track of the distance and strayed a good deal farther than they had intended. They had dismounted and were locked in a tender embrace when nine bandits surrounded them.

"They spoke a peculiar language," Masha explained, "so we could not tell what they wanted, but Vladimir Nikolaievich said I should not be afraid. He said they probably wanted money and would leave us alone if we gave them what we had."

"A wise decision," Aleksandr said, making Masha smile in fond remembrance of her beloved.

"He gave them what money he had, and I did not want to give them your necklace, madame, but I was afraid they would hurt us if I did not."

"You did the right thing, Masha," Katherina said.

"After that, some of the men started to get back on their horses—but one of them grabbed me and began to kiss me very brutally. Then two more started yelling and tearing at my clothes." Masha squeezed her eyes shut as if to block out the terrible memory. "Vladimir Nikolaievich could not bear to watch. He jumped on the back of one of the men and wrestled him to the ground. But the other two pulled him away and began stabbing and slashing at him with their knives. I screamed and kicked until they stopped hurting him and threw him aside, but the devils were not finished yet. While Vladimir lay there, his very life running out of him with each drop of blood, they pounced on me and—" She looked away, her cheeks flaming.

"You need not describe more," Katherina said gently.

Masha took several deep breaths, slowly composing herself. "I was too terrified even to scream, until I thought I heard someone riding nearby. For a moment I feared it would be more of the bandits. Then I realized there was nothing else they could do to us. Even if they killed me, it would be a blessing.

So I screamed with all of my strength, hoping that whoever was riding would come to our aid. At first the bandits tried to quiet me, and they slashed at me with their knives, but they must have heard the rider, too, for their leader called to them and they fled, leaving Vladimir Nikolaievich and me bleeding on the ground.

"I don't know how long we lay there before I realized that all was quiet again and no one was going to come to our aid. When I crawled to Vladimir Nikolaievich, his chest felt like one huge pool of blood. I tried to stop the bleeding with my petticoats, but they were not enough. I had to use your dress, too, madame. I had to try to save him!

"By the time I had bandaged Vladimir Nikolaievich's chest, I was so tired that I collapsed right there. But when the morning sunlight woke me, I was afraid again. I feared the bandits would be back to murder us both. I thought that Vladimir Nikolaievich was still breathing, so I dragged him to a low bush and tried to hide him and myself beneath it. I think then I must have passed out."

"Oh, Masha!" Katherina cried. "I'm only sorry it took us so long to find you. You could have di——" She stopped herself, ashamed that she had almost verbalized her fears.

Masha smiled weakly. "But you did find me, and I am so grateful to you both for the care you have given me. It is I who must be sorry—for causing you so much trouble and disrupting your plans."

"Disrupting our plans?" Katherina had been so consumed with her concern for Masha that their planned escape to Austria had not even entered her mind.

"You are too good, madame, I hope I am worthy of your kindness."

"Don't be silly, Masha. In a few days you will be well and strong again, and we can begin our journey then."

Katherina did not see Aleksandr Sergeievich shake his head, nor did she see the sad look in his eyes as he left the room.

Chapter 16

During the next week, as Masha grew stronger, Aleksandr Sergeievich never mentioned their departure. But when Masha began walking around the house and helping with the chores, Katherina became more and more impatient to leave Pyatigorsk. She was worried about being trapped there when Pavel Pavlovich returned. One night as she and Aleksandr Sergeievich prepared for bed, she said simply, "Masha has agreed to be ready to leave the day after tomorrow. Is that agreeable to you, Sasha?"

He walked to the window and stared out at the moon. "I wish it were," he mumbled.

"What do you mean? I can think of no reason why we cannot leave then."

"Then think a little more," he whispered hoarsely, still looking out the window.

Katherina went to him, put her arms around his waist, and rubbed her face against his back. She felt his spine stiffen. "Don't you want to go away with me, Sasha?"

He turned and took her face in his hands, gazing at the way the moonlight caressed her features and highlighted her eyes. "Katya, you know better than to ask me such a thing. Can you really question my love?"

"I don't think so. But why don't you want to go? What about the plans we made a few weeks ago?"

"Katya—think. Be sensible. Think of what happened to Masha. After all the days and nights you sat by her bed, can you really want to make her and yourself bait for more Circassian bandits?"

She tossed her head. "I think that is for me and Masha to decide."

"No, the risk is too great. How can we have a life together if one or both of us is murdered between here and the Austrian Empire?"

"How can we have a life together if Pavel Pavlovich returns and takes me back to St. Petersburg?"

"At least then," he said softly, "I would know that you are alive."

"Can't you see it is pointless for me to be alive if I must live without you?"

"Then how would you feel if I were murdered during our journey?"

"I suppose I would kill myself."

"Then the whole flight—all our plans—would be pointless!" He grabbed her shoulders and shook her roughly. "Can't you please admit that, Katya?"

"No," she insisted. "I won't give up my dreams so easily."

He sighed. "I don't intend to give up anything either, Katya, but I am not enough of a fool to follow our original plans. It would be sheer stupidity for three people to travel west along the Caucasus when we know there have been Circassian attacks."

"Then what do you suggest we do?"

"I don't know." Aleksandr went to sit on the bed, his shoulders slumped. "I don't know," he repeated, "but I won't expose you to the suffering Masha had to endure."

Katherina slid onto his knee, encircling his neck with her arms. "Sasha, there must be a way. If we delay much longer, I am afraid Pavel Pavlovich will return. Perhaps the Circassians are through attacking.

Perhaps the soldiers from the fort have subdued them."

"That would be impossible to tell. The Circassians are completely unpredictable. I think it was foolish of me to even consider riding through their lands."

"But couldn't you at least find out what has been happening? Perhaps the trip would be safer than you think."

"How do you propose I find out?"

"You could ride to the fort tomorrow and talk to General Bugov."

"And what would I say? 'General Bugov, sir, Katya and I are planning to run away together, and we wonder if you think we will be safe?' Better yet—perhaps I could ask him for an armed escort to the Austrian border. Come, Katya, be serious. After our last meeting I think the man can hardly stand me. I certainly can't visit him simply to ask for information."

"You could take him news of Masha's condition and her description of the attack. We did promise to keep him informed."

Aleksandr sighed. "I suppose we did. I'm surprised he didn't send someone to inquire about her by now. God knows I don't relish seeing the general again."

"Then you'll go?" Katherina kissed his cheek.

"Yes, I'll go and see what I can learn. But I will not make any promises. I still think the journey would be too dangerous for us. Yet—who knows?" He shrugged. "Perhaps something I see or hear will suggest a better route."

Aleksandr Sergeievich had been gone less than two hours when Katherina heard a commotion in the courtyard. Rushing to the window, she saw a wagon driven by a soldier of the Imperial Army. Two other soldiers were sitting in the back of the wagon, and it appeared that they were leaning over a fourth person, who was lying in the wagon bed. Oh my God, she thought as she held onto the windowsill to steady herself, I pestered and begged Aleksandr Sergeievich until he agreed to ride to the fort, and now something has happened to him. Are the Circassians so bold that they would attack a man in full daylight? He didn't want to go, and I forced him with my wheedling. Thank God there was someone near to save him.

But there was something strange—something that bothered Katherina. If Aleksandr had really been hurt, wouldn't General Bugov have been only too happy to keep him at the fort and send someone else to act as her protector? Had enough time passed for Aleksandr to travel all the way to the fort and be transported all the way back? Confused and unable to contain her nervous curiosity, Katherina rushed to the door.

The soldiers were carefully lifting a stretcher from the wagon. As Katherina threw open the door, the cry of "Sasha!" was on her lips. She stifled it just in time to see her husband.

She stumbled forward, completely stunned, feeling her knees about to give way. "Pavel Pavlovich?" she choked in a small whisper just as the driver jumped down from the wagon to support her.

The count's eyes fluttered open and his lips formed a faint smile. "Ah, Katherina Andreievna—my dear wife. Seeing you makes me feel better already."

His right arm was bound in a sling. With his other arm he reached out, groping for her hand. She gave it slowly.

"Pavel Pavlovich, what has happened to you? Why didn't I receive word that you were coming? Are you in pain?"

He gave her hand an almost imperceptible squeeze.

"All in good time, my dear—but for now could you please direct these good men to our bedroom. The journey has made me so tired."

Hearing him say *our bedroom* cut at Katherina's heart, but she led the soldiers into the house, hoping that none of Aleksandr Sergeievich's clothes were scattered in the room. It would be too cruel for Pavel Pavlovich to learn of their relationship at that moment. Katherina thankfully noted that Masha had already made the bed, which she and Aleksandr had left in disarray after their morning lovemaking. A quick glance assured her that none of Aleksandr's belongings were in view. She hurried to turn down the quilt for the count.

After the soldiers had settled Pavel Pavlovich in the bed, Katherina called Tamara and asked her to get the men something to eat. Alone with her husband, she cringed inwardly as he smiled and patted the bed, indicating that she should sit down beside him.

Looking for an escape, she backed toward the door. "Perhaps you would like something to eat, too, Pavel Pavlovich. I'll go myself and see if Tamara has any borsch or cabbage soup." As she reached for the doorknob, his voice stopped her.

"Please do not trouble yourself, Katherina Andreievna. I am far too tired to eat right now. What I would like most, my dear, is for you to sit beside me until I drift off to sleep. Your presence will be such a great comfort to me after all these weeks of our separation."

"Very well," Katherina said meekly as she walked to the bed. Only then did she notice that his right foot was also heavily bandaged.

"Is something wrong, my dear? If I were not sure of your devotion, I would almost think you are not pleased to see me."

Katherina flushed slightly. "Pavel Pavlovich, I am sure you cannot believe that. But I am surprised and upset to see that you are wounded."

"Ah—you must not be concerned, my dear. They are hardly major wounds, though I must admit they put me in quite an awkward position." He chuckled. "The foot injury keeps me from walking, and the shoulder keeps me from using crutches. But they will heal," he said. "Especially with you here to care for me."

"But you still haven't told me what happened."

"Yes, I suppose I should give you some explanation." He took a deep breath. "General Paskevich is a fine commander. Instead of sending his men into battle, he leads them. Naturally, to observe him, it was necessary for me to follow his movements closely, and last week, in a battle in the Kura Valley, south of Tiflis, I took a bullet in the shoulder and one in my foot."

Katherina winced. "Oh, my poor Pavel Pavlovich!" Her feeling for him was genuine.

Her husband smiled. "Actually, I was fortunate. I might well have been killed—as were so many of our fine young men—including my own Ivan."

"Ivan was killed! Oh—Pavel Pavlovich—I'm so sorry. I know how much he meant to you. But who saw to your injuries? Perhaps I should run into the village and get you a doctor."

"I assure you, my dear, that is unnecessary. The doctor assigned to General Paskevich's forces is very competent. He removed both bullets. Now all I have to do is rest and allow nature to heal my wounds." He yawned and closed his eyes. "Obviously, I was of little use in Transcaucasia when I could not even follow the general—so here I am. At least Pyatigorsk is a delightful place to recover. And with you beside me, Katherina, I can hardly become impatient or bored." He yawned again and shifted his weight, wincing slightly at the strain on his shoulder.

Filled with pity and guilt, Katherina sat with him until he was sleeping soundly. Then she got up from the bed and quietly left the room.

The soldiers had gone after they ate, and now Katherina was alone, pacing nervously in the small parlor. Once she went to the stable and stared at the chestnut mare, trying to convince herself to saddle it and ride out to meet Aleksandr Sergeievich. If she met him before he returned to Pyatigorsk, they could simply ride away as they were—never to return to the house. But could she really leave Pavel Pavlovich lying helpless in bed? Still, if they did not flee now, what would happen to Aleksandr Sergeievich? She hated to think of where he might be sent under the command of the distasteful General Bugov.

She had to talk to Aleksandr. Together they would decide what to do. Why was he taking so long at the fort? When would he be home? What would he say when he learned Pavel Pavlovich was there, sleeping in their bed?

Chilled by the crisp autumn air, Katherina went back into the house. She tried to sit patiently in the parlor, but the questions and fears racing in her head soon had her pacing again. No matter how she concentrated, there seemed to be no acceptable solutions. There was only the hard knot of anxiety that began in her stomach and mushroomed to take control of her body and mind.

It was twilight before she heard the clopping of Aleksandr's horse in the courtyard, and by then her head felt as if it were about to explode from the tension that had hammered away at her all afternoon. Katherina felt as if she were at the center of a terrifying tug-of-war. In the bedroom lay her husband, who had given her his devotion and his name. In the courtyard was her lover, the one spark in her life. Without bothering to take a shawl, she rushed outside.

"Sasha, we must talk," she whispered.

He dismounted and looked at her. "Yes—we must. The Circassians—"

"Forget about the Circassians for a moment." She cut him off, and he stared at her in surprise. "Pavel Pavlovich is home."

"The count? Here? Now?" The last question hung in the air as he stood open-mouthed. Even in the darkening light, Katherina could see his eyes begin to cloud as she nodded slowly.

Aleksandr broke the silence. "Where is he now?"

"Asleep. In our bed." She almost choked on the words. "Sasha, he's been wounded." Then, as he led his horse to the stable, unsaddled it, and gave it food and water, she told him the story of Pavel Pavlovich's unexpected arrival and of his injuries. When she finished, tears were streaming down her face. "What are we going to do now, Sasha?"

He led her to the garden and walked with her until her sobs subsided. Then he sat down on a large boulder, drew her into his lap, and kissed her swollen eyes. He massaged her back until the tension began to drain out of her muscles.

"Sasha," she whispered, "I am ready to leave with you tonight if you think it is safe."

"No," he said quietly. "It is not safe. And even if it were, we could not go now. You cannot leave your husband—who has been so good to you—when he needs you. Maybe you could pretend not to care, but something in you would always despise yourself for leaving him when he is begging for your care. And something in me would despise myself for taking you away from him under these circumstances."

"I know you are right, Sasha. The same thoughts have been plaguing me all day. But what will happen to us—to you and me?"

He curled a lock of her hair around his finger. "Well, with the count confined to his bed, we can be sure you will be staying in Pyatigorsk at least until spring. By the time his wounds begin to heal, winter will be upon us, and it will be too difficult for you to journey all the way across the snow-covered steppes and north to St. Petersburg. As for me, I suspect the bad news I learned at the fort today may actually work to our advantage."

"What do you mean?"

"Apparently the Circassians have been much more violent and much more persistent in their recent attacks than ever before. Most of the towns in the area are living in mortal fear of the tribesmen. It seems likely that a larger force of soldiers than usual will remain stationed at the fort in order to protect our loyal Russian citizens. I think I can contrive to be among them."

"But our life together will be finished!"

"We must be patient, Katya," he stroked her back. "We can still see each other. I am sure I can manage to get away from the fort at least once a week. Let us make a pact now that we must both try to meet at the spa next Wednesday afternoon. And perhaps when your husband has recovered, we can—" He left the sentence unfinished as his lips sought hers.

As they returned to the house arm in arm, they heard the count calling from the bedroom.

"Katherina! Katherina Andreievna!" His voice sounded weak and strained, and Katherina dropped Aleksandr's arm to hurry to his side.

"What is it, Pavel Pavlovich?" she asked as she burst through the door.

His face lighted up with happiness when he saw her. "Nothing. I'm sorry if I alarmed you, my dear. I was simply startled when I awoke and found you were not here. I've been away so long that I suppose I am a bit greedy for your time and company, but you must have become quite bored just watching me sleep."

"Not at all, Pavel Pavlovich," Katherina smiled. "I simply went to the garden to get some air."

"The garden? Do you really think it is safe for you to walk in the garden after dark? As we traveled north of the mountains, I heard the soldiers discussing how bold the Circassians have become in their nighttime attacks."

"You needn't worry. Aleksandr Belikov escorted me." Katherina hoped her husband would not notice how awkward she felt using Aleksandr's formal name.

"Ah yes—Belikov. I had forgotten for the moment that he was here. I don't recall seeing him when I arrived this morning."

"No. As a matter of fact, he rode to the fort today to inquire about the Circassian trouble. He returned only about an hour ago."

"Then you must ask him to come in and join us for supper. I can see he kept you quite safe while I was away, and I must thank him personally for that. You know, my dear, you have not yet told me anything of your activities in the last several weeks. But perhaps you can fill me in while we eat."

"Yes, of course. I'm so glad to hear you're feeling

hungry now. I'll call Tamara to bring us supper."

Katherina was relieved to have Aleksandr Sergeievich's company at supper. Throughout most of the meal the count questioned him closely about the Circassian hostilities, and Katherina was not required to talk much. But what would she do when Aleksandr was not there to support her? What activities could she describe as substitutes for all the days they had whiled away in sublime lovemaking?

"Well, I suspect that General Bugov will be glad to know I have returned and your assignment here is completed," the count said to Aleksandr. "From your descriptions I would assume he needs all the men he has to protect us from the barbarians. And, no doubt, you are anxious for some more exciting duty."

"I can assure you, Count Ostrov," Aleksandr said, "that my assignment here has been a great pleasure. But of course I will be returning to the fort tomorrow. As a soldier I cannot always draw such tours of duty."

The count nodded amiably, then noticed that the color had drained from Katherina's face.

"My dear, are you feeling quite all right?" he asked.

"Oh, yes," Katherina stammered, covering her embarrassment with a wide yawn. "It's just that I suddenly feel so tired. It's been such an emotional day, Pavel Pavlovich. And hearing the stories of the Circassians has been terrifying."

Tomorrow—our life together ends tomorrow! The phrase repeated itself again and again in her mind. She had known all day that Aleksandr would have to return to the fort, but hearing him say it to her husband made the departure frighteningly final.

Aleksandr Sergeievich rose quickly. "Perhaps I had best remove my belongings from the room you so graciously provided for me. I'll be happy to sleep in the servants' quarters so the countess can have the room."

"What a kind suggestion," Katherina said. "Then you will be able to rest peacefully, without my disturbing you, Pavel Pavlovich."

"Disturbing me? How could your presence disturb me, Katherina Andreievna? For weeks I have ached to have you beside me while I slept. You do not mean to deny me the one thing that will most hasten my recovery?" The count's eyes twinkled as he gazed at his wife. "I appreciate your kind concern, Belikov, but you need not surrender the comfort of your bed. That would be poor thanks, indeed, for the peace of mind you gave me knowing Katherina Andreievna was under your capable protection. I'm sure my wife and I shall manage nicely."

"In that case, I shall bid you both good-night." Aleksandr Sergeievich's face was a perfect mask of indifference as he left Katherina and the count alone in their bedroom.

Lying in the dark beside her sleeping husband, Katherina felt cold despite the two heavy comforters that covered them. Before drifting into sleep, Pavel Pavlovich had snuggled against her, whispering endearments. But now that he was sleeping soundly, Katherina inched away from him, thankful that his injuries at least prevented him from demanding his full rights as a husband. My God, she thought in disgust, have I become so low, so immoral, that I can rejoice in my own husband's pain! She shuddered. If only Pavel Pavlovich had not returned. If only he had not been wounded. If only she had not married him! How could the happiness she felt with Aleksandr Sergeievich turn so suddenly to unhappiness?

She listened to the floorboards creaking in the next

room, telling her that Aleksandr Sergeievich could not sleep either. It was their last night together under this roof, and they were not even sharing the same bed! Katherina could not lie there while their last moments slipped away. Her burning desire smothered any feelings of guilt, and she knew she must go to him. She slid out of the bed, listening for any change in Pavel Pavlovich's breathing. The floor felt cool and inviting under her feet, and she stood for a moment, making sure that her husband did not stir. When she was satisfied that he was sound asleep, she crept to the door.

Aleksandr Sergeievich's room was dark, but as Katherina opened the door she could see him outlined in the starlight, standing at the window. Lost in his own melancholy, he did not turn as she came into the room. She walked up behind him, slipping her arms around his waist and burying her face in the warm hollow between his shoulder blades. Absentmindedly, he took her hands and raised them to his lips, covering them with tender kisses. She gradually realized that his tears were running over her hands. Still not turning to face her, he squeezed her hands and spoke slowly, and she could feel the words tearing painfully at the back of his throat.

"Katya—you must go."

"No," she said, hugging him tighter, "I won't go, Sasha. I can't."

"Please, Katya. Don't torment me like this. In another moment I won't be able to control myself."

Her hands slipped lower, and her heart thumped furiously as she felt his rising desire. "Don't control yourself, Sasha. For my sake—please don't."

"Katya, be sensible. Your husband is in the next room." But even as he spoke, the craving surged through his body, drowning all remnants of sensibility.

She slid around to face him, covering his mouth with her own. "Let's not waste any more of the night," she moaned.

If he had wanted to argue, his body and hers would not permit it. As they embraced, she slipped out of her nightgown, exposing her perfect ivory flesh to the magical starlight. Forever awed by her smooth curves, Aleksandr gasped with euphoria. Their bodies melted together, unable to wait even for the few steps that would take them to the bed. The floor was cold and hard, but neither Katherina nor Aleksandr was aware of anything other than their own throbbing passions.

Later Aleksandr carried her to his bed, where they sealed their love over and over again until they both fell asleep in satisfied exhaustion.

When Katherina, still clinging to Aleksandr, awoke, sunlight was beginning to spill into the room. Her eyes traveled slowly over the walls and furnishings as she tried to remember why they were sleeping in this room, in this bed. The realization crept into her brain, and she wondered if the sun's rays were awakening her husband in the next room and what he might think if he found she was not there. She sat up slowly, debating whether to return to his bed.

As Katherina sat up, Aleksandr opened his eyes, drinking in her early-morning beauty. He ran his hands through her hair, drawing a few strands to his mouth to kiss. Then, with a sigh, he sat up beside her.

"I suppose I should be preparing to leave," he said, looking away from her.

"Surely you could stay until afternoon, Sasha."

"No. That would only make it more difficult for both of us. I will go this morning, while we still hold fresh memories of last night."

While Aleksandr dressed and packed his few belongings, Katherina went back into her room. Pavel Pavlovich did not stir as she dressed. When she returned to Aleksandr Sergeievich's room, she found it empty.

Chapter 17

When Pavel Pavlovich awoke a few hours later, Katherina was at her desk writing a letter to her mother in Novgorod. Katherina imagined for a moment that he watched her somewhat curiously, but she pushed the thought aside when he did not question her in any way. I must not let myself begin to feel guilty again, she told herself. I must be patient, and, when Pavel Pavlovich's wounds heal, perhaps we will all be able to work things out. She tried not to think too much about the details, preferring to leave them for the future.

Since his shoulder injury prevented him from writing, Pavel Pavlovich enlisted Katherina Andreievna as his secretary. He dictated detailed reports to the Czar about the worthiness of generals Yermolov and Paskevich. His recommendation was that Paskevich replace Yermolov, and he seemed to have endless bits of evidence to support his conclusions. Katherina found the long discussions of military tactics tedious, but she never complained. The work provided a welcome escape from any real conversation with Pavel Pavlovich, and by the time he had finished several hours of dictation each day he was much too tired to question her about her activities.

On Wednesday, Katherina meekly suggested that she might like to relax at the spa that afternoon.

Pavel Pavlovich heartily agreed. "But of course, my dear. Forgive me for not suggesting it myself. I'm afraid I've been working you far too hard. Perhaps we should inquire as to whether there is a clerk in Pyatigorsk whom I could hire as a secretary."

"Oh, no—I wouldn't hear of it, Pavel Pavlovich. It's so interesting helping you with your work—but I feel the need for a slight break in the routine."

"Then you must take one of the servants and go. Stay as long as you wish. Just be sure to return before dark. We don't want to tempt the Circassians."

She kissed him and left the room feeling quite gay. For a moment, Katherina considered asking Masha to accompany her. She knew she might have a long, impatient wait at the spa, and she could not even be certain whether Aleksandr Sergeievich could get away from the fort to join her. But she decided not to bother Masha. The place might arouse too many unhappy memories of Vladimir Nikolaievich. Besides, where could she send the girl if she and Aleksandr Sergeievich wished to be alone?

She was fifty paces from the well when she saw him lounging on a bench, his dark hair ruffling in the autumn breeze. Without thinking, she rushed to his arms as he sprang from the bench to greet her.

"Oh Sasha, I'm so glad you are here. I might have gone mad with uncertainty if I had been forced to wait for you, not knowing whether or not you would come."

"I have already gone mad with waiting," he whispered, "and I haven't been here more than ten minutes." Seeing that people were starting to stare at them, he gently pulled away from her.

"Oh," she flushed. "Perhaps we should not meet in such a public place. But—seeing you—I just couldn't stop myself."

He smiled. "I feel the same way, my love, so I have decided we will not meet here anymore. Come, Katya, I have a surprise for you."

He led her down the hill from the spa, across the main boulevard, and into a narrow side street. They stopped in front of a small whitewashed house—really no more than a cottage.

Katherina stared at Aleksandr. "Whose is it, Sasha?"

"Ours!" he announced as he swung her off her feet and carried her through the door. "I'm afraid it can't compare with the exquisite mansions and palaces you're used to, my sweet little countess, but it *is* private."

Still carrying her, he showed her the small kitchen, parlor, and dining room, all comfortably furnished. The tour ended as he dropped her on the cheery patchwork quilt in the little bedroom.

Her eyes danced as she looked up at him. "But Sasha—is it really ours?"

"At least until summer," he replied as he pulled his shirt over his head and began to take off his trousers. "A merchant from Kiev rents it each summer, but it lies vacant the rest of the year. The landlord was only too happy to collect some extra rent."

"But how did you find out about it?"

"Too many questions," he teased as he bounced down beside her on the bed and began to unfasten her dress. "If I had known you just wanted to talk, we could have stayed at the spa and I could have saved myself some money."

She giggled and fluttered her eyelashes. "Why, Monsieur Belikov, I cannot imagine what you are hinting at."

"Can't you, madame?" His eyes sparkled as he tossed her dress aside. "Then, by all means, you must allow me to demonstrate."

His lips began to trace teasing patterns all over her body, causing gooseflesh to erupt wherever they touched, and she became blissfully powerless. Thus, the afternoon passed.

Wednesday became their regular day at the little house, and Katherina found herself barely living on other days, existing only so that Wednesday would come again. Even when the winter dampness and rains enveloped Pyatigorsk, Pavel Pavlovich accepted without question her need to get out of the house. After all, she was such a devoted wife all week, faithfully attending to his reports to Czar Nikolai, and he could hardly expect her to spend all her time sitting in a stuffy room with a bedridden old man.

On most Wednesdays, Katherina and Aleksandr arrived at the house at almost the same moment, but if he arrived first, he started the fire in the little bedroom fireplace. If she got there before him, she let herself in and started the fire. The cottage quickly became their home, overflowing with all the love they could give one another.

One rainy Wednesday a few days before Christmas, Katherina hurried down the narrow street to the cottage. Pavel Pavlovich had watched her with more curiosity than usual as she prepared to leave, but she had insisted that she wished to do some shopping at the village bazaar. Now her felt boots and heavy woolen cloak—designed for St. Petersburg's cold and snow—were soaked through from the downpour. A chill crept through her body, and she hoped that Aleksandr Sergeievich had already arrived at the cottage. She looked forward to casting off her drenched clothing and warming herself by the fire.

With relief, Katherina saw that Aleksandr's black stallion was already hitched in the small path beside the house. As she opened the door, a welcome blast of warm air told her that he had arrived some time ago and the fire was already crackling at full force.

"Sasha," she called, "where are you hiding yourself?"

He emerged, smiling, from the bedroom, carrying a bottle of champagne. "I'm afraid it's impossible to get your Novgorodian *braga* in these parts," he explained as he held the bottle aloft, "so we will have to make do with champagne to toast the holidays."

Katherina laughed gaily, but the thought of cold champagne made her shiver. She would rather have had an entire samovar of bubbling hot tea.

Aleksandr put his arm around her. "You're soaked to the skin, Katya—come in and warm yourself by the fire." He led her into the bedroom, and she stopped and stared with amazed delight.

"Sasha, how did you manage it?" she breathed, forgetting how cold and uncomfortable she felt as her eyes took in the details of the room. Brightly lacquered ornaments hung from the ceiling and the furniture, reminding her of her childhood Christmases in Novgorod. In the center of the bed lay an oddly shaped package.

"Merry Christmas, Katya." He kissed her tenderly as he helped her out of her soaked clothing. "Now perhaps you would be so kind as to get that package off of our bed."

"But, Sasha, I didn't expect—I didn't even think to bring a gift for you."

"Of course you did," he said, sitting on the edge of the bed and pulling her into his lap. "You brought yourself. Now open your package before I open it for you." He plopped the unwieldy parcel into her lap.

Excitedly, she tore away the wrappings. It was a balalaika carved of dark wood, apple blossoms lacquered in a decorative border on its face. She strummed a string absently, filling the room with a sweet melodic tone. "It's beautiful, Sasha—exquisite—but I hardly know what to say. I don't know how to play such an instrument."

"Perhaps not yet," he said as he smiled at her, "but I was sure you could learn. Certainly someone as beautiful as you are could coax perfect sounds even from a battered and worn instrument. After all," he teased, "think of what you have done with me."

"You underestimate yourself," she said, laughing. "It seems to me that you are the most perfect instrument I could ever expect to encounter."

They spent the afternoon strumming the balalaika, singing holiday songs, sharing the sweet champagne, and sharing the even greater sweetness of each other.

On the third Wednesday in January, Katherina was surprised to see a dapple-gray horse tethered beside the cottage. That seems strange, she thought as she walked up the path to the door. Sasha never rides anyone else's horse. He has always seemed attached to that black stallion. Well—perhaps his horse went lame during one of his patrols in the mountains. Somewhat perplexed, she let herself into the cottage.

"Sasha," she called, "what happened to your horse? Did all his color fade away from this incessant rain?" When no one answered, Katherina assumed he was waiting in the bedroom with another surprise for her. As she cast her cloak aside and hurried through the parlor, she heard him strike a chord on the balalaika. The bedroom door was closed, and she wondered what he was hiding.

"What kind of mischief are you up to today?" she laughed, throwing open the bedroom door.

She froze in the doorway and her laughter stopped.

Lying on the bed, in the spot where Aleksandr Sergeievich should have been, was General Bugov. Despite his full-dress uniform and the saber buckled at his waist, he looked perfectly relaxed, his arms propped behind his head, and his feet, in their shining black boots, crossed at the ankles. A wicked smile creased the corners of his mouth.

"Do come in, my dear countess."

"You!" Katherina hissed when she finally recovered her voice. "What are you doing here?"

"I'm so sorry to disappoint you," he said, the sarcasm in his voice becoming heavier, "but I'm afraid your lover will not be coming today. It seems he was assigned to an emergency patrol, so he asked me to come in his place."

"That is hardly likely."

"Well," he shrugged, "believe what you wish. The fact remains that Belikov was detained for the day, and I thought I would save you some worry by bringing you a message."

"How did you know to come here? I'm sure he didn't tell you."

"No, as a matter of fact he did not." Bugov's smile became broader. "But haven't you heard, my dear, every man in the army quickly learns where to go to seek a whore."

"Get out of my house!" she screamed as her initial wariness gave way to rage.

He sat up slowly, lazily swinging his heavy leather boots to the floor. "You must forgive me if my bluntness has offended you, Countess Ostrova. Perhaps you prefer to be called a mistress. Does the title Belikov's mistress have a more delicate ring to your sensitive little ears? Perhaps your husband has not noticed—but I was not too blind to perceive the intimacy between you and Belikov."

"You scum. How dare you break into my house and insult me with your filthy innuendos?"

His tone became harsher. "Perhaps you should avoid calling me names, my dear. Unless of course you wish me to carry stories of your activities to your husband. Does the good count know he is married to someone else's mistress?"

"I don't care what you threaten to tell him. He would never believe you!"

"Are you sure you want to take that chance?" the general taunted.

Katherina swung around and started out the door. "I won't stand here and listen to any more of this."

The general leaped off the bed, drew his saber, and swept it around her. He stood behind Katherina, forcing her body against him as the saber pressed threateningly just below her breasts.

"I suppose you thought I was too old and over-weight to move so quickly," he said. "But when one visits a whore, one usually expects more than spiteful conversation."

Despite the tightening saber, Katherina's tone remained defiant. "And are you such a desperate man that you can only get what you want by force?"

"No, of course not," he chuckled. "I prefer to think of this as a gentle instrument of persuasion. It will simply persuade you to listen to what I have to say. When I tell you the manner in which I propose to pay for your services, I think you will agree to my demands most readily."

The first barb of understanding began to prick at Katherina Andreievna's brain, sending a cold shudder through her body. "What are you planning to do to Sasha?" she demanded hoarsely.

"Ah—I can see that you are more intelligent than you at first appeared." Bugov relaxed the saber a bit and steered her back to the bedroom, kicking the door shut behind him. Savoring her tension, he waited a few moments before replying to her question.

"I have a request from General Paskevich for a reinforcement of one hundred men, to leave tomorrow. Your Belikov could be among them. On the other hand, I could arrange for him to remain at the fort to continue in his patrols against the Circassians. The decision is entirely up to you—if you understand what I mean—my dear countess."

"How do I know I can trust you?"

"Can you really afford not to? By way of persuasion, perhaps I should explain to you that Paskevich is an excellent general, but his losses have been considerable. The Persians are very cunning and devious warriors, and they have succeeded in killing vast numbers of our young men. Others have been wounded in ways that prevent them from ever being, shall we say, of use to a woman again." He paused to smile. "But, I repeat, the decision is yours entirely."

Katherina swayed uneasily, thinking of all the war losses Pavel Pavlovich had described in his reports to the Czar. She thought of Pavel Pavlovich's own injuries. But most of all she thought of the unutterable pain of having Aleksandr Sergeievich sent to Transcaucasia, knowing she might never see him again, knowing she could have saved him. If she gave in to Bugov now, both she and Sasha might be spared so much suffering. She would only have to endure a few moments of agony today, and Aleksandr Sergeievich need never know. But could she trust General Bugov to keep his word? Did she really have a choice? Looking away from him, her face burning with embarrassment, she began to unbutton her dress.

"Ah—now you are being sensible," General Bugov

said as he resheathed his saber and sat down on the edge of the bed to watch her. "Who knows, perhaps you will even find me more adept at lovemaking than your young officer. My age most certainly gives me more experience."

Katherina did not answer and she refused to look at him. Her dress dropped to the floor and she stood in her petticoats.

"Please remove everything, my dear," Bugov said softly. "It's been a long time since I have gazed at such exquisite loveliness. You know," he continued as she peeled away her underclothing, "I have wanted you since the first time you entered my office. I never intended to take you in this way. I tried to court you, you may recall, but apparently Belikov had already ensnared you. It's a pity our first union must be under these circumstances, but—" He stopped in mid-sentence to stare at Katherina's body.

He reached out to fondle a breast, weighing it lightly in his hand, pinching the nipple between his thumb and forefinger. Then his hand ran down her side to her waist, continuing until it ended at the velvety skin between her thighs. His fingers felt repulsively coarse and rough, and her churning stomach made her wonder if she could live through the afternoon without vomiting.

"Spread your legs a bit, madame," he whispered. "It is customary for a whore to allow her client to examine the merchandise."

Katherina stiffened at his sarcasm, but she complied and forced herself not to flinch under his exploring fingers and leering expression. He told her to turn around, and he ran his fingers down her back and over her buttocks, ending again between her legs. For a moment Katherina allowed herself to hope that he would be satisfied with looking at her and touching her. Then he commanded her to turn around and look into his eyes, and she shrank from the uncontrolled lust she saw there.

He jerked at her golden braids and said, "Unbraid your hair. I don't want a woman who wears her hair like a peasant or some filthy tribeswoman."

Katherina was almost glad to follow his command, for her hair fell over her breasts, concealing at least some of her nakedness. Then he told her to get down on her knees and pull off his boots. When she hesitated, battling against the humiliation, his hand flew back to the hilt of his saber, and she dropped to her knees as commanded and removed the boots. He left her kneeling uncertainly as he rose and slowly undressed, drawing out her moments of agony.

Finally, casting the last of his clothing aside, he flung her onto the bed and, without any preliminaries, thrust into her. Katherina bit back her cry of pain. He slid his hands under her buttocks, forcing her against him, but when he buried his face in her neck, she could not keep herself from fighting back, and she chomped down angrily on his earlobe.

"You little slut," he roared, digging his fingernails into her buttocks and thrusting more furiously into her.

Only stubborn pride kept Katherina from screaming. She fought against the cries erupting in her throat, swallowing furiously to keep them locked within herself. I must not give him the satisfaction of knowing my suffering, she told herself again and again, until she was numb to the pressure of his body against hers. Soon it will all be over, and Sasha and I can go on with our meetings, free from this ugly menace.

She concentrated so completely on the inevitable joy of future meetings with Aleksandr Sergeievich that she scarcely noticed when General Bugov, finally satisfied, cast her body aside. He lay there for several minutes, sweating and panting heavily, then he slowly rose from the bed and lumbered across the room to retrieve his clothing. Katherina stared at the fire, impatiently waiting for him to finish dressing and leave her house. She could feel his eyes traveling over her body, trying to bore into her soul, but she still refused to look at him.

"It's a pity that duty calls me back to the fort so soon. It would be pleasant to have another round, now that we have become so intimately acquainted." He laughed loudly.

"You got what you came here for," she snapped. "Now get your filthy body out of my house."

"I warned you before about name-calling, madame." He grabbed her wrist, squeezing it until she turned her head to look at him. "Actually, I did not get quite what I came for. To be candid, your performance disappointed me." He pronounced each word slowly, letting her feel its full impact.

"What did you expect, you brute?" Katherina wrenched her wrist away.

"I expected a bit more response on your part. After all, a woman of your experience must be capable of a good deal of passion. I suspect even the old count demands his conjugal rights from time to time. And then there is your lover, Belikov. And God only knows how many other perfumed young dandies you have taken to your bed in St. Petersburg and Moscow—and all the other little towns along the way."

His words cut into her, driving her to a white-hot rage. "There haven't been any others!" she screamed.

He shrugged. "Well, perhaps there have and perhaps there have not. It really makes no difference.

The fact remains that now there is me. And I expect you to treat me with a bit more respect and affection the next time we meet."

"If it's up to me, there won't be a next time," she said icily.

"Ah—but that is where you are wrong. I think you will be meeting me here again next week."

"That was not part of the bargain."

He shrugged again. "But in my opinion you did not fulfill your end of the bargain. As I pointed out, your performance was rather disappointing. You should be grateful I'm giving you a chance to redeem yourself —and Belikov."

"And if I refuse?"

"It matters little to me whether your Belikov remains at my fort or is sent to General Paskevich. If you wish him to depart tomorrow, I certainly will not disappoint you." He pinched her cheek. "Perhaps you have tired of him and wish to move on to a new lover—eh?"

Katherina stared into the fire, wishing she had never ridden to the fort with Aleksandr Sergeievich and had never met this detestable man. To think she had once laughed at his attentions—and his chestnut mare still stood in her stable. How well-founded were Aleksandr Sergeievich's jealousies! Revulsion gripped her body. If she did not agree to yield to Bugov again, her afternoon's suffering would have been wasted—she knew the general would relish sending Sasha away—but how could she face another afternoon like the one she had just endured? Bugov's voice intruded on her thoughts.

"Your silence is difficult to interpret, my dear. Am I to assume it means agreement?"

Katherina continued staring at the fire, as if it could offer her an escape. What if she went to Aleksandr

Sergeievich? Could he help her? Or would he be repulsed by what she had done? Certainly he would murder General Bugov, and what would happen to him then? Could he possibly escape without being discovered?

"Come, come, my dear, I have important business to attend to. Are you going to meet me or not?"

Katherina nodded.

"Good girl." He patted her head. "I will certainly make the meeting worth your while. And, just to show you how understanding I am, we will make our rendezvous on Tuesday. That way you will still be free to meet your other lover on Wednesday."

Katherina cringed at the way he said "other lover" —as if he considered himself equal to Aleksandr Sergeievich. "But what will I tell Pavel Pavlovich?" she cried. "I'm not sure he will understand if I want to go out two days next week."

General Bugov was striding toward the door. He flung his answer back over his shoulder. "I'm sure you will think of something, my dear little whore. After all, you have lied to your husband before."

Chapter 18

All week Katherina struggled to find a way to escape from the impending Tuesday meeting without hurting Aleksandr Sergeievich. If only she could see Sasha before then, he would certainly have a solution, but what could she possibly tell him? Could she ever bring herself to reveal what had happened between her and General Bugov? It was useless to even speculate on seeing him before their usual Wednesday meeting. He could not get away from the fort, and, even if she could contrive to ride there, General Bugov would probably prevent them from so much as greeting one another, much less sharing a private talk. Even while she agonized over the problem, Katherina knew in her heart that she would go to the little house on Tuesday and that she would pretend to please the general no matter how repulsive she found him. She could see no other choice if she wanted to see her beloved again. It seemed as if Sasha was actually in prison, and only she had the power to free him.

As the days dragged by, Katherina Andreievna became more and more irritable. General Bugov had denied her last Wednesday's meeting with Aleksandr Sergeievich—the one thing that renewed her spirits and enabled her to face each week—and she felt robbed and cheated. She complained to Tamara about the wretched cooking, reprimanded Lizaveta for leaving a speck of dust on the vase in the parlor, and sent Masha flying to her room in tears, snapping at the poor girl for pulling her hair while arranging it.

Even Pavel Pavlovich, still confined to his bed, suffered from her nervousness. On Monday she upset the inkwell as she took his dictation, spreading a soggy black stain across the paper and her dress. In frustration, she cleared the desk with one furious sweep, sending the inkwell clattering to the floor where it shattered into fragments. Then she collapsed in sobs on the desk top.

Alarmed, but unable to rush to comfort her, Pavel Pavlovich sat watching his wife in silent amazement. Finally, when her sobs began to subside, he addressed her in an almost cautious tone. "My dear Katherina Andreievna, what has been troubling you these last few days?"

"I don't know," she choked. "I'm sorry that I ruined your letter. I just can't seem to control myself."

"The letter is not important right now, my dear— but you are. Have you been feeling ill?"

She shook her head as she sat up and dried her eyes.

"Does my condition annoy you so much? I know you must be weary of waiting on me, being my hands and feet, but I can assure you I will do everything possible to make it up to you."

"Oh, no, Pavel Pavlovich! Please don't think you're to blame." She burst into sobs again, ashamed at having made her husband feel guilty for something he had no part in.

"But my dear Katherina, what is the problem? You can tell me—your own husband."

She shook her head again, fighting a sudden urge to confess everything. "I just don't know, Pavel Pavlovich. I'm sorry—but I just don't know."

"Very well," he said quietly, "I won't pressure you more, but it seems to me you are badly in need of something to relax you, some diversion to take away the drudgery of your existence here."

"But I go out walking every Wednesday with Masha."

"Yes, and those walks appear to do you a world of good. You seem to come back with lighter spirits and an attractive bit of flush to your cheeks—" He stopped. "Except last week—you returned rather agitated. Did you see or hear something that upset you?"

Katherina blushed slightly and looked away, embarrassed that her mood had been so obvious. "I can't think," she stammered. "Oh—yes, now I recall. There was a dead bird in the roadway. I don't know why it upset me so much. Perhaps because I almost tripped over it—and because death in any form is unpleasant to look at."

The count smiled at her. "Oh—my dear wife—I'm afraid you are far too sensitive. The world is, unfortunately, full of ugly and distasteful things. Perhaps your parents and I have done you a disservice by shielding you too much from life's unpleasant realities." He paused again. "But as I was saying, I think you need a bit more diversion. Perhaps you need the chance to chat with and confide in another woman. I know you talk to Masha, and you feel quite close to her, but I suspect you need the company of someone nearer to your own social status. Is there no one in Pyatigorsk with whom you could visit from time to time? Perhaps once a week?"

Katherina's mind raced. Could he actually, unknowingly, be suggesting the perfect excuse for her to leave him tomorrow? "I don't know," she replied slowly. "You know most of the society people from St. Petersburg and Moscow only come for the summer—and they returned to their homes months ago. But," she closed her eyes, "there was someone I met at the spa last fall. I think her name was Princess Golovine. She told me she had been widowed recently and planned to stay through the winter rather than face the sad memories evoked by the winter balls in Moscow. Perhaps I should call on her tomorrow. No doubt she is feeling rather lonely herself."

"That sounds like an excellent idea, Katherina Andreievna. No doubt the visit will do both you and the princess a great deal of good."

"Yes." Katherina went to the bed and kissed her husband's forehead. "Thank you for the suggestion, Pavel Pavlovich. I feel much better already."

In fact, she did feel a trifle relieved, knowing that her excuse for the next day was set.

When Katherina Andreievna arrived at the little house on Tuesday, no one was there. As she carefully checked each room, a new possibility occurred to her, and she began to hope that General Bugov would not come, had never intended to come. Wasn't it possible that he had simply forced her to agree to the rendezvous in order to torment her with the days of apprehensive waiting? Perhaps it was his way of punishing her for not responding to the attentions he had given her from their first meeting. Katherina felt a surge of bitter rage for his cruel schemings. Still, she knew she could endure the rage far more easily than she could endure another afternoon with the pompous general.

She started for the door, eager to leave the house and the hideous memories of the last Wednesday.

She would feel happier coming back the next day, knowing that Aleksandr Sergeievich would be waiting for her. As she lay her hand on the doorknob, a sudden thought held her back. Suppose General Bugov had simply been waylaid, and he arrived after she had gone? The certainty that he would keep Aleksandr Sergeievich from coming to her on Wednesday forced Katherina to turn away from the door and walk back to the bedroom. It was better to wait now than to be disappointed again tomorrow. If necessary, she would wait the whole afternoon, but she desperately hoped that nothing more would be required of her than passive waiting—for a man who would not appear.

Not bothering to light a fire, Katherina sat huddled in her cloak, wishing for the afternoon to pass quickly, without any intruders. After a time, she picked up her balalaika and began to entertain herself by playing and singing the folk songs her nurse had sung to her in Novgorod. More than an hour passed, and Katherina became so caught up in her music that she did not hear the cottage door open. As she paused between songs, a gruff, sarcastic voice interrupted her thoughts.

"My, my—a singing whore. I see your talents surpass anything I might have hoped for, my dear countess."

Katherina looked up, and her eyes met the mocking gaze of General Bugov, who lounged lazily in the bedroom doorway.

He stepped into the room and closed the door. "Please don't let me interrupt this charming performance. By all means, continue, my dear."

Defiantly, Katherina put the instrument aside as the general removed his cloak. He raised his bushy eyebrows at her. "Am I to understand that you are too anxious to get on with our other activities?" He snatched her cloak from her shoulders and tossed it aside. "I'm sorry to have disappointed you by being late, madame, but I suspect we shall find enough time for everything, eh?" He winked at her viciously.

"For the moment, I think I would like to hear you finish your little serenade. That is, of course, after you have removed all your clothing."

Katherina stared at him in disbelief, making the general chuckle heartily. "Come, come, my dear. Surely you can't find my request so unreasonable. Have you forgotten how well I've agreed to pay you for your services? Or am I to understand that you wish to suspend our agreement?"

Still not speaking, Katherina slowly rose and undressed. She shivered in the unheated room as she reached for her balalaika and tried to conceal as much of her body as possible behind the instrument. General Bugov surveyed her shivering flesh approvingly.

"Don't mind the cold, my dear," he taunted as a smile twisted across his face. "Just think how delightful it will feel when our bodies are at last consumed by the burning fires of our mutual passion." He laughed.

She played for him and sang for him, and she allowed him to use her body, even trying to fake a response. But she refused to speak to him all through the interminable afternoon. As he prepared to leave, General Bugov shocked some words out of her.

"It seems you are reluctant to honor me with your conversation, my dear, but perhaps you will feel differently next week."

The words penetrated her mind like a blow. "Next week?"

"But of course! You didn't think I was fool enough to abandon a treasure like you after only two meetings, did you?"

"Don't you have any shame?" Katherina screamed. "Don't you have a wife somewhere?"

The general threw back his head and laughed long and loud. "How strange that you should talk about shame, *Mistress Belikov.* As for my wife—she is a fat, ugly nag I gladly left in Kazan. You may put your mind at rest, she is quite well taken care of. But the less I see of her, the better I like it."

"And the less I see of *you*, the better *I* like it," Katherina spat as she jumped from the bed and began to dress. "I won't be here to entertain you next week!"

"What a pity. But I'm sure General Paskevich will be requesting more reinforcements soon. Perhaps next week—perhaps the following week. It takes a lot of strong young men to fight a war. Particularly when the Imperial Army's losses are so heavy."

Katherina paled, and her voice trembled with fury. "How long do you intend to persecute me? How long do you expect to keep me enslaved?"

"Enslaved? My dear countess, you are not enslaved. You are free to refuse my attentions whenever you please. Of course," he shrugged, "you must be prepared to accept the consequences that ensue."

Katherina's hands were shaking so violently that she had difficulty fastening her dress. Watching her, the general burst into laughter. He came up behind her and dropped his hands heavily on her shoulders.

"Two o'clock next Tuesday, my dear?" he asked as he bent to nibble at her ear.

Stiffening at his touch, Katherina responded coldly, "It seems I have very little choice in the matter."

"Oh, but you do have a choice. You must always

remember that. Where your own future—and Beli-kov's—are concerned, the choice is yours."

After the general strode out with a hearty laugh, Katherina spent another hour in the little house, furiously cleaning the room. She wanted no trace of Bugov's visits to be apparent to Aleksandr Sergeie-vich, and she did not want anything in the room to remind her of the despicable general when she returned the next day for a happier rendezvous.

Though she tried to mask her anger and depression, Katherina's ashen face told Pavel Pavlovich something was wrong the moment she walked into their bedroom.

"Did you find the Princess Golovine was not well, Katherina Andreievna?" he asked gently.

"No," Katherina stammered, "she was—quite well. But I'm afraid I found her conversation quite depressing. She spoke so much of her dead husband and how lonely she has been without him. The only thing I could find to be cheerful about was that I still have my own dear husband. And of course I could hardly say as much to her. It would only depress her more."

Pavel Pavlovich smiled. "Perhaps you should not visit her again. It might be better for you to seek more cheerful companionship."

"Oh, I promised to return next Tuesday. The poor princess is so lonely she really needs a sympathetic listener. Perhaps I can think of some way to cheer her up."

"Sometimes, Katherina Andreievna, I think you are a bit too kind for your own good."

"Nonsense," she said, laughing nervously. "What a poor example of Christian charity I would be if I turned my back on those who need me."

"I just worry that you are overextending yourself,

my dear. You have quite enough to handle, caring for me. You should save some time for yourself."

Katherina sat down on the bed beside him. "Caring for my own husband is certainly not a chore," she said. In fact, she thought, compared to entertaining General Bugov, it is sheer joy. "And I have time for myself on my Wednesday outings, you know."

"I suppose," the count sighed. "I just wish there were some way for me to lighten your load. Perhaps you could suggest that the princess come here to visit you. Away from her own home she might feel less inclined to talk about her departed husband."

"Oh—no," Katherina protested almost too quickly, "I'm afraid she would feel very uncomfortable here, knowing my own husband is so near. Besides, I wouldn't want you to be disturbed while you are resting."

"Well, do whatever you think is best, my dear. I learned long ago in St. Petersburg that you will always contrive to do as you wish anyway." He chuckled, and Katherina surprised and delighted him by kissing him full on the lips.

On Wednesday, Katherina approached the narrow street with a pounding heart. Would Aleksandr Sergeievich be there? Had General Bugov simply tricked her, or would he keep his part of the bargain? She turned off the main boulevard, feeling a mixture of fear and excitement. Before she was fifty paces from the boulevard, she saw Aleksandr Sergeievich's black stallion tethered beside their cottage. Barely stifling a cry of joy, she ran toward the house, imagining the feel of his strong arms cradling her against him. She threw open the door and rushed to embrace him as he walked from the bedroom to the parlor.

Tears of relief streamed from her eyes as he enfolded her in his arms, rocking her breathless body and stroking her hair.

"Oh Katya, I have never missed you so much. One week away from you is torture, but two weeks without you was intolerable."

"I know, Sasha," she said. "These two weeks I have felt like I was in hell."

"Katya, I know you must have been worried about me, but I could think of no safe way to send you a message." He lifted her head and looked into her tear-glazed eyes. "Do you forgive me?"

She nodded. "There is nothing to forgive. I'm sure you suffered as much as I."

Aleksandr held her. "It was very strange. Last week I was preparing to ride here when General Bugov himself came out and assigned me to an emergency patrol. He stood and watched while we rode far into the mountains toward Kislovodsk. I wanted to slip away and ride to you, but it was impossible." He stopped. "It almost seemed as if he knew where I was going and purposely prevented me from coming here—as if he knew about you and me."

Katherina shuddered in his arms, and Aleksandr mistook her reaction for fear. "Please don't worry, Katya," he whispered. "I'm sure he can't really know. It was foolish of me to imagine it or even mention it to you. And even if he did somehow manage to find out, what could the general possibly do to harm either of us?"

Oh Sasha, she thought, I pray that you never come close to even imagining what he could do.

Aleksandr carried her to the bedroom then, and they spent the rest of the afternoon lost in the blessed oblivion they always found in each other's arms.

The weekly Tuesday rendezvous with General Bugov stretched on into spring. After the first three or four horrible encounters, Katherina Andreievna became numb to the pain and humiliation, and she accepted the situation as some sort of divine retribution for the hours of sublime joy she shared with Aleksandr Sergeievich each Wednesday. The rest of the week passed in a blur.

Pavel Pavlovich's wounds healed slowly. Both his collarbone and the bones in his ankle had been fractured by bullets, and his age was a decided deterrent to the healing process. The shoulder injury healed first, and by March he was able to begin moving around on crutches, but his ankle still could not bear any weight, and the crutches irritated his tender shoulder muscles, so he could scarcely stand the few steps he took from one room—or one piece of furniture—to another. Despite his condition, he became increasingly restless, and he finally suggested to Katherina one night that they should attempt to resume conjugal relations.

Since she was already giving herself to both Aleksandr Sergeievich and General Bugov, Katherina knew there was no way she could in good conscience deny her own husband. In fact, his consideration so far exceeded General Bugov's that, by comparison, making love with him was pure ecstasy. Although the delicate condition of his shoulder and his bandaged foot made the act somewhat awkward, Pavel Pavlovich seemed thoroughly satisfied, and their relations fell into a regular routine. Perhaps, Katherina thought hopefully, he would soon be able to abandon the crutches—and she and Aleksandr Sergeievich could leave Pyatigorsk without feeling too guilty.

Katherina had become accustomed to General Bugov's strange demands. She stopped feeling self-con-

scious when she played her balalaika in the nude.
She accepted without question, although without
enthusiasm, any position and any location he chose—
from the cold kitchen floor to the precariously balanced straight chair in the parlor to the tame confines
of the bed. When he insisted that she call him Fyodor
Petrovich, she complied because it facilitated matters, although it sickened her when he called her
Katherina Andreievna or, worse, Rina—the pet name
he had chosen for her. Just as often, depending on his
mood, he called her whore, though Katherina had long
ago become immune to his taunting.

Throughout their afternoons together, she concentrated on Aleksandr Sergeievich and the fact that
her actions on Tuesday might well determine whether
she saw him on Wednesday. And, much as she de-
spised Bugov, she granted him a grudging respect
for his own distorted sense of honor. Since that first
Wednesday in January, he had never kept Aleksandr
Sergeievich from her.

Then came a Tuesday early in April. Bugov had
been especially demanding that day, dragging her
from room to room and using her until she was exhausted and it was beginning to get dark outside.
Katherina had worried about how she could explain
her lateness to Pavel Pavlovich. She had already exhausted her imagination with stories about Princess Golovine, and she was growing uneasy thinking
about the possibility that someday Pavel Pavlovich
might actually meet the princess and recount her stories. But she had not complained to Bugov and had
remained totally submissive to whatever he suggested.
She had something important to tell Aleksandr Sergeievich the next day, and it was imperative that
she see him.

As Fyodor Bugov dressed to return to the fort, he

smiled slyly at Katherina. "I must thank you, my precious little whore, for your attentions in these last months. It's a pity that we won't be able to continue this liaison."

"What do you mean?" Katherina whispered hollowly.

"Quite simply, I have no further use for you. You have been most generous with your considerable charms, but I find that my interests and desires are beginning to wander. Perhaps I neglected to tell you about my new Circassian maid. Such a wild one! A real tigress!" he clucked. "Frankly, my dear, I find that she submits to me with far more abandon than you ever did—or probably ever will. And, of course, having her there in my quarters makes it so much more convenient. I was beginning to get bored with the long ride from the fort each week."

"You can't do this to me!" Katherina shrieked.

The general widened his eyes in mock surprise. "My dear Rina, do I mean so much to you? I thought you would be only too glad to be rid of me. Of course, if it will soothe your feelings, you are welcome to ride out to the fort to visit me from time to time. I'll be most happy to take you to my bed, for old times' sake. Or, if you like, I could arrange for one of my junior officers to visit you here each Tuesday, just so you can keep in practice. One man is as good as another, isn't he?"

"You pig!" Katherina lunged at Bugov. "You know very well what I'm upset about. What are you planning to do with Aleksandr Sergeievich?"

"Oh—Belikov?" The general caught her arms in a crushing grip. "I'm afraid I can't say right now, but since our arrangement is terminated, I feel no further obligation to either you or him."

Katherina tried to struggle out of his grasp, beating

her fists against his chest. "You brute! You scum! You despicable demon! You used me and now you intend to cast me aside and do as you please."

"Please, my dear Rina," the general chuckled. "Such behavior hardly becomes you, and it will do nothing to convince me to keep your lover nearby. If you wish to know his fate, why don't you ask him yourself when you whore for him tomorrow?" He flung her back on the bed and left her sobbing in grief and fury.

Chapter 19

It was dark when Katherina Andreievna trudged into the courtyard. She had lain—sobbing—in the little house, gripped by the terrible conviction that there would be no tomorrow for her and Aleksandr Sergeievich. It was useless to wait and hope that tomorrow would be a Wednesday like any other because she was sure that Bugov had no intention of allowing them to meet. The only thing for her to do was to find Aleksandr tonight—provided that the scheming general had not already sent him south across the mountains to die with Paskevich's troops.

As she crept toward the stable, she looked for one moment of longing at the house where she and Aleksandr Sergeievich had shared more than a month of happiness. Her eyes caught a glimpse of Pavel Pavlovich in the lamplight of the parlor as he struggled on his crutches toward a chair. She considered rushing through the door to help him, but she forced herself to look away. She had to find Aleksandr Sergeievich before it was too late, and she could not allow any sentimentalities to stand in her way.

Katherina Andreievna had never saddled and bridled a horse, but she had often watched Aleksandr Sergeievich, and now she was sure she could do it. Still, her tension made her fumble in the dark stable, and she dropped the bit with a loud clatter. She froze for a few moments, then went to the stable door and looked warily toward the house. Certain that no one was coming to check on the noise, she returned to the

horses. Her task was doubly difficult since she chose
to saddle Pavel Pavlovich's brown stallion, who was
not at all familiar with her touch. The horse pawed
the ground nervously as Katherina adjusted the bridle;
however, she couldn't bring herself to use the gentle
chestnut mare General Bugov had lent her. She
would never again, under any circumstances, ride
that horse.

After more than a quarter of an hour of struggling,
Katherina finished preparing the horse. With a pounding heart, she led it out of the stable and through the
courtyard to the gate. After a quick glance at the
house, she mounted and cantered to the bottom of
the hill, and when she reached the main boulevard,
she coaxed her mount to a full gallop.

The mountain area was desolate. There was no
moon that night, and the dark shadows seemed to
swallow up Katherina and her horse as the lights of
Pyatigorsk disappeared behind her. As they galloped
at top speed, Katherina's eyes darted among the trees
and shrubbery searching for would-be attackers. For
the first time in months, she thought of Masha's ordeal, and she wondered how she could defend herself
if a band of Circassians held her at their mercy. She
would be a helpless toy, tossed from one barbarian
fiend to another, and she had not even brought a
knife or a gun.

Still, she consoled herself, whatever the savages
might devise to do with her could not be any worse
than the humiliation Fyodor Bugov had forced on
her. Besides, she was foolish to imagine things. In all
likelihood, she would ride all the way to the fort
without being disturbed, and then she would have to
face the more realistic worry of what General Bugov
might do with her, particularly if Aleksandr Sergeievich was not there to protect her. Of course, if her

Sasha had already been sent away, she could hardly care what the general might do.

Katherina continued riding, her hair flying and the wind rushing in her ears, until she sensed a reluctance in her horse. The horse slowed before she even reined him in, then stopped moving completely. Katherina waited, blood pounding in her ears, straining to discern what had upset the horse. Suddenly she became aware of the sound of hooves thundering toward her.

It did not sound like a large group of horses, and there were no sounds of men's voices calling to one another. In fact, she thought hopefully, it might be a solitary rider. Then her heart sank as she realized how much harm even a solitary rider could do. Did she dare wait for the rider to pass, hoping she could keep her horse quiet and go unnoticed on the moonless night?

The sound of hoofbeats continued straight toward them, and Katherina's horse began to shift uneasily. As she began to discern the dim outline of a horse and rider, Katherina realized that she must be visible as well. She pulled sharply on the reins, turning her mount, to flee from the approaching rider.

Concentrating on galloping away, Katherina would not permit herself to look back. She dug her knees into the horse's sides and leaned low against his neck, whispering words of encouragement. She thought she heard the rider behind her yell something, but the wind carried away the words. Katherina shuddered, imagining the rider was demanding her surrender, and fear forced her to spur her mount more insistently. In the distance she could see a few scattered lights. If she could reach the safety of the main boulevard of Pyatigorsk, surely her pursuer would not dare to accost her there.

Feeling her horse begin to tire, Katherina patted his neck and whispered, "Just a bit more. Please. Come on. You can make it. Just a bit more." Then the straining horse stumbled on a rock, lurching forward and almost throwing Katherina over his head. As Katherina steadied herself in the saddle and the horse struggled to regain his footing, their pursuer rode up beside them. Before Katherina had time to urge her horse forward, the other rider reached over and grabbed the bridle. Katherina screamed as the rider caught her and steadied her on the horse.

"My God, Katya," the rider panted, "what are you doing out here? Trying to get yourself killed?"

Hearing Aleksandr's voice, she collapsed against her horse's neck. "Sasha, what are *you* doing here?"

"Coming to visit you—and the count—but I hardly expected to find you out here alone in the darkness. Don't you realize how dangerous this is? Come on, let me take you home. Your husband must be worried to distraction."

"I'm not going home," she whispered.

Aleksandr peered at her in the darkness. "Why? Has Count Ostrov mistreated you?"

She shook her head. "No, nothing like that."

"Then what?"

"I—I just can't bear to live this way any longer. I can't be without you. I was coming to tell you. We must go away together, now."

"Katya, I still don't understand. Why did you have to come in the darkness? Couldn't you have waited to discuss this with me tomorrow? Why did you take the risk?"

"I thought there might not be a tomorrow," she whispered slowly.

"Why?" Aleksandr Sergeievich looked at her closely, wondering how she could know.

Sensing his suspicions, Katherina spoke carefully. "I don't know why. I just had this feeling. And I had to talk to you. I've been waiting all week, and I couldn't wait any longer." She paused, then blurted, "Sasha, I'm going to have a baby!"

He stared at her for a moment, dismounted, and lifted her from the saddle. Cradling her body against his, he whispered, "You're sure?"

She nodded, and she felt his chest rise and fall in a long sigh. "I waited this long to tell you because I wanted to be sure. But—you're not happy about it, Sasha?"

"I don't know," he admitted. "A baby is a wonderful thing. A miracle. But it complicates our situation so much."

"No it doesn't, Sasha. It just means that you and I must go away together now—as we had planned before Pavel Pavlovich returned. He is almost better now. It won't be as great a blow to him as it would have been before."

Aleksandr steered her to a large boulder, sat down, and pulled her into his lap. "Katya, I was riding to your house tonight to pay my respects to the count and to tell him that I am being sent tomorrow to join General Paskevich's forces at Tiflis. But most of all, I had hoped that you and I would be able to talk privately. I meant to ask you to leave with me tonight. If you were willing to risk the dangers, I would desert the army and we would flee together to the Crimea and then to Austria."

"Sasha, the answer is yes," she breathed. "Let's be on our way now. By morning we can be a great distance from the fort."

He shook his head. "Not far enough, I'm afraid. Even if we rode to exhaustion, it would be days before we reached the straits connecting the Black Sea and the Sea of Azov. And we would be pursued the whole time. My absence would be noticed at the first light of dawn."

"But surely we can hide out in the mountains. How could they guess where to look for us?"

"It's too great a risk. If the army did not find us, the Circassians or the Abazans would."

"But only a moment ago you said you wanted to flee with me."

"That was before I knew you were carrying a child. It would be foolhardy to go now. The way is too treacherous. The trip would surely endanger your health—and the child's."

"So what will you do?" Katherina asked. "Leave me here to bear our child alone while you go off to war?"

Aleksandr responded gently, "Do you want to risk losing the child?"

"I don't want to lose you!" She pressed her face against his shoulder, her tears flowing freely.

For a long time they sat silently, until Katherina became aware of Aleksandr's tears. When she lifted her head and looked at his face, she could see the tension contorting it as he struggled to form a question.

"Katya—is there any chance the count might be the father?"

"No—I'm sure the child is yours." For an instant a horrifying thought flashed through her mind. Could the child be Fyodor Bugov's? She shuddered and looked away, hoping Aleksandr would not see the frightened expression on her face.

"Katya," he pressed, "you must think. Is there any chance at all?"

She was silent a moment, not wanting to answer.

Then she mumbled, "He is still my husband, Sasha. I could hardly refuse to fulfill my marital obligations."

As he expelled a long sigh, she added, "Please don't blame me, Sasha. I did not want to be untrue to you, but I had no choice. What could I do?"

He stroked her hair. "I don't blame you, Katya. In fact, I am relieved. It simplifies matters. You must tell the count about your condition—tonight if possible."

"That's quite out of the question. He'll want to take me back to St. Petersburg."

"Exactly."

"But if I wait to tell him, if I hold off for at least a few months, it will be too late for me to make the journey."

"Which is precisely why you must tell him immediately."

"Sasha, I don't understand. If you won't take me away with you, at least I want to stay near you. You sound as if you don't even want me here."

"I don't." He felt her start to stand up, and he held her back. "Katya, listen to me. I want you to be safe and to bear the child in safety. That is most important right now."

"You are not making sense. Don't you think women in Pyatigorsk bear children in safety?" Katherina was becoming indignant. "Even the barbarian Circassians manage to give birth without going to St. Petersburg to do so! I have been safe in Pyatigorsk for more than half a year. No doubt I can survive a bit longer."

He shook her roughly by the shoulders to quiet her. "For God's sake, listen to me, Katya. If you won't think of yourself, think of the child. If it is mine, I want it born far from the dangers of any battlefield."

"But we are far from the fighting."

"We are—now—but I am afraid to guess how long it will last. Even if Paskevich succeeds in routing the Persians, there will still be the Turks to contend with. The talk at the fort is that hostilities may break out at any time." He took a deep breath. "If that is not enough to convince you, consider this: There are rumors of a cholera outbreak in some districts of the Caucasus. It could easily spread to Pyatigorsk."

"That's a foolish thing to worry about. I've heard the health officials themselves say the disease is not contagious."

"Then why does it spread so rapidly?"

Katherina had no answer. She knew Aleksandr Sergeievich was right, but she could not bring herself to admit it. She was sure that if they parted again there would be no more reunions. "If I go to St. Petersburg," she said slowly, "what will happen to you?"

"I will go to Transcaucasia as I have been ordered. Then, in less than a year and a half I will be free to join you—and our child—in St. Petersburg."

"But you could be killed in Transcaucasia."

"I won't be killed," Aleksandr said. "You've heard too many war stories—too many stories about the hundreds who die. Have you forgotten about the hundreds more who survive? I intend to be a survivor."

"I don't know," she mumbled. "How can you be so practical and so optimistic. You act as if it doesn't pain you at all to send me away."

"Is that what you think, Katya?" He brought his face close to hers, and her heart almost burst when she saw the tears glistening in his eyes.

"I'm sorry, Sasha," she whispered. "It was cruel of me to say that."

He kissed her gently. "I understand. But you must

promise to tell the count you are expecting a child. Do it for me, Katya. I know he will take good care of you and will always be kind to you. And if I know that you are safe in St. Petersburg I will be able to concentrate all my strength on keeping myself safe so I can return to you."

"All right, Sasha, I promise." Katherina forced herself to smile at him.

"Good." He carried her to her horse. "Now I think I should take you home before Count Ostrov sends the whole city of Pyatigorsk in search of you."

Despite the hour, Katherina and Aleksandr could not resist stopping for one last farewell in their little cottage, where they lingered longer than they should have. Riding up the hill to the Ostrov house, they could see that the courtyard was ablaze with lanterns. As they came through the gate, they found the count struggling with his crutches as he attempted to mount General Bugov's chestnut mare.

"Katherina Andreievna!" he cried. "Thank goodness you are home!" Then his initial relief gave way to irritation, and he barked, "Do you realize it is almost ten o'clock? The servants retired hours ago—while I sat waiting and imagining all sorts of things that might have happened to you. I was about to go and rouse your friend Princess Golovine—wherever she is —to ask where you might be. And now you come riding in, gay as you please, with Belikov of all people. Perhaps I should treat you as the peasant men treat their wives—give you a good beating now and then. Would that help you to remember to come home at a decent hour?"

The count's words shocked Katherina. Aside from a few stern admonitions about not traveling alone in

St. Petersburg, he had never spoken to her with anything but kindness, particularly when others were present. She shifted uneasily in the saddle. "Pavel Pavlovich, please—you're embarrassing me!"

"Do you think I wasn't embarrassed when the servants asked where you were and I couldn't say?" he roared. "Do you think I wasn't in pain, sitting alone all evening wondering what had become of you? Where *have* you been, my dear wife? Why do you arrive now, with this young man?"

Aleksandr broke in. "I was on my way to pay my respects to you and your wife, sir, when I met the countess near the foothills. I simply accompanied her home."

"And what was she doing at night in the foothills?" The count eyed Katherina suspiciously.

"Perhaps I should explain in the house, where you can sit down, Pavel Pavlovich." Katherina hoped the count would be more understanding when he was sitting comfortably, so that neither of his wounds were bothering him.

"Very well. This should be quite an interesting story." The count started toward the house.

Dismounting, Aleksandr helped Katherina from her mount and whispered, "I'll unsaddle your horse and bed him down. That will give you a chance to talk privately." When Katherina looked at him fearfully, he added, "Don't worry, I'll be right here at the stable. If he begins to abuse you in any way, just scream for me, but I think his attitude will change when he hears your news."

Katherina followed Pavel Pavlovich to the house and stood in the doorway as he settled himself into a chair.

"Well, my dear Katherina Andreievna," he said,

"perhaps you should begin by telling me why you rode off on my horse—and precisely where you were going."

"Yes," she said meekly, shuffling into the parlor and sitting down in a chair opposite him. "I'm sorry if I worried you, Pavel Pavlovich. I hope—"

"Never mind the apologies," he waved her words away. "Just begin with the explanations."

"All right. There was something about my conversation with the princess today that left me rather disturbed."

"Disturbed?" The count raised his eyebrows.

"Well, perhaps *confused* would be a better word. I found there was something I had to tell you, and I was not sure of how to approach the subject. I was not sure what your reaction might be. I thought if I went out to the mountains to think about it I would be able to get things clear in my mind. I'm afraid I rode much farther than I should have and as it got dark I completely lost my way. Fortunately for me—"

"Please get to the point, Katherina," Pavel Pavlovich interrupted. "What is it you learned from Princess Golovine that you found so disturbing?"

"It was something I had suspected for some weeks, but I felt I needed the counsel of an experienced woman to confirm my suspicions." She stopped, aware that the count was studying her closely. Finally, she forced out the words. "I am going to have a baby."

The count struggled to his feet and clomped toward her on his crutches, his eyes alight with joy and awe. "But that is wonderful news, my darling. To think that at my age I am to become a father. I must admit that I had despaired of ever having children of my own. Won't Pyotr Dmitrievich be surprised. Come—kiss me, my dear." He bent toward her and she rose to accept his gentle kiss.

"But my dear Katherina Andreievna, I cannot understand why you were so hesitant to share your news with me."

"I—I don't know," she faltered. "I assumed you would want to take me back to St. Petersburg, and I was not sure it would be an easy trip for you in your condition."

"Don't be foolish. I am almost completely mended. A trip by carriage will most certainly be no strain for me."

"I also feared that after all these years you might not welcome the change of a child coming into the house. A baby can throw a household into quite an uproar, you know."

"I'm sure we will manage nicely." The count smiled. "I shall engage the finest nurse in St. Petersburg for the child. As for the change, do you think I would have married you after all my years of living alone if I could not accept change?"

Katherina laughed nervously. "I suppose not. I'm afraid my willfulness has demanded quite an adjustment on your part—I hope life with me has not been too hard on you."

"Well, there have been a few trying moments," the count chuckled. "Can you excuse the way I jumped on you, my dear? You must understand that I was frantic with worry, my foot had been hurting me all evening, and I had to sit here feeling totally useless and unable even to go out looking for you."

"I'm afraid I am the one who must apologize, Pavel Pavlovich. I was so engrossed in my own worries that I neglected to think of you."

The count struggled back to his chair. "You are forgiven, Katherina. I have always heard that women experience all sorts of confusing and conflicting feelings when they are carrying a child. Now that I know your condition, I will make every effort to be more patient."

A light tapping at the door interrupted their conversation, and Katherina sprang from her chair. "Oh, my goodness, I completely forgot about Sas——" She stopped herself. "—Monsieur Belikov." She rushed to the door to let him in. The smiles on her face and the count's told Aleksandr Sergeievich the crisis was over.

"Well, my dear boy, what brings you to Pyatigorsk this evening?" the count asked in his usual jovial tone.

"I came to bid farewell to you and the countess. I leave tomorrow to join General Paskevich. I must apologize for the late hour, but I did not receive my orders until evening, and I couldn't think of leaving without thanking you again for all the kindness you have shown me."

"No need to apologize. If you had left the fort earlier, perhaps you would not have found the countess. I can't thank you enough for seeing her safely home."

The count waved Aleksandr into a chair. "So you are off to join Paskevich, eh? I'm sure you will find him an excellent leader. No doubt you are aware that at my urging Czar Nikolai has placed him in command of the Transcaucasian forces."

"Yes, sir, and I would be happy to carry your greetings to the general."

"Please do. And you might also give him another message. Tell him I am soon to become a father!" The count's eyes twinkled.

"No!" Aleksandr cried in perfectly feigned surprise. "What a marvelous announcement! I must congratulate you both."

Katherina blushed, and Pavel Pavlovich beamed.

"Yes, the countess has just given me the news, and

no one could be more pleased or more surprised
than I. I suspect that the coming months will fly for
both of us. Of course we will be departing for St.
Petersburg as soon as possible. I want the countess
to have the very best care when her time of confinement arrives."

"I'm sure that is a wise plan. By the way, Count
Ostrov, I am pleased to see that you are up and
around. You must be feeling much better."

"Yes, thank you, Belikov. My only regret is that
this foot and these crutches make it all but impossible
for me to get into the town, and I'm going to have to
find a carriage and coachmen to take us back to St.
Petersburg. It's a pity that you won't be available to
help us. Katherina Andreievna is quite capable, but I
feel it would be unfair to send her to do a man's
work."

"Nonsense, Pavel Pavlovich," Katherina said quietly. "I don't mind at all. I'm sure we will not have
any problems."

"Well, perhaps I can help after all," Aleksandr offered. "If I mention your situation to General Bugov,
I am sure he will send someone to help. Perhaps
even a military escort to accompany you at the outset
of your journey."

Katherina blanched at the mention of Bugov's
name, and both men eyed her with curious alarm.

"My dear, are you feeling all right?" Pavel Pavlovich asked.

"Yes." She smiled weakly. "I'm afraid I've just discovered how hungry I am. You know, I had forgotten that I missed supper tonight."

"Then you must have something. It's very important that a woman in your condition eat properly.
Shall I call Tamara?"

"No, please don't bother her. I'll go to the kitchen myself and see what I can find. Can I bring you something, Pavel Pavlovich?"

"Nothing, thank you. But perhaps Aleksandr Sergeievich is hungry after his long ride from the fort."

"No, thank you," Aleksandr rose and started toward the door. "I really should be returning there now."

"Won't you stay the night?" the count asked. "The guest room has been empty since you left."

Katherina's eyes rushed to look at Aleksandr. Please say yes, they pleaded, one last night would be heaven, and I could fly to you the moment Pavel Pavlovich fell asleep.

With an effort, Aleksandr Sergeievich tore his eyes away from hers. "Your generosity is most touching, Count Ostrov, but I'm afraid it is impossible for me to stay the night. My detachment leaves tomorrow at dawn, so I must say farewell and wish you a safe journey to St. Petersburg—and a healthy child."

Katherina's heart sank, but she struggled to conceal her feelings. "There is no need for you to get up, Pavel Pavlovich," she said. "I'll see Monsieur Belikov to the door."

As they slipped through the door, Aleksandr whispered, "I told you he would be overjoyed with the news."

"But Sasha," she whispered, "I don't know how much longer I can keep up this deception. He thinks the child is his."

"Perhaps it is. At any rate, he must go on believing that."

"But I feel so guilty."

"Then think of the child. I don't plan to get killed, but if anything does happen to me the child will still have an excellent father who will take good care of you both."

"Oh, Sasha, I hope we are doing the right thing." She clung to him, not wanting to let him go.

"It is the only rational thing to do," he said. "I will write to you at every opportunity, and you will be so busy with the child that the year and a half I still have to serve will be over in no time."

He kissed her and the fires of passion begin to burn in her lips. His own body trembled with overwhelming desire to make her his again, but he tenderly untwined her arms from his neck, kissing her fingertips before softly dropping them and turning to mount his black stallion.

Long after he rode through the gate and down the hill, Katherina stood in the darkened courtyard, blinking back tears that seemed to come from her very soul.

Chapter 20

At midmorning, Pavel Pavlovich and Katherina Andreievna were still in their room. Katherina had awakened long before dawn, but, remembering that Aleksandr Sergeievich was on his way south, she had seen no reason to get out of bed. The months ahead would be unbearably dreary without even their Wednesday meetings to revive her. Of course she could look forward to his letters, but the mail between Tiflis and St. Petersburg would be excruciatingly slow, so it might be months before she received his first message. At least she would be able to blame it on her condition if she closed herself in her room and lay in bed for long listless hours.

When Pavel Pavlovich awoke, he had insisted that Tamara serve them a leisurely breakfast in bed. "We must pamper our mother-to-be," he had said, smiling happily.

So now, though it was nearly eleven o'clock, Katherina had just finished dressing and was sitting impatiently as Masha arranged her hair.

Just as Masha placed the last hairpin, they were startled by a loud knocking at the front door. Katherina, who had been daydreaming about Aleksandr Sergeievich, jumped up so suddenly that the hairpin jammed into her scalp. To Masha's surprise, she scarcely flinched. She was much too engrossed in her own wild hopes. Perhaps Aleksandr Sergeievich had changed his mind after all; perhaps he was standing at the door, waiting to carry her off to a new life.

"I'll get the door," Katherina called over her shoulder as she rushed out of the room.

She was trembling so with anticipation that she could scarcely open the latch, but when she at last managed to throw open the door, ready to leap into Aleksandr's arms, her eyes refused to focus on the person standing before her. She felt her knees buckle, and rough, ugly hands reached out to keep her from falling. The hands pinched playfully at her waist as General Fyodor Bugov entered the house.

"Surprised?" His smug voice penetrated Katherina's shocked silence.

Regaining her balance, she wrenched her hands away and whirled from him in disgust. "What do you want here?" she whispered hoarsely.

"My dear Countess Ostrova," he said in a mocking tone, "I'm afraid you have the situation rather twisted about. I don't want anything here. It was my understanding that you, or at least the good count, requested my presence."

"I'm sure I don't know what you are talking about."

"Your friend Belikov informed me that you would need someone to help you prepare for a journey, so I have come to offer my services."

"I'm afraid Aleksandr Belikov was mistaken. We don't require your help, General Bugov."

"General Bugov? Your formality stings me, my dear Rina. Why not call me Fyodor Petrovich, as you did in our more intimate moments?"

"Why don't you simply leave my house?"

"Because I would feel lacking in gallantry if I did not offer my aid to a woman in your condition."

Katherina turned and eyed him angrily.

"Oh yes, sweet Rina, Belikov told me that, too. As a way of explaining why you are returning to St. Petersburg and why you need assistance in making arrangements. He seemed to think that both you and the count are in far too delicate conditions to manage by yourselves. Actually, it was quite touching the way he pleaded your case." The general chuckled heartily and slapped his knee.

"You could have sent someone else. It was quite unnecessary for you to tear yourself away from your spirited Circassian maid."

"Oh, but it was! I had to be among the first to offer my congratulations. Or should I say condolences? You know it is hardly customary for a whore to become pregnant. It can put such a disturbing damper on your activities. Whatever will you do with all the passion that is locked up inside that marvelous little body of yours?" He leered at her and his eyes seemed to strip away her pieces of clothing, one by one, until she stood naked before him. Then he shrugged. "Well, I suppose I need not worry about you. No doubt you can find at least a few men in St. Petersburg who are perverse enough to take a woman even when her body is grossly distorted by a pregnancy."

Katherina put her hands over her ears. "Get out of my house! I won't listen to any more of your insults."

The general raised his eyebrows in warning. "Very well, then I won't force you to listen, but perhaps your husband would like to listen to me. Perhaps he would be interested in learning how you spent your Tuesdays and Wednesdays these many months."

"You wouldn't," she whispered hollowly.

"Well, you may do and think whatever you wish. Just remember that I shall also do as I choose."

Katherina turned away from him and saw Pavel Pavlovich hobbling through the bedroom door.

"Who is it, my dear?" he asked; then he added before she could answer, "You're quite pale, Katherina Andreievna."

"I was just telling the countess the same thing," General Bugov said as he stepped into the count's view. "Perhaps I can help her to a chair. A woman in her condition should be very careful not to overtax herself."

Katherina allowed him to take her arm and guide her to a chair. When she was seated, Bugov turned to embrace the count. "Well, my dear Count Ostrov, I must congratulate you on your good news! Belikov informed me this morning, and I must say I am overwhelmed with happiness for you. Imagine becoming a father at your age!"

"Thank you, my dear general. I still cannot believe my good fortune. But you did not ride all the way from the fort merely to congratulate us."

"No, as a matter of fact I came to offer my services. Belikov told me you need someone to engage a carriage and coachmen to transport you to St. Petersburg."

"Actually, just to Moscow. We left our own carriage there at the house of my friend, Prince Dolgochev—so we can continue the journey ourselves from that point. You see, we traveled from Moscow in Czar Nikolai's own carriage, but I sent it back immediately after we arrived. I felt it would be a great imposition to keep it when we were unsure of how long we would be staying in Pyatigorsk."

"I am sure the Czar appreciates your consideration. I will be happy to do whatever I can to help you arrange for your journey."

"You are most kind, Bugov. Were it not for my foot injury I would do everything myself."

"Think nothing of it. It is a great honor and pleasure to assist you and your lovely wife."

The count smiled broadly. "Good. Let us have a glass of cognac to celebrate our good fortune."

In the next week, General Bugov came to the Ostrov household every day. He made a habit of sharing the noon and evening meals with the count and Katherina, and Katherina made a habit of retiring to her room immediately after the meals. Assuming a woman in her condition required a great deal of rest, Pavel Pavlovich saw nothing strange in her behavior. In fact, he watched her so closely and insisted that she rest so often that Katherina became irritated by his concern. She hoped that when they arrived in St. Petersburg his injuries would be healed, and he could resume a full schedule of activities at the Council of State. At least then she could suffer in privacy.

As their day of departure grew nearer, Katherina wished desperately to return to the little whitewashed house to get the balalaika Aleksandr Sergeievich had given her. Aside from the military button he had presented her with on their first Christmas Eve, the balalaika was the only gift she had ever received from him, and if she left it behind it would be claimed by the merchant from Kiev when he came to occupy the house in the summer. But Pavel Pavlovich watched her so closely that it was impossible to slip away, and even if she did manage to get to the cottage, she would have trouble explaining her bulky bundle when she returned.

On their last day in Pyatigorsk, in a rare moment of privacy, Katherina summoned Masha and explained about the cottage and the Wednesday rendezvous. Masha had begun to consider the situation highly romantic, and she readily agreed to go to the house and retrieve the balalaika. Katherina almost wept, knowing that her most prized possession would not be left behind.

While Masha went to get the balalaika, Katherina sat sorting the few belongings she had in her desk. In the bottom drawer, she found the letter she had written to Pavel Pavlovich the day before the planned departure with Aleksandr Sergeievich. All these months she had kept it hidden, hoping there would come a time when she could use it. Now, staring at the letter and thinking of the way fate had changed their plans, Katherina's eyes clouded, and a tear fell on the envelope, blurring her writing. As she gazed at the letter, wondering how to dispose of it, Masha entered the room, bubbling with enthusiasm.

"Madame—it is the most beautiful instrument I have ever seen."

"I know, Masha. Only Sasha could find something so exquisitely fashioned." Katherina took the instrument from her servant and held it tenderly.

The appearance of her beautiful, beloved gift buoyed up Katherina's spirits, and she absent-mindedly dropped the letter into her lap as she lovingly ran her hands over the polished wood.

"Can you play it, madame?" Masha asked.

"I've learned some. Songs I remembered from old Natasha."

"I would so love to hear you play."

"And I would love to play again." Katherina began to pluck a string, then stopped and asked, "Where is the count?"

"Still in the dining room with General Bugov, enjoying their after-dinner brandy."

Katherina nodded. "Good. Come with me to the garden and I will play a bit." As she stood up, the letter in her lap fell to the floor.

The apple trees were beginning to bud, and the garden smelled with all the sweet freshness of spring. Katherina seated herself on a boulder near her favorite apple tree, and Masha sat on the ground beside her. At first Katherina felt uneasy, but soon the songs flowed out of her as freely as if she were singing and playing for Aleksandr Sergeievich. In fact, she imagined him sitting beside her, sharing spring in the garden as they had shared the autumn. Now she fully realized what a perfect gift the balalaika had been. With its mellow tones recreating her most precious moments with Aleksandr Sergeievich, she could never feel too far from him.

Katherina played and sang for more than an hour, not feeling at all tired, and becoming oblivious to everything around her. She did not hear the crunch of boots on the gravel paths, and her husband's voice startled her as she began another chorus of "Daleko, Daleko."

"Katherina Andreievna, I had not realized what a musical artist you are."

She stopped singing, almost dropping the balalaika in her confusion.

"Ah—but I'm sure your lovely wife possesses many talents of which you are not aware," General Bugov said, smiling.

When Katherina glared at him, and the count eyed him curiously, Bugov hastily added, "I only meant that you have been married a relatively short period of time. It takes many years to unfold the charms and abilities of a woman as exquisite as the countess."

The count smiled with pleasure. "Ah, yes—and how lovely to know that my discoveries have just begun. I have so much to look forward to. I hope I will be treated to your singing often in the future, my dear. But it's strange, I don't remember seeing that balalaika before. It is such a perfectly crafted instrument that I doubt if I would have forgotten it."

"Oh, no. It was a gift," Katherina said before she realized what she was saying.

"A gift? From whom?"

"A gift to Masha from one of her admirers in the army," Katherina said, quickly recovering. "We played it often to pass the time while you were away. Since you returned from Transcaucasia, I have been too busy to play."

Masha blushed at being drawn into the deception.

"Oh," the count said simply. "How kind of you to let the countess play your instrument, Masha. It appears to be a very special gift."

"It's really my pleasure, sir," Masha said meekly. "Madame sings and plays so much better than I."

"Your admirer must be quite rich to afford such an expensive gift, and his feelings for you must be profound," Bugov cut in. "Tell me, child, is he stationed at my fort?"

Katherina quickly interceded. "I hardly think it is appropriate for you to question Masha about her personal affairs, general."

"Quite so," the count nodded, and for once General Bugov looked embarrassed.

Katherina returned to her room feeling so triumphant that she did not even notice that her letter to Pavel Pavlovich was missing.

In order to see them off, and to close up the house after they left, Bugov spent the night in the guest room. Katherina tossed uneasily all night, afraid that at any moment he might creep through the door and demand that she give herself to him one last horrible time. She knew he had not forgiven her for turning the tables on him out in the garden, and he would love to make her pay for embarrassing him. When he said good-night, she read the unmistakable lust in his eyes and shuddered at the memory of the ways he found to appease his passions. But the night went by without intrusion. Perhaps he thought it was sweeter torment to leave her wondering.

When the first rays of dawn crept into the bedroom, Katherina rose and dressed quickly. She wanted to say good-bye to all her special places in the garden before anyone else was up to disturb her.

As she stepped into the courtyard, she thought of how easy it would be to slip away. She could take any one of the horses and ride to the mountains. If she followed the range southeast she would reach the Terek River, which would lead her south to the Daryal Pass through the Caucasus Range. Then, if she continued south along the Kura River, she would eventually reach Tiflis—and perhaps be near to Aleksandr Sergeievich. She had studied the map so many times that she felt she knew the region by heart. The trip would actually be easy, she told herself, and without further consideration, she walked away from the garden and into the stable.

She stood there staring at the horses, trying to decide which would serve her best. Pavel Pavlovich's brown stallion had served her well last week, but the gray horse that General Bugov had ridden from the fort yesterday was probably more accustomed to long, hard rides. She patted the gray horse nervously, but the horse seemed quite docile, and she saddled and bridled it without problems. As she began to adjust the stirrups, a pair of hands grasped her around her waist.

"What are you doing, my dear little Rina?" Bugov's

voice rasped. "It's most kind of you to saddle my horse, but I don't plan to leave for at least a few hours. And I'm afraid you've made the stirrups far too short."

He turned her roughly by the shoulders, clamping one hand firmly over her mouth so she could not cry out. "You conniving little slut. So—you thought you'd steal my horse and make off to your lover, eh? Did you really think you could get through the mountains? And what if you did? Can't you imagine the welcome you'd get as you rode into a military encampment? You'd be raped by every soldier who could get his hands on you. Of course," he said, smiling wickedly, "you might enjoy the experience."

"It would be better than being raped by you," she spat as he took his hand away from her mouth.

"Do you really think so? May I remind you, my dear, that you have never been raped by me? It seems to me that you always submitted willingly. How many times did I find you at your little whorehouse, anxiously awaiting my arrival? But perhaps you would like a taste of rape—something to add to your collection of interesting sexual experiences."

In one horrified instant, Katherina envisioned what he had in mind. She threw back her head to scream, but the sounds stuck in her throat.

"Come, come, my dear. I had expected you to be a bit more vocal in your protests." He covered her mouth before she could recover her voice, and he swung her around, forcing her to walk ahead of him out of the stable and into the garden. All the while he kept her arm twisted behind her back—where he could exert pressure if she attempted to struggle.

She stumbled before him down the gravel paths, wishing they would meet Masha, Lizaveta, anyone— even a robber who might startle him into letting her go. As they moved near to the sundial, he tightened his grip on her mouth, dropping her arm for a moment while he fumbled in his breast pocket. Then, as she tried to beat her fist backward against his chest, he stuffed a silk kerchief into her mouth and tied it securely at the back of her neck.

Throwing her roughly to the ground, he jumped astride her and pulled up her dress and petticoats. With a small dagger he took from his belt, he swiftly sliced away her remaining undergarments while she whimpered helplessly into the kerchief. Katherina tried to wriggle away, but the general kept her pinioned between his knees until the first violent thrust, when he dropped his whole body heavily onto hers. He grunted out his pleasure as he thrashed on top of her, bruising her with his military medals and decorations. Katherina squeezed her eyes shut and clamped down her jaw, praying for a swift end to the experience. Why did this beast of a man have to defile all the places she had shared with Aleksandr Sergeievich? Would he still find time to take her in her own bed while Pavel Pavlovich was in another room?

It was over within minutes, but Bugov lay atop her, sweating and panting and gloating over his conquest. As he sat up, he picked up her ragged linen and waved it in her face before stuffing it into his pocket. "An appropriate souvenir of the occasion, don't you think?" He chuckled. "I shall look at them often to evoke fond memories of this moment."

Still astride her, he got to his feet and stood leering down at her. "Now, my dear," he said deliberately, "you may consider yourself raped. I hope that you now have a better understanding of the word." His toe delivered a slight kick to her ribs as he began to walk away. "You may keep the kerchief, to remind you of this little lesson."

Katherina struggled to untie the kerchief, but her fingers trembled so violently that it took her several minutes to loosen the knot. When she finally managed to withdraw the gag, it was just in time for her to vomit next to the path. Her stomach was almost empty, for she had not eaten since the previous night, but she could not stop the sickening reflexive action. When her stomach muscles were exhausted, Katherina struggled to her feet and forced herself to walk up and down the garden paths until she lost her nausea. Rage and humiliation churning within her, she passed by all the places that held special memories of Aleksandr Sergeievich—without even stopping to notice them.

An hour passed before she could compose herself enough to return to the house. By that time everyone in the household would be up, preparing for the trip, so it would be futile to try to escape. When she opened the door, the clink of china and the sound of voices told her that Pavel Pavlovich and Fyodor Bugov were sharing breakfast. Would her dear husband laugh so if he knew what the general had just done? Katherina brushed the thought from her mind. It was silly to speculate when she knew she could never tell the count. The best thing she could do was to go to breakfast.

"Ah, Katherina Andreievna," the count greeted her, "I was about to send Masha to find you. You'd best eat heartily in preparation for our journey."

For Bugov's benefit, she bent to kiss her husband's cheek with more affection than usual. "I went to say good-bye to the garden. I think it is the one thing in Pyatigorsk I shall miss the most."

"No doubt it holds all kinds of precious memories," Bugov smirked.

Katherina ignored his remark as she sat down and began spooning kasha into her mouth. For the rest of the meal she said very little, speaking only when her husband directed a question to her.

The carriage and coachmen Bugov had engaged for them arrived at half-past eight. Another wagon followed and was loaded with their belongings, except for the balalaika, which Katherina insisted they take with them in the carriage to be sure it would not be broken. When all the preparations were completed, Bugov, with exaggerated graciousness, helped Pavel Pavlovich, Masha, and Katherina Andreievna into the carriage. As he swung her into the seat, he grasped Katherina's waist more intimately than necessary, sliding one hand upward to brush her breast.

Shoving the matted silk kerchief into her hand, he whispered, "I believe you forgot something," and when she thought he would finally be gone, he stopped to add, "do write and tell me if the child resembles me."

Chapter 21

Returning to Moscow, they followed the same route as they traveled when they had first come to Pyatigorsk, and within ten days Katherina became bored with the rolling wheat fields, the peasants in their gray caftans, and the red vests of the Don cossacks. At least the Circassians and the other mountain tribes dressed more flamboyantly, she thought. Pavel Pavlovich insisted that they travel slowly, stopping long before dusk each afternoon so that Katherina would be sure to get enough rest. She suspected that he was just as bored and tired as she and that he, too, welcomed the chance to descend from the cramped carriage each day. Watching the endless steppes roll by the carriage window, Katherina wondered why she had ever dreamed of traveling. She would gladly trade her title, her fortune, and all her traveling experiences for the chance to spend the rest of her life with Aleksandr Sergeievich on some small secluded plot of land.

They generally stayed in small towns that offered rude inns with small, bare rooms. Although they shared a bed, Pavel Pavlovich, in consideration of his wife's condition, never asked her to make love and for that, at least, Katherina was thankful. The cooks at the inns appeared never to have heard of French cooking and served only the simplest peasant fare. Katherina relished the borsch, cabbage soup, and fresh vegetables, but she found the heavy portions of lamb, pork, and fried potatoes totally indigestible.

She wondered whether her condition made the food seem even worse than on the original journey, or whether her emotional state was to blame. Some nights she felt that even Tamara's spicy food and yogurt would have been preferable.

Katherina often found herself musing about where she would be if she had succeeded in stealing Bugov's horse. In her more romantic moments, she imagined herself crossing the mountains in less than a day—to find Aleksandr Sergeievich waiting at the other side in a whitewashed cottage. But when she was more rational she admitted to herself that Bugov had painted a far more likely picture. She thought of her first visit to the fort, when only Aleksandr's presence kept the lusting soldiers from plucking her from the horse, and she knew it would be almost impossible to reach Aleksandr untainted. And how would he receive her if their child turned out to be harmed by her impulsive journey? He had wanted her to stay with Pavel Pavlovich for their own good, and she owed it to him to respect and uphold his wishes.

However, understanding the reason for their separation did not make it any easier to bear. Though she tried not to show it, Katherina was moody and easily irritated. Attributing her brooding to her pregnancy, her husband was particularly patient with her, and that made Katherina even more irritable. The only time she relaxed and forgot her problems was when she played the balalaika. For an hour or more each afternoon, she played and sang, bringing cheer to herself, Pavel Pavlovich, and Masha. At times, even the coachmen joined in the songs that transformed the dreary little carriage into a warm, gay traveling home. But her depression seemed deeper each time Katherina emerged from her music to realize that with each turn of the carriage wheels she was traveling farther from Aleksandr Sergeievich. Then, even with Pavel Pavlovich dozing beside her and Masha sitting opposite her, Katherina felt completely alone.

On the twenty-fifth day out of Pyatigorsk, the dusty, bumpy road suddenly became smoother, and Katherina knew they must be approaching Tula. In less than three days they would arrive in Moscow, and from that point their journey would be easier. How often had she heard Pavel Pavlovich declare that the road from Moscow to St. Petersburg was the finest causeway in all of Europe?

By midafternoon on the twenty-eighth day, Katherina sighted the gilded domes of the Novodevichy Monastery. Remembering her joy the last time she was there, she felt her eyes fill, and she quickly averted them, but Pavel Pavlovich had already noted her reaction.

He placed an arm around her and whispered in her ear, "Does returning to Moscow make you so unhappy, my dear?"

"No, of course not," she sniffled.

"Then perhaps those are tears of joy I see." He touched her cheek. "It is good to be back in a familiar city, isn't it? I could almost weep for joy myself."

"Yes," Katherina said.

"If it suits my friend Prince Dolgochev, perhaps we will stay a few days in the city. It will give us all a chance to rest, and perhaps we can explore more of the city together. You remember that I promised to bring you back when our last visit was cut short."

Katherina cringed.

"You look somewhat dismayed, Katherina Andreievna. Are my plans not agreeable to you?"

"You mustn't think that. I was just remembering how horribly I acted when we left Moscow. I'm afraid I made you feel guilty for taking me away when

I should have felt guilty for questioning the Czar's plans. Please don't extend our stay here on my account. Perhaps it would be better to continue on to St. Petersburg to prepare for our child's arrival."

"Nonsense, my dear. You will be confined to the house quite long enough in the weeks before the birth. You should enjoy yourself a bit before that."

"Whatever you say," Katherina said.

"No doubt the prince has at least a few doctor friends. I believe he even introduced us to a Dr. Ponumago at a ball last summer. To put your mind at rest, we'll ask the good doctor to examine you—although I'm quite sure both you and the child are in excellent health."

Prince Dolgochev welcomed them warmly, and he was delighted when Pavel Pavlovich announced the impending birth. As he led them to a suite of rooms, the prince mentioned that his nephew from St. Petersburg—Boris Ivanovich—was also staying at the mansion. However, the Ostrovs could expect to see very little of the young man since he spent most of his time dashing from one social engagement to another. Not finding the nephew's name familiar, Katherina pushed it to the back of her mind and soon forgot it.

They stayed in Moscow for two weeks, and Katherina enjoyed the luxury of lying in bed till midmorning, taking her breakfast—and sometimes even her midday meal—in bed, knowing that she would not be subjected to a day of listening to the creak of carriage wheels. Doctor Ponumago examined her and, as Pavel Pavlovich had predicted, pronounced her in perfect health.

The doctor also examined the count and announced that his wounds had healed nicely. Within a week, the count abandoned his crutches and began to rely only on a polished birch cane. He even managed to dance a few steps with Katherina at the parties and balls they attended almost nightly.

The night before they were to depart for St. Petersburg, Prince Dolgochev insisted on hosting a ball in their honor. As they mounted the marble steps to the prince's ballroom, Katherina caught sight of his nephew for the first time. There was something familiar about Boris Ivanovich Dolgochev, but Katherina pushed aside the feeling of foreboding that swept over her when she saw him. No doubt she had simply recognized him from one of the dozens of balls she had attended in St. Petersburg. When Prince Dolgochev presented his nephew to the Ostrovs, Katherina offered him her hand to kiss, and when he drifted back into the crowd, she turned away and lost herself among the other guests.

Not until hours later, when Boris Ivanovich asked her to dance, did Katherina again begin to wonder where she had met him. His blond hair, blue eyes, and thin lips seemed hauntingly familiar.

As they moved to the music, Boris tightened his hand against her spine and inclined his head to whisper in her ear. "I've been wondering ever since uncle introduced us this evening—is your lover in Siberia now?"

Katherina jerked her head up and stared into his cold eyes. "I beg your pardon!"

The corners of his eyes crinkled in amusement. "You must forgive me. I most certainly did not mean to offend you. I simply assumed that, since you were willing to pay so much to see him, he had to be more than a mere acquaintance."

Katherina suddenly realized why Boris Ivanovich looked so familiar. He was the guard she had bribed

when she had gone to see Aleksandr Sergeievich at
Petropavlovsky Prison. Well—let him try to taunt her.
He did not even know Aleksandr Sergeievich's name,
and she would not give him the satisfaction of ad-
mitting anything.

"I'm sure I do not know what you are talking
about, Monsieur Dolgochev," she said, smiling sweetly, "and at any rate I find this talk of lovers im-
pertinent. Have you forgotten that I am a respectable
married woman?"

"Not at all, countess. Neither have I forgotten that
you are exactly the same woman who approached me
one cold December day in St. Petersburg. I would
say you displayed admirable spirit and devotion
on that occasion—and I have never ceased to be impressed by that."

Katherina stiffened. "Really, monsieur, if you per-
sist in this fairy tale, I'm afraid I'll be forced to seek
another dance partner."

He tightened his grasp and steered her toward the
terrace. "Please hear me out," he said. "We have a
great deal to discuss. Perhaps you will feel more inclined to talk in private."

Moscow was still quite cold in May, and Katherina
shivered in the chill on the terrace, but when Boris
Ivanovich pulled her close she shook him away defiantly.

"Surely you have other—unmarried—friends who
would welcome your embraces," she snapped.

"Forgive me, countess. I simply thought you appeared cold."

"It *is* cold out here, and I'm anxious to return to my
husband in the ballroom. Why don't you say whatever it is you have to say, and get it over with?"

"I had hoped that you would not force me to be so
blunt. What I have to say concerns your lover—or

should I say your former lover? I have a proposition to put to you."

"What sort of proposition?" Katherina asked. She wasn't going to fall into another trap such as Fyodor Bugov had set, although she had to admit to herself that, under different circumstances, she might have found Boris Ivanovich Dolgochev rather attractive.

"One thing at a time." He chuckled. "Since you are willing to listen to my proposition, am I to assume that you admit to having a lover?"

"No doubt you have already assumed whatever you wish—and what I say is hardly likely to change your opinion."

"Very well, then. I will assume that you have, or had, a lover. And, since he was ill-advised enough to be involved in the revolution, he has probably indeed been sent to Siberia. Unless, of course, he was among those unfortunates who were hanged."

"Monsieur Dolgochev," Katherina whispered impatiently, "enough of your assumptions. Please get to the point."

"All in good time, Countess Ostrova. No doubt you've heard that the road to Siberia is wide, but the lane back is narrow."

"Who hasn't heard that?" she snapped. "Did you bring me here simply to repeat old proverbs?"

"Of course not. I repeat it merely to point out to you that your lover will probably never return from Siberia."

"So?"

"So perhaps you would be considering a replacement for him."

Katherina whirled and walked toward the ballroom door. "I've heard quite enough," she said.

Boris Ivanovich caught her by the arm. "You do yourself a disservice if you refuse to hear me out."

Katherina sighed, wondering how he might retaliate if she pushed him away. "All right," she said coldly, "finish what you have to say. But quickly. The night air is giving me chills."

He drew her back into the shadows. "I simply wish to offer myself as your most humble servant."

"I am touched by your offer, monsieur," she replied sarcastically, "but I'm afraid all of your assumptions have led you astray. In truth, I am not the least bit interested in taking a lover."

"Forgive me," Boris said sincerely. "Perhaps there is already someone else. Uncle tells me you are expecting a child."

"Yes, I am expecting a child. What is so peculiar about that? I am a married woman."

"But all who make love do not make marriages."

"More proverbs! What is that supposed to mean?"

"Simply that your good husband, Count Ostrov, seems a bit old to be fathering a child."

"I'm sure he would not agree. In the Caucasus, where we have just lived for several months, it is not at all unusual for men almost twice Pavel Pavlovich's age to father children."

"Interesting. But quite beside the point."

"It seems to me that this entire conversation is without any point. Now—if you'll excuse me." She started for the door again.

"You know, I'm offering you quite an honor," Boris Ivanovich said.

"I beg your pardon?"

"The chance to be my lover. You would be the envy of all the ladies in your social circle."

"I'm afraid you flatter yourself, Monsieur Dolgochev."

"Not at all. Hasn't uncle told you we are relatives of the Czar?"

"Distant relatives."

He ignored the disdain in her voice. "In St. Petersburg I spend a good deal of time at court. Surely you have heard of the great honor attached to any liaison with the Imperial family? Most noblewomen would fight like wolves for the merest chance of having their names linked with one of us. The gossip alone would immeasurably increase your social standing."

"And what do you think my husband would think of all this?"

"He would be overjoyed. Such a liaison is a sure sign of your own desirability and of his wisdom and good fortune in acquiring you as a wife."

Katherina burst into laughter. "Forgive me, but this conversation has become absolutely absurd. To begin with, I happen to know that your link with the Romanov family is tenuous, at best. Secondly, Pavel Pavlovich would hardly be overjoyed to learn I was having an affair with anyone—even Czar Nikolai himself. Thirdly, can you really imagine yourself squiring me about the capital in a few months with my stomach distended by my pregnancy? The whole idea is a stunning joke."

"It's not a joke," Boris insisted. "By winter your child will have been born and you will be as beautiful as today—as beautiful as that first day I saw you."

Katherina narrowed her eyes to stare at him. "According to your uncle, you have beautiful girls, younger and more willing than I, pining for you all over Moscow and St. Petersburg. What do you want with me, Boris Ivanovich?"

"I told you before," he said quietly, "I admire your spirit. It's not often one finds a woman like you. I know because I have explored a countless variety of women."

"Your praise is too generous. Still, I am happily

married, and I'm afraid you will have to admire me from afar."

"Very well," he said, holding her wrists so that she was obliged to hear him out. "I am not a man who forces myself on a woman. I suspect we will meet from time to time, and I have other women to divert my attention, but someday, my proud little countess, you will find that you want me as much as I want you. When that happens, no matter how far in the future, I will be ready. And when we are finally united, you will wonder why you waited so long. Until that moment, let me leave you with something to remember me by."

Leaning over her, he held her in his arms and pressed his lips against hers. His tongue shot into her mouth, running along every tooth and every crevice as if to memorize it for future reference.

When Katherina rushed back into the ballroom, searching for Pavel Pavlovich, her lips still stung from the brutality of the kiss.

Chapter 22

Two weeks later, in early June, Pavel Pavlovich, Katherina Andreievna, and Masha arrived in St. Petersburg. After greeting the servants, all of whom received the news of her pregnancy with disdainful stares, Katherina went directly to her room. She was relieved when her husband announced that he would install himself in his old bedroom down the hall from hers, so that he would not interfere with the increasing amounts of rest she would be needing.

As she closed her door, she caught sight of a piece of paper lying on her bureau. She rushed to pick it up and immediately recognized Aleksandr's red wax seal. Could it be possible that his first letter had arrived in St. Petersburg before she did? How long had it waited there while she attended balls and soirees in Moscow? Sitting on the bed, she tore away the seal and began to drink in the words.

> My beloved Katya,
> When I found you had already left St. Basil's, my heart was almost broken. But I can truly feel it breaking at this moment as I must write to you that we will not be reunited—at least not for many months—in St. Petersburg . . .

Katherina stopped reading, confused, until she realized that this was the letter Aleksandr Sergeievich had sent her from Moscow before he left for Pyatigorsk. Well, it would have to sustain her until his first new message arrived. She scanned the remaining lines, full of information she already knew, then she kissed the signature and slid the message into the bodice of her dress.

Within less than a week, Pavel Pavlovich had proudly proclaimed to almost all of St. Petersburg that he would be a father before winter. Katherina found herself entertaining a steady stream of St. Petersburg society ladies who offered their congratulations and showered her with every kind of advice on pregnancy, childbirth, and caring for a baby. Everyone had a nurse, a doctor, or a midwife to recommend, and before long Katherina's head was spinning. Between entertaining women old enough to be her mother, she sandwiched her appointments with the dressmaker, who designed looser fitting dresses as the weeks went by.

Summer moved slowly as Katherina waited for her first message from Aleksandr Sergeievich. The marshy tracts of land on which St. Petersburg had been built simmered in the sun, blanketing the city in humidity, so that Katherina spent much of each day overcome by nausea. Toward the end of June, when she felt the child moving within her, she began to keep a journal. Someday, she would share her records with Aleksandr Sergeievich so he could see exactly how their first child had developed.

From the time she discovered her pregnancy, she had never doubted, at least consciously, that Aleksandr had fathered the child. She spent hours imagining the dark curls and shining black eyes their son or daughter would have. She pictured the three of them laughing as they traveled by troika through snow-covered birch forests. Aleksandr Sergeievich would be released from the Imperial Army in time to celebrate the child's first birthday, and, from that time, Katherina vowed, no matter what else might happen, she would never agree to further separations.

At night, when she slept alone in her room, her blissful visions of family harmony were replaced by scenes of horror. At least once a week Katherina awoke trembling, covered with sweat, from a recurring nightmare. Each time she had the dream she saw the child at birth, but instead of the perfect body she imagined by day, it was portly and bald, with sunken brown eyes. Worst of all, instead of greeting the world with the customary wail of a newborn baby, it opened its mouth and laughed—with the cruel sarcasm of Fyodor Bugov. In the dream, both Pavel Pavlovich and Aleksandr Sergeievich witnessed the birth, and both fled in disgust when the child laughed. No matter how often she had the dream, Katherina could not get used to it. She would lie awake until morning, afraid to close her eyes and see the monster infant who threatened to rob her of her beloved.

One morning at the end of August, Masha rushed into Katherina Andreievna's room so excited that she forgot to knock. Katherina was dozing, trying to overcome the effects of her nightmare, but she sat up when she heard Masha's words.

"Madame, I have a message for you. From Monsieur Belikov."

"He sent a message to you?" Katherina asked in confusion.

"No, madame," Masha laughed gaily. "He simply addressed the letter to me, with a short note of explanation. The letter is for you." She drew the papers from her bodice, where she had hidden them from the other servants.

As Katherina gratefully took the letter, Masha whispered, "I hope he sends good news, madame," and with a smile, she left the room, closing the door so that Katherina could enjoy her letter in privacy.

The letter was dated May 3, only a few weeks after they had left Pyatigorsk, yet it had taken almost four months to travel from the Caucasus to St. Petersburg.

My dearest Katya,

Lest you think I have deserted you for your Masha, let me explain why this letter arrived in her name. Since you have often mentioned the suspicious nature of the count's servants, I thought it would never do for you to receive regular correspondence from the Caucasus. So I am addressing these epistles to you, through Masha, knowing that she has proven herself more than trustworthy in all our months together. If anyone should question her about her abundance of correspondence, I feel sure she can explain that she met a young man of her own in Pyatigorsk. Enough of that.

I hope you did not find the trip home too difficult and that you and our child are resting comfortably in St. Petersburg. Our child! After all my years as an irresponsible nobleman and soldier, it seems strange to think of myself as a father, but I must admit I find the prospect rather pleasant, so long as it entails a lifetime spent with you, my precious Katya.

Please take especially good care of yourselves until I can be there to care for you personally. I am counting the months until I will be free of my obligations to the empire. When that day arrives, you can be sure I will set a new record for rapid travel from the Caucasus to St. Petersburg!

Know that I am well, Katya, and I think of you constantly. I am not in much danger here, so I hope you will not be too concerned for my safety.

If you send your letters to me in Tiflis, the army will see that they are dispatched to me wherever I might be stationed. Please write soon, beloved, so that I might have at least something of you to help me get through these interminable days and nights.

Your forever loving
Sasha

After that first message, new letters arrived from Aleksandr Sergeievich every four or five days. Masha faithfully carried them to Katherina and blushed shyly when some of the other servants teased her about her Caucasian lover. One of the older maids, Olga, who was so homely and ill-tempered that no man had given her a second look in all her sixty-five years, even went to Pavel Pavlovich and complained that it was scandalous for Masha to be carrying on such a torrid correspondence with a man at the other edge of the empire. But Pavel Pavlovich, who had remained in high spirits ever since Katherina announced her pregnancy, simply laughed and told Olga that she could use a bit of love to spice her own life. Besides, he pointed out, Masha was Katherina Andreievna's personal servant, and if Katherina had no complaints he certainly would not interfere. Olga retreated in a huff, muttering something about willful young wives who ruled their husbands, but no one made any further attempts to interfere with Masha's—or Katherina's—mail.

Katherina received each letter hungrily, reading it over and over until she had memorized every word. Aleksandr Sergeievich wrote very little about the progress of the war, except to say that peace seemed imminent within the next several months, but Katherina heard all the war news she cared to from Pavel Pavlovich, who gleaned it from discussions at the Council of State. Each letter overflowed with words of love, descriptions of how much he missed her, and fanciful plans for their future together.

By September, the ladies of St. Petersburg had tired of visiting Katherina to share their advice, and Pavel Pavlovich was again occupied full time with the Council of State. Katherina was free each day to write long letters to Aleksandr Sergeievich—describing how she felt, telling him how many times the child had kicked inside of her that day, and indulging in her own fantasies of the future.

No matter how inclement the weather, Masha dutifully posted the letters each day, but Katherina knew it might be months before the first of them reached Aleksandr. The lag between the time a letter was written and the time it arrived at its destination was frustrating to Katherina. She longed to know what Aleksandr was thinking that very day, not three or four months before. In her gloomiest moments, Katherina realized that he could have been killed in the time it took to receive his letters. He could be dead while she continued to receive his letters of hope for months afterward. And, unlike a wife, who could at least expect a notice from her husband's commanding officer, she would have no way of learning about his death until the letters suddenly stopped coming.

Whenever she felt herself dwelling too heavily on death, Katherina took out all of Aleksandr's letters and reread them. Though he was at the southern edge of the empire, his optimistic words always reassured her.

In mid-September she stopped accompanying Pavel Pavlovich to any social engagements. She was becoming a bit embarrassed with the knowing manner in which people assessed her profile, and it was customary for a woman to remain in confinement toward the end of her pregnancy. She was happy to be spared the boredom of sitting with the older women at the balls, unable even to dance. At a few of the summer parties, she had noticed Boris Ivanovich staring at her from across the room, but he never so much as approached her, and she stopped thinking of him as any sort of threat.

On November 19, exactly two years after the death of Czar Aleksandr at Taganrog, Katherina stood at her balcony doors watching the twilight settle over the frozen canal. She was thinking of another anniversary. In a few days it would be exactly two years since her first ecstatic union with Aleksandr Sergeievich. All day she had mulled over their first weeks together, when St. Petersburg had seemed so new and exciting. Now—any day—she was about to experience another beginning. How she wished that Aleksandr could share that moment with her. Tears welled in her eyes as she thought for the thousandth time that day how much she wanted him.

"Katherina Andreievna."

She turned slowly when she heard Pavel Pavlovich's voice. In the dusk she could see him outlined in her bedroom doorway.

"Pavel Pavlovich—I didn't hear you come in."

"The council adjourned early today," he said as he walked toward her. "It seems that almost everyone was anxious to go home and prepare for Madame Kislovsky's soiree."

"Then you must certainly do the same."

"I shall, in a moment. I thought I would come and sit with you. I suppose I feel a bit guilty leaving you again tonight—but why are you standing in the darkness, my dear?"

"Oh, I was watching the night descend over the city. Twilight seems to have a quieting effect on me."

"Well, it's past twilight now. In another moment

you'll be stumbling to find your way in here. I won't have you injuring yourself or the child." He lit the lamp on her bureau, then studied her face. "Katherina, there are tears in your eyes. Have you received some bad news?"

"No—I—" She moved awkwardly to perch herself on the edge of the bed. "I haven't been feeling too well today." She shrugged and smiled. "I suppose my time is almost here, and I'm getting a bit edgy."

Pavel Pavlovich sat down beside her and gently put his arm around her. "Perhaps it would be best for me to stay home with you tonight."

"No—please. No doubt I'll be asleep in a few hours, and you would miss a delightful party on my account."

"But I should be with you—in case."

"*No.*" She cut him off so abruptly that he jerked away in surprise. Instantly, she softened. "I'm sorry, I didn't mean to sound so harsh. It's just that it might be days before the child is born, and I can't have you disrupting all your plans until then. Please, Pavel Pavlovich, I would feel so much more relaxed if you would go on with your regular routine."

"But I think I am becoming as nervous as you."

"Then the social engagement will help take your mind away from your nervousness. Please say you will go. Tomorrow you can describe to me all the women's gowns and the food that Madame Kislovsky serves. It will be such a pleasant diversion for me to hear about it."

"All right." He laughed and kissed her on the forehead. "At your urging I will go—but only so that I may serve as your personal newspaper tomorrow."

As he left the room, Katherina swallowed the gasp that was forced through her throat by the first strong labor contraction.

By the time Pavel Pavlovich had dressed for the party, Katherina had felt two more pains, but she smiled brightly as he bid her good-night, and she admonished him not to dance with all the beautiful women at the soiree. After he left, Olga brought Katherina's supper tray, but she found she had no appetite, and she sent it away without touching any of the food.

She extinguished the lamp and dozed for a few hours, until she awoke, sweating, feeling as if her body were gripped in a vise of pain.

"Masha!" Katherina screamed.

Chapter 23

Katherina remembered almost nothing of the birth. She had vague recollections of Masha sending for the doctor, of someone clutching her hand when the pain seemed most unbearable. After what had seemed like an interminable amount of straining, she recalled hearing the first wail of the child. But she was acutely aware of one thing—throughout the delivery she had screamed, sobbed, and gasped "Sasha" more times than she wished to count.

She thought she remembered several people, none of whom she could identify, clustered around her bed during the ordeal, but when it was finally over and she focused her eyes in the dimly lighted room, she saw only Masha.

Before she even asked about the child, she feebly whispered the one question that was plaguing her. "Is Pavel Pavlovich here?"

Masha nodded. "He is in the hallway, speaking with the doctor."

"Oh," Katherina swallowed glumly. "How much did he hear?"

"I imagine very little," Masha reassured her. "He arrived only at the end, and by that time the entire house was in an uproar." Seeing the worried look on Katherina's face, Masha hurried to explain further. "The doctor himself did not even arrive until the child was almost born. It seems that he was invited to three different soirees tonight, and it took Dmitri several hours to locate him. Not that it mattered. We managed quite well without him. But it wasn't until the doctor arrived that I remembered to send someone to Madame Kislovsky's to summon the count."

Katherina smiled weakly. "You seem to have managed everything quite marvelously, Masha. Had you ever considered being a midwife?"

"Not really. But I haven't forgotten that my own mother told me much about the births she assisted in. In fact, she told me she was present when your mother gave birth to you." She stopped suddenly. "Oh—but we have completely forgotten the baby. Don't you want to see him? Shall I bring him to you now?"

"Him? I have a son?"

"Yes—a healthy, handsome boy. Olga took him to clean and dress him. I won't be a moment." She dashed from the room.

Instead of Masha, it was Pavel Pavlovich who entered a few moments later, gingerly carrying a small squirming bundle. He approached the bed, his face wreathed in joy and awe, and the tender way he looked at Katherina assured her that either he had not heard or had not understood her cries for Aleksandr Sergeievich.

Gently placing the child in her arms, he kissed her and whispered, "Well, Katherina Andreievna, what do you think of our son?"

Now it was Katherina's turn to gaze in awe. The child's face was a perfect replica of all her happiest dreams. A dark profusion of curls covered his head, and his eyes flashed as dark and deep as Aleksandr Sergeievich's. "I think he is the most beautiful person I have ever seen," she breathed.

Pavel Pavlovich smiled. "With the possible exception of his mother." He kissed her again and said, "You can't imagine how pleased I am finally to have a son. As soon as you are feeling strong enough, we must have a grand party to celebrate the event."

Katherina stared at the baby in her arms, only half listening to what her husband was saying. Looking at the wide, dark eyes, she could almost see Aleksandr Sergeievich's own eyes gazing back at her. If only he could be there now to see their perfectly formed infant.

She wondered suddenly if Pavel Pavlovich was conscious of how the child looked. No doubt the servants were already gossiping about how strange it was that the baby had dark hair and dark eyes. After all, Katherina had golden hair and blue eyes, and the count had gray eyes, and his gray hair had once been light brown. Which of them would be the first to tell him about her strange cries for Sasha? Would it be Olga? Dmitri? Anna? Alyosha? Petrushka?

"You know, it's strange—" Pavel Pavlovich's voice intruded on her thoughts. "The child has an uncanny resemblance to my uncle Fyodor. It's a pity he will never be able to see him."

"Fyodor?" Even after all these months, the name made Katherina shudder. "I don't remember him."

"Of course not. He died three years before our marriage, but you've seen his portrait any number of times."

"I have?"

"Yes, yes. In the house at Novgorod. Hanging above the mantel in the small eastern sitting room."

Katherina stared at the child, trying to see a resemblance to the faded portrait, but all she could see was the beloved face of Aleksandr Sergeievich.

"You needn't worry yourself about it, my dear. Perhaps we'll visit the estate in the spring. When you see the portrait again I am sure you will see what

I mean. For now, I think you should get some rest. I'll have Masha care for the child while you sleep, and tomorrow I'll engage a proper nurse. There's a woman I have been intending to interview for weeks. It seems I put it off a bit too long." He stood and kissed her. "Rest well, my little mother."

Katherina was nursing the baby the next morning when Pavel Pavlovich entered her room.

"How is my son today?" he asked.

"Hungry." She smiled.

"Just like his father. I always feel as if I could eat a wild bear in the morning."

Unnoticed by Pavel Pavlovich, Katherina cringed slightly. Yes, she thought, he is like his father. In the weeks they shared at Pyatigorsk, Aleksandr Sergeievich had always been ravenous at breakfast, especially after their strenuous morning lovemaking.

"Well, my dear," the count said as he sat down beside her on the bed, "did you choose a name for our boy yet?"

"Since he is our first, I assumed you would want to call him Pavel," Katherina said sweetly.

The count smiled broadly. "You are most considerate, Katherina Andreievna, but I think one Pavel Pavlovich in the house is quite enough. You know, my father and my grandfather were named Pavel, and as a child I always felt cheated that I was not given a name of my own."

Katherina laughed gaily, inwardly sighing with relief. She had hoped that Aleksandr's and her son would not have to bear the count's name. "What name do you suggest?" she asked.

"Well, of course Fyodor—for my uncle—comes to mind, but I've always detested that name, so I wouldn't think of saddling my own son with it."

Katherina heaved another inward sigh.

"Since he was born on the anniversary of Czar Aleksandr's death, what about naming him in honor of that great man?"

"That's a splendid idea!" Katherina exclaimed. She could hardly wait to write to Aleksandr Sergeievich and tell him he had a son named Aleksandr.

"Yes," Pavel Pavlovich continued thoughtfully, "I've always admired the name Aleksei. How does that sound to you, Katherina? Aleksei Pavlovich."

"Very fine," she said. It was not Aleksandr—but it was close enough. The baby finished feeding and she pulled him gently from her breast. Hearing the clock in the hall strike nine, she asked her husband, "Shouldn't you be going, my dear? You must be late by now."

"Oh, I am not going to the Senate today. I have far more important things to do."

"Pavel Pavlovich, I've never heard you speak of anything as being more important than your duty to the empire."

"Until now," he said, smiling, "nothing was more important. No doubt the Council of State will spend the day discussing the realignment of administrative districts—without coming to any sort of decision. I am going to find a nurse for our Aleksei."

"I really don't think that is necessary, Pavel Pavlovich. I'm sure I can manage with Masha's help."

"No—I insist. The doctor says that, except for nursing the child, you must rest and regain your strength. After that, there will be times when you will want to go out, and you will appreciate having someone capable here to look after Aleksei."

"All right," she relented. "For now, at least, I'll accept your decision."

"Good. And while I am out I think I will stop at Our

Lady of Kazan to make arrangements for the baptism. Do you have any godparents in mind?"

"Surely your friend Pyotr Dmitrievich would be an excellent godfather." Besides, she thought, Aleksandr would be pleased with the choice.

Pavel Pavlovich beamed with pleasure. "I had hoped you would suggest him. In fact, with your permission, I will make one other detour while I am out. I'll call on Pyotr Dmitrievich to tell him about the birth and to ask him if he will be godfather. I'm sure he won't hesitate." The count paused and looked fondly at his small family. "No doubt you will wish to write a note to whomever you choose for godmother."

"I don't think that will be necessary," Katherina said.

"Oh?" the count raised his eyebrows. "Don't tell me, my willful wife, that you asked someone to be godmother before the child was even born—and without mentioning it to me."

"Not at all, but I am sure the person I have in mind will readily agree. And I expect to see her at any moment."

"Katherina Andreievna, I really must insist that you not begin entertaining visitors so soon after giving birth. I doubt that the good doctor would approve."

"You are absolutely right, Pavel Pavlovich. And I have no intention of entertaining anyone for several days."

"But—"

She cut him off, laughing. "The godmother I have in mind lives here—in this house. It's Masha!"

"Masha? Why that's preposterous, Katherina Andreievna. I'm afraid I can't agree at all."

"Why not? She's a fine, loving, God-fearing, capable young woman. She has been invaluable to me, both here and in Pyatigorsk—as much a dear friend as a servant. And she proved her devotion and her ability last night, when she attended me so perfectly."

Pavel Pavlovich sighed. "Katherina, please try to be sensible about this. I can't deny that Masha is a fine girl. But she is hardly of the caliber to be godmother to our firstborn."

"You can't question her character."

"Not her character—her background. She's a peasant—a mere house serf. I doubt that even the priest would agree to allowing a serf to be godmother to the son of a count."

Aleksei began to wail, and Katherina shot a reproachful glance at the count. "You see? Even our son disagrees with you. He knows Masha would make a fine godmother. If you won't agree, perhaps he will just have to remain unbaptized."

"Katherina!" The count tried to sound stern, but his wife's shocking pronouncement and the baby's wails had him flustered. "Let us not put our child's soul in peril because of a disagreement on our part."

"Then agree with me that Masha is the best choice," she said simply.

"Well," he relented, backing toward the bedroom door, "perhaps Masha could act as godmother in proxy. You might write to your friend Princess Golovine in Moscow and ask her to be the real godmother. Of course she wouldn't be able to get here in time for the ceremony, so Masha could stand in for her. If you lend her a suitable gown."

"I don't know," Katherina pouted. "I'll think about it."

"Good." The count smiled. "Good-bye, Aleksei Pavlovich," he called as he backed out of the door.

Katherina looked down at the baby, now asleep in her arms. He may call you Aleksei Pavlovich, she thought, but I will always think of you as Aleksei

Aleksandrovich. And someday—someday before you are too old—you and I will go away with your real father and you will know your real name.

In the end, Pavel Pavlovich capitulated. When Aleksei Pavlovich Ostrov was baptized in Our Lady of Kazan Cathedral, his godparents were Pyotr Dmitrievich Belikov and Masha Semyonovna Zemlyov.

For the first few weeks after the baby's birth, Katherina enjoyed the luxury of having a nurse in the house. The nurse, Natalya Vasilievna, was gentle and efficient, and Katherina found it comforting to know that she need not jump out of bed or stop writing her letter to Aleksandr Sergeievich in mid-sentence the moment she heard little Aleksei begin to cry. Natalya was there and could be relied on to bring the child to her when it was time to nurse him.

But gradually Katherina began to resent Natalya's constant presence in the nursery. During the long winter afternoons, even while Aleksei slept, Katherina liked to sit close by, observing him as she wrote to Aleksandr or made entries in her journal about their son's progress. At such times she wanted privacy, so she could imagine herself alone with Aleksandr and Aleksei, but Natalya Vasilievna refused to leave the room, as if Katherina were incapable of caring for her own child. Katherina was constantly aware of the click of the nurse's knitting needles, which stopped only when she sat staring curiously at her young mistress.

On a cold day in January, Masha knocked at the nursery door to announce that the dressmaker had come to fit Katherina's newest gowns. Aleksei was sleeping soundly, and even Natalya had dozed off in her rocking chair. Without thinking, Katherina lay aside her half-finished letter and went downstairs to greet the dressmaker.

When Katherina returned less than an hour later, Natalya Vasilievna was stooped over the writing table, her lips moving slowly as she read Katherina's letter to Aleksandr. Katherina flew to the table and snatched the letter away from the startled nurse.

"How dare you pry into my personal correspondence!" she screamed.

With a smug smile, Natalya simply walked back to her chair and resumed her knitting.

Katherina stomped after her. "Well—have you nothing to say? Won't you even make some feeble attempt at an apology?"

"It seems, countess," Natalya replied tartly, "that—compared to you—I have very little to be embarrassed about."

"Exactly what do you mean by that?"

"I think you know well enough. Who is this 'Darling Sasha'? Why does your letter keep calling little Aleksei his son?"

"That's none of your affair, you old witch!" Katherina screamed so loudly that she awakened Aleksei. The child's eyes opened wide and he began to wail. Natalya hurried to pick him up before Katherina could even approach the cradle.

"Anything that affects this innocent baby is my affair," the nurse retorted. "Had I known that his mother was a sinner, I never would have accepted employment in this house."

"Then why don't you leave now, before you become tainted by my presence?"

"I would, gladly, but I fear for the soul of this child."

"Let me worry about Aleksei. He is *my* son!"

"But he is my responsibility. I am his nurse—and I

won't have it on my conscience that I left him in the care of an immoral woman. The things I read in that letter were enough to make me shudder. Things no decent, moral, modest woman would write to her own husband, let alone to another man. I'll have to seek confession just to purge my soul from the sight of such words!"

"Then I suggest you go to the cathedral immediately," said Katherina. "And you needn't return when you have finished your confession. I'll have your belongings sent to you wherever you go."

Natalya's eyes narrowed, and she stared at Katherina. "Am I to understand that you are throwing me out of your house?"

"Exactly."

"Count Ostrov might think differently. I believe it is more his house than yours. At any rate, he is the one who engaged my services."

"That hardly matters. My husband will not question my decision."

"He might if he knew what prompted it," Natalya said quietly.

"Do you mean to threaten me, Natalya?"

The nurse smiled slowly and returned the calmed baby to his cradle. "Not at all, countess. I am simply offering you a small compromise. Although I find your character distasteful at best, your home is quite comfortable, and the child, though I now understand he is a bastard, is quite easy to care for. It might be difficult for me to find another position now, in the middle of winter, so I am prepared to bargain with you."

"But perhaps I am not willing to bargain with you."

"Oh—but I think you are," Natalya said shrewdly. "You may be a tainted young woman, but you have never impressed me as stupid. I have served some of the most prestigious families in St. Petersburg, and I still retain connections with most of them. As you must know, there's nothing like a juicy bit of gossip to warm up the cold winter months. Madame Kislovsky, for example, would be so pleased with a new tidbit to enliven her conversations."

Katherina cut her off. "I think you have made yourself clear."

"Yes." Natalya smiled broadly. "I knew you would understand. It seems to me that if I can endure your sinful presence you can surely endure me. In the spring, if I hear of another position, I will be only too happy to leave. At that time we can discuss suitable additional compensation for my silence."

Katherina nodded, her lips pressed tightly together. As she turned to leave the nursery, she could not resist saying, "It's obvious that you don't understand how it feels to love someone enough to devote your whole life to him."

"On the contrary," Natalya said softly. "Thirty years ago I loved a man with all my heart, but my family was too lowly for him to consider me as more than a passing flirtation." As Katherina passed through the door, Natalya's voice followed her. "His name was Pavel Pavlovich Ostrov—but a count does not marry a merchant's daughter."

Natalya's words cut at Katherina's heart, and she was overcome with sympathy for the nurse—and for Pavel Pavlovich. How different might his life have been if he had married Natalya Vasilievna! It was hard to imagine that she had ever been a beauty, but at least she would have been a faithful wife. Katherina wondered if the young count had ever loved with a passion similar to what she shared with Aleksandr Sergeievich. Had Pavel Pavlovich and

Natalya ever experienced the full physical liaison of uninhibited love?

In the next months, Katherina tried to treat Natalya with more compassion, but the older woman made it clear that she was not moved by Katherina's gentleness and that nothing the countess could do would restore her respect. Eventually, they learned to treat each other with indifference, exchanging as few words as possible.

It was April, and little Aleksei was five months old before Katherina received Aleksandr Sergeievich's letter rejoicing in the birth of his son. By that time she had known for more than a month that the Persian war had ended with the Treaty of Turkmanchai, by which Persia had surrendered most of Armenia and Azerbaijan to the Russian Empire. At first she had hoped that the Czar, pleased with his new acquisitions, would release Aleksandr from his military responsibilities before his two years of service had expired. But with every passing day, as she listened to the count describe the affairs of state, her hopes grew dimmer, and they disappeared completely when Pavel Pavlovich announced, on the same day that Aleksandr's letter had arrived, that Czar Nikolai had declared war on the Turkish Empire.

Chapter 24

Natalya Vasilievna left the Ostrov household in early June. Madame Kislovksy's grandniece had given birth to twins and, being assured of the young mother's virtue, Natalya Vasilievna happily agreed to become their nurse. Her departure relieved Katherina, although she pretended disappointment to Pavel Pavlovich.

"Of course," she told him, "Natalya is an excellent nurse, and with twins to care for I am sure Madame Kislovsky's grandniece needs her much more than we."

"Perhaps we can find a new nurse," the count suggested.

"Oh, no," Katherina protested. "Whomever we found could not possibly be as good as Natalya Vasilievna, and I would constantly be comparing her. Besides, I so enjoy my time with Aleksei that I see no need for a nurse."

"That may be true, my dear, but there should be someone capable with whom you can leave him when we go out for the evening—or if you should wish to go out during the day."

"There is always Masha," Katherina said firmly. "As his godmother, I think she is quite capable." She actually hoped that Aleksei would become a ready excuse for her absence from social events.

The count shrugged apprehensively, but he did not argue, and he never again mentioned finding another nurse.

Summer dragged on. Most of the nobility abandoned the steamy swampy environs of St. Petersburg to relax at their country estates. Even Czar Nikolai left the capital to personally direct the western offensive in his war against Turkey. Content to watch her son's progress, Katherina was glad to be spared the unending boredom of balls. But Pavel Pavlovich seemed listless with neither the Council of State nor society to occupy his time.

When her husband suggested that they travel to Novgorod for a few weeks, Katherina rejected the proposal with the excuse that Aleksei was still too young to travel. In fact, she could not bear to imagine even one week without receiving mail from Aleksandr Sergeievich. She convinced the count that he should take a short journey without her.

As Aleksei grew, his eyes and hair became darker, and Katherina could see a greater and greater resemblance to his father. At bedtime, and sometimes in the afternoons, she would sing and play the balalaika for him, and his eyes seemed to take on the same dreamy quality that had shone in Aleksandr Sergeievich's eyes when she played and sang for him in their cottage at Pyatigorsk.

Every letter from Aleksandr Sergeievich overflowed with his feelings about how much he looked forward to being discharged from the army in the fall and seeing his son by the child's first birthday, or at the very least by Christmas.

But Aleksei's birthday passed without his real father; and Katherina cringed every time the child called Pavel Pavlovich "papa."

In December, a letter arrived from Aleksandr explaining that his discharge had not been approved. The war was going well, but the Czar was unwilling to release any of his troops. Still, Aleksandr Sergeievich wrote, there was every indication that the war would be over the next year, and surely then he would be free to return to St. Petersburg.

He spent the winter at the newly captured fortress of Akhaltsikh, while Katherina brooded in ice-covered St. Petersburg and Aleksei giggled happily as Pavel Pavlovich bounced him on his knee. Pavel Pavlovich was good to the child, and she could not begrudge him the happiness he found with little Aleksei. But she couldn't help worrying that the boy would become so attached to the count that he might never be able to accept Aleksandr Sergeievich as his real father. If only the war would end soon!

They had suspended their marital relations at the time she announced she was pregnant, but now Pavel Pavlovich began to hint that something was missing from their marriage. Katherina could not bring herself to encourage him, but she was not surprised when, on Christmas Eve, he crept into her bed. Though she accepted the inevitable, she lay rigid throughout the experience, turning her face away from his as tears dropped silently onto her pillow.

When Pavel Pavlovich asked gently if he was hurting her, she simply shook her head and bit back the sobs that rose in her breast. He visited her bed regularly for the next several months, but her response was always the same. Finally, the unions became as painful for him as they were for her, and he stopped disturbing her at night. He began to spend more and more time at the Council of State or visiting his many friends in St. Petersburg, and when summer came and he announced that he wished to follow Czar Nikolai's court to Moscow, he seemed almost relieved when Katherina firmly told him to go alone—that she preferred to stay in St. Petersburg. Perhaps, she said, her mother or one of her sisters would come from Novgorod to pass part of the summer with her.

Pavel Pavlovich left early in July. From all reports, the war with Turkey would be over at any time, and Katherina was overjoyed at the fact that she and Aleksei would be alone—except for the servants—when Aleksandr Sergeievich swept back into her life! She ordered a dozen new gowns so she could look her best when she greeted him. For Aleksei she had a small suit made that was an exact copy of his father's uniform. Every morning she waited excitedly for Masha to bring the mail, and when Aleksandr's letters said nothing about his impending return, she convinced herself that he would probably arrive personally before his message could, so she spent the remainder of each day waiting for him to knock at the door.

It was late September, and Pavel Pavlovich had already returned from Moscow when word arrived that the Russians and the Turks had signed a peace treaty at Adrianople. Surely, Katherina thought, her beloved was already on his way home to her. Their reunion would be more difficult now, with Pavel Pavlovich present, but they would manage somehow. Surely, after their last strained months together, Pavel Pavlovich would readily agree to divorce her. But would he give up little Aleksei—even when he learned that another man had fathered the boy?

Katherina's worries turned out to be premature. The Neva was already freezing for the winter when she received a short, unhappy note from Aleksandr Sergeievich.

My beloved Katya,

No doubt by now you have heard that Turkey has surrendered a number of cities and the war is over. I was ecstatic at the end, dreaming of my

joyful return to you. And I suppose you, too, have
been waiting every day for my arrival in St.
Petersburg. But it seems the Czar has a long
memory of the revolution of December, 1825, and
a much shorter memory of the promises he made
since that time. At any rate, it seems that my
tour of duty is still not ended. There is continued
trouble with the Circassians, and I am to remain
here, stationed near Pyatigorsk, of all places, to
aid in quelling the disturbances.

Oh, Katya, it is so painful! Everything about
the fort, the town, the mountains reminds me of
moments shared with you! Lying in my lonely bed
at night, I sometimes despair of ever holding you
again, of ever seeing our son while he is still
young enough to bounce on my knee.

At times I wonder if good Czar Nikolai knows
about us and is purposely keeping us apart as a
favor to the count. There are rumors here that his
secret police open at least one-tenth of the mail
that passes through the post office—and every letter sent by supposed subversives.

But I fear I am worrying you unnecessarily. In
time, I know we will be reunited. And at least until then I know you and Aleksei are being well
cared for. Kiss Aleksei for me, and know that you
both have all of my love.

Your own
Sasha

Katherina crumpled the letter. "I sometimes despair. . . ." The words reverberated in her head, and
she envisioned his eyes as he wrote the letter. Her
own despair, which she had hidden even from herself all these months, now flooded her mind, and she
fled to her balcony. There, with the Baltic wind
stinging her face and whipping the pins from her
hair, she felt a new relief.

If he could not come to her, she would go to him.
This time, nothing would stop her. She had thought

enough of Pavel Pavlovich's feelings. Now she had
to think of Aleksandr Sergeievich and herself. She
had traveled the route between St. Petersburg and
Pyatigorsk twice, and she was sure she could find
her way again. No doubt Masha would agree to accompany her, and they would remember at least
some of the landmarks. Besides, they could always
refer to the map General Bugov had given her, still
hidden away in her personal belongings.

The wind seemed to slice through Katherina
Andreievna's clothes, but she stayed on the balcony,
exhilarating in the sense of freedom she felt the moment she made her decision. Glancing at the frozen
canal, she realized that it would be foolhardy to
leave immediately. The harshest months of winter
were still to come, and she had no desire to be lost
on the snow-covered steppes with Aleksei shivering
beside her. He was almost two years old now—a
strong, healthy child who walked without a hint of
a baby's toddling. But the trip would be too long and
too brutally cold for him to survive in winter. When
spring came, it would be easy—because Aleksandr
Sergeievich waited at the journey's end.

With her decision came a complete change in
Katherina's temperament. She so looked forward to
her planned reunion with Aleksandr Sergeievich that
she was suddenly consumed by an overwhelming
joy for living. She happily accepted social invitations,
dancing and laughing with her husband until
many a dawn. She even planned a lavish party at
their own mansion and watched Pavel Pavlovich puff
with pride when she appeared in a new gown to
greet her guests. And when they returned from a ball
in the early-morning hours and Pavel Pavlovich followed her to her bedroom, she did not reject his at-

tentions. After all, she reasoned, she owed him something for his years of caring for her. Only hours
later, when she was sure he was asleep in his own
room, did she light a candle and take out her precious map, studying for the thousandth time her route
to Pyatigorsk.

When the spring suns again began to melt the ice
on the Neva and its network of canals, Pavel Pavlovich brought disturbing news from the Council of
State. The year before, merchants had carried cholera
from the Asian town of Bokhara across the Ural
Mountains to Orenburg. Now the disease seemed to
be spreading through central Russia at a rapid pace.

"But is it really something we need be concerned
about?" Katherina asked. "I have always heard that
cholera is not contagious. If it were, surely the
health authorities would have imposed a quarantine
when it appeared in the southern districts during
the last decade."

"It appears that our doctors know less about the
malady than they thought," Pavel Pavlovich sighed.
"If it is not contagious, why does it spread so rapidly?
Czar Nikolai wishes to convene a special commission
to examine our public health policies regarding
cholera, and he has appointed me a member."

"Why you, Pavel Pavlovich? Of course, it is always a great honor to be chosen to serve the Czar,
but I should have imagined he would want doctors to
compose his commission."

"There will be doctors," the count explained, "but
there is also a need for government officials to help
implement any new programs deemed necessary. Our
esteemed minister of the interior, General Zakrevsky,
will head the commission."

"I suppose this means you will be locked up in the Senate building for longer hours than ever," Katherina sighed, although she was secretly pleased. If he left the house in the early morning, it would be easy for her to slip out of St. Petersburg and begin her journey while the streets were still empty.

"Unfortunately, it will not be quite so easy. The commission convenes in Saratov. The Czar thought it better to be near the actual incidences of the disease."

"I suppose that is sensible—but Saratov is such a distance. It must be more than a week's journey southeast of Moscow."

The count smiled faintly. "Your knowledge of geography seems to have improved considerably since our marriage. I can remember when you thought Taganrog was a palace."

Katherina laughed. "I had plenty of time to improve myself while I was in Pyatigorsk and you were in Transcaucasia. And General Bugov was good enough to lend me a map."

"Well, I can see you used it well," he said, kissing her on the forehead. "Anyway, my dear, I'll be required to leave for Saratov within the week. I only regret that I'll be forced to leave you and Aleksei behind. I'm afraid it will be another boring summer for you."

"But why can't we come with you?" Katherina pictured the map in her mind. Saratov was farther east than she wanted to go, but it was on the Volga River. Perhaps she, Masha, and Aleksei could sail down the Volga until it neared the Don River. At least, with Pavel Pavlovich, they would be assured of a safe journey as far as Saratov.

"Much as I long for your company, I would not

hear of it. With all the uncertainty surrounding this cholera scare, I could not think of exposing you to it. You and Aleksei are my most precious possessions. I couldn't risk losing either of you."

Katherina looked away, blinking back tears. But then another plan began to crystallize in her mind. "Are there reports of cholera in Moscow?" she asked.

"I don't believe so. From all reports, Czar Nikŏlai himself plans to travel there with his family this summer."

"Then at least let us go with you as far as Moscow! Aleksei is old enough now for his first look at the ancient capital. And you know Prince Dolgochev said his house is always open to us. Wouldn't you like to show him our son?"

"Well—," Pavel Pavlovich said, "Moscow would be more pleasant for you. I suppose there would be any number of social events you could attend."

"And think of how much closer to us you will be. We could have a holiday in Moscow before you begin your work—and another longer one when you return from Saratov."

The count laughed and kissed her again. "My dear, you are too convincing for me to resist. Can you be ready to leave in three days?"

"Of course." She kissed his cheek excitedly. "You won't object to my bringing Masha?"

"No. She will be good company for you—just as in Pyatigorsk. And perhaps she will agree to bring her balalaika, so you can entertain us on the road to Moscow." He paused and beamed with joy. "My dear Katherina Andreievna—you are an angel in disguise. I arrived home feeling so glum about leaving you, and now you have me looking forward to a holiday in Moscow with my family."

As he left the room, Katherina felt a slight twinge of guilt. What would this good, kind man think of her when he returned from Saratov and found he no longer had a family?

Chapter 25

They arrived in Moscow in time for Holy Week. Pavel Pavlovich had sent a messenger ahead to warn Prince Dolgochev of their arrival, and the prince was waiting in his courtyard when their carriage rolled in. He embraced both the count and Katherina three times and offered them the customary Holy Week greeting—"He is risen"—to which they gave the customary response, "Risen indeed."

On Easter Eve they fasted all day, then spent the evening at the traditional Easter service at Saint Basil's Cathedral. Emerging after midnight, weak and famished, they hurried back to the Dolgochev mansion where they were greeted by a banquet table laden with more than thirty traditional dishes, including Easter eggs painted with brilliant, intricate designs. The prince presented Katherina, Pavel Pavlovich, and Aleksei with exquisite imitation eggs. Katherina's was white china, covered with tiny pastel china flowers, a fragrant lavender sachet concealed in its base; Pavel Pavlovich's was china, too, and on it was a miniature painting of a birch forest; Aleksei's was made of sugar, with bright sugar decorations of childhood toys. Though Katherina tried to keep her eye on him, the wide-eyed child consumed half the gift as soon as she turned to speak with another guest.

"Aleksei," Katherina scolded, "what have you done with your lovely present?"

The prince laughed heartily. "Let the child enjoy

the gift however he wishes. It's better for him to eat it than to have it consumed by ants this summer. I'll have another egg made for him next Easter."

"You are very understanding," Katherina said.

She enjoyed the Easter celebration, partly because it reminded her of her family holidays in Novgorod. She could picture her parents, her brothers and sisters, her nieces and nephews, all gathered round the banquet table. But her underlying excitement came from the assurance that Pavel Pavlovich would be leaving for Saratov in a few days and at last she would be able to fly to her beloved in Pyatigorsk.

The morning Pavel Pavlovich left, Katherina had all she could do to keep herself from rushing to Prince Dolgochev's stable, saddling a horse, and galloping south toward the Caucasus, but she had decided that she would wait a week, to be sure her husband had almost reached Saratov. If she left sooner, it might be too easy for the prince to send a messenger to the count telling of her disappearance. In that event, her husband himself might overtake her before she was more than a few days' journey out of Moscow. If she waited, he would be too far away to be quickly recalled, especially since she might be gone a full day before the prince or his staff discovered her absence. This time she would not even leave a letter for Pavel Pavlovich. Eventually, she consoled her aching conscience, she would write to him, explaining everything and instructing him to apply for a divorce.

All week she kept an erratic schedule, flitting from teas to soirees, never appearing in the Dolgochev mansion at the same time each day. She hoped her unpredictability would help to hide her flight. If the prince and his staff never knew when to expect her, they would be less suspicious when she did not appear for dinner or supper. As an added precaution, she sent Masha to procure peasant clothing for her and Aleksei so they would be less conspicuous when they left the city among the stream of early-morning shoppers.

On Tuesday, the day before their departure, Katherina went alone to the Smolensky Cathedral in Novodevichy Monastery to pray for a swift and safe journey. All day she knelt on the cold stone floor, asking that she, Masha, and Aleksei be granted a safe reunion with Aleksandr Sergeievich. She was aware that there was something contradictory about asking God to bless an adulterous union, but she was convinced that He could not find fault with her love for Aleksandr. She thought of the Smolensky Cathedral as a special charm for their love, for it was there that they had savored their first reunion after their first long separation.

Late in the afternoon, Katherina heard the swish of fabric on the stone floor and then she felt someone gently touch her shoulder. Her eyes flew open and she saw a gray-bearded priest, his gold crucifix shining against his black caftan. His kindly gray eyes looked so much like Pavel Pavlovich's that she jerked away in fright.

"Is something wrong, my child?"

"No. Nothing, father."

"I have been watching you for a long time from behind the altar," he prodded. "I have seldom seen anyone pray as fervently as you. Perhaps you are seeking confession?"

"No, father," she mumbled.

"Is there a sin for which you wish to atone? A falsehood you carried against your neighbor? Another woman's jewel that you coveted?"

"No, father."

"Ah—then perhaps you have sinned against your husband?"

Katherina flinched, but she did not answer.

"Don't be afraid to tell me, my child. If a woman did not sin, she would have nothing to atone for, and then she would not be a woman, but a saint. You must bare your soul to me so that I can devise a penance to win you absolution."

When Katherina remained silent, the priest's tone became less gentle. "You cannot seek God's grace alone. You must trust me to intercede for you, or your soul will surely perish. And you must remember that God visits the iniquities of the parents on the children, even to the third and fourth generations. If you will not confess for yourself, do it for your children."

At that, Katherina brushed past the priest and fled from the cathedral.

Behind her, she heard the ominous tone of the priest's voice. "I will pray for you to find the strength for confession before you and all your children are consumed by the fires of hell."

All the way back to Prince Dolgochev's, Katherina tried to put the priest's declaration out of her mind, but his eyes haunted her for the rest of the evening, and that night when she tried to sleep they appeared before her again. Still, she refused to change her plans. Before retiring, she dressed in the embroidered peasant skirt and blouse Masha had brought her. At the first light of dawn, she would wrap herself in her heavy peasant's shawl, load a few scanty provisions into Prince Dolgochev's oldest wagon, and she, Aleksei, and Masha would leave Moscow—perhaps forever.

At three o'clock in the morning, when Katherina had finally shaken off her image of the priest and drifted, exhausted, into sleep, she was awakened by noises coming from the room that adjoined her own. Lamplight filtered under the door, and she heard the tread of several pairs of feet, followed by men's voices, speaking in hushed tones. She groped for a dressing gown, threw it over her peasant outfit, and cautiously crept to the door.

She opened the door a crack until she could see Prince Dolgochev and several other men she did not recognize. They were clustered around a body that was lying on the bed, and their faces all wore the gravest expressions.

"I hate to wake her," the prince whispered, "but we ought to tell her now, before it is too late." Then he looked across the room to the partly opened door, and, before Katherina could step back and close it, he was striding toward her.

"Countess Ostrova," he said kindly, "I am sorry if our noise disturbed you, but I think it is best that you are awake. These men have just delivered your husband to us."

"Pavel Pavlovich!" Katherina gasped.

"Yes. And I fear his condition warrants your immediate attention."

Katherina swung open the door and took a few steps into the room. The men fell away from the bed, and her first glimpse of the count almost made her swoon. His skin looked lax and wrinkled, and his eyes and cheeks seemed to be sunken into his once-robust face. The skin around his eyes and lips had a pale bluish tint. It was impossible to believe that he had left Moscow only six days earlier in perfect health.

Feeling the prince supporting her, she turned questioning eyes to him. "What happened?"

"Cholera." The word hung in the air like a thunderclap.

"But he looks so terrible. How could it happen so quickly? Can nothing be done?"

The prince shrugged helplessly. "It is a terrible disease. It comes swiftly, and it moves rapidly. They say he was barely two days out of Moscow when it first felled him. His doctor advised against further travel, but he insisted on being brought back here to see you once more."

"Once more?"

The prince hesitated, then said slowly, "Recovery seems unlikely."

Katherina swallowed hard. In a few more hours she would have been gone, and even now a part of her longed to flee from the deathly image lying before her, but she would stay. There was no other choice. She squared her shoulders and turned to the waiting cluster of men.

"All right," she whispered hoarsely. "Thank you for bringing my husband to me. I will stay with him now."

As the men filed from the room, the prince touched her arm. "Are you sure you don't wish some company, my dear?"

She shook her head. "But perhaps you could send a samovar—to help me keep awake—and in case he awakens and wants some warm tea."

"Yes, of course. I will bring it myself."

After Prince Dolgochev left, Katherina moved uneasily toward her sleeping husband. His hand was cold, as she imagined a dead person would feel. His eyes opened slowly.

"Ah, Katherina Andreievna," he rasped in a husky, unfamiliar voice, "I am glad to see you." Then his eyes closed again and his face took on an anxious expression.

Prince Dolgochev brought the samovar and, with shaking hands, Katherina poured herself a cup of tea. In the next two hours, she drank nearly ten cups of tea as she watched her husband sleeping fitfully.

At 5:30 in the morning, Masha burst into the room. "Madame, are you almost rea——" She stopped in mid-sentence when she saw Katherina's face. Then her eyes fell on the emaciated form of the count, and she collapsed uneasily against the wall.

"We won't be going out today, Masha," Katherina said. "If I am detained, please take care of Aleksei when he awakes."

"Of course," Masha said as she backed out of the room.

It was midmorning before Pavel Pavlovich awakened again. He lifted his eyelids lazily and stared at Katherina for a long moment. In the same husky voice as before, he whispered, "Aleksandr Belikov will take good care of you and Aleksei."

"What?" Katherina whispered.

"I have already sent a messenger to General Paskevich asking him to release young Belikov to come here and care for you and Aleksei. In the time we spent together, Paskevich became a good friend. He will do it for me. I sent the messenger within a day after I took sick."

"But why, Pavel Pavlovich?"

He smiled feebly. "I am too old to recover from this illness. I suffered too much in the first days, and I can already feel it draining the last strength from my body. But I am not too old to realize how much you love Belikov—and to know he loves you, too."

Katherina blinked back the tears that flooded her eyes. Pavel Pavlovich knew! It would be useless for her to deny it. How had he discovered their love? How long had he suffered with the knowledge?

"Oh, Pavel Pavlovich," she cried, "I never wanted to hurt you. I tried so hard to hide it—to be a good wife to you. And now—I have failed you miserably. How you must hate me." She turned away as her tears started flowing.

"But I don't hate you at all, Katherina Andreievna." He took her hand and squeezed it weakly. "You have been a good wife, despite all the temptations that stood in your path. You nursed me in Pyatigorsk, and even when I was well you did not desert me. How many chances you had to run away with young Belikov—and yet you stayed with me."

His softly stated words made Katherina sob even harder. Would he be so understanding if he knew she had planned to leave that very day? If he knew how many times she had been on the verge of flying to Aleksandr Sergeievich? Did he know that she would have left him in Pyatigorsk, when she first discovered her pregnancy, if Aleksandr Sergeievich had not insisted that she return to St. Petersburg? She stifled a compulsion to confess everything, to bare her soul and bask in his forgiveness. But if he was really going to die, it was better to let him die in peace. Her confession might bring her full forgiveness, but the words would only torment him on his deathbed.

Taking a sniffling breath, she turned her face to meet his eyes. "Pavel Pavlovich, you are more understanding than a saint." Her shaking voice became steadier. "Until this moment, I have never completely realized how blessed I am to have you for a husband. You must believe how sorry I am—how ashamed I feel for all the pain I must have caused you."

"And I am sorry for all the pain I have caused you. I should have quietly divorced you long ago—so that you could have brought your love for Belikov to full flower—but I wanted you too much for my own self." He squeezed his eyes shut to conceal the tears in them. "I hoped, foolishly I suppose, that in time you would learn to love me as much as you love Belikov, but now that time is running out I can see how selfish I was."

Selfish! How could he call himself selfish when she had been so selfish all these years? He seemed to have twisted the whole problem, so that now she felt completely confused. He said he should have divorced her long ago. How long had he actually known? How long had he kept his disturbing secret?

Unable to contain her question, she blurted, "How long have you known?"

A weak smile passed across his lips again. "I think I suspected from the first—even from the days before the ill-advised revolution in St. Petersburg. You seemed to gain a certain joy for living after you spent time with him—a liveliness you had not exhibited during the first weeks of our marriage. Later, there were other clues—your poorly concealed relief when he was released from prison, and your obvious depression in the months after he left St. Petersburg."

"But wait." Katherina shook her head helplessly. "There is something I don't understand. If your suspicions were so strong, why did you choose Aleksandr Sergeievich to look after me in Pyatigorsk while you traveled to Transcaucasia? There must have been other soldiers at the fort who could have stayed with me."

"But who would have been more concerned for your safety than a man who loved you so completely? With Belikov there, I knew no harm could come to you."

Katherina sighed and went to the samovar, more because she needed a momentary escape than because she wanted a cup of tea. The china cup and saucer rattled in her hand as she pretended to concentrate on pouring the tea. If she looked at Pavel Pavlovich she would burst into sobs again. She had to strain her ears to hear his weak voice coming to her from across the room.

"The day before we left Pyatigorsk, I had my proof. I found a note on the floor of our bedroom. It was addressed to me and had been written by you—Katherina."

As the words penetrated her brain, Katherina sucked in her breath. Her hand seemed to lose control, and the cup and saucer clattered to the floor. So he did know that she and Aleksandr had planned to run away! Numbed by this revelation, she forgot to turn off the spigot of the samovar until boiling water soaked through her satin slipper and snapped her back to reality.

With a cry of pain, she jumped away and turned off the water. Kneeling, she began to pick up the pieces of china. When she finally felt capable of speaking, she said, "Why did you never confront me with the letter?"

"I suppose," Pavel Pavlovich sighed, "I was afraid of upsetting the delicate balance that existed between us. And I may have hoped that our return to the glamour of St. Petersburg would induce you to abandon any plans to leave the empire. In addition, you were pregnant at the time, and I did not want to disturb you in any way. To protect you and the baby, I thought it best to let you believe I knew nothing about your relationship with Belikov."

Katherina deposited the bits of shattered china beside the samovar and smiled sadly. "To think of all the women in the world who have never known love—and I have had the good fortune to be loved by two extraordinary men." She shook her head in wonder. "What have I ever done to deserve even one man's love?"

"You have done enough, Katherina Andreievna," said Pavel Pavlovich. "You must know that your presence has given my last years immeasurable joy."

Running to the bed, she fell to her knees and clutched his hand. "And you must know, Pavel Pavlovich, that I truly did love you. I do love you. If I could ever have imagined what the future held, I would never have accepted your marriage proposal —for all of our sakes." She bent her head and her tears covered his wrinkled hand.

His hand gently brushed away her tears. "Katherina, Katherina," he mumbled in a hoarse voice, "there is no need for further explanations. We all made mistakes. We all wronged each other in some way. Perhaps I made the greatest error of all by asking you to marry me. It was unfair of me to expect devotion from a girl thirty years younger than myself." He paused, stroking her cheek. "Now you must promise me two things—two things that will give me peace."

Katherina raised her head and looked steadily into his eyes. "I will promise you anything, Pavel Pavlovich. Anything."

"Promise that you will stay with me until I die."

"Of course I will stay with you. Did you really think you needed to ask? What else shall I promise?"

"Promise that you will marry Aleksandr Belikov."

Katherina gasped. "You cannot mean that, Pavel Pavlovich! How can such a promise possibly give you peace?"

"Because I know Belikov will make a good husband for you—and a good father for Aleksei. Because I know the union will bring you more happiness than I ever could."

Katherina covered her face with her hands. Her breasts heaved as she sobbed uncontrollably.

"You needn't say anything, Katherina Andreievna. Just nod your head so I know you will fulfill my request."

Katherina nodded slowly. Then she collapsed beside the bed.

Chapter 26

Pavel Pavlovich Ostrov died in the early evening two days later. During those two days, Katherina Andreievna never left his side. Although she was relieved that the count knew about her liaison with Aleksandr Sergeievich, his understanding attitude made her feel even more guilty for the suffering she must have caused him.

The prince sent food to the room several times each day, but Katherina only picked at it, and she could barely induce the count to so much as sample any of it. The flies that were drawn to the room appeared to eat more than either of them, and the prince's servants clucked disapprovingly each time they came to carry away the trays.

Katherina and the count exchanged few words. She did what she could to make him comfortable, but it was impossible to know whether her efforts pleased him, for his manner was apathetic. She missed Aleksei terribly, but she was afraid to leave the room to visit him, and she knew the boy would be terrified by the sight of the withered count. In addition, she was sure Pavel Pavlovich would not want Aleksei to remember him in that condition.

In the last hours before her husband died, Katherina began to feel weak and exhausted. She attributed her condition to strain, coupled with lack of food or sleep, and she began to hope, though not without feeling guilty, that death would claim Pavel Pavlovich soon. She dozed, her head beside him on the bed. When she awoke, he was no longer breathing.

She ran first to Aleksei's room. Masha was tucking the child into bed. Masha looked up as Katherina rushed into the room, and her mistress's eyes told her that the waiting was over.

"Mama!" Aleksei cried as Katherina rushed to embrace him. She held him tightly against her breast and rubbed her face in his curly hair.

"Did you miss me, sweetheart?" she asked as she fought back her tears.

"Yes, mama. I missed you."

"He begged to see you, but I told him not to disturb you," Masha said.

"You were right," Katherina said, patting Aleksei's back.

"Mama—is it true that papa is here?"

Katherina's eyes shot to Masha, who shrugged helplessly. "It is not my fault, madame," she whispered. "The child heard the talk among Prince Dolgochev's servants."

"Yes, Aleksei," Katherina said gently, "he is here."

"Then why doesn't he come to see me? Did I do something naughty?"

Katherina hugged him closer. "No—no—of course not. Your papa has just been ill."

"Oh." Aleksei pulled away from his mother and studied her face seriously. "Is he feeling better now?"

"Much better," Katherina assured him. She saw Masha frown, but she felt she was not lying to the child. There could be no doubt that Pavel Pavlovich felt better now than he had in his last days of life.

Aleksei's eyes lighted up. "Then may I go to see him now?"

"Not now, dear. He is resting, and it's time you went to sleep, too."

"All right." He lay back reluctantly. "But I will see him first thing tomorrow morning."

"We'll see, Aleksei," Katherina said slowly. She leaned down to kiss him, then she extinguished the lamp beside his bed, and she and Masha left the room.

"Madame," Masha whispered as they hurried toward Katherina's room, "do you really think it was wise to let the child believe the count is still alive?"

Katherina shrugged weakly. "I couldn't explain to him about death tonight. It will be so much easier tomorrow, when we have all had a good night's sleep."

They entered the room where Pavel Pavlovich lay, and Katherina walked to the bed to pull the comforter close around his face. His limbs were already as stiff as if he had been dead a full day. She lit a long taper and placed it on the small table next to his bed.

"Tomorrow we will have to make arrangements to return to Novgorod," she said wearily. "I suppose he would want to be buried at his family estate. But I can't think about anything more tonight. I feel as if I haven't slept in months."

Katherina went to her room and undressed, but she didn't sleep. Soon after she lay down, she began vomiting. And though she had hardly eaten in three days, the vomiting, followed by severe hiccups, continued for several hours. Then her legs and feet were convulsed by agonizing cramps that spread in sharp bursts of pain to her stomach and back.

She became vaguely aware of people around her, but she was too exhausted and too crippled by pain to concentrate on who they were or what they were saying. When she forced herself to focus on one of her hands, she saw with horror that it was almost as wrinkled as Pavel Pavlovich's hand had been. Would she die in a few days, just as her husband had? Was that to be her ultimate punishment?

She woke once to find Masha standing over her, staring anxiously at her face.

"Where is Aleksei?" Katherina asked, and she was shocked by the raspy sound of her own voice.

"He is being well cared for," Masha assured her. "You mustn't worry about him, but you must relax and rest so you can recover and care for him yourself. I think he misses his mother."

"Masha, do I have cholera?"

Masha hesitated, then answered softly, "That is what the doctor says."

"Am I going to die?"

"Of course not!" Masha said sharply. "The doctor says you are too strong not to shake off the illness. You mustn't even think about death."

"Oh," Katherina said, forcing a weak smile.

By the fourth day, Katherina began to feel stronger. The vomiting ended and the cramps disappeared. She accepted the bowl of barley soup Masha brought her, savoring the warmth that spread through her body. After eating, she sipped a cup of tea, and she smiled at her servant.

"When I have finished, will you bring Aleksei to see me?"

Masha looked at her uneasily. "I think that would be better left to another day."

"Why? Is he napping now?"

"Yes," Masha said. "I am sure you would not want me to wake him."

"Then perhaps you can bring him after his nap."

"By then you may be asleep, madame—and it would be best not to wake you. The doctor says you need a great deal of rest."

"It couldn't hurt to wake me for a few moments so I could see my son." When Masha did not respond, Katherina said, "Masha, bring me my hand mirror from the bureau."

Masha dutifully brought the mirror, and Katherina surveyed herself. Her face still looked lax and wrinkled, and her hair lacked its usual healthy sheen.

"Aha," she said. "Just as I suspected. My face is quite a terrible sight. No doubt I would frighten the poor child half to death. Did you think I was too vain to be told how horrible I look?"

"I simply did not wish to upset you, madame."

"Well, it is obvious that we cannot allow Aleksei to see me in this condition. Perhaps in a few days."

Masha sighed. "Perhaps—" She picked up Katherina's empty dishes and quickly retreated from the room.

The next day Katherina still did not judge her appearance suitable, but the following day she thought she looked better, and again she asked Masha to bring Aleksei to her. Masha began to make excuses.

"Perhaps you should wait. The doctor says you should rest in bed for at least another week."

"Masha," Katherina said irritably, "I am not going to get out of bed. I simply want to see my son. What could speed my recovery more than seeing my darling son? I insist that you bring him to me immediately."

"I am afraid that is impossible," Masha said.

"Why?" Katherina snapped.

"He—he went out for a ride with Prince Dolgochev."

"Why didn't you say so in the first place? Then you must bring him as soon as he arrives home."

"Perhaps," Masha replied as she hurried from the room.

Several hours later Katherina heard movements in the adjoining room.

"Masha," she called, "have you brought Aleksei?"

When no one answered, she turned in the bed to look at the doorway. There, lounging against the doorframe, was Prince Dolgochev's nephew, Boris Ivanovich.

"May I come in?" he asked as he strode into the room.

"It appears that you are already in," she replied coolly.

He continued smiling, and without invitation he sat down on the edge of her bed.

"I really should not have visitors," Katherina said as she pulled her comforter closer and slid away from him. "I've been ill, and I am supposed to rest and recover."

"So I have heard. But you look even lovelier than the first time I saw you."

"I really must insist that you leave. I'm feeling rather tired."

He settled himself more comfortably on the bed. "I'll be happy to honor your request in a moment, Countess Ostrova, but there are a few things I wish to say to you. To begin with, let me offer my heartfelt condolences on the death of your husband, the count. I'm sure it was a difficult loss for you."

Katherina nodded absently. "Thank you."

"Secondly, I wish to remind you of the proposition I made to you here, on the terrace of this house, more than three years ago."

"Have you forgotten my reply?"

"Not at all. But since circumstances have changed considerably since then, I thought your reply might also have changed."

"No, Monsieur Dolgochev, my reply has not changed."

"You must understand that I am quite willing to marry you now. Of course we would be required to wait a year, for the sake of propriety, but in the meantime we could see each other regularly, if you understand my meaning. Perhaps I could even escort you to some of the balls in St. Petersburg. I assure you, I would exercise the greatest discretion at all times."

Katherina sighed. "Monsieur Dolgochev, you don't seem to understand. I am not in the least interested in either marriage or a liaison."

"But you are much too young, and much too beautiful, to be alone in the world. Perhaps I should give you more time to think. You might regret your hasty decision."

"I doubt that anything would change my mind. And may I remind you that I am not alone? I have Aleksei, and he is all the company I need."

"Aleksei?" Boris Ivanovich said uncertainly.

"Yes. My son."

Boris looked away and his face paled slightly. "Then you don't know?" he whispered.

"What are you talking about?"

"Forgive me. I simply assumed that they had told you." He started to get up from the bed, but Katherina took his arm and held him back.

"I demand that you explain your words."

He hesitated, then shrugged uncomfortably. "I suppose someone must tell you." He paused again and took a deep breath. "Your Aleksei is dead."

"What!" Katherina sat upright in bed, not noticing as the comforter fell to her waist. She pounded her delicate fists against Boris Ivanovich's chest. "What a cruel lie! Do you really think you can win me by playing such wicked games with my heart? Get out of my room!"

"It is not a lie," Boris said slowly. "I wish it were. The child died of cholera three days ago."

"I don't believe you," Katherina cried, pounding harder against his chest. "I'm expecting my servant to bring him to me at any moment."

Boris caught her wrists and shook her roughly. "Katherina, listen to me! I have told you the truth."

"No!" she sobbed. "Masha would have told me herself." She slowly remembered Masha's evasiveness and uneasiness whenever she had asked about Aleksei. Her Aleksei—Aleksandr Sergeievich's son— was really dead!

"Aleksei! Aleksei!" she wailed, and she collapsed against Boris Ivanovich's chest.

Boris wrapped his arms around her, pulling her closer to him. Without thinking, feeling only the welcome strength of his arms, she put her own arms around him and continued to sob for her lost son.

Immersed in her grief, Katherina Andreievna scarcely felt Boris Ivanovich's lips pressing urgently on her neck and then her face. She was not conscious of his hands gliding through her unbraided hair and gently massaging her spine, and when his tongue flicked lightly into her ear, she only pressed her heaving body closer to him.

Suddenly Katherina became uncomfortably aware of the thinness of her nightgown, which barely shielded the soft points of her breasts. She started to pull away in embarrassment, but he tightened his arms around her and covered her protesting mouth with his own.

This kiss was not like the harsh, bruising kiss he had given her on the terrace three years before. This time his lips were soft and tender, coaxing her to accept him, begging her lips to open and admit his hungry tongue. Too spiritually drained to push him away, Katherina gave in to his desires, and she found a strange solace in his caresses.

When at last his lips moved away from hers, he murmured in her ear, "Don't be ashamed, my little golden-haired beauty—don't be ashamed to admit you need me now."

He kissed her again, this time more boldly, his tongue flicking nimbly in and out of her mouth. Then, pressing his lips to her throat, he began to untie the ribbons on her nightgown. When she started to pull away again, he whispered, "Relax, my little princess. Don't be afraid. I won't hurt you."

He lay her against her pillows and folded the gown back against her ivory skin. He kissed one breast, then the other, burying his face for a moment in the warm, throbbing hollow between them. Then, as Katherina watched silently, he got up and closed the door to her room.

She did not protest as he undressed and slid beneath her comforter. Or as he pulled her nightgown from her trembling body. What did it matter now, she wondered. Her heart, her mind, her body felt numb. She would never see Aleksei again, never again would she hear him laugh or speak, never would she present him to Aleksandr Sergeievich. Aleksei would never know the identity of his real father, and Aleksandr Sergeievich would never meet his son.

Boris Ivanovich was a slow, gentle lover. He murmured tender words of reassurance as his body moved against Katherina's. Gradually, she abandoned herself to the feeling that spread through her.

For a long time afterward, Boris Ivanovich lay beside her, clutching her close to him and running his fingers through her hair.

Chapter 27

Katherina slept for a few hours, but she awakened in the middle of the night, her head throbbing with tension.

Aleksei is dead! The thought pounded through her mind. What did the future hold for her now? What could she tell Aleksandr Sergeievich? Assuming that General Paskevich complied with Pavel Pavlovich's wish, Aleksandr might arrive in Moscow in a few weeks—and he would expect to see his son.

She became aware that she had been sleeping in the nude, something she had not done since she and Aleksandr Sergeievich had shared her bed in Pyatigorsk. And then the memory of her encounter with Boris Ivanovich engulfed her. Had she really submitted to him? Why had she allowed it to happen? How could she ever explain it to Aleksandr Sergeievich? At least with General Bugov she had acted to save Aleksandr, but she had accepted Boris only out of her own selfish need for comfort.

Of course, she need not tell Aleksandr, but it seemed unlikely that Boris Ivanovich would let them go away together unchallenged. He had talked yesterday about their future together, and now he was sure to pursue the subject. As they made love, he had been gentle and considerate, but Katherina had no doubt that he could be ruthless if another man threatened to disrupt his plans.

Aleksei's death—Aleksei—dead. No matter how she

tried to get away from the thought, she felt responsible for her child's death. She must have infected him. She should have been there to care for him. She should have listened to the warning of the priest at Smolensky Cathedral.

Aleksandr Sergeievich had entrusted their son to her care—and she had failed. She wondered if she could ever face him again. She ached to feel joyful in the knowledge that Aleksandr was coming to her and that she was free to marry him, but she felt only grief, fear, and guilt.

Katherina was still awake at dawn when Masha quietly opened the door and looked in on her. She motioned Masha to come in, and the servant tiptoed to her bedside. Masha stared uneasily at Katherina's sunken eyes.

"Madame, did you not sleep well last night?" she whispered.

"No, Masha—I did not sleep well."

"Can I do something? Get something to make you feel more relaxed? Perhaps some tea."

"No. Nothing can make me feel better." Katherina paused. "Aleksei is dead."

Masha gasped and looked away. When she spoke, her voice was heavy with tears. "How did you find out?"

"It doesn't matter," Katherina said quietly, "but I wondered why you did not tell me, Masha. Why did you let me learn the news from someone else?"

Masha sobbed. "I couldn't tell you. Not right away. I thought in time I would be able to talk about it and in time you would be strong enough to bear the grief. But how could I tell you when I myself was torn in two by the pain?"

"Masha, Aleksei was my son! I deserved to know!"

"But you were so sick. I was sure the news would be too much for you. And I couldn't bear to lose you, too, madame."

Katherina's tone softened. "I'm sorry, Masha. I know you tried to do what was best for me. Forgive me for being so harsh. Could I at least see his body one more time before it is taken away?"

Masha shook her head. "I'm sorry, madame, but he was buried immediately. The health authorities insisted. If you wish, when you are well, we may visit his grave at Novodevichy Monastery."

"And what of Pavel Pavlovich?"

"He was buried there as well. The authorities would not allow us to transport his body to Novgorod for fear of somehow spreading the disease." When Katherina made no comment, Masha continued, "We are very fortunate that you came through this experience, madame—but you must try to get some rest if you ever expect to fully recover. You must sleep."

"I can't sleep, Masha. There are too many problems tormenting me. With Aleksei gone, I have no reason to want to recover. I've no idea what I will do with myself when I finally get out of this bed."

Masha stared at her in dismay. "You can't mean that, madame. What about Monsieur Belikov? If you wish, I will still go with you to Pyatigorsk as soon as you are well. I am sure we can make the trip safely. And now there is no reason why you two cannot be married."

Katherina shook her head. "I no longer wish to go to Pyatigorsk. At any rate, Aleksandr Sergeievich may already be on his way here."

"What makes you think that?"

"Pavel Pavlovich sent for him before he died."

"The count sent for him? I'm afraid I don't understand at all."

"It's too difficult to explain, Masha, except to say that the count was even a finer man than I had ever imagined."

Masha nodded thoughtfully, then her eyes brightened with excitement. "If Monsieur Belikov is coming here, we must prepare for him! If you rest, I am sure you will be well enough to be up within a week. I will find you a dressmaker to make you some stunning new gowns. He will be overwhelmed when he sees you again!"

"I can't see him, Masha."

"Madame—do you know what you are saying? Of course you will see him. I am anxious to see him myself."

"No—I cannot see him. How can I tell him I let his son die?"

"His son?" Masha whispered.

"Surely you saw the resemblance, Masha. You, of all people, must have known Aleksei was Aleksandr's son."

"I suppose I did know," Masha admitted slowly. "But how can you even think that you are responsible for Aleksei's death?"

"I just know it. I feel it. It was my fault."

"Don't talk nonsense," Masha said sharply. "You know better than to believe that, and you certainly cannot think that Monsieur Belikov will blame you. Only God decides when illness may claim a life— you and I have nothing to say about it."

"I made Him decide to take Aleksei," Katherina said softly.

As Masha opened her mouth to reply, a hearty voice from the doorway interrupted them. "And how is my lovely fiancée today?"

Katherina winced, and Masha looked at her in curious disbelief as Boris Ivanovich strolled into the room. Uncomfortably aware of her nakedness, Katherina pulled the comforter closer to her chin.

"It appears that you awaken very early, Monsieur Dolgochev," she said coolly.

"No earlier than you," he said. "And please call me Boris Ivanovich. If we're to be married, you must not address me so formally."

Masha continued to stare, and Katherina carefully restrained herself. "If, indeed," she muttered, and she turned to Masha. "I won't be needing you for a few moments, Masha. It appears that Monsieur Dolgochev and I have a great deal to discuss."

Masha nodded and left the room slowly, a perplexed expression creasing her face.

"It seems your servant does not approve of me." Boris Ivanovich chuckled.

"I'm not at all sure I do either."

He settled himself on the bed and touched her nose playfully with the tip of his finger. "You disappoint me, Katherina Andreievna. Yesterday you seemed to approve of me most heartily."

Her eyes met his, and her voice was cool and steady. "Yesterday you offered me consolation in my grief. I was grateful to you for that—but there was and is nothing more."

The corners of his thin lips quivered in the beginning of a smile. "Marry me, and I can give you that kind of consolation whenever you like."

"As I told you before, I have no desire to marry you."

"That is what you said with your mouth, but your body told me something quite different. You need me. I thought perhaps by the morning's light you would be willing to admit that."

"I don't need you," Katherina said. "What I need is peace and quiet. A chance to rest and a chance to think. Leave me alone, Boris Ivanovich."

He rose, laughing. "As you wish, madame. Of course I will leave you. But I will still be here, in this house. And I think when I come to see you again you will have changed your mind."

"Never!" Katherina flung the word at his back as he sauntered toward the doorway.

He turned and smiled broadly, his white teeth glistening in mockery. "We shall see, my spirited little beauty. We shall see."

After he left, Katherina stared at the empty doorframe, quivering with rage. Who was he to act so smug? How dare he embarrass her in front of Masha? How would she ever explain his words to her servant? She would not, she decided, allow him to bully and intimidate her. She would not stay under the same roof with him while he mocked and embarrassed her. She would leave that very day.

Her decision made, Katherina sat up and swung her legs over the side of the bed. She found her nightgown on the floor, slipped it over her head, and reached for her dressing gown. Then she stood and took a few steps. The cool wooden floor felt strange under her feet, and her head seemed to reel with every step. She staggered toward her wardrobe cabinet, falling heavily against its carved wooden doors. She leaned against the wardrobe, panting from exertion, and, summoning all her strength, she opened the heavy doors and selected a gown.

Katherina managed to stagger back to the bed and dress herself. She quickly plaited her hair into two long braids, then she stood again and walked unsteadily toward the bedroom door to go in search of Masha.

She stopped to rest against the doorframe, then, taking several deep breaths, she forced herself to continue through the room where Pavel Pavlovich had died. His bed was empty now, covered with fresh linen and a bright new comforter. The samovar that had seen her through her last days with him had been taken away.

Katherina was halfway across the room when the queasiness began to overtake her. It's just the smell of death lingering in this room, she told herself. She took a few more timid steps before the room began to spin before her eyes and she lost her balance.

When she awoke, it was evening, and Masha was sitting beside her bed.

"Masha—what happened to me?" she whispered.

"You fainted," Masha said. Then she added in a reproving tone, "You should not have been out of bed yet. Where did you think you were going?"

"I was looking for you. I wanted to leave this place immediately." As her memory came back, Katherina started to sit up in bed.

"You are being very foolish," Masha said, firmly pushing her back against the pillows. "The doctor said you must allow at least a week to recuperate. After that you will have all the time you wish to travel, but for now you must be sensible. We were fortunate to have Monsieur Dolgochev so near."

"Monsieur Dolgochev. You mean the prince?"

"No, his nephew, the young Monsieur Dolgochev."

Katherina froze. "How were we fortunate?"

"Because he carried you back to your bed. I could never have managed alone. He seemed most concerned about your condition."

"Oh." Katherina stared at her hands, aware that Masha was watching her.

"Madame?" Masha ventured timidly.

"What is it, Masha?"

"Is it true that you are going to marry Monsieur Dolgochev?"

"Do you think I should?"

"I think that is not for me to say."

"Well," Katherina mused, "I would be well cared for and I would certainly have all the money I need—"

She saw Masha's eyes filling with tears. "But you needn't worry, Masha. No matter what he may say, I have no intention of marrying him. I don't love him, and I'll never marry a man I don't love."

Masha smiled. "I was hoping you would say that. Monsieur Belikov's heart would surely be broken if you married another."

"I'm afraid I may already have broken his heart," Katherina said softly.

"Oh, no, madame—"

"Please, Masha," Katherina cut her off with a wave of her hand, "I can't discuss it now. You said yourself that I must rest."

"Yes, madame," the servant answered weakly.

When Boris Ivanovich visited Katherina the next day, he demanded more discussion. He perched on the edge of her bed and riveted his eyes on hers.

"Have you decided yet to accept my proposal?"

"My answer remains unchanged."

"Surely you don't expect me to drop to my knees and beg you?"

"Of course not. I simply ask you to honor my decision and leave me alone."

"But that's impossible. As I told you before, you're much too beautiful—and much too capable a lover— to be left to face the world alone."

Katherina blushed at his reminder of their experience in bed.

"But perhaps," he continued tauntingly, "that is precisely why you continue to refuse me. Could it be that—now that you are free of your husband—you wish to sample the delights of a number of men? Would you prefer that I prove myself as one of your many lovers?"

White-hot fury coursed through Katherina's body, and she slapped him hard across the cheek.

When he spoke again, it was in a softly penitent voice. "Forgive me, Katherina Andreievna. I did not mean that—but it is beyond my powers of understanding to perceive why you will not agree to marry me."

"I have my reasons," Katherina said. "Most of them have nothing at all to do with you, but if you must have some explanation, perhaps you will accept this: Quite simply—I do not love you."

Boris Ivanovich sighed. "But that is not a problem. I do not demand that you love me. I suspect that few marriages are based on love, anyway. Only say that you will marry me, and I will be satisfied."

"Why? So you can display me as one of your possessions?"

"Surely you do not think me as callous as that, Katherina. Of course I would be proud to go out in public with you on my arm as my wife, but I would also like to take care of you and enjoy that spirit of yours that I have always admired so much."

His unexpected sincerity touched her, and tears filled Katherina's eyes. She shook her head helplessly. "It's no use, Boris Ivanovich. I can't agree to marry you. I shan't agree to marry anyone."

He rose slowly and started toward the door, but he

hesitated in the doorway and turned back to face her again. "Is it because of your other lover? The one who was in the December revolution?"

She looked away without answering. Rushing back to her bedside, he clutched her hand and cried, "Katherina, only tell me his identity and I swear I will use all my influence to bring him back from Siberia. If I bring him back, will you agree to marry me?"

She shook her head.

"I won't be a jealous husband. I won't even demand that you give him up. You may enjoy him all you wish if that makes you happy. Just marry me."

"Please, Boris. I told you it is no use. I do not intend to marry again—ever!"

"All right, Katherina, I won't bother you again. I wish you well in the life you have chosen for yourself, but I warn you, don't expect it to be easy. I won't be the last man to propose to you. No doubt your suitors will become quite a nuisance, and, in the end, you may find it would have been easier to accept my proposal."

Boris Ivanovich's words hung in the air long after he was gone, and Katherina Andreievna had to admit that much of what he said was true. As a prominent young countess, she would no doubt be besieged by men who wanted to marry her—for a variety of reasons. Even if she retired to Novgorod, some of them would pursue her, and the country gentry would also begin to court her.

If only she could marry Aleksandr Sergeievich. She desperately longed to be enfolded in his arms, but she was sure she could never bear to see the hurt, the despair, perhaps even the accusation in his dark eyes. She had to find an escape—but where could she go to be out of reach of everyone—including Aleksandr Sergeievich and all the bittersweet memories connected with her love for him?

By the time Masha brought her dinner, Katherina had found the solution. "Masha," she said, "tomorrow you must ask Prince Dolgochev to visit me. I want to consult him about the necessary steps to giving you your freedom."

Masha gasped as she set down the tray on Katherina's lap. "You are very kind, madame, but—since I wish to remain with you—it is unnecessary to give me my freedom. You have always treated me fairly and I have never wished for anything else."

"Still, I think it would be for the best, Masha. Where I intend to go I will not be permitted to take servants."

Masha stared openmouthed at her. "I don't understand, madame."

"I intend to enter a convent."

Masha turned white. "But you have not given this very much serious thought, madame."

"I have—and no one can say anything to change my mind."

"But Monsieur Belikov will—"

"Masha," Katherina interrupted, "perhaps you did not hear me. I said my mind is made up."

"Perhaps the convent will not accept you. It is hardly customary for a woman of your status to enter a convent."

"I can think of no reason why they could refuse me." Katherina began to pick at her food.

Masha's eyes brightened. "But there is a reason for them to refuse you! Have you forgotten that the law forbids any woman to enter a convent before she has reached the age of forty? Perhaps in another ten years, when you are legally of age, you will have changed your mind. Perhaps by then Monsieur Belikov will have changed it for you."

"No!" Katherina said, pushing the tray from her lap. "I don't care about the law! I won't be stopped! I must enter a convent. And before Aleksandr Sergeievich arrives in Moscow."

"But you will never be permitted."

"Then I shall find another way. I shall go to a monastery. Surely the monks must need someone to clean and cook for them."

"I had always understood that the monks did all those things for themselves, madame—that it was part of humbling themselves before God."

"If I throw myself at the mercy of the brothers, I'm sure they will find some use for me. They cannot refuse to help me."

Masha shook her head doubtfully. "Where do you propose to go? To Novodevichy, here in Moscow?"

The thought of her last visit there made Katherina shudder. Even if she could cast off her image of the priest and his ominous warning, there would always be other, more painful, memories of an afternoon spent in Smolensky Cathedral with Aleksandr Sergeievich. "No. Definitely not Novodevichy."

"Where then? Will you return to Novgorod? Perhaps to the monastery on Lake Ilmen where Countess Orlova used to go for her retreats? It always looked to me like such a cheery place, with the bright blue domes sprinkled with gilded stars. As a child I always thought that God had given the monks a bit of the sky to tend on their cathedral domes. If you went there, I could visit you from time to time. And perhaps, when you have recovered from your grief, you might rejoin the world."

Katherina cut her off. "I will never rejoin the world

—and I don't deserve the cheeriness of the monastery on Lake Ilmen. I won't return to Novgorod. It is too near to the people and places I hold dear."

"Then where will you go?" Masha asked desperately.

"I think perhaps to Kiev. I've heard of a monastery there called *Pecherskaya Lavra*—'the Monastery of the Caves.' I think it would be fitting for me to spend the rest of my life in a cave."

Tears welled in Masha's eyes. "But you can never be at home in Kiev. The people there do not even speak true Russian. Just some Ukrainian form of the language."

"Ukrainian is close enough to Russian to understand. And I imagine the brothers may use Old Church Slavonic. Besides, I am not going to the monastery to be comfortable or to have conversations."

"Madame, why do you insist on being so harsh on yourself?"

Katherina looked away, and she repeated the warning given her by the priest at Novodevichy Monastery —words that had plagued her since she learned of Aleksei's death. "The Lord visits the iniquities of the parents on the children, even to the third and fourth generations."

Shaking her head in confusion, Masha gently touched Katherina's arm. "Madame—you are not making sense at all."

"My sins caused Aleksei's death!" Katherina cried.

"Madame, that is not true. I won't believe it, and I won't let you believe it."

Katherina shook her servant away. "I do believe it, Masha, and nothing you say will convince me otherwise. Just do as I have directed, and ask the prince to visit me tomorrow."

Masha's voice became heavy with tears. "If you

won't think of yourself, think of me. After all my years of faithful service, will you simply cast me away like a worn-out boot? Where will I go? What will I do with myself? This is the only life I know."

"As a free woman, you will go where you wish, do as you wish, and marry whomever you wish. You are a young woman, Masha, with a great deal to recommend you. I'll see that you receive a considerable sum so you need never worry about money. If you wish, you may return to our house in St. Petersburg. Stay there as long as you wish. My bedroom is yours, and you may take whatever pleases you among my gowns and other possessions."

"And what will I say when Monsieur Belikov comes, as I know he will, to ask me where you are?"

Katherina froze, battling her emotions. Then she turned her head and met Masha's wide eyes with her own steady gaze. "Tell him I have disappeared. That you have no idea where I am. Perhaps you should even tell him that I am dead."

Masha gasped and looked away from Katherina. Staring uncomfortably at her hands, she mumbled, "I don't think I could lie to Monsieur Belikov."

"You must. You must swear that you will never tell anyone where I have gone."

"How can you want to hurt him," Masha blurted, "when you have always claimed to love him so much?"

"Love cannot keep me from hurting him," Katherina whispered hoarsely. "It's too late to keep from hurting him now. When he learns of Aleksei's death it will hurt him more than anything he may have suffered in the wars or in the Czar's prison. It's a terrible burden to know you have hurt someone you love. Can't you understand, Masha, I want him and need him now as much as ever. Perhaps more."

"Don't you think," Masha said quietly, "that he needs you too?"

Katherina shook her head. "He may think so, but he will find that life is better without me. I can't risk causing him more pain. If we never again see each other, there will no chance of my hurting him again."

Masha sighed. "And yet you know you will hurt him by your very disappearance. If you'll forgive me, madame, your reasoning is impossible to understand."

"Then don't try to understand it. Just promise me that you will never reveal my whereabouts."

Masha shook her head. "I can't promise that. My heart will not let me."

"Very well then. I will choose a different monastery. And I will not confide my destination in you."

Masha hesitated, struggling with her conscience; then she said slowly, "No. Go to Pecherskaya Lavra. It seems—suited to you. I'll do—as you ask." Before Katherina could thank her, she fled from the room, sobbing.

Chapter 28

They left Moscow six days later, as soon as Katherina was strong enough to travel. Although they hired two carriages for themselves and their belongings, Katherina and Masha traveled together in the first carriage on the first day. Since they had been so close during their stay in Moscow, Katherina did not want to arouse the prince's suspicions. Only the carriage drivers knew of their separate destinations. When she had explained earlier in the week that she wished to reward Masha for her years of faithful service, the prince had, without question, helped her draw up the papers declaring the servant a free woman.

After their first night west of Moscow, Katherina and Masha separated. As they embraced in the chilly dawn, Katherina was tempted to go with Masha to St. Petersburg, but she forced herself to enter her own carriage, directing the driver southwest toward Kiev; and Masha's carriage turned northwest, toward St. Petersburg.

The journey to Kiev took almost three weeks. Katherina remembered almost nothing about it, except for the seemingly unending wheat fields as they traveled through the Ukraine. The monks at Pecherskaya Lavra were reluctant to take her in, but her constant flow of tears, aided by her offer of a huge endowment for the monastery, convinced them of her sincerity.

During the first weeks, Katherina thought she would never adjust to the damp passageways and the eerie flickering of candles in the caves. In one section, dead monks, some of whom had lived and died seven hundred years before, were actually buried in the sides of the narrow passageways. Katherina shivered and quickened her pace whenever she passed there.

After a time, life in the monastery settled into a dull monotony. Katherina discarded the few fine dresses she had used for traveling and she wore a loose-fitting gray peasant caftan. She spent most of her time working in the kitchen, but she often went to the monastery gardens to gather vegetables for preparing the simple meals. At such times, she always found an excuse to stay outside, breathing the fresh air for a few extra minutes.

Despite an apparent adjustment to her new life, Katherina still suffered silently in her bare monastery cell. She lay awake each night, imagining the warmth and strength of Aleksandr Sergeievich beside her. Even when she managed to sleep, she awoke to find her cheeks wet with tears of loneliness and longing. Some nights, she thought she heard Aleksei calling her, and she bolted up from her cot before she realized she was only dreaming.

As the weeks passed and the nightmares refused to disappear, Katherina began to wonder if she had made the right decision. Perhaps she should have returned to St. Petersburg with Masha, perhaps she should have waited for Aleksandr Sergeievich in Moscow, but it was too late now to change her mind. Aleksandr Sergeievich was probably on his way back to the Caucasus, expecting never to see her again.

Katherina had been at Pecherskaya Lavra for six weeks—six long weeks in the musty underground corridors, six weeks of monotonous routine, and six weeks of terrifying sleepless nights. Every day she worked harder than the day before—cooking, cleaning, doing laundry—hoping to drown herself in exhaustion and thereby escape the horrible visions and the loneliness that threatened to swallow her each night. However, no matter how exhausted she felt, when she extinguished her candle and crawled beneath her rough blanket, sleep refused to come.

On the first evening of the seventh week, Katherina hurried down the damp passageway. She felt almost too tired to hold her flickering candle, and she prayed that tonight, at last, she would sleep peacefully. She pulled aside the ragged curtain at the entrance to her cell, and the candle's wavering light fell on a bulky object resting on her narrow cot.

Katherina froze in the doorway, still holding the edge of the tattered curtain. She tried to hold the candle steadier as she stared in disbelief. Could it be another vision, here to torment her? When would she ever have peace? She stepped forward hesitantly. The candle's flickering light swept over a polished triangular wooden surface, and painted apple blossoms swam in the unsteady light. She moved the candle until the light swept over the handle of a balalaika. Still not believing it was there, and not understanding how it could have gotten there, Katherina reached out uncertainly and plucked a string. Its familiar mellow tone flooded the tiny cell, filling Katherina with a warmth she had not felt since she had left Aleksandr Sergeievich in Pyatigorsk. As if afraid to dispel the miraculous vision, she plucked another string and again felt enfolded in blissful warmth and security.

"Go ahead and play it. It won't disappear."

The voice startled Katherina. She whirled toward the corner of the cell, dropping the candle in her excitement. The flame sputtered and died on the floor, but she needed no light to recognize who had spoken to her.

"Sasha!"

Before she took a step, he was there, holding her. She buried her face in his shirt and breathed in the familiar smell of his body as she sobbed uncontrollably against his chest.

"Oh, Sasha, I've missed you so much. I don't think I've lived at all since we've been separated."

He smiled. "Well, you certainly didn't make yourself very easy to find. I've been over half the empire searching for you. My God—what a hiding place you chose. I think even a dungeon might have been preferable." He tilted back her head and covered her mouth with his own.

She rubbed her face against his cheek. "But how did you know to come here?"

"How do you think? I got the news of your whereabouts from the same place as the balalaika."

"Masha?"

He pulled her closer and nuzzled her ear. "Yes—Masha."

"But she swore she would not tell anyone—especially you."

He laughed softly. "You're forgetting that you gave Masha her freedom, and as a free woman she is no longer obliged to follow your orders." He began to unbraid her hair. "Would you rather she had kept her promise?"

"No." Her feelings slipped out before she could stop herself. Then she shook her head. "I mean—yes. I don't know. It's just that I thought life would be better for you without me—that I couldn't cause you any more pain if you never saw me again."

Aleksandr Sergeievich grabbed her by the shoulders. "How can you talk of pain! Have you any idea how I've suffered these last months, searching for you, wondering where I would find you—wondering why you deserted me?"

"Sasha, I didn't desert you, I—"

"Yes, I know," he cut her off. "You needn't try to explain. Masha told me everything. Thank God she has more sense than you."

"She told you—everything—," Katherina stammered. "Even about Aleksei?"

"Yes—she told me everything."

"Did she tell you I am responsible for his death?"

"Don't talk nonsense, Katya. She told me that's what you believe. She also told me it isn't true."

"She doesn't know! She didn't speak to the priest at Novodevichy Monastery," Katherina cried hysterically.

"What are you talking about?"

"The day before Pavel Pavlovich returned to Moscow with cholera—the day before I planned to come to you in Pyatigorsk with Aleksei and Masha—I went to Smolensky Cathedral. The priest there begged me to confess my sins. When I refused, he told me that God punishes children for the sins of their parents. I know Aleksei would not have died if I had confessed and repented."

"Repented for what?"

Katherina's voice was small and strained. "For sinning against my husband. For breaking my marriage vows."

He stroked her cheek, tenderly wiping away the tears that covered her face. "Don't you think you are being a bit greedy, taking all the blame?" he chided. "If you sinned, my sins are at least equal to yours. Perhaps greater—because I pursued you from the beginning. But I think we must remember that your own dear husband forgave us both. If a mere man—and one who has been wronged—can find it in his heart to forgive, don't you think that God, in His infinite mercy, forgives us too?"

"I don't know," she sniffled.

"Yes, you do know, Katya. Look into your heart and you will see the answer—if you will only accept it. We don't need a priest's forgiveness—we have Pavel Pavlovich's. Even Masha, who has always struck me as being a great deal more pious than you, accepts that fact."

He was silent for a moment, stroking her hair, which now hung loose around her shoulders. Katherina was equally silent, enjoying the touch of his hands and the nearness of his body, trying to digest his words.

"You know," he mused, "Masha is a good deal wiser than I had ever imagined. She loves both of us, and she loved Aleksei—and she wouldn't have brought me here if she didn't know in her heart it was right for all of us."

"Brought you here? Is she here too?"

"Not here at the monastery. But yes, she is in Kiev. She insisted on coming to see you. I found her a room at an inn. You can see her tomorrow when we leave here."

"But I can't simply leave. I have responsibilities—promises I made to the monks."

He sighed in desperation. "Katya, Pecherskaya Lavra has existed for eight hundred years. Its passageways won't crumble when you leave. Surely you cannot think the brothers need you more than I do."

When she did not answer, he prodded her. "Katya, you are not happy here, are you?"

"No," she admitted slowly, "but I am so afraid I

cannot make you happy again. I can't let myself ruin your life, Sasha."

"The only way you can ruin my life is by refusing to become my wife. But I won't give you that opportunity. I'll stay in this cell, day and night, until you agree."

Katherina giggled. "What a scandal that would cause! I can just imagine all the monks breaking the grand silence to gossip about our sinful relationship! I ought to put you off for a day or two, just to see their reaction."

Aleksandr slapped her buttocks. "That sounds a bit more like my willful, playful little Katya. But you won't keep me waiting—will you?"

She pursed her lips. "I don't know. I'll have to give it some thought."

"Perhaps you need a bit of persuasion." He gently pushed her back toward her cot.

"Sasha," she whispered, "not here!"

"Why?" He laughed as he picked her up and carried her the few remaining steps. "Are you expecting someone else to visit you tonight?"

"Don't be silly. There's no one here but monks— and none of them has even given me a second look."

He set her down on the cot and began taking off her caftan. "If they ignore you, Katya, they must all be blind."

She pushed his hands away. "Please, Sasha. Don't forget we are in a monastery, a sacred place."

"And I can think of nothing more sacred than our love." He threw the caftan across the room and pressed his mouth to her throbbing breast. "Don't deny me now, Katya," he said. "My body is starving for you."

She lay back without further protest and pulled his

mouth to hers. Every muscle in her body quivered, scolding her for all the weeks she had denied herself his love.

"Oh, Sasha," she breathed, "can you ever forgive me for how foolish I have been?"

His tongue moved to her ear, teasingly flicking in and out of its tiny crevices. "We have a lot of lost nights to make up for," he whispered. "And a lot of lost days."

Together they peeled away his clothes. And then he lay beside her, and their bodies melted together. When he entered her, she felt sure she would scream with joy and all of the monks would come running to her cell to find out the cause of the disturbance. But, as she and Sasha loved each other with all the intensity that had been locked in their hearts and bodies during the years of their separation, she forgot about the monks and Pecherskaya Lavra.

Later, as she slowly became aware of the scratchy monastery blanket beneath her delicate skin, she propped herself up on an elbow and touched her lips to the tip of Aleksandr's nose. He stirred slightly and, with a moan of pleasure, gave her buttocks an affectionate pat.

"Sasha," she whispered.

"Ummm?"

"Where shall we be married?"

"Wherever you like, Katya. Only I hope you will say in Kiev, for I'm not sure I can wait much longer to make you completely mine."

"Perhaps I could talk to the abbot tomorrow."

He grimaced. "I have no desire to be married in a cave. Besides, beauty like yours ought to be displayed in a cathedral. I suggest Saint Sophia's."

"Oh, Sasha, Saint Sophia's is too grand! I've nothing

to wear in a place like that. My gray caftan would never suffice."

He gently stroked her breast, feeling the nipple grow hard. "My love, you could go naked and be more magnificent than any icon in Saint Sophia's. But that won't be necessary. Masha brought you a selection of gowns."

"Dear Masha! She seems to have thought of every-thing."

His fingers moved casually down her body. "I suppose you will want to return to St. Petersburg?"

"Oh, no! I'd be content never to return there again, as long as I can spend the rest of my life with you, Sasha."

"Good," he sighed as he licked the hollow between her breasts. "I would like to start a new life for us. Somewhere we have never been before—where we can build a lifetime of memories."

"I'll go anywhere with you, Sasha," Katherina whis-pered. "Where shall we start our new life?"

"Perhaps we can honeymoon in Odessa—I hear it is just like an Italian city. And then we can continue into the Crimea. It is green—and wild—and free. We can build our own little house somewhere among the grapevines—and we won't leave it for at least three months!"

"Mmmm," Katherina closed her eyes and envisioned the green hills of the Crimea waiting for them. "It will be perfect."

"Enough talk," Aleksandr Sergeievich said, nibbling at her ear.

"I'm sorry," Katherina whispered. "I guess I forgot myself. You must be tired after the long journey from St. Petersburg. I'll let you sleep now. We have thousands of tomorrows in which to talk."

Aleksandr laughed. "It wasn't sleep I was thinking of." He pressed close to her, and his hardness made her body tremble with passion.

"I think," she moaned, "that I am not sleepy either."

ABOUT THE AUTHOR

LYNN LOWERY is a student of Russian history and culture, so that nineteenth-century Russia was a logical choice for her first romantic historical novel. With her husband, she has written several juvenile books. Ms. Lowery lives in Evanston, Illinois.

A Preview of
MY LADY'S CRUSADE
by Annette Motley

A sweeping new novel of
exotic danger, coming in April
from Bantam Books

CHAPTER ONE

Hawkhurst

The torches flared and shuddered in their dozen sconces about the walls and the candles flickered on the long table as the sudden draft gusted down the hall.

Eden knew there would be a storm. She signaled to Rollo, stretched on the straw beside the two great dogs, content and dreaming after his meal. The serf got up at once and took the long curtain-pole from its place behind the settle; he drew the heavy, hide-backed russet folds across the tall, shuttered windows, his shadow scaling the high, stone walls to reach them unaided.

"Shall I feed the fire again, my lady? It'll be a cold night. Snow, mebbe."

Eden shivered and drew her cloak of fine, dark-green wool close across her breast. She hated the winter. It seemed that she had always been cold since Stephen had left. It was at moments such as these, when the demons took their spurs to the winds outside, and the doors and shutters creaked and rattled their hinges, that she felt her isolation most.

It was small consolation to her to be the sole mistress and sovereign lady of Hawkhurst, if she must keep her state alone at her board every night, with nothing but the prospect of a cup of wine with her chaplain or a game of backgammon with her bailiff to call her pleasure. True, they would speak to her of Stephen, calling up visions of the Holy Land as if it were a country in a minstrel's tale. They did so to bring her comfort, she knew, but as she listened, it was as if her husband had gone from her into the flat dimensions of a map or the exotic scene of a tapestry, so far from reality were their pictures of turbanned knights and veiled women, of silken luxury and barbarous cruelty.

At first, she could not believe that he had indeed take the Cross. Stephen had lived with her, here at her manor of Hawkhurst, since both of them were children. She had been her father's only heir and was betrothed to him at the age of seven. He had entered the household, when she was ten, so that he might learn the virtues and responsibilities of his future inheritance. To the lonely girl, by now motherless, the handsome, thoughtful boy became the adored elder brother she had never had. He was sixteen and he came to represent to her all the heroes of her favorite legends; he was Launcelot, Roland, Tristan, all in one. They had married when she was fifteen and there had been three years of this changed state of existence; just three brief, ecstatic, confused years of darkness and brightness, and then the cry had gone up for the Crusade. Stephen, idealistic, fervent in his Christianity, in love with the concept of Chivalry, eager to serve his great, golden giant of a King, had been among the first to sew the white silk token on his shoulder.

He had been gone for nearly two years. There had been no news. It was scarcely expected. It was known that his troop had been present at the seige of the great city of Acre; it was possible that he was still in that region and alive; the city was still beleaguered, no news had come of its relief . . . and some men must live on when others die.

Eden prayed nightly for her husband. At times, when the task of maintaining the well-being of six hundred acres of land and some one hundred and twenty souls became overwhelming, she wept . . . though whether for his absence, for his return or simply on account of his desertion of her, she hardly knew. There had been, there would be, too many nights like this one. She was not formed to sit and stare into the fire, feeding her cold heart on memories, like a woman three times her age. She was only twenty; she was bold and bright and quick as sunlight, and her body cried out with her spirit for rescue from this penance that had been laid upon her . . . for no sins of her own. Why should she not dance, run, make love, bear children, enter into all of life's rich rhythms, as other women did? Granted she was clerk, steward, justice, overseer of her lands, ruler of her household, but she was no longer a woman; she felt herself almost anonymous, a wraith without a sex. She did not think she could bear it much longer. As she did so often on these lonely evenings, Eden sent away the serfs and tried to arouse her tired senses with music. She was learning to play the lute, an accomplishment which, she had heard from a pilgrim last month, was much admired among the ladies of Queen Eleanor's court. Her father had used to promise that one day she should go to Winchester or to London and see the wonders of life among the Plantagenets for herself, but time had passed, and more time, and the promise had never been kept. Perhaps, one day, when Stephen returned . . .

She swept the soft strings of her instrument, caressing its swollen belly with loving hands. "My love rode away to Jerusalem," she sang, determined to allow no break in her voice. She finished the verse and poured herself a brimming hanap from the pot of mead that was simmering on the hearth; it was spiced with some of the precious cinnamon brought by Sir Godfrey, her father, from the second Crusade, so long ago; it was still fresh; she had wrapped it in leaves and kept it in a box with a firm lid. Thus seasoned the mead became metheglin, the fairy drink, beloved of King Arthur and his knights, balm to the weary bones and the humorless mind.

She watched the flames leap and dart, sending the nameless troops of unquiet shadows out into the long room where they climbed the walls and hid behind settles and swarmed across the board where none had supped tonight except the lonely Lady of Hawkhurst. It was a fine, high-roofed hall, made for feasting and dancing and the cheerful companionship of friends and neighbors; its efficient and elegant hearth and chimney were the envy of the entire county of Kent. There were tapestries on its walls and warm woolsacks on its seating. There was good pewter in the kitchen, to dress the board, and a wealth of fine wines from France, down below in the undercroft. Eden felt its emptiness as she felt her own.

She was tired to the bone; she had ridden twenty miles that day, to the house of Isaiah the Jew, to ask for a further loan against the next season's wool. She had got her money, but the interest had gone up; she didn't know where she was going to find it, but find it she must.

She drowsed, only half aware that she had drunk more deeply than usual. Her head drooped sideways and rested upon the carved back of her tall chair; she scarcely noticed how hard it was as she drifted willingly into sleep.

Outside the storm furies lashed the winds to a fine frenzy and the rain fell mercilessly upon the cowering earth making flooded trenches of the farm furrows, tearing at thatch and croft and turning the roads into rivers. It was not a night on which to ride out. Nevertheless, while Eden slept a heavily cloaked and booted troop of men were directing their unenthusiastic horses along the almost indistinguishable path to Hawkhurst. Their leader crouched low in the saddle, turning now and then to hurl encouragement at his followers, cursing as his mount stumbled over a loose rock.

"Not long, now, lads! We'll soon be home and dry! And remember . . . not a sound, do you hear? We want to surprise the Lady Eden! The storm will keep our secret till we gain the house!" His laughter scattered before him on the wind as he spurred his horse to greater effort.

As the Lady of Hawkhurst slept on in exhausted ignorance in her great hall, the cloud of dark shadows rolled toward her with the storm. She did not stir as the broad gates open to them, nor did she wake at the sudden outcry from the undercroft, where the serfs and servants caroused to keep out the weather; she heard nothing as the leader of the sodden and weary troop gave curt orders which were immediately obeyed, nor when his henchmen stole like ghosts through the quiet chambers, going quietly and efficiently about their several duties.

Their captain, having assured himself of their obedience, left them to stride purposefully toward his own object, though taking the time to make an interested inventory of the eye as he passed through the great kitchen with its silver and pewter, up the twisting stairway, warmly tapestried against the cold, through the small family solar, where hung the late Sir Godfrey's treasures from the Holy Land, chased and jeweled swords and scimitars, exquisite metal and enamel vases and cups, hangings whose colors sang in brilliant silks, and the strange, flat, deeply-hued paintings of slant-eyed virgins of the Greek church. He smiled, his look satisfied and proprietorial as he looked upon them. Then he passed through the curtained doorway which lead to the heart of the house and looked, at last, upon its lady herself.

She presented an exquisitely vulnerable picture as she slept. Her face had lost its tension and her skin gleamed, translucent in the firelight. There was strength there as well as beauty; dark golden brows curved boldly above long-lashed, heavy lids; the full, red mouth held a resourcefulness that its owner would not have recognized and the memory of a sensuality now suppressed. The fine bones were beginning to reveal their line beneath the rose-gold surfaces of her skin, the cheek high and proud, the chin resoulte. Her mouth had fallen open slightly and her small, well-shaped teeth showed white and strong. A yard of deep gold hair, unbraided and left loose, spilled over her lap and gilded her blue-green gown. The darker cloak had fallen from her shoulders and framed her body in graceful folds.

The man who stood before her derived a slow and sensual enjoyment from the sight. He was tall, broadly built with powerful shoulders and strong limbs, heavily muscled. His face, as he stared down at Eden, was cruel and clever, its structure half buried in coarse black hair. His eyes, too, were black, and sparkled like sea-coal. His red cloak clung, soaking, to his tunic. He let his eye roam delightedly from the parted lips to the full, round breasts beneath the soft, woollen dress; he followed the line from small, neat waist to splendid, flaring hip, from long thigh down to a slender calf and tiny elegant foot. He noted the mud on her green leather boots, the heavy keys on her woven girdle, the callous on one finger where her rein had rubbed it.

"You give yourself too much work, lady! It becomes neither your position nor your beauty."

The voice was crusty deep and filled with confidence. It brought Eden back to herself swifter than a cold ducking.

"Sir Hugo!" She sat up pulling her cloak around her again.

"I sorrow to disturb your sleep, lady, but I told you I would come for my answer." The pleasure had left his face, a deeply etched, customary scowl taking its place. Heavily he waited. Eden stared at him in distaste, forcing herself fully awake. Sir Hugo de Malfors, who had so arrogantly thus availed himself of her house, was not the least of her present problems. Importantly, and unfortunately, he was her overlord. Baron of Stukesey Castle, to whose honor the Lord of Hawkhurst did homage, he, in turn, held his lands as tenant-in-chief of King Richard himself; it was said that the King was also his friend.

She sighed briefly with a tired impatience. "You have had your answer, a dozen times. It has not changed. It will not do so." She was careful to keep her voice level and pleasant. "And I wish you will cease these importunities; they add no dignity to the relations we must have with each other."

The frown deepened between the black brows. "You speak as though I sought to do you some dishonor! You are harsh Eden. All I wish to do is to offer you my hand and my name." He laid one fist over his heart in a gesture that, knowing him, she could only understand to be sarcastic.

"As I have repeated so frequently," she said, her voice very slightly unsteady as her anger rose, "I already have a husband."

Sir Hugo shrugged. He dragged forward a broad, low-backed chair and made himself comfortable, stretching his black-booted legs to the fire. "Your father gave you to the wrong man; now he is gone, and likely will not return. It is time to right the matter. You know I wanted you, when they married you to Stephen! Your father was a fool!"

"How dare you slander his name in his house!" Eden's control had broken its leash. "He preferred Stephen because he knew you to be the man you are!"

There was silence. Then, "Indeed?" said Hugo quietly, his eyes dangerous. "And what kind of man is that?"

But she would not be drawn. "He did not think you would ensure the welfare either of Hawkhurst or myself. And beside," she added, remembering suddenly, "you had recently buried a wife."

"A green girl who had not the strength to bring a healthy child into the world! I was well rid of her. A man without an heir is like a tree without a leaf."

Eden recalled the small, unhappy figure she had once seen at a church festival. "She was too young to bear; you could have left her to grow," she said.

He grinned, then spat.

"What use is a wife, if not in bed?" Eden shuddered.

Sir Hugo was becoming restles. "I'll speak once, for the last time of asking. Our lands march; you are my liege-woman; it makes good sense that we should marry. Will you be my wife?"

"For the last time, Sir Hugo . . . and right glad I am to have your word on *that* . . . I will not!"

The black eyes glittered and a certain satisfaction appeared in them. "Then I have to inform you lady, that I rode here tonight with thirty armed men at my back. I have become tired of asking. I have courted your vanity like a lovesick squire for overlong. Now I shall *take* what I want."

She stared at him, unbelieving, her hands clutching at the arms of her chair.

He nodded, the truth triumphant in his smile. "I admit that I had a little help from within your walls. One of your men had a mighty fear of losing both of his hands . . . if he did not employ them in opening your gates to me."

She ground her teeth to prevent the cry that welled within her. She could not bear to face the treachery.

Hugo looked at her in mock regret. "Alas even so! Loyalty is a mere, fleeting thing. I verily believe I will take off his hands anyway, to teach him a better morality. What do you say?"

Her look of disgust was his answer.

Sir Hugo's mood changed, the amusement fading from his eyes. "I've not come here for conversation, lady. I've come for what is mine. I have Hawkhurst and can hold it . . . and I will have you, too . . . tonight. Make up your mind to it, and we shall do very well together. I'll marry you as soon as may be."

"I am married to Stephen," she shouted furiously then, losing all reason as the full wretchedness of her situation was borne upon her. Married indeed, and to a man who had taken every able-bodied man off the domain, leaving her with boys and well-meaning graybeards to guard what was hers.

His contemptuous laugh dispersed her fractured syllables like blown leaves. "Are you so?" The dark amusement and unholy pleasure returned to his face. "Then why," he asked with quiet obscenity, "have I heard it said that Stephen de la Falaise was no true husband to you? I can have it attested before the Shire Court that there was no blood on your fine, white sheets, after your wedding night . . . nor ever."

He grinned, satisfied with her incredulous gasp.

"Poor Eden! Your miserable clerk of a husband could not do a man's part by you, confess it! He was fit only for the monastery. And my good friend, the Bishop, will therefore take pity on such a lusty young woman as yourself . . . and grant you the annulment of this mismatched marriage . . . on the grounds that it was never consummated."

"It isn't true! No one would believe you!" she cried, distressed beyond measure.

"Would they not? You've been wed nigh on five years, Eden. You should have three or four fine sons by now. Where are they?"

She could not bear his triumph; he had sought out her secret sorrow and now defiled it with his ridicule.

She had hoped so agonizingly to concieve before Stephen left; she had hoped, also, to bring forth the heir to Hawkhurst while her father still lived. He had enjoyed no son; she had greatly longed to give him his grandson. But it had not happened, not then, not now.

She hated Hugo de Malfors with all her spirit. She summoned her strength and spoke coldly and clearly. "No Bishop would put his soul in peril to do what you suggest."

"You would be amazed at what even the Pope might do, if he were offered a great enough inducement," said Hugo dryly, shifting his bulk for a moment to lean and help himself to a cup of metheglin.

He gave her a grin of encouragement. "Put off that whey face! You'll change your tune, right enough, when we've made a proper marriage of it, as we should have done long ago. Why, I'd have tupped you like a ram every night of your life. You'd have those four strong sons by now, and your breasts filling with the next." His eyes raked her body and she began to be afraid.

There must be something she could say that would turn away his purpose. Her throat was dry: she swallowed. No words came.

"You are lax in your duty as a hostess," he complained, holding out his hanap for more of the mead. "I don't like to see that. I trust you will not see my friends go dry when I am master of this excellent hearth."

"That will never be!" she raged, finding her voice at last.

He opend his throat and sent down the wine in one long stream, then wiped his mouth with the back of his hand. He belched.

"Indeed! Will it not? I think it may already be accomplished!" He rose from his seat. "Now, my lady . . . you will show me the way to your bed. I have a mind to take my pleasure of you . . . most thoroughly."

She made no sound, but sat rigid in her tall chair, confounded by an incredulous horror.

"You were Stephen's friend!" she whispered, loathing him from the very core of her being.

Hugo nodded agreeably. "I was his good lord, and as such, gave him wondrous good advice. In truth, Eden, I cannot understand why you insist on remaining so pitifully loyal to the memory of one who was so eager to forsake the pleasure of your person for those of Outremer."

She understood him well enough. "Your 'good advice' told him to take the Cross?" She already knew the answer; it turned in her like a sword.

Hugo's strong teeth showed in his wolf's grin. "He was remarkably easy to persuade. He had a true devotion to his Christian duty."

"Christian duty!" she spat. "What do you know of that . . . who are as much a Christian as Saladin and all his race of devils?"

"My friend the Bishop would take issue with you," he replied amiably. "It was, perhaps, above all, his sermon that tipped the balance with Stephen. Who could resist that ringing eloquence, filling the vastness of the cathedral at Canterbury? The great call to all faithful knights of Christ to wrest his Holy Sepulchre from the violation of the Infidel. Most moving! Why, when I saw Stephen sink to his knees and cry 'For Jesu' . . . I nearly took the Cross myself. But then he would have had none to look to his lands . . . and his lady."

"Blasphemer! You are very bold in tempting the wrath of God! You will be less so when He sends your punishment. Be sure that if you do harm to myself or to Hawkhurst, you will die at Stephen's hand when he returns!"

There was a guffaw of genuine derision. "Stephen will *not* return, my lady, believe me! It is most likely he is already dead, of a Saracen arrow or his own incompetence. If not, you have my promise that, in any event, he will not reach Hawkhurst again . . . alive. So put him from your mind, Eden. You will soon have much other matter to fill it . . . aye, and other parts too."

At first she thought she would vomit. Then, with a cry of rage and hatred, she seized her heavy pewter hanap and hurled it with all her force in his face. The black hair dripped wine upon the floor. He dashed the liquid from his eyes. His movement was controlled but his look struck terror to her belly.

He hung over her and she was instantly reminded of the first time she had set her eyes on him. A child, she had sat dreaming by the river; he had ridden up and reined his horse in close to her, a red-lipped scowling boy who had subjected her to a minute's discomforting, brooding scrutiny before she had leaped to her feet, and, following some deep, uncomprehended instinct, she had taken to her heels and raced back to Hawkhurst as if a devil were after her. He had not followed but his black, speculative look had troubled her dreams. He bent this look upon her now.

"Get up!" he ordered her thickly.

She did not move. Her heart raced like a rabbit's.

He took her roughly by the wrist and jerked her to her feet. "Do not think yourself too fine for me, lady. You are not. There are many who would envy you this night. I have bastards enough about the county to prove it."

She stood, helpless, pinned beside her chair, the tears gathering and falling down her cheeks. Her sense of desolation was greater than anything she would have believed possible. Hawkhurst had always been her ultimate security, her pride, the warm place at the heart of her life; now the knowledge of its vulnerability, as great, it seemed, as her own, tore at her heart. . .

Without knowing it, she screamed, then found herself reeling back from his sickening blow to her mouth. She steadied herself on the back of her chair, tasting blood on her lips. He came, scowling, toward her.

"Take your taper, Eden, and light me a bed," he commanded.

She shook her head, unable to speak.

With a foul oath he hauled her toward him and threw her across his shoulder. Seizing a candlestick from the table, he held it uncomfortably close to her swimming head. "If you struggle or seek my harm, I shall set fire to your admirable hair. I can quite well do my will upon you without the added pleasure of winding it around my fingers."

She shuddered and kept still, hopeless tears salting her hurt mouth.

He carried her deliberately into the solar, where he flung her onto the bed with a force that winded her. She longed to cry out, but who, even hearing, could aid her?

When Eden finally escapes the clutches of Sir Hugo, she sets off in search of Stephen, a journey which takes her from Queen Eleanor's Court to Cyprus and the Holy Lands. This passionate quest leads her into exotic dangers and haunting temptation.

DON'T MISS
THESE CURRENT
Bantam Bestsellers

WE DELIVER!
And So Do These Bestsellers.

RELAX!
SIT DOWN
and Catch Up On Your Reading!

Bantam Book Catalog

Here's your up-to-the-minute listing of every book currently available from Bantam.

This easy-to-use catalog is divided into categories and contains over 1400 titles by your favorite authors.

So don't delay—take advantage of this special opportunity to increase your reading pleasure.

Just send us your name and address and 25¢ (to help defray postage and handling costs).